DAYS of CAIN

DAYS of CAIN

J.R. DUNN

AVON BOOKS ◆ NEW YORK

fic

This is a work of fiction. Names, characters, places, and incidents either are the product of the author's imagination or are used fictitiously. Any resemblance to actual events, locales, organizations, or persons, living or dead, is entirely coincidental and beyond the intent of either the author or the publisher.

AVON BOOKS
A division of
The Hearst Corporation
1350 Avenue of the Americas
New York, New York 10019

Copyright © 1997 by J.R. Dunn
Interior design by Kellan Peck
Published by arrangement with the author
Visit our website at **http://AvonBooks.com**
Library of Congress Catalog Card Number: 96-48527
ISBN: 0-380-79280-X

First Avon Books Trade Printing: August 1997
First Avon Books Hardcover Printing: August 1997

AVON TRADEMARK REG. U.S. PAT. OFF. AND IN OTHER COUNTRIES, MARCA REGISTRADA, HECHO EN U.S.A.

Printed in the U.S.A.

QPM   10   9   8   7   6   5   4   3   2   1

JAN 1 5 1998

Acknowledgments

My thanks to Mike Kandel and Matt Bialer for talking me into this, Judith Solomon for coming through with historical documentation, Paula May for long-term support and assistance, Margarete Driver, Joe Held, Iren Ruschak, and Robert M. G. Thomas for assisting a pitiful monoglot Anglophone with translations, Amy Goldschlager for her sharp eye, and Jennifer Brehl for making it work.

1917

Dawn came slowly to this sector of the front. It brought a cool morning, the brassy sky promising damp heat later in the day. A low mist clung to the ground, obscuring anything farther than fifty metres off.

The mist embraced an artillery landscape. No touch of green was visible, no color at all aside from the gray-brown of muck and clay churned repeatedly until all variations of hue were lost. What had once been an open field was now carved into a frozen sea of shellholes, countless shallow craters flowing endlessly into the fog. A cluster of stumps stood in the near distance, their tips blackened and splintered. Beyond, dim in the mist, sat a shapeless pile that might once have been a farmhouse or a barn.

There was no movement, no sound of insects or birds, only the low rumble of distant gunfire, broken by the occasional sharper crack of a rifle or the chatter of a machine gun. Other places might echo with the voices of men, the rumble of wheels, the whinny of horses. Here there was nothing.

The mist was beginning to rise when a man appeared. At first only a shape within the fog, he resolved into a running figure moving swiftly through the shellholes. Loping at an easy pace, he kept to the lips of the craters where there was no chance of stumbling across an unexploded round.

He wore the gray of the Imperial Army, the coal-scuttle helmet that had become its symbol in this war. The leather pouch of a courier banged against his hip. His collar bore the tabs of a Gefreiter, and at his throat hung a black Maltese cross.

When he passed the stumps, there was a sudden flicker. The runner slid into a shellhole without slowing down, raising his hands to his ears as he thumped against the dirt.

He had been at the front for nearly three years, this runner. Volunteering when the war began, arriving at the trenches only a short time after the opening attacks subsided into stasis. He had survived every aspect of death that combat had shown him. Heavy shells landed elsewhere. Gas flowed only where he was not. Other men died beside him, or went mad, or were carried off maimed to the field hospitals in the rear. Once, early in the war, he helped his injured commander to safety while machine gun rounds stitched the ground at his feet. Not one had touched him. Later that year a shell had struck the group he had only a moment before been eating with, exploding directly over their heads. Only he survived.

Those events had convinced him that he would live through the war, that he had a destiny beyond the trenches, a role awaiting him that no other could fill. He had begun looking for ways to test that conviction, for a sign that would confirm it.

The seconds passed with no concussion or roar of detonation. Lowering his hands, the runner bit at the end of his thick mustache and rolled to the edge of the crater. He listened for a few seconds, catching only the muted rumble of artillery before looking out over the rim.

A hundred metres away a figure stood, silhouetted by receding mist. The runner narrowed his eyes. The man was facing him, turning slowly, his weapon held high. The runner ducked into the crater as the man's gaze reached it.

The uniform was unfamiliar, the weapon strange. Not a poilu, or a Tommy either. No helmet, though he seemed to be wearing driver's goggles and some kind of covers over his ears. A Yank, perhaps, new to the lines and inexperienced. Not that it mattered what he was. They were all worms, degraded and tainted, not true men at all.

The runner raised his head again. The man was now approaching, seeming to shrink as he stepped into a crater. A grimace creased the runner's sweat-streaked face. Reaching for his holster, he pulled out his Mauser and clicked off the safety.

The man instantly froze, one foot poised outside a shellhole. Weapon rising, he looked directly at the runner's hiding place.

The runner fell back as a flash passed overhead. A wave of heat struck him, followed by a shower of dirt from the edge of the crater. He fought down an impulse to leap to his feet and fire off the entire magazine. An impulse fueled by rage, the deep-seated anger that had always boiled within him. It had controlled him once, in Linz and in Vienna, but he had mastered it long ago. The rage was now his tool, a flaw transformed into virtue, another weapon in the arsenal of his will.

Pulling himself by his elbows, he crawled into the next hole, a lip of dirt keeping him hidden. He heard running footsteps, growing steadily louder. Raising the pistol, he aimed it at a spot just above the crater's edge. He recalled the voice that had spoken to him just before the round killed his comrades, telling him to rise, to go to the other end of the trench. He wondered if it would speak again now.

Another flicker came, as dim as the first had been. The runner heard a shout, followed by a whisper of movement. Hesitantly, he crawled to the rim of the crater.

Two more men had appeared. One was hunched over next to the gunman, who was swinging about to face a second man circling to his rear. But what held the runner's gaze was a patch of darkness behind them. Nearly rectangular, half again as high as a man, it hung a hands' breadth above the ground, looking as if a slab of night had punched through the mist. The runner squinted, trying to see what lay within it, squeezing his eyes shut when he failed.

The gunman was now sprawled half into a shellhole. The other man looked down at him, stuffing something into his uniform before turning to his partner, who had sunk to one knee. After a moment, they closed in on the gunman. One of them picked up the weapon and slung it over his shoulder before bending to help the other drag the limp form over to the dark curtain.

Careless of being seen, the runner got to his feet. He vaguely pointed the Mauser but let the barrel fall. He drew a breath, about to call out, only to gasp when the figures reached the patch and two of them—the gunman and the man who had taken his weapon—disappeared within it.

The remaining man turned to scan the landscape. He became very still when his eyes reached the runner. For a second or two they regarded each other in silence, then the figure swung away and was gone. A moment later the black pane vanished as well.

Holstering his pistol, the runner climbed slowly out of the crater. Instinctively, he looked about him. The mist was nearly gone, and the clatter of small arms had grown louder as the enemy trenches became visible.

Making no attempt at concealment, the runner walked to the place where the men had stood. His eyes never wavered, even when he almost stumbled into a crater. Reaching the spot, he halted to gaze at his own long shadow, nearly as black as the occult curtain had been. Finally he raised his head and gave a short bark of laughter. The sound came again while he reached up and unfastened his helmet. Letting it thump onto the baked earth, he dropped beside it, laughing wildly as his empty eyes stared into a sky nearly as colorless as they.

M3/REL

The image froze: a lone figure on a bleak landscape, head thrown back, mouth wide.

"Any recognition?"

Gaspar looked wearily over at Coriolan. He'd just completed an absolute week orienting a group of novice researchers when the message had arrived asking him to report to M3 Center. He still had no idea what the intendant wanted, which was nothing unusual where Coriolan was concerned. He hoped it was something minor. He'd been looking forward to a few days back home, in his own now, away from the responsibilities of the Moiety.

He glanced again at the holo. It said nothing to him. Early 20th, or perhaps late 19th, far outside his specialty. An echo of an echo, at most. "I'm not sure," he said. "The face strikes a chord, but there's something off. The mustache, perhaps."

"Very good," Coriolan trilled. "He changed the style in honor of his warlord, a monarch called the 'Caesar' in his language—"

"German, I take it? That would be 'Kaiser,' then."

Coriolan's head bent to one side, as if listening. "So

it is, James. 'Kaiser'—quite correct. He adapted another term himself—'Führer,' I believe. In any case, he reverted to a clipped pattern
after the war. Rather puzzling—the style was originally Greek.''

''And he wouldn't have cared for that?''

Coriolan chuckled, an oddly musical sound, almost feminine except
for the depth of tone underlying it. Gaspar had heard plenty of spec-
ulation as to what exact personal pronouns might apply to Coriolan.
The intendant was from well upline, where emphasis on such matters
was often different.

''No, James. He would not.''

Gaspar examined the image once again. A stumpy, unattractive man
in primitive costume overwhelmed by some unknowable emotion, one
with little apparent connection to what had just occurred. A disturbing
sight, in a way that Gaspar couldn't quite define. It was the eyes, he
decided. Whatever might be going on in the man's mind, the eyes
revealed nothing. ''Who tried to negate him?''

''We'll touch on that.'' Coriolan gestured with a motion of almost
grotesque delicacy. The floating image switched to a view of a street,
Medieval in character, the buildings crowded close, the pavement
made up of rough stones. A mob surged over them, aimed directly
for the focus, filling the entire width of the holo.

No, not a mob, after all. They were too intent, too controlled. It was
more of a march, almost a military charge. Most of the men were in uniform, in fact, a near-comical brown getup of laced boots, flaring trousers, and high-necked shirts. All wore a red armband featuring a black
wheel inside a white circle . . . or was it two stylized Z's superimposed?
Historical clothing tended to look silly, but these in particular . . .

Then the eyes caught him again. That extraordinary, seldom seen
blue-white, the innate deadness behind them hidden now by excitement, almost a sense of exaltation.

He was marching in the center of the mass, next to a plump, aging
man in dark formal wear and a flat round hat. He wore no uniform,
merely a belted coat all the more impressive for its simplicity. Or
perhaps it was the way he carried himself.

Gaspar noted that the mustache had been trimmed to a short, almost
nonexistent dash beneath the nose. He felt a twinge, a tickle at the
bare edge of memory. Little attention was paid to Terrest history on
his homeworld—Arpad had been settled to escape it in the first place,

after all—but this face called forth a response regardless. "Istra," he whispered to himself. "Hister—"

"Hitler," Coriolan said.

Yes; Hitler—that was it. Oswald—Adolphus—The twinge deepened to a chill. Adolf, the Wolf Prince.

The crowd pressed closer, a ripple of emotion—fear or nervousness—moving through it. Shouts in German rose. Gaspar was turning his head to Coriolan when a sudden crack of gunfire erupted.

His eyes darted back to the holo. Several of the marchers had fallen in ways that showed they'd never rise again. The others—all of them, stretching back a city block or more—threw themselves facedown onto the street. Only the older man in the overcoat continued moving, plodding stolidly onward as if nothing unusual had occurred.

Almost anxiously, Gaspar leaned forward. The big man was blocking the view, but now he passed outside of the image and there was the subject, lying prone along with all the others. As Gaspar watched, he flung one arm over the opposite shoulder and raised his head. A lock of hair had fallen across his forehead, and the eyes squinted in pain, but a sense of infinite burning malice came through clearly enough to shock.

Coriolan froze the image. "An attempted coup. A 'Putsch' in German . . . is that pronunciation correct? Good. It occurred in Munich in 1923 . . . A.D., that's to say. But you still use C.E. in your period, don't you? Of course you do."

"Who was the big man?"

"A retired soldier named Ludendorff. A tool. Of no real interest." A gesture and the image swung wildly to focus on a window some distance up the street. A shape was visible behind it.

Gaspar had been about to ask why the officer had marched on through that hail of bullets, but he supposed it wasn't important. Instead he concentrated on the image, trying to make out what it represented, going so far as to engage his optical implants. But the picture was too blurred to come together.

Coriolan whispered a command. The image wavered, flashing as pixels danced across it. The shape became clear: a man aiming a weapon. "Karas—I don't think you've met—guessed that this episode would be critical and put a number of operatives in place. On rooftops, street corners, and such. They spotted this one just before the government troops began shooting. Notice he's wearing goggles—a targeting system, we assume. Karas beamed an all-frequency burst that fogged them as he fired. Otherwise . . .'' Coriolan shrugged. ''Three pellets struck a bodyguard. Very close.''

''Assume? They didn't catch him?''

''No. Too much uproar. Streets full of troops, fleeing Nazis—the marchers, those.''

''They're using contemp weaponry,'' Gaspar observed.

''Where there are witnesses, yes.'' Coriolan gave him a chilly smile. ''They've dropped that now.''

''Who are they?''

''A moment.'' Slim fingers rose to change the image. Coriolan showed him two more attempts—a bomb in a summer home and another sniper shot during a political rally in 1932. Neither came as close as the first two episodes. The last wasn't noticed by anyone present, not even the intended target.

''After 1933 access is poor and he's too well guarded for any conventional methods. There are several other incidents during the war decade, but these are on record as legitimate eral activity. It's astonishing how many attempts he escaped. A dozen or more, some of them quite close. As if he was invulnerable until the moment he chose to destroy himself. Almost enough to make one believe in fate.'' At a clap of the hands the final image—Hitler facing a large crowd, his clenched fists high—vanished, replaced by dim-glowing lights. ''In any case, the focus appears to have changed.''

Coriolan got up and swept across the room, leaving Gaspar to mull over that last remark. There was no point in asking about it. Coriolan would provide an answer in his own good time, and not one second before. That was the way the intendant operated, slowly unfolding the puzzle leaf by leaf until it stood revealed in its totality. As if by ritual, as if it had to be done in that way and no other. Again Gaspar wondered what kind of society could produce a Coriolan. But it seemed to work well enough. Coriolan had been M3 intendant since Gaspar's recruitment, and that was a long time past.

Coriolan occupied himself with something or other at a counter across the room. Not quite an office, though they seldom were. Longer than it was wide, the far end lost in dimness. Odd decorations on the walls that might be artwork, signs, or neither, objects on the flat surfaces that could be machinery or sculpture or both. The whole reflected Coriolan's personality with accuracy—mysterious, ambiguous, oddly inviting. You wanted to go poking into things.

Coriolan returned, loose white clothing bright as a flare against the dark background, an effect that Gaspar guessed was carefully chosen. The fabric was shiny and of different shades, the overall tone a perfect balance. The top part might be called a chemise, although Gaspar was not at all sure of that.

Gliding toward him, Coriolan handed Gaspar a long-stemmed glass, smiling as if it was the most gracious gift in his power. Gaspar nodded his thanks and took a sip. Spicy, not too sweet, a smooth aftertaste.

Head resting on one hand, Coriolan lay back on a couch. A striking face: well sculptured, skin smooth, bone structure prominent, the most memorable features the wide violet eyes above the high cheekbones. Just now they were closed, the long eyelashes resting on the cheeks. " 'Renegade,' " the soft voice whispered. "A fine term, a useful one. Strange how words fade over time. I'd never heard that one before I was assigned to this period. It covers all aspects, doesn't it? The stupidity of the act, the nastiness, the futility. Have you ever tried to understand what motivates them, James?"

Gaspar shook his head, letting his expression speak for him.

"Of course you haven't. Who would? Misfits, disloyal to their oaths, putting the continuum itself in jeopardy in favor of their own short-term visions. Best left to counselors and such. Though you may modify that opinion when you become an intendant yourself." Coriolan made a face and sipped at the wine. "We may be facing another rash of them. It almost seems to be a cycle—long periods of stability broken by bouts of impulsive outbursts. Inevitable, I suppose, humans being what they are. You don't recall the last such spasm, do you? Before your time."

This was becoming convoluted even for Coriolan. Gaspar shifted impatiently in his chair. "Who is it now?"

A languid hand brushed Coriolan's forehead. "The boy involved in the Ypres attempt is named Campbell Smith. A child, still in his twenties. Origin early 21st-century Canada. An apprentice researcher, no specialty as yet. Smith was perfectly rational when intercepted, but developed extreme psychotic symptoms immediately afterward."

Gaspar let out an involuntary grunt. Coriolan cocked an eye at him.

"Oh, he's not permanently damaged. Some kind of drug." Coriolan gave his glass a twirl. "But it did leave us stymied. The most we've been able to discover is that the renegades number between twenty and thirty—quite a large group, really. That they're using a transit station, which means that a control AI must have been subverted. That the leaders' names are Rissa Surat, a forecaster, Joseph Walzer, an operations specialist, and Alma Lewin."

Coriolan paused expectantly. Shifting in his seat, Gaspar gulped at the wine, no longer tasting it. "That's not . . . the same Lewin that's in research."

"So it is." Coriolan smiled. "Do you remember her?"

Gaspar pictured gray eyes, a face edging more to handsome than anything softer, a presence that made looks irrelevant, a voice saying, *How long does it take to gain a temporal perspective?* He must have processed a hundred recruits in his day, and he remembered none of them. Only a series of half-familiar faces that he'd sometimes encountered in various eras. But he remembered Alma Lewin. "Yes. Yes, I do."

"You should." Coriolan rose on one elbow. "You rated her good-to-excellent on her training evaluation."

Was that what this was about? A rebuke for recommending a novice who'd gone bad? He wondered what Coriolan would say if he knew the full circumstances, the events that hadn't made it into any forms or files. Gaspar could have given Lewin a negative rating. Oh yes. Possibly should have—there had been plenty of grounds for it. But he hadn't. "Are you certain it's her?"

"Absolutely. The boy Smith responded to imagery. Waved at her picture and shouted, " 'Hi, Alma.' "

"And that's proof?"

The intendant's eyes rolled. "The state he's in, yes."

Gaspar sipped at the wine to gain a few seconds' silence. It had been years since he'd thought of Lewin, and he'd had no reason to believe that they'd ever cross paths again. But the years made no difference; the memory remained distinct. Her personality—he'd never been able to think of a word to describe it. Self-contained, serious, quiet—all that was true, but it didn't begin to cover the impression she made. Someone who spoke so little shouldn't have so large an impact. But her charisma was undeniable. Along with her skepticism, which never descended to insult or sarcasm, but was always there, always ready to jab. Her coldness—many of the younger recruits had actually been afraid of her. Her way of influencing people to do things against their better judgment, their own interests, without ever making a demand or even pleading a case.

A sudden certainty gripped him: if Lewin was involved, she was in charge. There was no need to look further, consider any other names. If he'd been asked to pick which of the millions of beings working in the temporal extension of the Moiety would go renegade out of sheer conviction, one name would come first.

He felt a sense of dull anger, as if she'd betrayed him personally. Which, in a way, she had. Not that he needed an excuse to be angry where Alma Lewin was concerned.

He leaned forward, cupping the wineglass in both hands. "Tell me the rest."

Coriolan went through the story quickly, voice ascending the scale at certain points, fluttering hands illustrating others. A dozen individuals were known to have abandoned their duty stations and were believed to be involved. In fact, it was Walzer's absence that had alerted Roger Angiers, the C20 monitor. A half-dozen others were out of contact, while the same number had arranged for leave with requests now known to be false.

It was unknown whether the renegades were using an empty transit station or had acquired equipment of their own. Inspection of recent records revealed unusual activity by several different modules. It was taken for granted that the conspirators were basing themselves in a remote area of 20th-century Europe, using the Channel only for operations. It appeared that their current activity was confined to the period of the Second World War, roughly 1939–1945. Whether they were utilizing timelike shunts or other methods of shorting despite the inherent dangers was unknown.

Problems facing Angiers's unit included not only the ongoing war, but the fact that contemporary Europe was controlled by a totalist government—the Third Reich established by Hitler himself—rendering covert operations tricky. Another difficulty was lack of access. Quantum fluctuations in the Channel during this era could be extreme, with apertures opening and closing rapidly, often after a relative duration of only a few weeks. The morale of the continuity team was reported as dismal.

"How is Angiers handling it?"

"Angiers is not handling it," Coriolan said quietly. "Angiers has requested that he be relieved."

"What?" Gaspar sat back. A monitor dropping out of a continuity emergency was unheard of. That was the very purpose of the Extension, of the Moiety itself. The Moiety was the name that described—at least for entities here on the short end—the ultimate union of consciousness in the late epochs of the universe. Organization, community, denomination, alliance—the Moiety was all of these, and considerably more as well. Its creed held all intelligent life to be sacred, part of some vast but knowable pattern imbuing the continuum. The goal of the Moiety was to trace that pattern across the deep eons, the empty light-years, from the first appearance of intelligence two gigayears after the Emergence up into the final state, the dark epochs when the universe had gone quiescent and only self-sustaining systems remained. Its ultimate ends Gaspar did not and perhaps could not understand.

What he did understand—had made his life's work—was that the continuity of universal history must be maintained. The base state of the timeline was sacrosanct. The pattern could not be marred: changes might eradicate lives, perhaps entire races in the deep future. The task of the Moiety's temporal extension—with its monitors overseeing the centuries, intendants the millennia, and beings whose titles were drawn from processes at the far edge of understanding regulating vaster chunks of time—was to defeat its own errors, protect the continuum from the effects of its own research. The Extension was a snake preventing itself from swallowing its own tail.

Protecting continuity was what a monitor did. Oh, there was administration and overseeing standard intertemporal operations, the kind of thing that Gaspar had seen too much of in the last few years, but that was trivia. The core of a monitor's duties was to act against continuity breaks: any attempt, deliberate or otherwise, by any entity, for any purpose, to change the course of history. A monitor turning his back on an intervention was like a general deserting his army in the midst of battle, a captain abandoning a ship facing a typhoon.

Worse than that: it wasn't simply a victory or a vessel at stake, but the stability of the historical continuum itself.

"Yes," Coriolan said, the very picture of a disappointed woman from one of the more feminine eras. "Twelve hours ago, relative."

Gaspar made no response. "He seems to have been overwhelmed by some kind of eral preoccupation," Coriolan went on. "Something offensive to contemp sensibilities. I mentioned that the renegades' focus had shifted. The target is no longer Hitler, but an event he was instrumental in triggering. It's known by various names, but the most common is the Holocaust."

Gaspar frowned. Individual responsibility for a historical event was a strong claim, particularly in a period like the 20th, with a large number of powerful actors.

"You've heard of it?"

A vague memory stirred. "Some sort of atrocity . . . a massacre, was it?"

"It could be defined that way. Several magnitudes larger than a simple massacre, I'm told. It's viewed in period as *the* mass killing, though I understand there were several even larger. This being the 20th, they have a term for it: a genocide. The murder of an entire people. In this case, the European Jews."

"Why the Israelis in particular?"

"Not Israelis, James. Simply Jews. This was the last period in which they lacked an actual nation."

A people without a nation? Gaspar grimaced. An absurd idea. But it was the 20th century they were talking about. "What does this have to do with Angiers skipping out?"

Coriolan gave him a reproachful look. "I wish you'd be more gentle, James. Roger is in for a difficult time. I'm not at all sure it's his fault. Our birth eras leave marks on us all. Roger is late century and grew up with knowledge of this Holocaust event. It seems to have preyed on him. And not him alone. Karas is another example. He requested relief after the Putsch episode. He was recruited from the '50s, and several close family members were executed while Hellas was occupied by Reich forces. Two others have left as well. So it's not simply Roger—it's an eral problem. They have strong feelings about the nature of the mission."

Gaspar looked at the floor, covered with something that could not be called a carpet but was soft and yielding all the same. It was clear to him now what Coriolan wanted. A replacement for Angiers: someone willing to take over where he'd failed, to beat this intervention before it could go transcendent, blossom into a change that would require half the Moiety's resources to correct. Someone capable of carrying it out quickly, ruthlessly, and effectively. Someone not looking for a pat on the back from the hierarchy. Most important, someone who wouldn't turn Intendant Coriolan down.

By this time Coriolan should have gone upline. Far upline, to one of the advanced epochs, the High Interstellar or Galactic periods, inhabited by entities no longer biological, perhaps not even baryonic. A situation this critical required their matchless technology, their incomprehensible style of thought. Going upline was standard procedure for any serious continuity emergency.

Gaspar could guess why he hadn't. The Moiety—the Extension, at any rate—operated on merit, with merit judged by results. A crisis this serious would call for an investigation, carried out by minds that it was nearly impossible to communicate with, much less persuade. No telling what the verdict would be; perhaps forced retirement or reassignment to a period where a more sophisticated entity could keep a close watch. Gaspar didn't know why Coriolan had worked his way this far downline from whatever his homepoint was—maybe he liked primitives or was fleeing from something dark and personal. It didn't matter. Everybody had their reasons.

Gaspar knew he was being manipulated, maneuvered into operating outside of channels, over and around the call of duty. Asked to wash a broken plate, as they put it on his homeworld. It was odd how little difference that made.

He looked up. "I've never served in the 20th."

Coriolan relaxed just enough to show how much tension he'd been feeling. "I know this is out of era for you." Suddenly all energy, he bounded from the couch. "But there's plenty of data. And we'll make time. Gain some duration at the cellular rifts. Say a day and a half."

Going to what must be a computer, though it looked like anything but, Coriolan whispered a command. A data wafer extruded. Coriolan snatched it and approached Gaspar with the same grave air he'd shown with the wine.

Gaspar was just then finishing his glass. "Did that please you?"

Coriolan asked. Gaspar nodded his appreciation. "Good. I'll send you a flask."

Getting up, Gaspar slipped the wafer into his pocket. "I'll need to talk to this, uh ... Smith, is it?"

A sorrowful look crossed Coriolan's face. "I fear that would be useless. Do you know what cartoons are?"

"Some sort of primitive visual entertainment. For children, I believe."

"Yes. That's what the boy is doing. Sitting in a med suite viewing cartoons. He'll be in that state for weeks to come."

"I'll see him anyway."

"As you wish, James." Coriolan took his elbow, a light touch, barely felt. He told Gaspar they'd speak again before he dropped. At the door he stood back, as always, and gave him a strange ceremonial half-bow. "I am in your debt, James."

Gaspar hesitated, wondering again what the answer would be if he asked Coriolan whether he was male, female, or some combination necessary or customary to his period. He let it go, guessing that something would be lost if he knew. "Not worth mentioning. I look forward to it."

Outside he paused. The center was nearly silent. Two men passed by wearing long woolen robes, their hair in elaborate pompadours, just in from a period unfamiliar to Gaspar. He walked on, taking his time.

Gaspar had been C24 monitor for nearly a decade now—a relative decade, of course. A quiet century, the 24th, the kind that was looked back on as a golden age, like the 2nd or 19th: civilized, easygoing, and dull. He'd overseen only three operations during his entire term, all of them involving personnel trying to find a congenial now to lose themselves in. Not one continuity emergency among them. There was nothing anybody would want to negate in his century.

A continuity crisis was the highest-order mission that a monitor could perform. If being an intemp operative was an art—and Gaspar believed it was—then suppressing a negation was an operative's masterpiece. Continuity breaches were rare. The limitations of intemp transfer itself presented barriers, complicated by the Moiety's security procedures. It was a wonder that breaks were even attempted, much less that any ever went transcendent. But there were always people willing to take on a challenge.

Gaspar had been part of only one continuity operation, and then only as backup. It had occurred well upline, in M10, and he'd never been able to grasp the point of the mission or what had been at stake. But it remained the most satisfying thing he'd ever done.

Then there was Lewin. Gaspar despised renegades. He'd been recruited at the worst point of his life, a lost man, with no place to run. His wife dead, his child claimed by her people, Gaspar left with only a seething black hatred of the world as it was. The Moiety had returned him to himself, given him structure, something to live for. To Gaspar's mind, striking against the system that had saved him was an attack on the very source of order and sanity itself. Gaspar went after renegades in person, whether they were simply hiding or more active. And Lewin was not only a renegade, but one he'd trained and recommended. A smile crossed his face. Errors always found their way back home, didn't they?

At the office door he paused. A day and a half, Coriolan had said. Enough time for a short trip home. A few hours spent under Arpad's large and gentle sun. He'd been looking forward to seeing Rici again. Rici was his granddaughter—Ricia Theresa, after his wife. Eight years old now, which was . . . yes, six Terrest. Rici fascinated him, and he visited her as much as possible. Twice a year at least, every couple of months, relative. It had been nearly three, this time around . . .

But the thought was merely a pledge of the heart, a promise to himself. His daughter Elena believed him to be a businessman with interests in Eridani's Kuiper Belt, dependent on irregular shuttles to get home. Dropping in for only half a day would be difficult to explain. And as always, Moiety duties dominated. After this mission he would take several weeks off to spend at home. It was late spring there, the days long and lazy. He would take Rici to the shore to watch the medusae migration. She'd enjoy that.

He entered his office. The window was ablaze with light. A cascade, a spectacular one, covered the sky outside. Vast waves of color, matching the brightest of auroras, rolled overhead, cut off by the dark line of the apron surrounding the center. An artifact of the transfer process, high-energy chronons striking the singularity that encased M3. Operations was running heavy traffic today.

Going to his comp, he ordered the system up. Accomplice, adversary, event: those were the important factors. Smith wasn't going anywhere, from what Coriolan had said. He could wait. As for Lewin . . .

He called up her file. Lewin, Alma Maria. Researcher specializing in the late-20th-century Anglo-U.S. horizon. Recruited in the early 22nd from the Columbia Free Republic, a buffer state in the Pacific Northwest between the Yamatists' coastal holdings and the old American Republic. Her family was mercantile, acting also as couriers between the Diehards—the native guerrillas—and the U.S. military. A brother had achieved minor historical standing during the Liberation in the mid-22nd. The only other item of interest was that Lewin had been brought up as a Teresist, a neo-Catholic sect whose doctrine held all intelligence to be interactive, with every action affecting all souls equally. Her training record—he read through his own evaluation, chuckled to himself. He *had* gone overboard there, hadn't he? Apprenticeship, promotion, commission, each accompanied by an evaluation no more insightful than his. A rundown of her research projects, the standard list of trivial individuals important to the Moiety for reasons of its own.

He shook his head. He needed more. He told the machine to compile a list of everyone Lewin had worked with, the most recent at the top, those present at the center highlighted.

That left the event. He slipped the wafer from his pocket. The Holocaust. Yet another of the Great Wheel's gouges across the face of history. Like Sligo, like Bokhara, like Jerusalem. The picture of Lewin in that last now rose in his mind, in her guise as a woman of the Hebrews. He put it aside. There weren't many things that Gaspar wanted to forget, but Jerusalem was one of them.

Instead the image of Hitler's face returned, laughing in the wasteland. He felt a touch of the same disquiet as when he'd seen it first, as if someone had spoken the devil's secret name. What had he thought when he saw the portal? Gaspar wondered. What did they ever think? The hand of destiny, unknown forces looking after him, supernatural protection. In a way, he was right.

He slapped the wafer on the comp and watched it meld into the surface. The holo displayed a new image. Another wasteland: lines of wire, crude buildings, a tower in the distance. He sat back, telling the system to proceed. Behind him colors flared and rolled anew. He paid them no attention.

1973

Reber clutched the wrought-iron railing, caught by a wave of dizziness, a swift whirlpool of the senses. A serious matter when it happened, as now, at the top of a flight of steps. He closed his eyes. " 'All will be well,' " he whispered to himself. His grandmother's old prayer, or as much of it as he could call to mind. *All manner of thing will be well.*

Steadiness returned. He let go of the rail and brushed off his hands. These sudden fits had been coming all too often lately. One of the payments exacted by age; as with so much else, they could only be endured.

Taking a deep breath, Reber looked out into a fine autumn day. It was warm for October, perhaps as high as eighteen degrees, and he fingered the lapels of his overcoat, debating whether to leave it behind. But he still felt a mild briskness in the air. It seemed that he was always cold, these days. Straightening his hat, he made his way carefully down the apartment house steps to the sidewalk.

It was almost noon, and the street had been awake for hours. He saw children running about, which puzzled him until he recalled that it was Saturday. He liked the weekdays best, when the neighborhood was left to the old folk. He always took his walks during the quiet afternoon hours, after a morning spent in his customary manner: reading the paper, listening to music—the old cabaret tunes long forgotten in this age of Yankee noise—and carefully dressing for his daily stroll.

The street itself, this entire section of Hannover, was a throwback to earlier days. Miraculously untouched by Allied bombers during the war, even more surprisingly left alone by the building programs decreed from Bonn. It reminded him of his youth, which was why he'd chosen the city for his retirement. He passed an older woman sweeping her stretch of sidewalk, touched his hat brim when she wished him guten tag. He went on his way, as pleased with himself as he ever got. Gerd Reber, fixture of the neighborhood, the ancient fellow who stuck to the old ways, the proper ways.

At the corner he paused, trying to think of what he might need from the shops. Yet another burden of age, memories beginning to fade, though often enough not the ones he most wished to lose.

Shrugging, he walked on. It didn't matter. If it came to him, fine. If not, there was always tomorrow. He needed no excuse for a pleasant walk, followed perhaps by lunch in a beer cellar. He'd treat himself to a Römer of wine. Forbidden by the doctors, but what was life for? And after that, where? The Grosse Garten? A museum?

He paused on hearing a burst of laughter from up ahead. At the center of the block a gaggle of youths spilled from a building stoop halfway across the sidewalk. Too distant for his faltering vision to make out their ages, though he could perceive their mode of dress clearly enough. Denim trousers, jackets the same, or else of leather, hair hanging to their shoulders. Modern German youth in its full glory, more resembling New York hoodlums than anything else.

Reber walked to the curb. He'd had an encounter with their kind before, too recently for his liking. Last spring, it had been, in the evening. He'd accidently brushed against one, loafing in a pack the same as these. When the young thug turned to him, Reber had said something that offended him—he couldn't recall what; everything seemed to offend them these days. They'd followed him, the whole gang, dogging his steps almost all the way home, hurling their customary foul oaths, varied by comments that struck even deeper: *What*

*did you do in the war, Grandpa? . . . An SS-Gruppenführer, were you,
you old fuck? . . . how many Jews did you murder, old man?*

He'd wept for over an hour that night and was unable to sleep. He'd taken to avoiding that street . . .

The thin bleat of a horn rooted him with one foot on the pavement. He stumbled back as a Volkswagen whipped past, less than a metre away. Another bout of dizziness overcame him. Gasping, he leaned against the wall behind him.

Someone called out. Reber saw a boy approaching. With scarcely a pause, he hurled himself across the road, halting there to catch his breath before moving on. A surreptitious glance revealed the youths eyeing him, the one who had stepped forward shaking his head. Feeling his face redden, Reder looked away.

Trashy, vulgar, disobedient . . . No sense of respect in them. Though perhaps it was best that the ingrained discipline of his own generation was a thing of the past. And as for respect . . . well, that question was best not considered too closely.

He relaxed as he turned another corner. The canal lay ahead, and beyond it the business district. The Wagenheim Palace was visible, framed by the mountains. As always, Reber's eyes shot to the one where Phillips had operated a labor camp. As always, he tore them away.

This being the weekend, the stores and restaurants would be having a busy day. He'd walk a little longer than usual, give them time to empty out. Perhaps he'd sit in the park for a while. The sun, the sweet soft breeze . . . Yes, he would do just that.

A man preoccupied with a newspaper swept past him. Reber noticed he was wearing a yarmulke and felt that indescribable flash of emotion that always came whenever he encountered a Jewish person. He frowned as he turned away. The skullcap—you didn't often see those, even on the Sabbath. German Jews, the nominal number who remained, tended to be circumspect. They usually displayed signs of their religion only during . . .

A flash of recognition struck him. Of course! It was Yom Kippur! How could he have neglected that? Now that his memory had been nudged, he could recall marking it on the calendar. Rosh Hashanah had only been ten days ago, after all.

The park lay just ahead. He went past the lions guarding the en-

trance, the Hohenzollern statue overlooking the fountain, and found
an empty bench. Plopping himself down on hard white-painted wood,
he gave out a sigh. He was getting old, to forget that date.

But no wonder he felt so fine, so appreciative of the wealth of the
day. His unconscious had remained true, even if his waking mind had
not. The Holy Days always brought him a sense of relief, an easing
of guilt, as if their meaning somehow extended to him as well as the
People of God. Yom Kippur, Chanukah, the Passover—he always felt
close to her on those days.

Her face rose to mind once again, as it had ten thousand times
before. The memory that had saved him, that had kept him sane. The
only thing he could recall from the war years without being overwhelmed by disgust and self-loathing.

Her eyes, that was what he remembered most clearly. The only trace
of life left to her. The light growing within them, amid that pale bony
face, as she realized—as she decided—that she would yet live.

He wondered what she was doing now, this minute. Celebrating the
holy day, he was sure. She was a child of the Orthodox, the shtetls
of Poland, the ancient rites of Torah and Talmud. At the synagogue,
perhaps, in her small suburb outside of Jaffa, her children about her.
Yom Kippur, the Day of Atonement. How appropriate that was.

It would be warm in Israel today. Again he wondered what the
country was like, how the ancient Oriental landscape had adapted to
the overlay of European culture. He would have loved to have seen
it. He'd considered traveling there once. But that was Zion, the sacred
ground. He had no business setting foot there.

And besides, he would be tempted to see her, to lay eyes on her
again, and if he went that far, one thing leading to another, he would
speak to her, and that would never do. She wouldn't know him. It
was all those years ago, and he, after all, had been merely another
tormenter, another fiend in a field-gray uniform. And what if she did
recognize him, only to curse him or turn away?

Yet he did so long to see her one last time. Perhaps then the dream,
that nightmare that had dogged him since the war, would fade, leave
him in peace . . .

He drew himself up on the bench. No. It was better this way. The
checks, anonymous, once a month, sent in secret to her account. He
fumbled at memory, trying to assure himself that he'd mailed this

month's check out on schedule. He always sent them himself. It pleased him to write her name.

A word caught his attention. "Israel," someone had just now said, as if echoing his own thoughts. He raised his head. Two men in suits, looking far too young for any serious responsibilities, passed by on their way to the street. ". . . damn fool Egyptians," one was saying. "They'll have the Russians down on us all next."

The other laughed. "Hail Allah, if you ask me. About time somebody put the Yids in their place."

Reber felt a rush of anger. No better than the hoodlums in their long hair and leather, that one, despite his neat appearance. He felt an urge to rise from the bench and accost him, give him a piece of his mind. But he'd never been able to confront those who talked that kind of trash. Oh, a few occasions now and then when he'd been drinking, no more than that.

Still, what had the young fool been talking about? Egyptians, Russians, putting the Yids in their place? What the devil could that mean? Ill at ease, he glanced around the park. A few metres away a group of boys and girls sat on the grass, within the low railings that no one would have dared to cross in his day. They were listening to a radio. A moment before it had been playing the sort of barbaric American yawp that his mind automatically tuned out, but now a voice came steadily from the speakers. The news, it must be.

He got up and walked over. As he drew close, a few words reached him: tanks, battles, the U.N. He cocked his head to listen, gritting his teeth when the voice was replaced by a commercial. Tottering slightly, he counted the seconds as the advertisement droned on. Finally it ended, and the announcer's voice returned. But it was only local news now.

The youngsters were dressed in ragged, sloppy clothing, like that gang he had seen earlier. Hesitantly, he took a step toward them. He needed only to ask. They couldn't be insulted by that, could they?

But then one youth looked up at him, his gaze narrow and challenging. Reber dropped his eyes and headed for the gate.

The park was emptying now, the workers going back to their jobs, women guiding baby carriages home. He pushed through them, out past the lions and onto the sidewalk. There was a news kiosk a block down. He turned in that direction.

Smiling couples on the sidewalk, well-dressed older women, a policeman in uniform. Old, aging, young faces, enjoying a fine weekend. Their jokes, their gossip, their small talk. It must have been much the same in 1943, when the smoke had poured forth in the nameless towns to the east. Laughter and chatter while the Chosen were killed off like insects. Thirty years had changed nothing. *All will be well, and all will be well . . .*

His breath came in short gasps as he ran toward the kiosk. He saw again the mounds of corpses, the laughing men in gray uniforms, his own hand raising a pistol, the light dying from bright eyes. " 'All will be well,' " he whispered to himself.

He thrust a man aside with a strength he'd believed he no longer possessed, snatched at a paper, *Die Zeitung.* The headline leaped out at him: EGYPTIAN ARMY ADVANCES IN SINAI. He scanned the paragraphs beneath: . . . surprise attack . . . three armored divisions . . . Syrian forces pushing through the Golan . . . Israelis falling back on all fronts . . .

A cry rose of a kind that he had not heard since the war. He looked around for the source, saw with shock the paper crumpled in a hand he could no longer control, felt the gritty coolness of the sidewalk against his cheek. His hat lay brim up some distance away. A shoe moved into view just beyond it, a voice shouted for someone to call 115.

Reber reached for his hat—a man should never be seen in public without a hat—only to spin into a darkness filled with flames and screams and barbed wire.

M3/REL

Gaspar paused at the head of the corridor—little more than a shaft, really—while lights flickered on before him. He couldn't recall ever seeing the maintenance level of M3 before, but he must have been through it as a recruit, when he'd explored every metre of the center open to him. But that was three decades ago, and the memory had faded. The thought of anyone living down here was little less than grotesque, but Lisette Mirbeau was a ghost, and they tended to be rather strange.

Mirbeau had turned out to be the name most closely associated with Lewin's. He'd been surprised to learn that she was still onstation. Operatives who suffered breakdowns usually retired to one of the Moiety's proprietary worlds or were sent upline for therapy and eventual enhancement. Still, it was a piece of luck: no one else who had worked with Lewin was available, a fact that somehow failed to astonish him.

He stopped at the door that the section AI had indicated, convinced that he'd been misdirected. He saw no sign that anything living had passed through here for years. But this was where he'd been sent: second corridor, third entrance. He gave the door a hesitant tap, then repeated it with more vigor.

Nothing happened. There was no handle—this entire section was automated. He snorted with disgust and suppressed an urge to kick at the door. As if he hadn't had enough trouble already today at the med center. He supposed the next move was to contact the AI and issue an override using his monitor's code. He was lifting his workcase to do exactly that when the door slid open.

Eyes wide, Gaspar stepped back. What the open door revealed made no sense, not here or anywhere else in M3. The entire space was filled with vegetation, some type of plant unfamiliar to him. Vines of varying thickness, leaves differing in color, shape, and size. He'd seen offices upcenter featuring large arrays of plant life, but nothing resembling this jungle.

He was reaching for one of the vines when they moved of their own accord. Gaspar retreated once again. With a rustle of leaves, a circle, like a window or porthole, opened in the center of the mass. He watched as it drew wide, the vines coming to rest about an arm's length apart. Leaning forward, he tried to make out what lay within. A face appeared in the opening.

At first Gaspar thought that it was too young to be the woman he was seeking. But then he saw that the shadow of the plants had softened the light, and that it was an old face, older than any he could recall seeing at the center. The face of someone who had long ago ceased ågathic treatments.

"Mme. Mirbeau?"

She inclined her head. "And you are?"

"Gaspar James, monitor, C24."

"Ava Sharif is no longer 24th monitor?"

"Not for some years."

A hint of expression crossed her face. "Time passes," she said. Her accent was thick. "How may I assist you?"

"By talk alone. Concerning a protégée. Alma Lewin."

"Come in," Mirbeau said, vanishing quickly enough to surprise him. He was about to ask how that trick could be accomplished when the plants unfolded further, creating a hole wide enough for him to walk through.

He hesitated at the threshold. Floor, walls, ceiling, the entire interior were covered with the same vegetation that had blocked the entrance. Or not quite the same—he detected variations, splashes of color denoting flowers. It occurred to him that it wasn't a single plant at all, but different species growing in harmony. A symbiosis, probably gengineered.

The plants held at his first step. Mirbeau was nowhere in sight along the green corridor. He walked on, eyes adapting to the diffuse, steady glow emitted by some of the leaves. The scent was powerful but not overwhelming. A close look at the blossoms showed them to be Terrest in origin.

He found Mirbeau about twenty steps in, seated on what seemed to be a natural ledge within a spherical bower or grotto. A sense of oppression swept him as he entered the space and saw that it was closed at the far end. Not a bower at all, he decided. More like a cave. A good place for a ghost.

"Sit down." Mirbeau indicated a spot behind him. A glance showed nothing but smooth green.

"There," Mirbeau insisted. She rose, both hands raised, as if to push him into the plants. "*Sit*. Sit down. Yes—that's it."

He backed into the mat of green. When the longest fronds brushed him, he heard a whisper of leaves and saw that the vines were shifting, forming what looked for all the world to be a bench. Rici would like this, he thought as he took his seat. She was at that age where she was fascinated by the Gothic—the eerier the better. There was much in the Extension, both weird and homely, that he knew she would enjoy, things she would never have a chance to see. He made up for that with stories and presents. Tales about the striking things and the odd characters he came upon while on duty. He'd even written one about Alma Lewin. Little items picked up from one era or another— bits of paper folded into the shapes of animals, a watch with the picture of a mouse on the dial, a plant that moved and did tricks when it was watered but safely dried up when it wasn't. It was a challenge to find a gift Rici would like that wouldn't attract too much attention. He often thought he was stumped but always came across something before he was due back.

He doubted he'd find anything for Rici on this trip. Not unless the 20th offered something more cheerful than barbed wire.

He smiled at Mirbeau. "Quite impressive," he told her.

Mirbeau made no response. She was a small woman, with the deceptive look of fragility common among those raised in microgravity. She wore a white gown, high at the throat, far more elegant than the casual wear commonly seen around the center. It lent her a deathly appearance in the dim light.

Lisette Mirbeau originated in the 22nd, recruited from the frontier culture remaining in the inner solar system after the near collapse of Earth's industrial society early in the period. She'd cut an impressive swath during her career, serving as monitor in not one but three centuries—unusual in that most monitors remained with their home periods, doubly so in that Mirbeau had once served in an earlier millennium, acting as C19 monitor for nearly two decades. She'd been considered an obvious choice for the next intendant M3, or even M2, whenever Coriolan or Rodrigo chose to step down.

Then she had thrown it aside, with no explanation or comment, only a few years ago. She'd become a ghost, someone who opted out of the Moiety, giving up all duties, refusing the alternatives open to her. The most pitiful end that an operative could face: burned out and unwilling to do anything about it. Though Gaspar had to admit that there was nothing pathetic about the woman who sat across from him.

He recalled that her home language was Francette, the trade tongue of the Belt and the Jovian Trojans during her era, a combination of French, American, and Japanese. That furnished him with a smooth diplomatic opening. "Would you prefer using your birth language?"

"No. We will speak English." Her voice was low, the tone flat. Gaspar noticed that she wasn't actually looking at him as much as focusing on a point between them. "Tell me, M. Gaspar. What do you yourself make of the Moiety?"

"Beg pardon?"

"The Moiety, Monsieur. Our section of it, this extension through time. What are your views of it? Its work, its methods, its purpose."

Gaspar began to rapidly revise his opinion. The purpose of the Moiety? That was the kind of thing you heard novice recruits discussing. Some of them, anyway; Gaspar hadn't wasted much time on it. A useless exercise; as well speculate about the purpose of the universe as a whole. He forced back a surge of annoyance: he'd finished speaking to Campbell Smith only minutes ago and was in no mood for any more nonsense. "Well, Madame . . . since I am myself part of the work and methods of the Moiety, I'll leave you to judge. As to the purpose—I believe what I was told. That the Moiety is the space-time expression of the final evolution of intelligence in the universe. That the temporal Extension is the means by which that evolution is overseen and secured. That my own role and duties are a crucial part of that effort."

"That this is the best of all possible worlds?"

Exactly what a novice would say. "That this is the most possible of all possible worlds." He waited for a reply. There was none. "Do I pass?"

Her expression changed not at all. "Oh, there's no such thing as failure, M. Gaspar. It's to inform me how to properly address the questions you wish to ask."

"I haven't come to ask questions, Mme. Mirbeau. Simply to hear what you have to say about Alma Lewin." He smiled. "Her work, methods, and purpose."

"I'd heard that Alma had impacted difficulties."

"The worst difficulties imaginable. She's gone renegade."

Mirbeau frowned slightly, as if at a vague personal worry. "You have met Alma, Monsieur?"

"Yes. I ran her just before you did. My candidate, your apprentice."

"Then you know her. The Alma Lewin that everyone knows. The hard-faced, brusque, impolite . . ."

"Obnoxious," Gaspar offered.

She nodded. "Yes. The woman in a hurry. The outsider. The bitch. The girl who was constantly asked whether she didn't wish to have friends. That is the Alma you know."

"Not the real Alma Lewin, I take it."

"Not at all, Monsieur." Mirbeau reached to one side and stroked a protruding vine. Something resembling a fern uncurled beside it. The end burst into flame, then subsided to a dull glow. Snapping it off, Mirbeau brought it to her lips and inhaled. "We all construct masks, personae to hide our real natures. It is of necessity, true of the habs where I grew up, of the surface worlds, of the Extension itself. You have done it, and I as well. One of the duties of a society is to teach its young what style of mask is acceptable. Often the most intelligent are the least capable of decoding the signals that a culture uses as guides in constructing a useful mask. Alma was one such. She grew up in a harsh culture and attempted to abide without a persona, presenting herself as she actually was. When she failed—inevitably— she responded by creating a mask so cool that none apart from those she chose would wish to look behind it.''

''I'll take your word for that.''

What might have been a smile on anyone else's mask crossed Mirbeau's. ''Oh, you must. I am one of the few she trusted. She lowered her mask more for me than any other, I think. She was sent to me— and I was not accepting apprentices at the time—because the hierarchy, our good Intendant Coriolan among others, believed us alike. I had much the same reputation as hers in my early days. As a rebel, directed by my own thoughts before all others.''

''What did you see,'' Gaspar said, ''when the mask came down?''

Several seconds passed before Mirbeau answered. ''A saint, Monsieur.''

She took another puff of the herb, drawing it well out, and Gaspar saw it for what it was: a prop, an extension of Mirbeau's personal mask.

''You are skeptical. That sour young creature, deliberately undermining her own attractions, given to asking cynical questions in a voice not her own. Could such a one be a saint? You came from a secular culture, M. Gaspar. Yes. A believer can always tell. Your impression of sainthood derives from that of the Moderns, the era that attempted to live apart from God. To you a saint is a strange being, pale of skin, weak in constitution, guided by fixations and compulsions, a person unable to deal with the world as it is. Correct, yes?

''This is ignorance, Monsieur. Of a particularly shabby sort. The saints of the great periods—of the Medieval age, of my own—were beings of tremendous strength, both of body and of will. Their role— to look behind the mask of the world itself, to force others to take the correct path against their own wishes—requires this. Saints are superhuman, in a way that even our masters of the advanced epochs are not. You have heard of martyrdom, M. Gaspar? How mere humans could defy the rack, the flames, the worst cruelties devised by the hands of man, without denying their faith? Were they weak? Do you think Paul of Damascus was a weakling? Barbara? Campion? But you don't know those names. I do. I was raised a Christian, and I have returned to that. The Belt and the Home System beyond were settled by Christians, led by the Lunar monastic communes. Saints as well, in their own fashion. I know what a saint is, Monsieur. And I say that Alma Lewin is a saint.''

She paused to slip the ember of the herb back within the plant from which it had come. A leaf folded over, extinguishing it. Gaspar remained silent. He couldn't see that any comment was called for.

Hands in her lap, Mirbeau looked about, eyes contemplating the flowers as if seeing them anew. Her gaze returned to Gaspar. ''A saint,'' she said. ''But a saint of a peculiar kind: a saint without a Deity, without a church. Oh, she was brought up a Christian, of a sort. A portion of the Mother Church that had deteriorated into a sect, a cult. Religions often take that path when confronted by powerful enemies. The Teresists began as a lay group devoted to charitable acts, but by Alma's time they were separated from their founder by a century or more and were essentially worshippers of Jehovah, the Lord of the Old Book, the God of Battles, seeking only vengeance against the Asians. Alma rebelled against that. She knew—had always known—that the Yamatists were not the subhumans of Teresist doctrine, forever outside the communion of souls. Though she was surprised to find that some—among the Japanese members of the Asian coalition—were Catholic themselves, and even more shocked to learn that the founder, St. Teresa of Calcutta, had not in fact been martyred by the Yamatists after all.

''It was those lies that she rejected, which led to punishment, and loss of faith, and ostracism. Eventually to recruitment into the Moiety. Since that time she's been seeking a faith, a vocation that will allow her to fulfill what she is. She has been looking for a cause.''

Gaspar regarded her for a moment. ''Do you think she's found it?''

''Perhaps. What has she involved herself in?''

Gaspar hesitated, his mind suddenly flooded with imagery. The ghastly record of the Endlösung, peak moment of the Age of Massacre: trenches filled with bodies, naked and so thin as to seem deformed. Figures scarcely more alive staring through barbed wire. A little girl dropping the food hidden beneath her dress while a soldier smirked behind her. Two men in striped clothing hanging from a gallows. A blackened shape jammed beneath a wall, hands become claws, scalp burned down to bone. Another child standing in line, waiting for the final horror to come ... "An event in mid-20th Central Europe. An episode known as the ... Holocaust."

"Ah," Mirbeau whispered. "And you have studied the episode, Monsieur?"

Gaspar sighed. "The Germanic peoples, calling themselves the Aryans for reasons of their own, attempted to depopulate the areas absorbed into their empire. Their primary target was the Jewish nation, in exile at the time."

Mirbeau's gaze intensified, as if she was noticing him for the first time. "And this perturbs you."

Gaspar stiffened. First Smith's gibberish, now this. He pointedly kept his voice level. "Not to speak of, Madame."

Mirbeau seemed ready to continue in that vein, but instead she dropped her eyes. "M. Gaspar, what is your interest in this? You being C24 monitor, I fail to see a connection."

"The monitor for the 20th has requested relief," Gaspar said curtly. "In the middle of an operation. I'm to replace him. That's the connection."

"Angiers? Roger Angiers? Why is this?"

"Not at all sure. Haven't spoken to him." He bent forward, the vines shifting under his weight. "But you see, I myself will be going after Alma Lewin. I'm going to take her down. So if you know anything, Madame, I think you'd best tell me."

For a moment he was afraid he'd struck too hard. Her face took on a lost expression, and one small hand lifted to the neck of her gown. But with a deep breath she regained control of herself. Dark eyes bored into his. It required an effort not to blink. "Alma visited me several weeks ago. She'd learned of the Holocaust some time before, after speaking to someone who had lived through it. It had become an obsession with her. She spent several years—absolute—researching it, talking to aged survivors living in her area of interest, the American Republic of the late 20th. The Republic itself is in a state of decadence at that time, both political and social. A long witches' Sabbath of hedonism, irresponsibility, selfishness. It astonished her that the Holocaust could have occurred with so little effect.

"But then she had an epiphany—"

"A what?"

"An insight, a vision. It occurred at a place called Flatbush, near—
or within, I'm not quite sure—one of the great megalopolises of the
era. She met an old woman who saw her entire family executed at a
camp called Auschwitz, four decades previously. She had worked in
the camp, in the offices, the department handling correspondence. In
that now—the early '80s of the 20th—the woman was living off of
a state pension that wasn't enough to serve her needs, and she was
afraid to leave her dwelling at night for fear of criminals . . ."

"How did Lewin locate this subject?"

"I don't know, M. Gaspar. She did have a pastime of tracing her
own ancestry, as so many do. Is it important?"

Gaspar shook his head.

"Very well," Mirbeau continued. "It was on the street outside that
Alma realized—the idea was thrust upon her—that the two were con-
nected. The predicament that the Republic, the entire West, had fallen
into wasn't despite the atrocities, but in some way caused by them.
She saw it as a great shadow, falling across history from its point of
origin, distorting everything it touched. Those living beneath it are
unaware that it exists . . . She herself had lived beneath it, a century
and a half farther on in time, all unknowing. The shadow grows as
time passes, tainting and debasing all it contacts, even the Moiety
itself.

"She told me that the Moiety could not be worthy if it embodied
such an event."

So she's out to pull down the Moiety, Gaspar thought. A laudable
ambition for a saint. And out of every period in the continuum, she
decided to start with Central Europe in the '40s of the 20th. It made
as much sense as anything else he'd heard today.

Mirbeau caught his expression. "You don't sympathize, Monsieur."

"Madame," Gaspar said, collecting his thoughts. "Let me put it
this way. I witnessed the sack of Jerusalem. From a distance, true. I
saw Black '47, when one of the oldest original cultures on the homeworld was effectively destroyed from the inside . . ."

"The Irish Famine, yes."

He paused. She would know about that, having been monitor for
the period. "And Red '83, the closing massacres of the Pacific War,
and—"

"And Arpad. You are from Arpad, aren't you? Something terrible happens there."

Gaspar had been about to confirm to her that he didn't sympathize, that everyone in the Extension, from trainees on, had seen those events or others of the same nature and knew firsthand that history was nothing more than a cycle of blood. But Mirbeau was about to make a point. He decided to let her. "Yes. Ash Thursday, it's called. After my time."

"I thought as much. You couldn't talk so if you held it in memory. Because you have seen none of these events from within. Always from an exterior viewpoint, from the viewpoint of the Moiety, our own little portion of eternity, which you always carry with you. You are free to leave. The victims are not."

He lifted a finger to silence her, but she went on without acknowledging him.

"The Holocaust differs from other historical events, both in degree and nature. It was the last time on the homeworld that humans could descend that low, commit such acts, without bringing the world itself down. It occurred at the very cusp, where it was possible to destroy a people without destroying all. That could not be done afterward, not for a very long time.

"Oh, there are worlds where similar events occur, in this millennium and far into the High Interstellar. But they annihilate themselves or are annihilated by their neighbors, as a cancer is burned out. And that comes much later, when the nature of humanity itself has changed, grown more capable of dealing with such events. You are aware of the formal name of the crime of Auschwitz, Monsieur? It is the Genocide. The Holocaust was the first and most terrible of these, as the first of anything always predominates. So Alma told me, and so I believe."

"And did she tell you what she was going to do about it?"

Mirbeau remained momentarily still before drawing herself up, arms gripping two vines as if she was about to thrust herself to her feet. Eyes slitted, she stared down her nose at him, and for that single instant Gaspar saw what she must have been like as a monitor.

"I'm certain, Monsieur, that I do not see the purpose of that question."

Gaspar inclined his head. She saw the purpose of it clearly enough, but she wasn't so much a ghost as to let the implication that she'd ignored an attempt against continual integrity slide past unchallenged.

"I hope this discussion has been of assistance," she said softly. She hadn't moved a muscle, as far as Gaspar could see. He got up, sensing the vegetation rearrange itself behind him. "It will suit, Madame."

"I wish you good fortune, M. Gaspar." Her eyes dropped to the leaf-covered floor. "A final comment, a piece of advice. Keep in mind that the shadow of Auschwitz touches you as well."

"Did Mlle. Lewin tell you that too?"

"We did not discuss you."

Gaspar allowed himself a smile. "Mme. Mirbeau, very few people are aware that Magyars reverse the order of their names. I'm constantly addressed as CM James. Yet you've been calling me M. Gaspar since the moment we met."

"We have spoken of you in the past," Mirbeau admitted. "You left an impression on her, Monsieur." Her eyes shifted, held his for a moment. "I see the regard is not mutual. Don't despise her, M. Gaspar. The error does not lie with Alma. Her actions are beyond her power to control. She should never have been recruited. Don't—" She dropped her head and looked away.

"I don't plan on harming her." Gaspar turned to where the entrance had been. It was now closed up, with no seam visible. He waved a hand at the mass, watched it open wide. Quite elegant, he had to admit. It would come in useful in some environments, say . . .

He swept his eyes about him, suddenly realizing what the plant was for. It was habitat growth, designed for microgravity. Used in the Belt colonies of the 22nd for food and life support. Mirbeau had re-created the world of her childhood, right here in the center.

"You'll take her upline, I suppose. To one of the proprietary worlds. She will be better off there. She doesn't belong in this place, where the ultimate good is wedded to the ultimate compromise. Do you remember your recruitment? I do mine. Far above the ecliptic, no fuel, no hope. The plants dying and myself to go soon. Alma was never that desperate."

That remark stung—Mirbeau was assuming a bit much for Gaspar's liking. He swung in her direction. She stood at the far end of the space, the vegetation opening up before her. "Tell me something," he said. "Why did you drop out?"

"I don't discuss that," she said over her shoulder.

"It was Lewin, wasn't it? Something she did, something she said. What could that have been, I wonder?"

"Yes," Mirbeau said calmly. "It was Alma. But not any one special thing. She simply—made me see what I was doing. Put me inside events. Saints have that power."

"I see." Gaspar clapped his palm against his workcase. "And one thing more, if I may: What *is* the purpose of the Moiety?"

For the first time he saw a plain emotion on her face, though he could not have said for certain what it was. Her eyes narrowed, her lips pursed: it was as if she was gazing into another life. It struck him that she must have looked much the same as a child.

She twisted her head away, hiding the expression. He had to listen closely to make out what she said: "You have no reason to know, Monsieur."

Then she was gone before he could respond, the plants closing behind her. Gaspar backed off a step or two. When he turned, the growth had receded, and the door lay wide open. He made his way out.

1943

The train swayed through one last turn. The clicking of the wheels began to slow. A shadow passed the length of the car. Then came the stink.

It was unlike anything that Rebeka had ever smelled before. Sweet and smoky, yet sharp enough to be perceptible above the stench of the waste and unwashed bodies within the car. She shivered and pulled her coat tighter around her shoulders. There was something about it that made her want to gag, that assured her that she would do that and worse if it grew any stronger. She caught the eye of the sharp-faced woman at her left, child in her lap, suitcase placed between herself and Rebeka as if to demark a firm border. Blinking rapidly, the woman dropped her head. The child whined softly, jolted awake by the shaking. The woman whispered to it, her voice high and fierce.

Quiet voices spoke as the train slowed further. "They have to feed us," a male voice said. Rebeka sighed, wishing she hadn't heard that. Her stomach had been empty since yesterday. Even worse was the thirst—they'd been given a bucket of water at a stop late last night, but since then there had been nothing at all to drink. Her lips were dry and beginning to crack.

A shudder ran through the train as it came to a halt, throwing Rebeka against the broad back of the old woman lying beside her. She twisted away quickly; the woman hadn't moved or spoken since yesterday evening.

A hush fell over the car. From outside came the sound of footsteps, voices speaking in German, the occasional snuffle and growl of an animal.

"Oh no," a woman whispered. "They have dogs."

Rebeka grimaced. Of course they had dogs. When didn't they? They always had dogs. All the same, her spirits fell sharply. There would be no chance of making a break now, not with guard dogs around. She'd have to think of something else.

The door slid open with a squeak. Light dazzled her eyes. Squinting through her lashes, she saw a man silhouetted from the chest up, a peaked cap on his head. Behind him stood two others in helmets, rifles slung across their shoulders.

"All right, people, let's go," the German said in fluent Polish. He backed off, the two soldiers moving with him, one of them bent over as if dragging something.

Around her people rose, some groaning at stiff muscles—there had been no space to lie down in the car. Rebeka, not that far from the door, decided to wait. "Watch your step there," the German called out. "No rush. You've got where you're going."

People pushed past her as the car emptied out. Rebeka leaned against the wooden slats, lest her legs, weak from being twisted beneath her for hours, betray her. Next to her the sharp-faced woman bent over to poke timidly at the old lady. "Excuse me," she said. "But we've arrived—"

"Don't," Rebeka said. The woman looked up, eyes wide. "She's dead."

With a retching sound, the woman jerked her hand back and clenched it into a fist. A dog barked outside the car. "Give that old fellow a hand there," the German said.

Scattered about the car Rebeka could make out other still forms beneath the feet of the departing passengers. She raised her head when she found herself counting them.

A moment later she was at the door herself, eyes watering in response to the unaccustomed light. Squatting down, she swung one leg out. A hand clutched her arm to guide her. She looked up at a tired, unshaven male face and smiled her thanks.

The German officer was a plump specimen, red-faced, thumb stuck in his belt. As Rebeka had guessed, one of the soldiers had a guard dog, a big Alsatian. It yipped as someone passed close by. The soldier patted its side and crooned a few soft words.

Smiling broadly, the officer waved them toward the front of the train. Rebeka moved past him, nearly running into a man in an overcoat and homburg, who stopped to speak to the German in a low voice. "No water on that train?" the officer cried out. "You don't say!"

Rebeka looked back. Hat in hand, the man made a bow. Behind him stood a small exhausted woman, one child in her arms, another leaning against her hip. The armband was slipping down the older boy's sleeve. Noticing it, the woman reached over and pulled it up.

"Well, you'll have water soon enough." The officer grinned. "Soup too. Bread, all you want. Soon as you get registered. Now get along."

"Danke," the man said clearly. Gripping his wife's arm, he hurried on. "Ahh," the officer called out. "The missus goes to that side. The kids too."

With a little bow to the officer, the man released his wife. She whispered something to him, her face hidden behind the short veil hanging from her hat. "Go on," he told her impatiently, his smile growing strained. "It's just for a little while."

"Keep close," she said as she moved to follow Rebeka. The older child let out a whimper.

"Yes, yes," the man said. He threw a glance at the officer. "It'll be fine, Moshe. Be a man now."

The officer swung away. He must have given the dog handler some kind of look; the soldier's eyebrows rose and his jaw moved as if he was trying to keep his face straight.

Rebeka stumbled against a suitcase. The throng was tightening up, forming a queue. She collided with someone else, apologized, finally found her feet. Moving with the flow now, she took the opportunity to look around.

She was on a long concrete ramp, the train to one side, the other blocked by a wall, armed soldiers lined atop it. Rebeka peeked beneath the train, saw nothing but another stretch of concrete. No, there'd be no escaping from here.

She considered what she'd heard about the camps. In the Łódź ghetto, from peasants, from the few friendly Home Army units. All rumor, but there had to be at least a grain of fact to it. You could survive, if you were strong enough and made the necessary effort. Most important was to find decent work first thing. Someplace inside, where you'd be warm, where contacts and arrangements could be made. The camp kitchen, the hospital . . . did they have offices here? They must.

She stepped over a joint in the concrete. It was filled with something, grime or ash. Bending over, she gathered some on her fingers and patted it on her face, rubbing it into her skin. That would do the trick—she'd tell them she was ill. Get herself sent to the hospital, talk to someone there, show them she was a good worker . . .

True, she'd heard other stories, the ones that said that no one lived, that Jews were murdered as soon as they arrived. But that was absurd. What could they do, shoot everyone? Rumors always exaggerated things. The Germans weren't Poles or Russians. There had never been pogroms in Germany.

The lines moved slowly on. Something was happening up ahead, but Rebeka couldn't see what it was. Only a group of men in gray uniforms with the Jews bunched up before them. Behind her the German officer was still shouting, moving people out of the rear cars. Numbers were chalked on the sides of the ones already emptied—169, 174, 172. But they were all out of order . . . Then she realized that it must mean the number of people in each car.

She heard a growl. A dog, poised atop the wall, snapped at the women moving below. She ducked as she slipped past.

Her shock was giving way to exhaustion. She needed to rest, at least for a minute, but there was no place to sit. She was filthy, dust from the car all over her, hands covered with the soot she'd scraped up. Her back ached from sitting on the floor all night. She took a deep breath to clear her head. At least the stench was no worse out here.

But she was in better shape than some of the others. There they stood, the Jews of Łódź, thin, pale, their clothes dirty, the single bright thing about them the armbands bearing the mark of Israel. A suitcase nudged her hip, nearly sending her sprawling. That was one advantage she lacked—they were all carrying something; packages, suitcases, bundles. But not Rebeka Motzin. She'd brought nothing into the ghetto with her and had taken nothing out.

. . . and so *quiet*. She'd never been in a crowd as silent as this one. It was eerie, so many people—there must be a thousand, no; two thousand or more—and barely a sound. She knew that silence. It was a silence born of fear, the silence of Jews cowering before their masters. Poles, Russians, Germans, it made no difference. Anyone could make a Jew quiver, back down and wait quietly for whatever blow was to fall. Or thought they could. Which was the same thing, after all.

"Now, now." A voice spoke beyond her, unnaturally loud. "The man said we'd be fed soon. You heard him, Moshe."

It was the woman with the veil, patting her son on the shoulder. From the other line her husband waved. He wore glasses, and Rebeka saw that one of the lenses was cracked. His smile had grown horrible, the teeth bared, his eyes nearly slits.

There it was again: the fear, nakedly displayed for the world to see. She had sworn to herself many times that she would never let that fear touch her, never let it control her as it did her father, her friends, her whole village. But now, in this mass, she could feel it seeping into her, turning her very steps into the puppet dance of the victim, marking her for what she was more clearly than any yellow armband ever could.

She passed beneath two more soldiers. One was clearly German, but the other had the blunt, square face of a Slav, and his uniform was different—a cap instead of a helmet, the insignia, all except the lightning bolts at his collar, of another style. He caught her gaze and, giving her a gap-toothed grin, raised his thumb to his throat. With a click of his tongue, he made a slicing motion. He chuckled as the German elbowed him in the ribs.

The head of the line lay only a few steps on. An officer waited, standing slightly higher than the waiting lines. The ramp must slope up at that point. He was an extremely striking man, suave in high boots and cavalry trousers. He studied the passing Jews wordlessly, arms crossed over his chest. Beside him stood a soldier with a clipboard, gazing at his handsome superior as if enrapt. The people who had already passed through stood behind them in two distinct groups, separated by soldiers with dogs.

A woman blocked her view. She craned her neck, trying to see past. Something important was taking place. That much she could tell. The expressions of the guards, the way the clerk studied the officer before jotting on the clipboard, even the nervous whining of the dogs, all told her as much. But she couldn't see what it was.

She was getting the feeling that she'd made an awful mistake. She thought again of the rumors. But she could hear no gunfire, no screams or shouting. Of course, they wouldn't kill anyone here, on the ramp. No, the Germans were too efficient, too methodical. They'd wait, calm everyone, give them hope, then take them off someplace where no one would see.

But they wouldn't kill everybody, would they? She had a terrible conviction that they would. They'd murdered so many in Poland already . . . But why were they dividing them up, then? She went on tiptoe to see over the shoulder of the woman ahead. The people in the group to the right—young men, all of them. Her stomach started to turn but then she saw the women next to them, off to one side. The other group to the left—old folks, children, a man on crutches . . .

Yes, it made sense. They wanted people who could work, young, strong, and healthy. But the rest—the aged, the crippled, the sick . . .

Dropping back down, she wiped her face with her sleeve. But that was useless. The coat was just as dirty as the rest of her. She had nothing else with her, no spare clothing, not even a handkerchief.

She thought of the armband. It was new, given to her when she'd left the jail at Lódź. Quickly unpinning it, she raised it to her lips and spat. It took her several tries to so much as dampen it, her mouth was so dry. Rubbing fiercely, she wiped her face clean. A middle-aged woman beside her made a revolted sound and edged away. Ignoring her, Rebeka went through the process a second time.

Only a few people now stood between Rebeka and the Germans. She wrapped the armband around her sleeve, then realized that she'd lost the pin. A glance around her feet revealed nothing but concrete. She pulled the band tight and held her arm close against her side.

The elegant officer stood in regal silence. His right fist, the one nearest the clerk, was resting on his elbow. Rebeka saw something—a pen or pencil—within it. An older woman, her breath coming in gasps, paused before him. As Rebeka watched, his thumb rose and pushed the pen into his fist. A soldier gestured the woman to the group on the left.

A young man—the same one who had helped her off the train?—was next. The officer's thumb remained still. The man went to the right.

Rebeka glanced between both groups. How could she be sure? Her papa would have said that she was using incomplete data. The group on the left was far larger, with many children. Babies. Would the Nazis kill babies? Perhaps they were sending them all to another camp, one with better conditions. Or perhaps they wanted to rid themselves of the young people, who might cause trouble. That could be it.

Another woman, this one even older than the last, reached the officer. He pushed the pen into his fist without hesitation. As a soldier pointed the way, the woman behind her, much younger, took her arm. The officer's eyes followed the pair and he opened his mouth as if to call out. An unreadable expression crossed his face and he turned away.

An old man followed them to the left, and then it was Rebeka's turn.

Eyes fixed on the pen, she stepped forward. She caught her breath, feeling the officer's gaze. A second passed, another, and then his hand opened, turning over as if to display the pen to her.

The fist clenched once more. The thumb stroked the pen's tip. Rebeka felt a sound forcing its way up her throat. She raised her eyes to meet those of the officer.

She jumped as shouts in German rose behind her. A dog barked, echoed by others. The officer dropped his hands and walked to the edge of the ramp.

Rebeka waited, eyes to the concrete. She started as someone struck her arm, looked up to see a soldier glaring at her. "*Raus!*" he said, jerking a thumb over his shoulder. At the group on the right.

She stumbled past him, shaking uncontrollably. She had to sit down. No way around it; if she didn't, she'd collapse, she knew it. But there was nowhere to sit, so she simply took her place among the other women.

Two soldiers were leading a woman to the front of the queue. One of them spoke to the officer. "... caught her off the platform," Rebeka heard him say.

The officer gave her a quick inspection. "Eager to get in, is she? We can accommodate her." He gestured toward Rebeka's group. A soldier shoved the woman in that direction. She took the first steps quickly, then slowed to a graceful walk. She slipped into the first rank next to Rebeka.

The line started moving again. The man in the homburg was ushered to the left, his family following at his heels. Rebeka took deep breaths, striving for calm. She felt disgusted with herself. To be that frightened, with no real cause. And after all she'd been through! She couldn't remember being as scared as that. Not when she'd gone off into the woods with the Techeleth Lavan, out to overthrow the Reich with a pistol, three fowling pieces, and a handful of homemade grenades. Not in the few battles they'd fought—if you could call them battles; as many of them had been with anti-Semites in the Home Army as with the Nazis. Not even when she was picked up by the Wehrmacht while trying to contact the Jews in the Warthegau ghetto, after their food had run out and the peasants turned traitor. By rights she should have died then and there, shot as a partisan. But instead the Germans had dumped her at the ghetto gates, saying that Chaim I would see to her. And so he had; she'd spent two months in the makeshift ghetto jail before leaving with this transport. Imagine, being locked up by her own people!

She wondered where the rest of them were. Micah, who had wanted her so badly, Dov, Yisroel, Misha. They'd been two dozen to start, and they'd ended up with only a third that number, following the ambushes, the betrayals, the deaths. Had they contacted the Russians, as they'd planned? Joined a friendly Home Army detachment? Or were they dead, or in this place already?

And her father. What of him? He'd wept so when she left. He never did that before. Not even when Mama died had his eyes been wet. Her unit had passed close to Dobra several times over the last year. Not once had she tried to see him. She wouldn't have been able to bear it. But now ... how long until she saw him again?

Rebeka pushed the thought aside, becoming aware that the camp itself was visible for the first time. Wire and brick: that was her first impression. A high fence, cutting off the ramp from the area within. Beyond it stood rows of low buildings, dozens of them, receding until they seemed to meet the horizon. Ahead, well past the end of the ramp, she saw two large brick buildings surrounded by trees. Behind her, where the train had passed through only a moment ago, rose a structure resembling a church tower. She trembled. So this was Oswiecim.

A movement caught her eye. Rebeka stretched to look over the woman beside her. She frowned, unable to quite grasp what she was seeing. There, some distance away, a man in a striped uniform was climbing over the wire. But no—he wasn't climbing, wasn't moving at all, just hanging there, arms spread wide. And beneath him, escorted by gray-clad guards, two men in the same kind of clothing were reaching up with a long stick, sliding it beneath the hanging man, levering him upward . . .

She winced as he dropped to the ground with a nearly audible thump. Losing her balance, she nudged the tall woman in black, who lifted a hand to steady her. Rebeka came near to grasping it to keep it close. She had no idea what it was she had just seen, but she couldn't escape feeling that it was something horrible.

A low rumble, made up of a multitude of whispering voices, drew her attention. It was the group on the left, the old, the sick, the families. From where Rebeka stood they might be passengers waiting for a conductor to wave them aboard a late train. But only at first glance. Some of them had figured it out, just as she had. Those on the edges glanced wildly about, looking for a way past the guards and dogs. On some faces Rebeka could see the sheen of tears. Across from her, the man in the homburg stood with an arm shielding his son. Still smiling, though the rest of his face was contorted as if he was being flayed.

The dogs caught the change, crouching to growl and snarl, forcing their handlers to work to keep them calm. Other soldiers moved in, some sliding their rifles off their shoulders.

Only a few remained in the queues. The officer continued his game with the pen. The fat one walked past him, took in the crowd, and hitched up his belt. "Where are the damned trucks?" he said to the tall Nazi, who merely shrugged.

There was a shout, quickly cut off. A man pushed to the edge, knocking an old woman to her knees. He started cursing the guards.

Rebeka heard a whining, as from a frightened child. The fat officer's hand strayed to the holster on his belt. Rebeka covered her mouth with her hands. She was shaking again.

"Bogati," a voice called out.

The officer paused, eyes narrowed. A dog rose on its hind legs, barking wildly. The guards fidgeted.

"Gazalti."

The voice was much louder this time. Rebeka searched the mass, finally spotting a bearded man wearing a black hat in the second rank.

"Dibarti," he chanted, his head thrown back, eyes closed. A few other voices joined his.

The plump Nazi relaxed. The guards glanced at each other and slowly lowered their rifles. The rebbe spoke on, more voices joining his. "We have been deceitful. We have sinned. We have been proud. We have been disobedient . . ."

The last Jew having passed, the tall officer took the clerk's clipboard and signed it with a flourish, his pen back to its accustomed use at last. Stalking past his colleague, he clapped him on the shoulder and shot him a grin. The big man grimaced in response.

"My God, before I was ever created, I signified nothing, and now that I am created it is as if I had not been created. I am dust in life, and how much more so in death. I will praise you everlastingly . . ."

It seemed to Rebeka as if the entire group facing her was repeating the prayer, and she heard the words being spoken around her as well. She tried to voice them herself, but her lips were quivering too much. Finally it ended, the rebbe dropping his head. Taking a deep breath, Rebeka forced out an Amen.

Rubbing the stripe on his gray trousers, the overweight officer waved the throng on up the ramp, toward the distant brick buildings. The troops had already started them moving. She saw the man in the homburg, his face placid now, putting an arm around his wife. A single sharp cry arose, nearly drowned out by the yapping of the dogs. That was all, until the rebbe began chanting once again.

It was the Kaddish, as Rebeka might have guessed. Shaking her head, she raised her hands to cover her ears. She couldn't stand that. The last time she had heard that prayer was when her father had said it over Mama. It was too much . . .

She felt a hand on her shoulder, heard a voice saying that it would be all right. Rebeka looked up. It was the woman in black. Her face couldn't be called pretty, but it was attractive all the same, angular and strong, not unlike Rebeka's own, which tended toward the boyish. Her hair was worn shorter than Rebeka was used to seeing, her eyes a deep and unknowable gray. She gazed unblinking after the marchers, her face marked with tears.

Rebeka let her hands trail down her cheeks and clasped them across her chest. The rebbe was barely audible now, even with the other voices echoing his. It faded further as the ramp emptied. In a short time they were so far off that it was difficult to make out any individuals. Only a dark mass, diminishing slowly with distance as they marched toward the far-off buildings.

A change came over the remaining guards. They moved into place quickly, tightening the line, but accomplishing it in a sloppy fashion. It was as if they'd completed the hard part of their task and were looking forward to a bit of relaxation. A dog handler ran by. As he passed, his rifle slipped from his shoulder. Rebeka winced as the butt hit the concrete. Raising his arm, the soldier forced the strap back on, cursing all the while.

Another guard stopped a few steps away, struck a match on his boot sole, and lit a cigarette. He flicked the match at the women without shaking it out.

The fat officer walked to the locomotive engine. An aide handed him a baton. He banged it twice on the boiler. With a hiss of steam, the train groaned into motion, heading in the same direction as the vanished crowd.

The last car passed, revealing more barbed wire, another set of monotonous barracks. Beyond those stood high wooden structures of a type Rebeka had never before seen, with little huts on top. She saw a figure moving inside one and realized they must be guard towers.

Tapping his palm with the baton, the officer walked past the first rank of Rebeka's group. ''All right, Judensau.'' He sprang forward, lashing out at a young girl holding a suitcase with both hands. The girl shrieked and clutched her fingers. Rebeka looked away to see that the guard with the cigarette had a baton of his own and was squeezing it with both hands. Noticing that it bent, Rebeka realized it must be made of rubber. Not a baton at all then—a truncheon, a club.

"Dump your shit!" The officer lunged at someone Rebeka couldn't see. "Now, I say!"

He passed the women in front, striking at random. "This is a camp . . ." A woman pled; he hit her again for good measure. ". . . not a resort . . ." He moved on to the men. There was a scuffle as they tried to get away. ". . . and the sooner you get that straight . . ." He turned back to the women. Rebeka saw the club rise high, heard a sickening thud. ". . . the better."

His face flushed, the officer stepped back into sight. "Be good Yids, like that last lot." Smiling, he nodded toward the gate. "They said their little prayers. That I like. You can pray too—but you'll have to do it on the run."

His smile vanished, his eyes went wide with amazement. "I said *run!*" he bawled, swinging with all his strength.

Rebeka caught only a slight movement from the smoking guard before an arm pushed her forward and a voice said, *"Go."* Then she heard only screams and thuds and the frenzied barking of dogs.

She stumbled over a suitcase, another, nearly stepping on a woman who had fallen. A dog had a young girl by the arm and was pulling her down. The girl was crying and flailing at the snout with her open palm. Something pushed Rebeka on and around. From the corner of her eye she saw a black-clad shape strike at the dog and pull the girl away.

A woman sat between the tracks, gripping her leg and shrieking, "It's broken—it's broken!" Two guards loomed over her. Rebeka turned her head.

Buffeted by the mob, she left the ramp behind and ran across bare muddy ground. The guards kept pace, taking casual swings as opportunity offered. She spotted the glowing coal of a cigarette and looked that way. A mistake: she hit a rough patch and went to her knees. She tried to rise but someone collided with her, knocking her nearly flat. She crawled a few metres, running feet forcing her down every time she attempted to stand. A sharp heel ground into her hand. She snatched it out from under, lost her balance, and pitched forward.

A large hand grabbed her arm and hauled her up. She glimpsed a gray uniform, lightning bolts, a pale and grimacing face. Then the guard flung her onward without a word.

Gasping for breath, she ran on. A hand struck her face, momentarily blinding her. She smacked into someone and nearly fell again.

Her vision cleared and she saw a fence. High voices yelled, "Szybko! Szybko!" A truncheon struck her wrist, and she looked up in shock at a woman wearing the same gray uniform as the guards. "Get in there, bitch!" the woman shouted, shaking the club in her face. Rebeka ducked away, past more female guards and on through a wooden gate. Others waited inside. They too had clubs but were less frenzied as they prodded the women toward a brick building with a wide door.

Rebeka looked over her shoulder. Most of the women had already passed the gate. The fat officer strolled easily behind them, twirling his club as if it was in fact a baton. Farther back a woman crawled on all fours, three guards beating her steadily. It looked like the one who had broken her leg.

Then Rebeka was through the door, into dimness, and screams, and voices shouting at her to strip.

She had no idea how long she was in that building. So much happened: the shaving, delousing, the sharp pain as the needle bit into her arm. When she stumbled out the other side, the sky had grown dark, the afternoon fled behind a low overcast. Someone roared at her, telling her to join the rest of the scraps. She nearly cried out at what awaited her. Shaven heads, ill-fitting dresses, eyes wide in shocked, pale faces. A gathering of trolls, or beings from the Moon.

She raised her arm: 42358, the numbers dark and clear. The surrounding skin was reddened and beginning to swell. They had given her no ointment to put on it. The woman had simply laughed and said, "This is Auschwitz, dearie," before pushing her on. And the one who had thrown her the dress, cackling that the last girl to wear it had gone up the chimney. What could that mean?

Beside her a woman stood open-mouthed, shoulders shaking with small dry sobs. It took several glances before Rebeka recognized her as the sharp-faced one from the train. No sense wondering where her child had gone—

"No talking," a guard called out. Wardress, rather—that's what the women inside had called them. Behind her, dogs at their feet, stood three others. They were chattering, the conversation broken now and again by high giggles. Two male guards loitered to one side, and beyond them several men in civilian clothing.

"You!" Rebeka froze, holding her breath until she realized the wardress didn't mean her.

"Get up!" Slapping her thigh with a truncheon, the wardress stalked to the door. "Now, bitch!"

Two women were stepping away from a third who lay slumped against the side of the building. Rebeka gasped as her face came into view: a bloody swollen mass, the eyes nearly invisible.

"Her . . . her leg's broken," one of the others said. The wardress bent over and poked at the injured woman's leg. She shuddered visibly, her mouth falling wide.

"Cyla," the wardress called out.

A girl about Rebeka's age hurried over. She was very pretty, with long blonde hair that looked as if it had never been cut, much less shaved. She wore everyday clothes, an eerie sight in this place. "Block 25 for this one," she said, jotting on a clipboard. "Go on," she told the two women, who were inching quietly away. "Pick her up."

Rebeka thought she saw a yellow patch on the blonde girl's dress and leaned over for a closer look. A hand grabbed her chin and pulled her head around.

It was a man, one of the ones in civilian clothes. Panicked, Rebeka tried to push him away. He slapped her and gripped her face more firmly just as Rebeka realized that it wasn't a man after all.

"Going for monkeys now, Bubi?"

The creature looked at the wardress. "Eh," she said in a surprisingly feminine voice. With a final smirk, she flung Rebeka back. "Not this one anyway."

"Well, back your ass off for now. You can pick and choose later."

With a shrug, the woman walked away. Rebeka burrowed farther into the crowd. She'd heard of those people. The triangle on her coat had been green—did that mean that she was a manly woman or what? It would be nice to be able to tell—

"Here," a voice whispered. Rebeka nearly cried out with relief. It was the tall woman. Her head as bare as the other's, the dress no cleaner, but on her the effect was different: she didn't look frightened at all, and something remained of her previous dignity.

"Make sure they can't see you," she told Rebeka. "Rule one."

Rebeka bobbed her head rapidly. The woman gave her a ghost of a smile.

"Attention!" the wardress's voice rang out. "March out one at a time, call your number as you pass, line up in groups of three. You bitches got that?"

For a few minutes it went slowly, then the clubs went into action, accompanied by cries of "Szybko!" The mass was thinning out when the two who had carried off the injured woman returned. One shook visibly while the other was speaking nonstop.

"Did you see their fingers? Bones, they were. They kept snatching at me . . . What will they do with them?"

"Quiet!" a voice shouted. Still jabbering, the woman put her hands over her face.

It was Rebeka's turn. She crept forth, afraid to lose the tall woman again. "Right behind you," she heard as she moved away.

Checking her arm, she rattled the number off, fearful that her throat would dry out halfway through. The wardress waved her on with a grunt.

Finally they were all lined up, the wardresses and a few male guards alongside. At a command they began marching down the path between the low barracks.

The ground was muddy, and Rebeka's clogs were too big. It felt as though she was going to lose them with each step. Her thirst had returned with a vengeance, along with the hunger that had never really faded. She was tired enough to drop and ached all over where she'd been struck, stepped on, or kicked.

Still, she felt better than at any time since the car door had slid open. At least she knew she'd survive the day. As for tomorrow . . .

She glanced at the tall woman, walking in long strides beside her. She had to suppress an urge to take her by the arm. That would be embarrassing, and what if the guards saw?

The wardress called a halt in front of a building identical to the others. She walked halfway down the column and flicked her club carelessly. "This block from here down."

"Inside!" a younger wardress called, her voice almost girlish. As the women began mounting the steps, the tall one clutched Rebeka's arm. "Wait," she said and went on ahead. Bewildered, Rebeka trailed after. On hearing what was coming through the open door, she came to a complete halt. "Ah, what's this!" a voice shrieked. "Zugangi! About time—" "This one's due for the oven—Cyla's falling down on the job."

The tall woman pushed through the group milling uncertainly around the steps and vanished within. Rebeka looked about her. Full night had come, and lights had gone on all along the fences, with spotlights glaring down from the towers. Far off something was burning; gouts of flame poured into the black sky.

The others had gone on inside. Rebeka put a foot on the first step, hesitating as someone cried out in pain, to be answered with harsh laughter and a voice shouting about ovens.

She glanced at the wardress, who smiled and tossed her truncheon into the air. It whirled languidly, silhouetted by flame. The wardress caught it with a snap. "Move your ass, slut."

With a deep breath, Rebeka plunged through the door. It slammed shut behind her.

For a moment she couldn't make out what was happening, so crowded was the space. A medley of cries, curses, and outraged shrieks deafened her. Over it all a singsong voice chanted that there was plenty of room in the bakery.

"... money, gold, jewelry. Let's have it, scraps. We know you got it ..."

The mass of women pushed Rebeka against the door, threatening to crush her. She fought her way through, thrusting them aside with her elbows. None of them protested or for that matter even noticed her. Reaching a clear spot, she saw why.

Only an arm's length away a husky woman with a vest over her dress was slamming a new arrival's head against a post. Two others struggled with someone pinned to the floor. Between them, as if acting as master of ceremonies, stood an enormous woman with black greasy hair hanging to her shoulders. She wore a thick belt, and a club dangled from one hand. The top triangle of her Mogen David was dead black.

"Come on now, give it out," she bawled, her voice revealing no emotion whatsoever. "Make it easy on yourselves."

With a squeal of joy, one of the pair holding the woman down lifted a small sack and gave it a shake. "That's mine," a weak voice said, followed by the smack of a palm on flesh.

"There we go," the blank-faced woman said. She gestured with the club. "Let's have another . . . Come on, it's for your own good."

The one in the vest—Rebeka didn't see what had happened to her victim; unconscious by now, she guessed—leaped at the crowd. With a simultaneous scream, they all moved back, nearly knocking Rebeka off her feet. She could see the tall one nowhere, and felt a stab of despair not unlike that which had gripped her when Papa told her that Mama was dead—

A tall, slender shape sprang into the open. The big woman snapped the truncheon high. "You get back—"

Rebeka missed what happened next, seeing only the big creature slam against a bunk and slump to the floor. Something clattered and she felt a sting at her ankle. Bending down, she grabbed the club and held it against her side. She looked up in time to witness the one in the vest falling flat on her face.

The tall woman paused only a second before throwing herself at the one clutching the sack. A quick flicker of hands and that thief dropped as well, followed by her partner, whose shocked curse was cut off in midsyllable.

Hands still raised, the tall woman turned about, gray eyes sweeping the room. "No more fools?"

The black-haired woman rose on one arm. Rebeka let out a yelp and pointed with the club. A foot flashed and she slumped again.

Crossing her arms, the tall woman shouted, "I want the blockawa! Now!"

"Here," a voice said, muffled in the gloom. A pinch-faced woman wearing a scarf and a man's shirt over her dress pushed through the mass of staring women. "What the hell—"

She went silent as the rest, her mouth wide with surprise. The tall one stepped over to her. "We talk."

Nodding, the blockawa took in the prone bodies one more time, then gestured to the rear of the barrack. The tall woman paused. "Wait," she said. She stepped to the moaning thief and retrieved the stolen bag. Handing it to its owner, she left the room.

Rebeka went after her, afraid to let her get out of sight. The blockawa, muttering under her breath, led them to a smaller room. Rebeka stationed herself outside the door.

She caught only snatches over the sudden buzz of talk throughout the barrack. "... whores, thieves, gangsters' women. Like characters from a Brecht play. You can't control them ..."

"You can consider them controlled now."

Someone came close. Rebeka raised the club, feeling a flash of guilt when she saw mad eyes searching her face. "Have you seen my children?" Rebeka shook her head. The woman walked on without a word.

"... over and done with. From here on, I'm the stubowa of that front room. There's more to discuss, but that'll wait for tomorrow."

"I don't know if the wardresses will care for this ..."

"So don't tell them."

Three other women timidly approached the door. The one in the lead smiled at her. She wore glasses, and Rebeka saw that her triangle was bright red. "Who is she?"

Rebeka straightened up. "She's my friend."

"Ah."

"... I think it should be you who tells the others. I've no wish to undermine your authority."

"Very well. Probably for the best."

"I agree."

There was a rustle from within the room. Rebeka gestured the three women back.

"What is your name, by the way?"

"Alma. Alma Lewin."

A second later they swept out, the blockawa in the lead. The tall one—Alma, Rebeka repeated to herself—gave her a glance and waved her to follow.

At the door the blockawa announced in a flat voice that Alma Lewin was now in charge. A cry of protest arose, dying out as Alma came into view. She pointed around the room. "You, you, and you, get your things. Find another place to sleep ... I don't care where. Squeeze in under a bunk someplace. You're out. Now."

There was muttering, but nothing more. The criminal women left, all of them keeping their distance. Alma turned to the others. "It's been a horrible day. Find yourselves a bunk and try to get some rest. We'll have more to talk about in the morning."

The women scattered to the bunks, three or four to each. Alma herself waited until the rest were settled before stepping to the bunk abandoned by the stubowa. Rubbing her forehead, she sat on the edge.

Suddenly shy, Rebeka hesitated. As she was working up the courage to move, the woman in glasses slipped through the door and approached Alma. Looking up, Alma listened for a moment and swept an arm at the bunk. The woman sat down next to her.

Rebeka hurried to a nearby spot. As she leaned against a post, the barrack lights flickered once and went out. Exhaustion gripping her, she let herself drop into a crouch. A shimmer of sound filled the room, made up of whispers and low sobs. She heard a cracked voice whimpering about children. Turning her head, Rebeka listened to what Alma and the woman were saying.

"... I'm the block clerk. You can't imagine how long we've been waiting for someone like you."

"They weren't much."

"True, but they've been here longer than anyone else. It's hardened them. Slovak women, most of them. I'm German myself, and they hate us worst of all."

"Same here."

"Ah ..." The woman's voice dropped, and Rebeka bent closer. "... certain things you should know. Who to watch out for ..."

A dark shape appeared before Rebeka. She gasped and clutched at the club. The figure raised a hand. "No—it's all right."

It was another of the women she seen at the blockawa's door, an older lady, even smaller than Rebeka herself. "You scared me," Rebeka said, hand at her throat.

"I'm sorry. They didn't feed you, yes? They never do. Here." She thrust something into Rebeka's hands. "Bread. For you and your friend. I wish we had enough for everyone, but ..." She shrugged.

"Thank you." The woman said good night and moved off. Before Rebeka was really aware of it she was chewing on one piece. Soggy and tasteless, but that made no difference; all that mattered was that she had something in her stomach. She finished and wiped her mouth, hearing once again the noises of the barrack. She wondered how many of them were crying from hunger, and was glad the lights were out.

Forcing herself to ignore the second piece, she turned her attention to the bunk.

"... Cyla—that's the pretty one."

"Oh, she's adorable, but mad. Utterly so. She's Taube's creature.

God alone knows what sort of relations they have. Too macabre to think about.''

''I should imagine. We'll keep a low profile where she's concerned. Taube too.''

''Yes. Plenty others just as bad, though. Schillinger, Grabner, Boldt . . .'' The names went on. ''. . . I'll point them out to you tomorrow. As for the prisoners . . . Are you a Communist, by the way? No? A pity. Orli Reichert—she's the camp senior—can be helpful, but she saves her favors for party comrades. I'm a Social Democrat, so she doesn't have much to say to me. But the most dangerous is Bubi . . . Oh, you're tired.''

''No, go ahead.''

''Well . . . just this until tomorrow. The worst problem here is water. There's only one source, the bathhouse, and Bubi controls it. Get on her bad side, and you won't see a single cup . . .''

''I can get water.''

There was a pause, followed by an intake of breath. ''My God—are those all dollars?''

''Yes. Nearly five thousand. I'll need you to tell me the best way to spread it around. Not too much at once—we don't want to draw attention.''

''Yes, yes. I . . . could you . . . some of my girls need . . .''

''It's for everyone, Hester.''

There was an outburst of small sounds, as if someone were choking. Alma spoke too softly to hear. ''. . . you don't know how it's been,'' the clerk said finally.

''Well, we'll see it doesn't get worse.''

The clerk left a moment later. Rebeka went to the bunk, awkwardly showing Alma the rubber club.

Alma turned, her face a shadow. ''I don't need that.''

Rebeka slid into the bunk. It was made of hard damp wood, with only a ragged blanket to cover it, no mattress or sheets. ''Well, I do.''

Wordlessly, she held out the chunk of bread. Alma looked at it and moved her head. ''You eat it.''

''I had some already.'' Her hunger flared up again at the suggestion, exactly as if he'd eaten nothing at all. She shook the bread insistently. ''Here. I'll feel bad.''

A slight smile, barely visible in the dimness, crossed Alma's face.

With a nod of thanks, she took the bread and nipped off a piece with her fingers.

"You're . . . Alma? Can I call you that?"

"Of course." She slipped another piece in her mouth. "And you?"

"Rebeka. Rebeka Motzin."

She was wondering what else to say when yet another shape approached the bunk. As she was raising the club, Alma touched her lightly on the wrist. "What is it?"

The figure seemed to collapse in on itself. "Oh, missus, please . . . I beg you, don't send me back there . . ."

Rebeka realized that it was the big woman. Alma gestured her forward. "Come close. And keep quiet. Everyone's asleep."

The woman fumbled nearer to the bunk. "It's the others," she whispered harshly. "They hate me now—they lost their place because of me. They say . . ."

"Shh." Alma waved for quiet.

Several gasps sounded, as if the woman was building herself up to continue. "They say they'll cut my throat as soon as I go to sleep. I can't stay back there, ma'am. They'll kill me. Let me sleep in here. I swear I won't be no trouble . . ."

"All right, you can stay." Alma's hand flashed out, grabbed the other woman's thick hair. "But hear me: you sleep in this room, and you're mine. Don't you dare defy me. You do, you go up the chimney. I'll send you there myself. Understand?" She shook the woman's head. "Tomorrow you'll point out the rats. The informants. Don't tell me you don't know. I know you do."

"They'll kill me."

"I'll kill you if you don't. Now go on—find a bunk."

Muttering promises, the big woman backed off. Alma watched her go before turning to Rebeka. "You need sleep too."

"Is it . . . all right if I stay here?"

"Why not?" Alma lifted her arm. "You can't see it now, but my number is only one higher than yours. So who else?"

She reached to the back of the bunk. "Here—take the blanket."

"Aren't you going to sleep?"

"Later." Rebeka was going to offer to sit up with her, but Alma's tone was final. Instead Rebeka gathered the filthy blanket about her and lay back.

"Alma," she said after a moment. "What does 'going up the chimney' mean?"

The silence drew out so long that Rebeka thought Alma hadn't heard. But finally she spoke, her voice hushed. "In the morning" was all she said.

. . . *B*ear raised his paw and the children became silent. "Hark," he said after a moment. "The soldiers are on the march." Bear, of course, could hear many things that people could not.

Baby began to cry. Heart thumping, Mina quieted her. The other children looked among themselves. "But what shall we do?"

"There is a cave," Bear growled softly. "In the heart of the forest. The trees form a fence around it, so that none but the woodfolk may see. But first"—he waved a paw—"you must remove those stars. That is how the soldiers find you. Their dogs see the stars through the trees."

The children quickly pulled off the stars and made a pile of them. Fox ran forward and, working busily with his paws, buried them beneath the soil.

"Now we will go," said Bear, dropping on all fours. "But Baby must be still."

He showed them a path that only the woodfolk knew.

As the children started down it, Fox yipped and there came a hum from the sky.

"A flying machine," Bear said, breaking into a run. "Quickly now!"

The sound came closer, and dogs began to howl. Clutching Baby tightly, Mina raced after Bear . . .

Gaspar started guiltily at a sound behind him. But it was only the office system, counting off the hours until he dropped. He looked back at the holo. He was glad that Coriolan—not to mention anyone else at the center—couldn't see him now. There were a lot of things that an operative ought to be doing to prepare for a red-level mission, but writing a fairy tale for his granddaughter wasn't one of them.

The stories were something he often did, as a way to pass the time and as a kind of personal therapy, a means of clearing his mind when frustrated, as he was now. Rici looked forward to them, and Gaspar had discovered that he enjoyed writing the tales for her just as much. A kind of tradition had grown up around them. He often illustrated them using a graphics program and had been doing it long enough to become quite good at it. Rici believed that all the characters were real, people and entities that Gaspar had met on his travels. Often enough they were.

Reaching for the keyboard, Gaspar scrolled back and read through the story. It wasn't working out. No surprise there; everything he touched seemed to go sour ever since he'd first spoken to Coriolan yesterday—or was it the day before that? The story was already twice as long as what he usually sent Rici, with no end in sight. But the real drawback was that it was simply too bleak to give to a child.

He called up the image that had prodded him to begin writing. A grainy, colorless picture, a primitive type called a "photo." A line of people dressed in dark clothing with yellow stars prominent, in the center a small girl, no older than Rici herself, staring directly at the sensor. Beside her stood a woman, perhaps her mother, though Gaspar doubted it. Surely a mother would have faced her child, held the girl's hand, offered some gesture of protection, of reassurance. Gaspar's wife had done that, even at the moment of her death. And the woman at Jerusalem . . .

It was the girl's expression that revealed her solitude. Eyes wide, mouth twisted open, on the verge of endless screaming terror. It shook a man to know that any child had ever worn such a look. His gaze dropped to the caption: AUSCHWITZ/OSWIECIM—MARCH 1944.

He pulled an image of Rici. There was his girl: her smile wide, the soft sky of Arpad overhead. It had been taken at Conjunction last year, and three of Arpad's seven moons shone clearly behind her. He recalled her laughter as they had counted them together.

He glanced between the two images, a strange sense of relief flooding him as he saw that there was no true resemblance. Over the past few hours he'd imagined Rici in that line, helplessly waiting for the darkness to sweep over her.

Bending closer, he narrowed his eyes at the ancient photo, then squinted at his granddaughter. Or did they look alike? He thumped back against the chair. He could no longer tell. He slapped at the keyboard. His words reappeared.

He'd overdosed on data, that's what it was. Worked himself too hard over the past day and a half, running through the entire available base on the episode over and over again, trying to find a way in, to trace what the renegades were after, what their target could possibly be. A hopeless task: even in the Extension, time passed hour to hour, day to day, the same as within the continuum itself. Thirty-six hours was nowhere near adequate for mission prep. Only long enough to drown in a tide of data, to saturate the mind to a point where it could no longer discern between separate elements: Judenfrage, Heydrich, Einsatzgruppen, RSHA, Treblinka, Leichenkeller, Stangl, Mischlinge, Kapo, Birkenau . . . Transports, barbed wire, death chambers, all the lost doomed faces. Like Sligo, Bokhara, and Jerusalem piled one atop the other, then multiplied a thousand times.

The sky outside was dark, the view strangely quiet. No cascade was visible, no activity at all. It was as if he was alone, the single conscious entity in the entire vast expanse of M3 Center. He called for the time: 1108, a little under two hours before he was due to drop. It seemed like an eternity.

Studying the holo, Gaspar shook his head. No, this was no story for his little girl, even considering that he was writing for himself as much as Rici. She would have been pleased to see Bear once again, but . . . no. There would be questions, and he didn't want her to know that such things had happened. Enough would occur in her own lifetime, he was sure, though he no more looked into her future than he did his own past. It would come, and it could not be changed. Regretfully, he erased the file. No story for Rici today, he thought as the keyboard dissolved into the desktop. But there was no reason it had to be done now. He would be back, after all. There would be plenty of stories to come.

He rose, forming his lips into the command that would shut the system down. But once on his feet he paused to stare quizzically at the holo. He chuckled softly and resumed his seat. Clapping his hands for the keyboard, he began making notes for a story about a strange old woman who lived in a cave. The half-hour warning caught him quite by surprise.

Gaspar halted only two steps into Coriolan's office. The holo was on, displaying a scene familiar to him, if not from that particular angle. Tightening his grip on the workcase, Gaspar dropped his eyes, more embarrassed than he cared to show.

Campbell Smith lounged in a chair, one bare leg slung over the side. A bowl of chips sat in his lap. From outside the image the soundtrack of a cartoon blared.

"I saw da wabbit," Smith told the man facing him, a squat figure in a cream Arpadian worksuit. The man crossed his arms. "Smith . . . Campbell! I'm over here, if you please."

Gaspar winced. Had he really been that loud? Perhaps Ratchi was justified in throwing him out, after all.

Coriolan leaned around a chair to wave Gaspar over. "Come in, James."

The holographic Smith broke into a wild titter. Smith had been dosed with a type of nanon that produced a psychoactive compound rendering him temporarily but completely insane. The nanons automatically replicated until a specified level in the bloodstream was reached, rendering transfusions useless. The drug itself was molecularly camouflaged so that no antidote could be identified. A dicey but certain method of assuring silence in the event of capture.

"I've had no opportunity to review this until now," Coriolan told him. Offscreen a woman's voice rose, telling Gaspar he'd gone far enough.

Gaspar masked his expression as he took a seat. Likely story, that. He'd learned long ago that there was no such thing as coincidence where Coriolan was concerned. He wondered how many times the intendant actually had viewed it, looking forward to this precise moment.

"They're very annoyed with you down in medical," Coriolan told him cheerfully. "Director Ratchi filed a formal complaint charging 'abuse of patients.' "

Gaspar grimaced. He could well believe it. His own voice rumbled from the image, demanding that the video volume be lowered.

Lips pursed, Coriolan shook his head. "You were hard on the poor child, James."

"He's a renegade. He had it coming."

"True enough." Coriolan snapped a finger and the holo went dark. Relief swept over Gaspar. He hadn't wanted to relive the part where he'd shut off the video. Not one of his finest moments. Smith had cried like the child Coriolan took him to be.

"Ratchi claims that the boy will need considerable therapy to correct the damage you caused," Coriolan was saying. "An exaggeration, I'm sure. The young virtually lived off of psychotomimetics in his now. All types, no matter what the effects. A demented period." He swung the chair to face Gaspar. "What I don't doubt is that you learned nothing from poor Campbell."

"Not to speak of," Gaspar said evenly. He should have seen that coming. He'd assumed there must be some point to this little tableau. Coriolan had his own ways of prodding people—Gaspar ought to be used to it by now.

"And what of the other data?" Coriolan shot his hands from the sleeves of his robe, a bright purple and green creation a little too impressive for Gaspar's taste. "I'm anxious to hear your strategy."

"Not much to tell."

"How so, James?"

Gaspar paused to gather his thoughts. He liked to choose his words carefully with Coriolan. Clarity was important; while the intendant had a full understanding of the Extension's activities on all levels—including some that were quite vague in Gaspar's own mind—he was convinced that Coriolan had not risen to his position by way of operations. It was awfully difficult to imagine him running a mission dressed as he was now, for one thing. "The record to date," he began, "reveals nothing. No pattern to their activities whatsoever."

He raised a hand. "I'm talking about the war period here. Prior movements make perfect sense: they were out to kill Hitler. But from 1941 on, the picture goes to pieces. Verified chronon events show them to be all over the place. One end of Central Europe to the other. That does follow the empirical progression of the episode. This Holocaust is one of the largest undertakings on record up to that time. You told me that 'massacre' wasn't the correct term. Quite right. The Nazis are draining their victims from every area of Europe under their control—which, in effect, means the entire peninsula. There's considerable evidence that the program was to be expanded once they achieved victory."

Coriolan nodded silently. Gaspar went on: "My first guess was that they were looking for a weak spot, some crucial point that would allow them to stop the progression dead with one quick blow. A substitute for negating Hitler. But it's gone on too long, in the absolute sense. Their operational now, mid-1943—"

"Late 1943."

"Excuse me?"

"The most recent chronon shower occurred on 5 September, 1943. At . . . Aus-wiz, I believe it's called. Really, James. The data was forwarded to you. I sent it myself."

Gaspar let out a breath. "My fault—I haven't checked my incoming since last night."

"Quite understandable. Some of us do require sleep. Continue, please."

"Well, late '43 doesn't change matters. There are plenty of events to date screaming for intervention. Several uprisings by the Hebrews—sorry, the Jews—including a major episode in a town called Warsaw. Serious resistance to Nazi activities in several contemp nations—Denmark, Italy, Bulgaria. But no detectable response. It's as if they're acting at random. As if"—Gaspar gestured at the empty holo focus—"Smith was directing operations for them."

"I noted that," Coriolan said. "Your conclusion?"

"Deliberate subterfuge. Taking advantage of event parameters to throw us off."

"And your intentions."

"To dive in, get my hands dirty, and see what transpires."

"Ah . . ." Coriolan released the sound as if Gaspar had said exactly what he'd been waiting to hear. "Play it by ear then, as they say. 'By ear'—do you know, I was quite perplexed the first time I heard that phrase? A fascinating language, English. Such a richness of metaphor, even in the small things. Forces one to think. Probably a major reason for the historical dominance of the Anglo peoples. But you're familiar with that thesis, of course."

Gaspar allowed himself a slow blink, wondering if Coriolan recalled that English was a second language for him.

"But tell me, James, have you ever considered putting yourself in their place? The renegades? I'm not speaking of running virts of possible intervention paths, but actually adopting their mindset, convincing yourself that an intervention is a just and proper action."

"I wouldn't."

"No? You've had active career. You've seen things. Not one episode engaged your sympathies, tempted you to change the continuum yourself? A child dying needlessly, a grand nation dismembered? A lovely creature's looks destroyed by plague, a city vaporized?"

Gaspar abruptly looked up. The thought was so close to his own of the previous hours as to be identical. He recalled Jerusalem, and Sligo, and the fact that coincidence was no part of Coriolan's style. "What do you mean?"

"Oh, nothing of importance. Simply that I've made what you'd call a pastime of intervention. Creating virtual timelines in the dataspaces, entering episodes that strike a chord, changing one variable and running it." Coriolan jiggled pleasurably in his chair. "I see you're shocked."

"Not shocked—surprised, let's say."

"Yes, I know—an intendant behaving as frivolously as that. *Dangerously* so, some would say."

Gaspar bit his lip. "How do they turn out?"

"Not very well, in most cases. Chaotic factors, you know. Events seldom develop as desired. But that's precisely the point." Coriolan's hands rose, thumb and middle fingers flat against the palm, the first and fourth of each pressed together. An intricate gesture, one Gaspar assumed was used in his homepoint, usually suppressed except when he was preoccupied. "That type of play persuades my—soul? subconscious? My term would mean nothing to you—that interventions are, in fact, futile. We could wish that Lewin and her people had done the same. If it was up to me the practice would be a standard training feature. A kind of therapy. Some periods use it as such, you know.''

"You can count me out.''

A perfect eyebrow cocked. "I guessed you'd say that.''

"And what about the Holocaust?'' Gaspar said slowly. "Does that strike a chord?''

The violet eyes widened. "Oh yes. It's so fortunate that these . . . genocides failed to become standard state policy during that epoch. Some credit the democracies, but my opinion is that they were an evolutionary artifact, a product of the interface between medievalism and modernism. Much as you find human sacrifice common in tribal cultures but seldom later. If directly exposed to such an episode, I might very well wish to disrupt it. . . . but we've wandered, haven't we?''

Expecting the intendant to rise, Gaspar gathered his feet beneath him. Coriolan made no such move, instead remaining seated, with a faraway look in his eyes. Gaspar checked the time. He was overdue for dispatch by a quarter of an hour. Not that there was any such thing as a schedule in Extension procedure, but still . . .

"I also spoke to Lisette Mirbeau,'' Coriolan said quietly.

"Oh?'' About what? Gaspar wondered. Or had he handled her too harshly as well?

"She asked—pleaded, I would say—that you be relieved of this mission.''

"Did she just?'' Gaspar slapped his workcase on the chair arm. "For what reason?''

"Calm, please, James . . . No reason; I doubt that she knows herself. She no longer thinks as we do. But . . . I remind you that you're not dropping to the 20th as an avenger. Much as I share your disdain of our renegades, keep in my mind that they are not wicked. No one attempts an intervention for base purpose. They're . . . misguided. Do be kind, James.''

Clenching his jaw, Gaspar held back a remark about ghosts now making Moiety policy. Something told him this was not a moment for sarcasm. Instead he nodded curtly.

"You're a hard man, James, but not without the faculty of pity. You know when to use your harshness. I value that highly.'' The distant look returned, Coriolan's rosebud mouth twisted in what Gaspar might have taken for pique under other circumstances. "I once possessed closeness to Lisette," he whispered.

Then, quickly enough to startle, he was on his feet. "Come along. We're late. We must send you off."

On the way to operations they discussed mission dispositions: Alexei Proskurin, C21 monitor, was on call for backup, as was Yung in the 19th. Gaspar paid little attention; he wasn't in the habit of asking for assistance. Coriolan asked about Gaspar's arrangements for the 24th. He'd left Ishtar Jaynes, a Variant based on Pacifica, one of the first colonies requiring serious biological adaptation, in charge—not so much out of confidence in her abilities as to lend her experience. She was to contact Brave Song or Dulancy if anything out of the ordinary occurred while Gaspar was gone. Nothing would; nothing ever did.

"You station yourself on your homeworld, James." Coriolan was speaking smoothly, as if the last few minutes had fallen from memory. "Most monitors operate from Earth, or what Earth becomes in the high epochs. You remain on Arpad. I've often wondered why."

"Because it's home. As close a duplicate to Earth as has been discovered up to period. Better, in some ways. The UV level from Eridani is much lower, for one. The differences are subtle, but quite evident to a native . . ."

He went on to describe the mesas that dotted his area of the Twin Continents, not quite the same as what the word described on Earth. The mild climate assured by Arpad's negligible axial tilt. The small seas with their complex tides created by the moons. Vistas rose in his mind as he spoke, each of them featuring Rici's dancing gamine form. Strange how he always pictured her when he thought of Arpad. Not Elena, not his wife—it was as if Arpad had not been his home at all before Rici was born.

"I see," Coriolan said. Operations lay only a few steps ahead. "Forgive my curiosity. I visited Arpad once myself."

"Oh?"

"Yes. In the wake of Ash Thursday."

Gaspar glanced sharply at him, wondering what in the world could have brought him to Arpad then, in that now. A never-ending source of surprises, Coriolan.

The intendant floated on, raising one hand as they entered operations. "So quiet," he said.

The room was nearly empty, no sign of arrivals, no one waiting to go either up or downline. A large space, a hundred yards in length, half that wide. To the right stood the portal platforms, the main one in the middle, flanked by two subsidiary units. Across the sunken waiting level was a control station, seldom used and dark at the moment.

At the far end, where perspective twisted near the singularities, a group of techs was at work. One of them, Gaspar saw, was from far upline. A shape floating a metre above the floor, seemingly encased in an ebony shell that flickered in odd places. It appeared to have no legs, and its arms—if they could be called that—emerged from whatever spot was needed. Three were in sight as Gaspar walked in. When he looked back after crossing the room, only one was visible.

Coriolan had already approached the dispatcher. "Aye, Intendant, bit o' heavy weather the last hour or two. That's done and over now, though."

Gaspar tried to imagine what heavy weather might look like. The Channel was itself a singularity—the source singularity, the cradle of everything—created at the moment of the primal inflation, a flaw in superspace similar to the cosmic strings and walls of normal space, but along a temporal rather than spatial axis. Expanded by the same forces that had unfolded the universe itself, the Channel stretched from the Aleph point on through the misty epochs where nothing existed but black holes and slowly deteriorating particles. Gaspar didn't know if anyone had ever reached the end of it or if it even had an end.

His personal picture of the Channel was of a long dark tube made up of toruses representing the entropy levels dividing period from period, epoch from epoch. So what would a storm be? A fierce wind of chronons, whistling up the tube, leaving the rings of the eras trembling behind it?

But of course they weren't actually rings, or cells either. Those were simply the closest analogies that fit. More like changes in the geometry of the Channel itself—which wasn't really a tube. But why let reality ruin a powerful image?

"Well then, Monitor." The dispatcher turned to Gaspar. "Cleared for the 20th, are ye? A good now to be out of, and that's truth. On duty, is it? Sure—wouldn't be goin' there for pleasure, now would ye?''

Humming to himself, the man called up another holo with a wave of his hand. ''Need to reel in a few days as well. That can be done.''

The holograms shifted to enclose him. Gaspar and Coriolan moved away. It would take the dispatcher several minutes to set up a juncture with the station. A proper link was crucial: Gaspar needed to get as close to the station's operational now—the point when Angiers's message had been sent—as possible. To violate the timelike geodesic already existing between Center and station was to risk structuring a paradox. That was possible under some circumstances, but there was no point to it as things stood.

The intendant draped himself on a couch on the lower level. Gaspar remained on his feet, too keyed up to relax. A movement across the room drew his gaze. The upliner, armless now, had drifted out of the workspace and hovered silent and motionless, silhouetted by the harsh lights behind. He/She/It appeared to be regarding Gaspar with whatever sensors served that purpose. Gaspar nodded in he/she/its direction and deliberately turned away.

Upliners—those from the late epochs, the Interstellar and Galactic—disturbed Gaspar, as they did many operatives. Granted that they were as human as he, if not more so, he couldn't help but be on his guard with them. Too many difficulties in communication, in comprehending their thinking—given that they were thinking anything comprehensible to start with. Time had opened a wide gap between the naturals on the short end and the products of controlled evolution, made up as much of silicon and energy as organic material, of the epochs to come. Gaspar tried to avoid drawing their attention, particularly at times like this, when he had an operation on his mind. Dealing with Coriolan was ordeal enough.

His soft melody dying at odd intervals, the dispatcher moved within the holo. Gaspar shifted his stance, impatient to be on his way. The man paused, arms motionless. Gaspar stepped forward, thinking he'd made contact, but with a sudden blare of sound the holo vanished.

Coriolan leaped to his feet, moving more quickly than Gaspar had ever seen him. ''What is it?''

''An emergency call, your lordship—'' The dispatcher touched a glowing patch to his right, apparently a recovery program. Behind him the portal light flashed green.

"I can hear as much," Coriolan said. "What period—"

Two armored figures stepped from the portal, a litter floating between them. Another operative followed them through, stumbling to avoid the litter. She tore away her visor, revealing an ashen face, the expression manic. "What kept you?" she shouted. "We've been waiting twenty minutes—"

"Somebody call medical," said a man leaning over the litter. "My system's down."

"It's done," Coriolan said. Robe flapping about him, he ran to the platform. "What did you—" He fell silent as he got a clear view of the litter. Setting his case aside, Gaspar went to join him.

Still shouting, the woman bore down on the dispatcher. "Marisol, please," Coriolan said. He took her hand and led her away. "A technical delay. No one's fault . . ."

The litter lay just ahead. Gaspar halted, breath leaving him involuntarily at what it held. For a moment he thought it was some kind of upliner unfamiliar to him, or even a non-Terrest sophont brought in for some unknown purpose. But no—that was armor, blackened and bent in ways he would have thought impossible, above it a shattered and melted helmet visor, behind that a face scorched to an extent where humanity had been erased. It reminded him of nothing so much as the man burned to death by the SS.

Trauma units blinked and buzzed about the shattered figure. The man beside it, obviously a medic, raised his head. "Where is *medical*?"

Something brushed past Gaspar. He started when he saw it was the upliner. The being silently drifted to the injured man's side. An extensor of some sort shot out and touched his face. The medic looked up, ready to shout. Seeing who it was, he closed his mouth.

The second operative, a blond youth with a face battered by exhaustion, stood a few feet away. With a final glance at the litter, Gaspar went over to him. "Period?"

The man's voice was tight with shock. "Late 21st, 2082."

The tension gripping Gaspar eased. He'd been afraid that this team was involved in the Holocaust operation and had run into something unexpected. "What happened?"

"It was . . . at La Jolla. Just south. The Yamatist beachhead . . ." He fell silent as med units swept into the room, personnel trailing close behind. Gaspar pulled him aside as the units slid past. "A raid of some sort?"

"Raid?" Eyes fixed on the litter, the man chuckled sourly. "The whole West Coast is ablaze that year. Not even a name for it. Just 'collapse of Pacific defenses . . . ' " He wiped his forehead. "Hold on, willya? Let me get it straight . . ."

A glance showed the machines settling around the burned man, already at work. The medic, obviously reluctant to leave, was talking to what appeared to be a nurse. The upliner was nowhere in sight.

". . . got some weird EM activity down there, not like anything we ever saw before," the blond operative was saying. "No surprise. Enough electronics in that area to make your fillings ache. But we check it out. Nothing to it, far as anybody can see. Then we spot some lifters on the horizon. Big ones, Yamatist. No way they could detect us, but . . ." He paused to rub his face. "We get hit anyway. Don't know by what—the weapons are evolving on their own in that now, that's why the Chinese abandon them afterward. Some kind of plasma thing, I don't know. It's just *there*, one minute nothing, next . . . world's on fire. Knocked me over, busted me up some," he moved one arm. "This is broken. But Felix . . ."

At the platform the litter had risen and was floating to the door, med units clustered thickly about it. The medic followed, limping slightly and supported by a nurse. On the lower level a doctor hurried to where Coriolan and the team leader sat.

". . . just burned him down. I look over, and that's all there is, this silhouette, all lit up. Burned him down, that's all . . ."

Gaspar gestured to one of the med personnel. "Take him along. He needs treatment."

"No—" The man winced as his hands rose. "I'll only get in the way. I'm not that—"

Gaspar raised his voice. "Don't be absurd. You told me your arm was broken."

The man's expression suddenly cleared. "You're CM James, aren't you? What are you doing here?"

"On duty." The nurse took the young man's good arm. "Now go on." He watched the two leave before turning his attention to the room. Coriolan, protectively clutching Marisol's shoulders, was speaking to the doctor. The woman had her head in her hands. When she looked up, Gaspar saw tears. "I never lost a man before," she wailed.

"You have not now." The voice was deep, with unfamiliar overtones. Gaspar looked behind him. It was the upliner, floating in the dimness at the rear of the platform. "The individual will survive. Some psychic reconstruction will be required."

"Then it won't be *him*," Marisol said, weeping anew. Coriolan whispered to the doctor. The two of them helped the woman to the corridor.

Behind him the dispatcher cleared his throat. "Shall I complete your linkage now, sir?"

Gaspar threw a glance at the entrance. No telling when Coriolan would return. "Yes."

Retrieving his case, he began an aimless pacing. The techs spoke among themselves, not yet back at work. Probably discussing how much they missed out on not being part of operational staff—

"An uncommon sequence."

It was the upliner, floating only six feet behind him. "Not uncommon enough," Gaspar answered.

"You drop to the 20th."

He turned to the . . . being. "Yes," he said shortly as he ran his eyes over the shape. About a man's height, but far bulkier. The color was a matter of opinion; dark, but seeming to shift tone wherever the eye settled. It was armless, featureless, simply a long tapered shell with a semisphere set on top. Like a sarcophagus. A floating coffin.

"Not your home era." The voice was deep, not machinelike though lacking any organic quality, neither masculine nor feminine.

"True," Gaspar said. "Not even my own world. My origin is non-Terrest."

"The 20th is a period of interest. A time of bloodbaths, the worst ratio of willed death while the race was confined to one world. The Age of Massacre. It holds the name even in my epoch."

"I'm aware of that." Gaspar shot a glance at the platform. The dispatcher was still at work.

"To what event are you assigned?"

"The . . . Second World War." Gaspar considered that the being might be able to detect the falsehood even as he wondered why he was bothering to lie.

"Within the Iron Decade, then—the period 1932 to 1945. The epitome of human spite. A deficit mortality of nearly five percent of the race. Does your assignment impinge on these events?"

"Why do you ask?" Gaspar noticed movement and saw that Coriolan had returned, after all. But instead of approaching him as he expected, the intendant stopped to listen respectfully to the upliner.

"You're aware that transfer between eras involves considerable psychic shock, strains on the mentality that are well understood but difficult to control?"

Gaspar forced a chuckle. "Of course. That's the first—"

"Your aura—that is, your expression, gait, movements, scent, the entire gestalt of activity—reveals considerable agitation."

"You mentioned uncommon sequences."

"It was evident when you first entered this space." Gaspar eyed the being warily, wishing for some way to make out an expression. The voice alone revealed little.

"Is this stress associated with your assignment?"

"I . . . suppose it is. I'm usually drawn rather tight before a mission. Look"—he raised a hand—"it's nothing out of the ordinary. I don't know your home epoch—High Interstellar, I'd guess—but matters differ here on the short end. Stress is the least of our worries. We utilize it, in fact. It's a resource, a type of fuel. We're not as, uh, evolved as you are. If we didn't have anxiety to kick us along, we might never get anything done."

"That may be so," the upliner said. "But—there is a practice in my time . . . A meditation? A ritual? A game, perhaps. We construct emotional portraits of different eras. Outlines of the psychological states of centuries, decades, events. I would display an example, but you are not equipped to process it. There is a strangeness in you, Monitor. Your own aura is clear and strong. But it contains echoes of no period at all."

Gaspar stared wordlessly. The being's surface seemed fuzzy, as if it was constantly changing shape on some level at the edge of vision. But Gaspar knew that if he were to lay a hand on it, it would be rock-hard. And cold as ice.

"Opinion on this is your own. But I believe it deserves consideration."

Tearing his eyes away, Gaspar looked around the room. Coriolan contemplated them with a hand on his chin. The other workers—the normal ones, human ones—were watching with signs of puzzlement. And on the platform . . . He nearly gasped with relief. The portal was open, the dispatcher waiting.

He turned back to the upliner. "Strange words coming from a tech."

The being seemed to bend, as if in a bow. "I am also a . . . a priest."

"Ah, a priest!" Gaspar clutched the workcase more firmly under his arm. "Probably a good idea to consult with clergy before a mission. Not my usual habit, though." He took a step toward the platform. "I'm afraid the continuum awaits—"

"I've inserted my identity—name, you'd call it—in your files," the upliner said. Gaspar glanced down at his work case. It hadn't even beeped. "An address as well. Contact me on your return. I have an interest in the 20th. Your assigned decade in particular, the period of the ultimate crimes, the sin of Auschwitz—"

"What?" Gaspar's eyes narrowed. "You know of that place? In your epoch?"

"Of course."

Gaspar restrained himself from grabbing at the being; there was nothing for him to grab. That this creature should know of that site, with whatever thousands or millions of years separated it from the 20th . . . Gaspar had never heard the name before he'd been assigned the mission.

For a moment he felt hollow, as bereft of history and roots as the upliner had just now implied. But beneath that grew an excitement born of certainty: that he had just been handed his key, the lever he needed to pry open Lewin and her rabble. With an effort, he calmed himself. "Yes, I'll contact you," he told the upliner. "Be certain of that." A final nod and he turned to the platform.

"James!" Coriolan called out. He walked on, oblivious. The intendant caught up to him at the ramp. "James, I—"

"Thank you for stepping in," Gaspar snapped at him. "Did you hear what that thing was saying to me?"

Coriolan looked away. An intendant's duty, after all, was to mediate between the ages, to act as a bridge between epochs with nothing in common but time. "It seemed important, James."

"Oh? You read auras too, do you?" Gaspar said as he stepped to the platform. "I wonder if it reads omens as well. Plenty of them to be found here. Fine way to start a mission—"

"Oh, James, don't be such a primitive."

Gaspar swung back to him, making the most of his advantage of height. But Coriolan's head was turned, one hand to his lips, as if he'd tried to hold the words back. "Forgive me, James," he said in the voice of a very tired man. "This"—both arms extended to take in the room—"brought back horrors. Things best left buried."

With a long stride, Gaspar crouched down at the edge of the platform. "I know the feeling."

Only then did Coriolan look up. "Yes. We all do." He gripped Gaspar's free hand in both of his own. His ambiguous mannerisms had vanished—in fact, Gaspar hadn't seen any of that since the alarm had blared. It occurred to him that he might be glimpsing the true Coriolan for the first time.

The intendant squeezed his hand. "Safe return, James."

"I take that as an order, Intendant." With a wink, he drew away.

"Here we are, sir," the dispatcher said as Gaspar approached the portal. "As close as it be without shorting."

Gaspar glanced from the amber READY light to the portal itself, a blackness as impenetrable as the floor beneath his feet. Behind him Coriolan was asking the upliner if it was free to speak. He called the creature "Pater." It would be interesting to learn what Pater might make of Alma Lewin's aura. First Coriolan, now this upliner. He wondered what kind of game the dispatcher made of his responsibilities.

"There ye be!" the dispatcher called. The light went green. "Have a care, Monitor. God keep ye."

Gaspar snorted as he stepped forward. Was every entity in the Moiety trying to make him . . .

1943

A transport had arrived last night. The crematoria blazed until dawn, and number three was still spewing smoke, filling the camp with sticky ash and that foul stench unlike anything Reber had experienced, even in the east.

Reber sat at his desk, trying to lose himself in the paper. The *Völkischer Beobachter*, the party's morning sheet. Three days old, but what could you expect out here? The Auschwitz complex wasn't on the main route to anywhere.

He was going through the news, reading between the lines in order to put together an honest picture of how the war was going. Not the Mediterranean theater; he could care less about that. So the Allies had taken Sicily. What of it? Where could they go from there? Fight their way up the boot and then across the Alps? An absurdity. No, that operation had to be a mask for activity elsewhere. No other explanation made sense.

It was the eastern front, the war he knew, that interested Reber most. Strange, but when he'd been there, in the cold that pierced deeper than he could have imagined, on the steppes nearly as infinite as the sky itself, fighting Russians in numbers that matched, he'd have sworn he'd never look back. But now he couldn't get enough of it.

Not that there was much to grasp. The *Beobachter* held little more than propaganda. Plenty of heroic yarns, exhortations toward greater efforts on behalf of the Reich, the usual vilifications of Churchill and Roosevelt. Little in the way of hard facts. It would be nice to see other papers, perhaps from neutral countries. But Höss would never approve of that. If the Kommandant was satisfied with the *Das Schwarze Korps* and *Der Stürmer*, they'd have to be enough for everybody else.

From what he could gather, the front was now stabilized. Kharkov and Poltava were lost, evidently for good, but Manstein had pulled Army Group Center together on the line of the Dnieper. Little enough to ask for, after the fiasco at Kursk. For a while there Reber had been convinced that the Reds would simply sweep aside everything in their path and drive straight into Europe. That danger was past, for the moment at least. All the same, he'd like to hear word of an offensive, some kind of response . . .

He looked up, aware of a change, a slight shift in his environs just now. A habit acquired in combat, where noticing the smallest detail often meant survival for one more day. He glanced around the room. The desks opposite him were empty. He'd sent the staff to lunch early; it was either that or listen to them chatter. So what could it have been? The clock was still running. Telephones, clipboards, orders of the day, Himmler and the Führer admiring each other from opposite walls. No, it hadn't been in here. The sound of typewriter keys continued from the next room, and he could hear Knoblauch speaking on the telephone across the hall. Perhaps it had not even been within the building. He looked uneasily over his shoulder at the window and was about to get up when a distant blare of sound gave him his answer.

He sighed and sat back. It was the prisoners' orchestra. A moment ago they'd been playing some rinky-tinky classical piece. Mozart, he supposed. He'd never cared much for the stuff; that was his mother's kind of thing. Operas, symphonies—she couldn't get enough of it. You'd think she was an artist herself rather than the wife of a shop foreman the way she went on; comparing orchestras, conductors, pointing out differences in tempo and interpretation. It all sounded the same to him.

Reber himself enjoyed more sturdy music; jazz, show tunes, or marches, like the *Badenweiler*, the one that the band was playing now. He recalled the first time he'd heard that tune, and all the others too; the *Hakenkreuzschwur*, the *Triumphmarsch*. Nearly ten years, it was. He'd been a young man then, in his mid-twenties, held by the dreams and passions of youth. Proud of being chosen for the elite guard, of the black uniform and enameled helmet with the lightning bolts on the side, of the grand mission that awaited him. To turn Germany around, to seize its rightful place among nations, to astonish the world. He closed his eyes, trying to recapture the promise of those days. Nuremberg, the great rallies of the '30s. Reber had attended them all, as part of his unit. The vast ranks of the SS, in full regalia, a black host stretching across the stadium from where the huge swastika banners flapped and boomed in the breeze. Many of his comrades collapsed under the hot Bavarian sun, standing at attention for hours while the party leaders spoke. But not Reber. He'd always endured, back straight, waiting for the moment when the Führer appeared.

But he couldn't really say he'd ever heard him speak. He'd always been too far in the rear, and his helmet had interfered. He recalled turning his head, trying various positions in order to capture the words. But all he'd ever heard was a distant gabble that seemed completely unconnected to the tiny figure on the stand.

He'd met the Führer once, if only for a moment. In Paris, after the 1940 campaign. The Führer had driven by in his staff car and had stopped to chat with the troops. Reber had actually shaken his hand.

He glanced between the two portraits. It was said that the *Badenweiler* was the Führer's favorite march. As for Himmler—Reber suspected that the Reichsminister had little use for music.

Sarah Blaustein appeared at the door to the typing room. Ever polite, she bobbed her head before approaching the desk. "This morning's correspondence, Obersturmführer."

Reber nodded and accepted the sheets. "The Department IV-B-4 letter is on top, as you requested."

"Danke, Frau Blaustein."

With a short bow, she turned away. Reber watched her leave. A ragged but clean striped dress, sweater over that, a scarf covering her graying hair. A fine woman, capable and efficient. Kept her girls busy and out of trouble. You wouldn't guess she was Jewish without the star. She'd been here when he first arrived, three months ago. It was seldom that they said more to each other than what had just now passed between them.

He went over the letters. The first, as always, was to Eichmann's office. It concerned the transport that had arrived yesterday. Number sent out: 1,983. Losses en route: 223, leaving . . . Ah, but this was unusual: the numbers didn't tally. The count at the ramp had been 1,761, one high. The second paragraph was a complaint about the sloppiness of the Lódź SS office. How on earth could proper records be kept with this kind of thing going on? Reber gave a sour grunt, thinking about how much uproar there would be had the total been one short.

He skipped through the last part, detailing the percentage selected for special treatment, and went on to the other letters. Duplicates of the first, to Massute at Generaldirektion der Ostbahn, Globocnik at the Generalgovernment, the Lódź SS, the WVHA . . .

"Gerd!"

Reber looked up. Knoblauch leaned through the office door, eyes red, jacket collar unfastened. Holding back a frown, Reber set the sheets on the desk. "What is it?"

"I need a hand." Knoblauch rubbed the back of his shaven head. "It's the worker Kikes. I've run out of causes."

"Too many heart attacks, hmm?" Reber dropped his eyes. For reasons he was unable to grasp, the Arbeitzjuden—those actually working in camp—weren't allowed to die anything other than natural deaths. It was Knoblauch's job as personnel clerk to make up the death list, and he had difficulty thinking up suitable demises. A few weeks ago—possibly the result of an excess of brandy in the club the previous night—he'd filed an entire week's total as dead of heart attacks. Höss learned of it and raised the roof, appearing at the Stabsgebaeude to threaten Knoblauch personally with everything from demotion to transfer to the east.

"Well, they won't let us use disease, Gerd. Come on now, help me out."

"Septic shock," Reber said in a dull voice. "Apoplexy, noma . . ." What was he doing in this madhouse? Killing them like bugs, like vermin, at one end of the place and falsifying their deaths at the other. His eyes strayed to the wound stripes on his sleeves. He was keeping himself alive, that's what he was doing.

Writing quickly, Knoblauch jotted the words on a pad, occasionally asking for a spelling. As Reber finished, Knoblauch looked up with a wolfish grin. "What was that one from last week ... 'pull'-something?"

"Pulmonary embolism."

"Uh-huh. Good enough, then." Knoblauch shook his head. "Thanks, Gerd. Damned if I'll ever guess where you picked this stuff up."

"I went to school, you twit," Reber muttered as he disappeared. Brother SS man or no, Knoblauch was hard not to despise. Women and pay were his sole interests. If he wasn't whining about how much of his salary went to party contributions, he was detailing his sexual antics. Take this morning, for instance. Knoblauch had treated himself to a spree in the brothel at the main camp last night, and Reber choked down his breakfast listening to how the Yid whores would do anything, with plenty of illustration. Capped, as always, with Knoblauch's observation that Obersturmführer Reber "was a better National Socialist than any of us. No subhuman ass for him, eh?"

Knoblauch wouldn't have lasted an hour in the Waffen-SS.

Going back to the correspondence, Reber riffled through the sheets. No sense checking the rest. It would all be perfect; not a word misspelled, not a comma out of place. He gazed at the door to the typist's room, where the tapping went on steadily, ever present, seldom heard. They knew better than to turn in poor work.

A glance at the clock told him it was barely noon. He shoved the sheets to the edge of the desk. Not enough to do here, that was the problem. Nothing but think, and what the devil were you supposed to think about? What?

He got up and went to the washroom. When he returned, a thick envelope holding the afternoon's typing lay on his desk, along with a covered plate. He pulled it close, put the lid aside. Sausage—probably more bread crumbs than anything else—noodles, a buttered roll. Spearing a sausage, he slapped it on the roll and ate quickly, not tasting it, not trying to taste it. When he was finished, he pushed the seat back, loudly cleared his throat, and walked to the window. His hand rose, but he jerked it back before it could touch the pane. There was a film on the glass, of a smoky blue color. It appeared whenever a transport was processed.

The view was to the west, revealing most of the B.II section and the unfinished B.III. In the distance the chimneys of the crematoria stood. To his left number three was still belching smoke. He shifted his eyes, but what he saw to the north was little better: hundreds, perhaps thousands of inmates working on the new section, carrying dirt from the higher spots to level out the area. In wheelbarrows if they were lucky, on their backs if they weren't. Guards moved among the workers, many of them leading dogs. A frantic movement close to the wire caught Reber's eye. He gritted his teeth. A prisoner was being run around the site. As Reber watched, the man stumbled and the Alsatian pacing him took a nip out of his thigh.

Behind him he heard stealthy footsteps, the scrape of a utensil on a plate. He lifted his eyes to the sky, disregarding the smoke curling overhead.

A quick movement at the edge of the window pulled his gaze downward. Too late for a clear glimpse, but he'd seen enough: a figure in black striding purposefully toward the Stabsgebaeude.

Stemming an impulse to open the window, Reber swung back to the desk. The women had returned to the typing room—lord, but they were quick. He clapped the lid on the plate and pushed it to one corner. Folding the paper, he shoved it into a drawer and then centered the letters directly in front of him.

The outside door creaked and slammed shut, followed by the sound of bootheels pacing the hall more loudly than usual. Reber gazed blankly at the desktop, not raising his head. Then Knoblauch brayed, "Ah, Maxim! Heil Hitler!"

"Sieg Heil," a low voice replied. Knoblauch said something that ended with a laugh. The other voice went on, too quietly for Reber to make out the words.

He reached up and pulled at his collar. He'd guessed correctly—it was Boldt, on one of his unscheduled inspections of the Kommandantur offices. Reber bent forward, trying to hear what they were saying. All he could pick up was muttering, an occasional chuckle, the clink of glass. He sat back, continuing his pretense of hard work.

Hauptsturmführer Boldt was a well-known figure in the Birkenau camp. He was assigned to the political office as a liaison between the Gestapo and the Totenkopf-SS that ran the facility. As far as Reber could tell, he had no particular duties, instead simply keeping an eye on personnel for signs of corruption, disloyalty, and moral degeneration.

Reber had met Boldt only once, when he'd first arrived, but he'd heard a lot of stories. Boldt had supposedly brought down Aumeier, the old camp Gestapo head, on charges of embezzling funds from prisoners. Some of the rumors held that he'd arranged for his chief to be caught with a safe full of cash. While Reber had never been one to credit gossip, the facts in Boldt's case were stark enough: that he'd served in Einsatzgruppe B, that he wore his dress blacks as often as possible, as if constantly on parade, that people's behavior changed in his presence.

He shifted in the seat at a whoop of laughter from Knoblauch. "Ah, big man Voss! I wish I could have seen that."

Boldt's voice rose to match. "Yes, he was probably mumbling, 'Orders are orders' all through it."

Reber frowned. Voss was a camp guard, sullen and sour-faced, that he'd had little to do with. Now that he thought of it, Voss hadn't been present in the mess this morning. Once again he leaned forward, curious as to what had happened, but the low voices frustrated him.

Frau Blaustein entered with more correspondence. This time she said nothing to Reber, only setting the sheets down with a wide-eyed glance at the hall. Reber had to call her back to hand her the afternoon's typing. For a moment she just stared from a dead-white face, then, for the first time he could remember, she smiled as she took the envelope.

He was still looking after her when footsteps sounded in the hall. He turned in time to see Boldt enter the room. Shooting to his feet, Reber clicked his heels. "Sieg Heil, Hauptsturmführer—"

Boldt raised a hand. He wore one dress glove. The other was stuck in his belt. "At ease. Quite all right. Not what you'd call a formal visit."

Reber shifted his stance slightly. In the other room the sound of typing seemed to slacken somewhat, then increase to a frantic tempo. He heard a small cry, as from someone who'd made a mistake.

Boldt paced around the room, inspecting it as if he'd never seen it before. "Correspondence," he whispered to himself. He pointed at Reber. "It's not just you? Sit down, sit down. No sense going by the book. Not here."

"There are several enlisted men also," Reber said as he took his seat. "But not much for them to do."

"I see." Boldt was eyeing the framed copy of the SS oath on the wall with evident approval. Forcing calm on himself, Reber tried to relax. He dropped his eyes to the desk; he hadn't looked away from Boldt once since he'd come in. It wouldn't do to let the Hauptsturm-führer think he was staring. His fingers began to tap the desktop; Reber clenched his fist. He glanced up again. Boldt was humming *Lili Marlene* along with the prisoners' band. A good-looking man. Not quite a Gestapo posterboy; a little too dark and hatchet-faced for that. But still quite handsome, particularly in dress black. That uniform was supposed to be reserved for parades and state occasions, but perhaps regulations were different in the Gestapo.

Inspection finished, Boldt approached the desk with an easy swagger. Reber couldn't help but think that nobody swaggered once they'd been at the front. Propping himself on the edge of the desk, Boldt pushed back his cap. "So how are affairs here?" He gestured at the inner door. "They're doing what they're told?"

Reber answered with a simple affirmative. He wanted to watch his step. He'd noticed that reactions to Boldt took two forms: enthusiasm or fear, with nothing in between. He had no desire to learn the reason why.

Reaching into his pocket, Boldt took out a small cigar. Reber opened a drawer to look for a match. "No, no," Boldt said as he stuck the cigar between his teeth. "I don't light up. Not anymore. Bad for the wind." He smiled. "You didn't know that? Old joke in the mess. But we haven't spoken much, have we?"

Boldt noticed the sheets. "May I?" He picked them up. "Ah," he said. "This miscount business. Today's big news. What do you make of it?"

"An error at Lódź, I suppose."

"Must be." Boldt chuckled. "After all, they're not stampeding to get in here, are they?" He glanced through the rest of the letters. "You hear about Voss, by the way?"

Reber shook his head.

The cigar rose in Boldt's mouth. "You'll enjoy this. Same transport. Over at the bathhouse. They'd processed the first batch, and the rest were getting antsy, so Voss decided to shoot them, get it over quickly. One of them had her whelp with her, and Herr Orders started on them first, get the hard part over with.

"Well, he walks over with his pistol, and the woman turns to hide the kid. So Voss shuffles around in front of her, and she turns again, of course, and there they are, the two of them, waltzing away right in front of the chamber."

Boldt's hands whirled around each other in illustration. Reber kept his eyes on them alone.

"He finally managed to put a round into the brat over her shoulder. The bitch didn't approve, needless to say. So you know what she did?" Boldt slapped his thigh. "Turned around and flung it straight at Voss! Right in the chest!"

He shifted his cigar to the other side of his mouth. "And Voss— little blood on his grays—he cracked. Couldn't aim, even cock the gun. Had to ask his aide to finish up."

Boldt squinted at Reber over the cigar. "How do you like that, Reber? Little blood on his grays."

Reber grunted. "Hell of a story."

Plucking the cigar from his lips, Boldt frowned at it. "Knoblauch— across the hall there—got a big kick out of it."

"Knoblauch's a jolly sort of fellow."

Boldt bit down on the cigar. "So he is," he muttered. His eyes met Reber's. "But you're not?"

Looking away, Reber shrugged. "It depends. Duties, you know. They're to be taken seriously . . ."

"I see." Boldt set a hand on the desktop, all four fingers spread wide. A flash caught Reber's eye. Boldt was wearing a ring, of a type made by Jewish goldsmiths within the camp. It bore the Totenrune— two Y's, symbolizing life and death, set base to base, one up and one down. As Reber watched, Boldt clenched his fist and tapped the wood twice.

Boldt swung toward the door of the typing room. "Anything interesting in there?" He made a move as if to get up.

"Feel free," Reber said, waving at the door.

Boldt cocked an eye at him. "Well now, tell me."

"Nothing special," Reber said. "Secretarial types. Most of them older. Chosen more for skill than looks."

Boldt pondered that a moment, then seemed about to go ahead and check for himself. Reber tensed: actually, there was a pretty blonde girl among the typists, one who could easily have passed as an Aryan.

But instead Boldt swung back to face Reber. "No sense disturbing your Hafjuden at their work," he said.

"Court Jews, Hauptsturmführer? I wouldn't say that. They're workers, same as all the rest. I don't know how this office would run without . . ." Reber's voice trailed off.

"Without them?" Boldt threw his head back, studied Reber over the tip of his cigar. "Well, my friend, eventually it'll have to. Keep that in mind."

He reached for the second stack of correspondence and began idly going through it. As if to give Reber time enough to sweat. He read the top sheet, then handed it to Reber. "Still fighting with Topff and Sohne over the damaged ovens. Our fault, really. The Sonderkommando—we don't keep them long enough. No sooner do they learn how to operate the things than they go in themselves."

The next drew a chuckle: "The Kommandant replying to Pohl concerning complaints about staff drinking. You don't drink to excess, do you, Reber? I didn't think so. Nothing to worry about, then."

Boldt went through the next few sheets quickly—standard requisition letters, Reber saw. Looking closely at another, Boldt smiled. "Ah, more complaints," he said. "Conditions in the women's camp. A problem there, Gerd. The whores are running the goddamn place. Something has to be done about that, no?"

Boldt paused and lowered the sheet. "But you don't get into the camp much, do you?"

"Not . . . very often, no, Hauptsturmführer." Reber felt his face redden. In truth, he hadn't set foot in the camp proper at all.

"I see." Carefully restacking the sheets, Boldt set them down before Reber. "Well, it happens that a party is planned at burner three. There usually is whenever a transport is run through. To blow off steam, you know. Decent liquor, better food than this—" He nudged the covered plate. "Even a bit of sport. They've arranged a match between two of the Sonderkommando. A miner and an ironworker. Big husky fellows, unusually so for Jews."

He got to his feet. "I'm going over there now. Interested?"

Reber stammered out an excuse.

Putting the cigar in his pocket, Boldt pursed his lips. "I thought not. Well then—" He headed for the hall. "You seem to have matters nicely in hand. My compliments to your Hafjuden." At the door he stopped and faced Reber. "But one thing."

Risen from his seat, Reber stared at him

"In future, Obersturmführer, use the familiar 'du' when speaking to me." Boldt adjusted his cap. "It's encouraged, you know."

He raised his arm. "Heil Hitler," he said, and then he was gone.

Reber waited until the sound of bootheels faded before he sat down. He reached up to rub his forehead. It was sweaty; he searched his pockets for a handkerchief, wiped his face dry, then worked the flimsy cotton between his fingers until it tore.

He hadn't known it would be like this. When he was transferred to the Totenkopf-SS after being released from the hospital, the personnel officer had told him he'd be on special duties only until he was fully healed. "You'll be in action again soon enough, lad," he said. "Until then, the Führer will have work for you."

Reber had told him, with perfect bluntness, that he had no wish to be assigned to an Einsatzgruppe. And the man smiled, and said by no means, that the Einsatzgruppen had been disbanded, that he was being sent to POW camp in Poland. And he showed him, on the order form itself: KGL AUSCHWITZ.

But the joke had fallen flat. Auschwitz was not a POW camp at all, not even a Koncentrationlager, but something nameless, something he could never have imagined, even after hearing the rumors about the special actions in the east. A place where thousands arrived only to vanish within hours, as if they'd never lived. Where skeletal beings moved beneath the sun. Where men—German men, men he knew— laughed while blood dripped off their boots. Where the stink of burning flesh permeated everything, even his clothes, the food that he ate. A place where death walked regnant only a wire's thickness away.

He yanked open a drawer, the lowest one. It was filled with papers. He searched through them. Somewhere in there, near the bottom, was a transfer request form, blank and pristine, awaiting his hand.

But even as he scrambled through the mess he felt his resolution fade. Grabbing a handful of paper, he lifted it out of the drawer.

Copies, old orders, regulations, excess forms—all waste. He dumped it back in and slammed the drawer shut.

What choice did he have, what choice? They wouldn't reward him for backing out, that much was certain. The best he could hope for— the absolute best—was to be sent east. He didn't think he could bear that.

He recalled winter sunrise on the steppes. The eastern horizon at dawn: one glaring band of light stretching from north to south. Men bent over fires, so close that a smell of singed leather rose. Scarves under the helmets to keep the frost from stealing your ears. Someone had mentioned coffee.

Then white shapes rising out of the brush, as if the snow itself had turned against them. Russians, in quilted winter gear. Russians who should not have been within thirty kilometers of their position. The bark of the PPSh's, sounding too low and soft to do any harm. A scream as a man fell face-first into the fire, mouth gouting blood. Reber himself turning, pulling his Walther from inside his coat, getting off only two shots before a grenade knocked him on his back.

A Russian pumping two rounds into him—one in the gut, another creasing the ribs—before dropping himself. Shouts signaling the counterattack, German training and skill overcoming Russian numbers. But Reber hadn't seen that. He'd been lying there fighting off the pain, slipping in and out of blackness, feeling the cold bite into him, knowing that the next time he faded out might be the last.

It would have been, if a Panzergrenadier regiment hadn't arrived within the hour. He'd have died there, frozen in his own blood. And if not that morning, then a week later, or the week after that. His unit had fought at Kursk, and the papers said that SS Panzerdivision Das Reich was now being reorganized. Reber knew what that meant.

It could be worse than that. An SS officer must follow orders at all costs. The man who did not could be shot, sent to a punishment battalion, demoted, expelled. A man cashiered by the SS had no place in German society; he was unworthy, a pariah, a nullity. Reber had heard Obergruppenführer Eicke say exactly that, years ago, before the war began.

He jerked as a shot came from outside, waited with gritted teeth. Sometimes there were two. Swinging in the seat, he glared out the window. A shudder wrenched him at the sight of the smoke-blue pane.

My God, couldn't they even keep the windows clean in this place?

Hearing a sound behind him, Reber stiffened. He turned, afraid that Boldt had come back. But it was only Frau Blaustein, another stack of letters in hand. He nodded as she approached and set them down. For the second time in his experience she smiled.

He dropped his eyes. A fine thing. He, a German officer, an Aryan, receiving sympathy from a member of the Rassenfeind. He looked across the empty room. From the wall the Führer eyed him sternly. He reached for the letters. The top one was to Tesch und Stabenow, an order for 150 barrels of material for the Jewish resettlement. Reber quickly set it aside.

1943

Opening the door a crack, Rebeka scanned the Lagerstrasse. It was dangerous out there at all times, even at night. Anywhere that they could see you was dangerous, especially if they found you alone.

Seeing no movement, she pushed the door wider. Lights greeted her, thousands of them, more than there were stars in the sky. It reminded her of the time her father had taken her to Łódź. That was how it looked, like a big city. It seemed almost inviting.

She shivered as a cold breeze touched her. Behind her she heard the sounds of the block coming to life: coughing, groans, the voice of a sick woman still lost in a dream. Rebeka slipped out, shutting the door quietly. In a few minutes Alma would be awake.

She crouched to put on her clogs, remaining in that position for a moment while she looked about carefully. No sounds or sign of anyone watching, but you could never be sure. The guards sometimes wandered the camp at night, in groups or alone. Often they were drunk.

Taking a deep breath, she went down the steps. The mud, damp and clammy, squelched beneath her clogs.

In each direction she saw low mounds in front of the nearby blocks.

She went to the closest. It resolved into a mass of limbs and torsos, pale skin drawn tight over bone. Bodies, stripped and left outside for the Todtkommando to collect. Three women who had died this night.

Rebeka rubbed her hands on her dress. It had grown harder the last two mornings, but it had to be done. She'd learned that in the forest. Leave no tracks, no marks, nothing to reveal that you'd been by. No one had died in her block for weeks, thanks to the money and the little pills that Alma had smuggled in. No deaths meant no bodies. And if there were no bodies, someone would notice: Mandel, or the Owl, or the Dark One. Alma didn't seem to realize that.

Bending over, she grabbed a leg and started dragging a body though the muck.

She was trembling, even though it wasn't that cold. It had been a mild fall so far, warm and dry for all but a few days. That meant a chilly winter; it always worked that way. Last winter had been terrible. Mama Blazak told her that people had frozen to death even inside the blocks.

The steps were right behind her. She let go of the leg and straightened up. The sky was beginning to lighten in the east. In the near distance a gout of flame burst from the crematorium. Rebeka dropped her head. She knew what that meant now.

The woman's limbs were loose, her arms trailing. The body had been hidden for a day, so that someone next door could claim the food ration. Rebeka stooped down to arrange the hands over the woman's chest. The least she could do. She pictured her mother lying in the coffin on the table and bit her lip.

She hurried to the pile in front of the other block. As the body came loose, it rolled over and Rebeka saw that half the face had been eaten away by a noma lesion. Backing off, she retched on an empty stomach. She'd never known there were things like that before she came here.

Holding her gaze away from the face, she pulled the body alongside the first. This one was still stiff. Rebeka was rising when she heard a gasp behind her.

She whirled, automatically coming to attention. At first she saw only the wardress's cap and cape. But then the face came into focus. It was Klaus, one of the handful of decent ones. She pointed a gloved finger at the corpses. Even in the dim light Rebeka could see that it was shaking. "What . . . what are you . . . ?"

Snatching back her hand, the wardress let out a long sigh, shook her head, and turned away. Wrapping her cloak tightly about her, she made for the gate.

Rebeka waited until her heart settled down before going inside. The lights were on, the block slowly coming to life. Women walking about, low conversation, the Agudah saying their prayers. A line had formed at the wooden tub that served as a latrine. Rebeka had already used it—one of the benefits of rising early.

She paused with her back to the door, still shaken by her encounter with the wardress. Her head was aching, as it had been for the past few days. The pain seemed a little sharper this morning. Not that it mattered; she hadn't felt truly healthy since the first day here.

It could be worse. Her eyes fell on a woman perched at the edge of a bunk, staring blankly into space. Rebeka thought of the dead ones outside. This woman was going to join them. She'd given up—turned Moslem, it was called. Alma made certain that all such women got extra food, but it didn't seem to make any difference. It would take much more than food to help them.

Rebeka hoisted her shoulders. She wasn't going to end up that way. The Nazis would have to kill her themselves.

Elsewhere in the room a few of the women were eating bread they'd saved from last night. Others lay quietly, unwilling to move before the signal for roll call. Only Yenka was sitting up, rocking back and forth as she jabbered about the dream she'd had. The same one as always: that there had been a selection, that most of the block had been taken. No one was listening. Across from her Mama Blazak prayed, reciting the Shema as she did every morning. Rebeka could see her lips moving from where she stood.

To her right Alma sat on the bunk, tying a scarf over her head. She was talking with Hester, the barracks clerk that she'd met that first night. Yulka, the big whore—Rebeka still thought of her that way, though Alma disapproved—stood beside them, stolid as a watchdog.

Rebeka drifted over. Yulka nodded gravely as she drew near. Alma, still deep in conversation, took no note of her. They were talking about work assignments. Apparently women from the last transport were coming to the block as soon as they got out of quarantine. There had been sickness on the train, which had been delayed by Home Army activity. Many of the transportees—eastern Jews from what had once been Ukraine—had died on the way.

Rebeka stopped listening. Death—that was all she ever heard about here. Who had gone, how many, how it had occurred, how to avoid following them. She had not yet hardened herself to it. That would come—she knew she couldn't escape it. But it hadn't happened yet, not even with what she did with those poor women each morning. How she wished she was simple, like Mama Blazak!

And it had only been six weeks. A month and a half, and already it seemed like a lifetime. As if nothing existed, or ever had existed, but Auschwitz. Her village, Mama and Papa, Micah, the days at school—no more than a dream, a wistful illusion that had protected her, as a mother protects a child.

But only so far and for so long. The things she had witnessed in those six weeks! They should have withered her soul, driven her mad and screaming, to throw herself on the wire like that man she had seen from the ramp, not knowing what it was she saw. There must be something wrong with her. Perhaps she was hardened, her heart grown black and stiff, all without her knowing it. She thought of the bodies outside, hoping that the Todtkommando would carry them off before the block was called out.

She glanced at Alma, wondering how she could stand it. Alma was made of far finer cloth than most of the block—even Hester and the other intellectuals. Rebeka was certain of that, though she couldn't say how. It was in the way she moved, the manner in which she spoke, the words she chose. She seemed more *advanced* than the rest of the women, as far beyond them as Rebeka's father had been compared to the Polish peasants he was trapped among. The others didn't know what to make of her. The best guess was that she was a U-boat, a German Jew who had gone into hiding, the protected mistress of an industrialist or Nazi official. Rebeka had asked about her background, but Alma had simply smiled and said it didn't matter now.

What she was experiencing must strike her to her core. Rebeka knew it must; she remembered well how she had looked on the ramp, as the doomed were led away to be gassed. Yet she never revealed it. Apart from an occasional burst of anger, nothing ever ruffled her calm. It was as if the camp represented a problem to be solved, and the blockawas, wardresses, and Kapos only pieces to be moved toward a goal that she alone could see.

It had worked. So far anyway. Alma had started with the block itself, forcing the whores and stubowas to stop brutalizing the others. It took them a while to realize that things had changed; Alma was attacked the week after they arrived, an ambush while she was using the waste tub. But Yulka warned her, and she broke it up as easily as the thieving spree the first night. The informers got the same treatment.

She went on to organize the block—"organize" in the old sense, not in the camp use of the word. She made it clear that they'd all have to work together, that resources would be pooled, that they would cover for one another. It was hard—many of the women had gone Moslem or were right on the verge, and the petty theft and beatings went on in secret for nearly another month. But Hata, the blockawa, was not a bad sort and appreciated what Alma was trying to do. Between the two of them the block was brought under control.

Then, with Hester's help, Alma moved out into the camp itself. She bribed Bubi, the bathhouse Kapo, with cigarettes and liquor, arranging nightly water deliveries to the block. Through a connection in the kitchen they got extra bread rations—some of the women had actually been starving. From a guard she'd obtained cans of insecticide—the bugs had been horrible, thousands of them, of all kinds, infesting the entire building. They'd completely covered the wall the first morning. But most of them were gone now and wouldn't be a problem again until winter was over.

Now Alma was concentrating on work assignments, the next move in her game. She had contacted someone in the allocation office to assure that the women of the block had decent permanent jobs that would put them beyond reach of the irregular camp selections. Where that wasn't possible, she paid off the Kapos directly, so that the block women wouldn't be beaten or abused. Rebeka acted as a courier for much of this. It was far easier than cleaning up the block had been. American dollars spoke for themselves.

Alma hadn't spent much cash yet. It was hidden, split between several safe spots inside the camp known only to the two of them. She seemed to be saving the bulk of it for some purpose she hadn't yet confided to Rebeka.

It was all going very well. As well as could be expected in a place such as this. Yet Rebeka was still afraid. There were things that Alma did not see, or refused to see, like the bodies in front of the blocks. Eventually they—the rotsayachen, as Mama called them—would notice. That no one was dying in Block 37, that crisp new dollars had appeared in the camp. An informer would talk. The Gestapo would move in. There would be a selection . . .

Rebeka had seen Mandel staring at Alma a few days before during roll call, her harsh jaw moving as she regarded the tall slender prisoner. Alma noticed and turned her head to stare back, straight into the Oberaufseherin's eyes. Mandel's face reddened, and for a moment Rebeka had been sure she was about to punish Alma—Rebeka herself had been beaten by Mandel for not moving fast enough, the truncheon striking her shoulders while she begged the woman's pardon—but somehow Mandel simply snorted and strode off.

They all did. Even the hardest guards and Kapos, the ones who thought nothing of beating a prisoner to the point of death, treated Alma with respect. Not one ever raised a hand to her. Rebeka couldn't understand it. Neither could the guards themselves—she'd seen it in their faces as they walked away, often looking back at Alma, as if making note of her. And that frightened Rebeka worst of all.

". . . they're peasants," Hester was saying. "Allocation will want some for agricultural work."

"I don't like the farms," Alma told her firmly.

"We could contact Caesar. He's not that—"

"Joachim Caesar looks away while the enlisted SS molest the girls. He's as bad as the rest of them."

Hester sighed. "Well, the poultry farm at Harmense, then."

"I'd rather keep them inside the camp."

"I would think you'd want to get them out."

Alma chuckled. "I suppose you're right."

—and that was another puzzle. The knowledge she had of things that she couldn't possibly have seen. Caesar—Rebeka would have pictured a man prancing about in a toga. But Alma knew exactly who he was, what he was like, what his crimes were. Rebeka rested her head against the beam behind her. Frau Lewin was a mystery, be certain of that. And perhaps that would be enough. Perhaps her mys-

tery itself would be all it took to get them out of this. Alma had told
her that they would get out someday.

She reached up to rub her temples. Her headache still pounded, soft
but insistent. She hoped she wasn't getting sick. To fall sick here was
to leap into the grave.

She felt a soft touch on her shoulder and turned to see Alma regarding her, chin resting on one hand. "Gut Morgn," Alma said.

Rebeka smiled. "Gut Tog." Alma spoke Yiddish well. She knew
all sorts of languages—German, Polish, Russian, even English. She
must have been a woman of the world before! Rebeka tried to imagine
her in a fine gown, stylish hair—difficult, that; their hair was just
beginning to grow back—jewelry, cosmetics. She decided that if she
was a man, she'd like that face, even if it wasn't actually pretty.

"You look tired."

Rebeka shrugged. "A little, I guess."

"Here—" Alma lay her palm against Rebeka's forehead. "Hmm.
You're a bit hot. How do you feel?"

"Oh—I don't know. It's nothing. I'll be all right."

"Still, I wish I'd saved some pills."

"Oh, how could you have?" The pills—omnibiotics, Alma had
called them, a new kind of medicine from the West, maybe even
America—had been gone within a week. There had been a lot of sick
women in the block.

Alma was frowning now. Bending close, Rebeka winked and said,
"It's o-kay." It was a word Alma used a lot, one that had become a
private joke between them.

Eyes crinkling, Alma smiled. She looked much younger that way.
"Okay," she said.

The door banged open and their wardress, Liesl, walked in. "Block
37, prepare for work!" she called.

"This is a camp, not a rest home," someone muttered.

Liesl grimaced humorlessly. She was all right, as far as it went, but
the rest of the wardresses considered her inept and she tried to make
up for it with a tough front. Rebeka suspected that she was actually
afraid of them all.

The wardress left, and a moment later two of the kitchen staff—
plump things, as they always were—brought in two big pots. Gruel

and tea, the steam still rising. The women lined up in an orderly fashion, with none of the scuffles of the first days.

Rebeka handed Alma her bowl, hanging within the harness of straw that Alma herself had told them how to make. She always had the block at work, making items she herself had designed: little stoves out of used cans, capes like the ones the wardresses had—though she had warned them not to wear them outside just yet.

They filled their bowls and ate sitting on the bunk, sharing some bread from last night. They finished just as Liesl's whistle blew and then walked arm in arm out to the Appelplatz. There they separated. It wasn't good to let the guards see things like that. At the very least there would be nasty remarks. Some of the women prisoners had paired off as sweethearts, exactly as if one of them was a man. But Rebeka and Alma were camp sisters, in the same way that Mama Blazak considered them to be her camp daughters. There was nothing unwholesome between them.

Roll call went quickly. Only the junior wardresses were present, no sign of Mandel or Taube, for which Rebeka was grateful. With a transport just in, the guards were concentrating on the new arrivals. For a few days the workers would be left alone until, out of boredom and spite, the guards turned on them again.

The work units began to gather as the roll call ended. Alma touched her hand. "Home soon," she said. Rebeka whispered the words back to her. It was like a promise.

She went to the spot where the warehouse crew was forming. Only one wardress was overseeing them today, a stupid self-important thing from Bavaria. The warehouse detail had Kapos the same as all the others, but they held little power. The wardresses ran the clothing operation themselves.

Rebeka checked to see that her scarf was straight and the bowl hanging correctly from her belt. This one enjoyed making a fuss of such things.

And so she did, with a simple girl from Radom who had broken one of her clogs. The Bavarian struck her twice across the face before she was satisfied. She then spent several minutes making sure they were in perfect formation before starting out. It made no sense—the lines always became ragged anyway. It was merely another opportunity to be harsh.

"Heads up," the Bavarian called. They started marching. At least she didn't demand that they sing, as some of the others did. Or run to the warehouses either; that was common. But this one was too fat for that. Rebeka could hear her puffing as it was.

A shout from behind caught her attention. She looked back to see another wardress beating a prisoner. The woman pulled away, crying and waving her arms wildly. That, along with the short yellow mop of hair, told Rebeka who it must be: Yetta Novosti, the one who'd gone mad after losing her children. She'd no doubt asked the wardress—she looked unfamiliar and might be new—if she'd seen the babies.

The wardress was still for a moment, stupefied by resistance from a prisoner. Then with a shout she rained another flurry of blows on Yetta. Rebeka winced as the truncheon cracked against the poor madwoman's skull.

The mud nearly sucked away one of Rebeka's clogs. She hopped a step or two before wedging her foot in more firmly. When she looked back again, it was to see Alma approaching the wardress. With a deep bow, Alma began speaking. The wardress paused, then lowered the club. Yetta crouched, wailing and holding her head.

Rebeka smiled as the wardress slid her club under one arm. The smile vanished with a gasp when she saw a man in black loping eagerly toward the three women, as if attracted by the smell of blood. He was coming from behind, Alma couldn't see him . . .

Slipping in the mud, Rebeka lost her balance and collided with the woman beside her, a German named Bauer. "Watch it there, shorty," Bauer said, shoving her erect. She was looking back at the Appelplatz herself, a twisted grin on her face. "God help those two," she murmured.

Rebeka glanced over her shoulder, but another work gang was passing, blocking her view. "Up the chimney and bye-bye," Bauer said. Catching Rebeka's expression, she frowned and turned her head.

They neared the gate to the men's camp. Rebeka's worry about Alma was overcome by surprise at seeing two men in ordinary clothes slouching against one of the posts. Then she spotted the cardboard square slung around the neck of the one facing them and deliberately dropped her eyes. All the same, she glanced over as they passed to read what was written on the sign. The lust of the eye, Mama Blazak called it; the compulsion to take in everything, no matter how horrible or disgusting. The learned rebbes had much to say about that in the Midrash.

THREE CHEERS, WE'RE BACK! That was what the sign, which was in Yiddish, said. She caught a glimpse of the man's open mouth, the brown stain on his shirt, before swinging her eyes forward. Escapees, tracked down and shot, probably before they'd gotten a stone's throw from the wire. There were always rumors of escapes, but she'd never heard of a successful one. Not for certain. The wardresses said that no one had ever escaped from Birkenau.

Someone patted her shoulder. Mama Blazak, her face full of concern. She'd slipped up to Rebeka while the guard wasn't looking, simply to reassure her. Mama—everyone called her that, even Liesl—was a Moravian Jew from a small town near Brno. She was an Agudah, very orthodox and very pious. It was she who had given Rebeka the bread that first night. Rebeka forced a smile for her. "Say a little prayer, darling," the old woman whispered.

Rebeka turned to hide her face. What was prayer to this?

They reached the gate to the warehouse section. It was nicknamed "Canada." The new uncompleted barracks section to the north was called "Mexico." So was the main camp section, where the workers' blocks stood, called "America"? The Slovak women all laughed when she asked that.

Canada was where the belongings of the Jews were sorted and packed. All of them, from both the camp workers and the ones who had been gassed. When Alma told her that she'd arranged for her to work there, Rebeka at first refused. She couldn't imagine anything more horrid than handling dead people's clothing. But Alma explained that the clothes often contained money and jewelry sewn in the linings, that there was food and medicine in many of the packages, all of it waiting to be organized. So Rebeka gave in, much as she hated the thought.

She recalled the bodies she'd touched only this morning. She'd seen a lot since then.

As they went through the wire, she kept her eyes to the ground. She sensed that most of the other women were doing the same. Canada was located between two of the crematoria. Both were throwing black and stinking smoke into the sky. She thought of what Bauer had said and shuddered.

They reached the warehouse, paused as a count was made. The fat Bavarian saluted the Canada wardresses with her club and plodded back to the camp center.

The wardresses led them inside. This building was used for processing women's belongings. The others handled everything taken from the men. The Nazis didn't care for the idea of male prisoners touching women's underthings.

Rebeka went to her usual table. A pile of boxes and packages lay behind it, covered with women's coats. The coats were promising; people often hid things in coats.

She sat down and got to work, taking her time, trying not to think about Alma. She'd be all right. She knew how to deal with those people. Even that one. The Gestapo man. The one the prisoners called Blackie. Hauptsturmführer Boldt.

The camp orchestra began playing. She paused to listen for a minute. It was something classical and very pretty.

"You! Table 17! Get cracking!"

Bending her head, Rebeka opened the suitcase and made a show of looking busy. Pulling out the clothing, separating the items to be placed in different piles, surreptitiously feeling the seams as she did. She wanted to leave the coats until later, when the wardresses wouldn't be so alert.

She studied them from the corner of her eye. They were in a foul mood. This transport had come from the east, where even the Jews were poor. The suitcases were made of cardboard, held shut by twine or rope. Many of the easterners had lacked even those, carrying sacks or packages instead. The clothes were old and shabby, often patched.

Usually the wardresses had their own sorting to do. All the furs went to their table. People hid jewelry, diamonds, or coins in the fox heads, and Rebeka had gotten used to hearing squeals of delight whenever a new cache was found. But there were no furs in this batch, no diamonds or rings to vanish into uniform pockets before they could be listed. Rebeka had seen them do that.

Everything else—clothes, belongings, suitcases—went to the rear of the building to be loaded into train cars. For some time Rebeka hadn't quite grasped what it was all about, where the clothes and goods went after they came through here. It simply never occurred to her to wonder. Then one day during the lunch break she asked another worker.

Rebeka had been appalled at what she was told. They sent these clothes to Germany for people to *wear*. Germans were actually walking around in clothes stolen from dead men and women, murdered men and women. And the children . . . ?

Rebeka hadn't dared ask about that. But the same woman—her name was Giselle, a worker from another block, a Gentile, though she didn't detest Jews the way many of them did—had told her that wasn't all. They knocked gold teeth from the mouths of the corpses and even used the shaved hair to make special slippers for U-boat crews.

It was too much for Rebeka. How could anyone do such a thing? Even if they were Nazis. Aside from how gruesome it was, what about tempting fate? Soldiers were always warned against stealing a dead man's boots. A soldier who did that died horribly. The Germans were defying misfortune, committing such an unholy act. Something beyond description was going to happen to them all.

The Nazis, she supposed, didn't tell anyone where the clothes came from, though she wondered whether they'd even care if they knew. Still, it made her feel better about what she was doing. She was helping them seal their doom.

She finished emptying the suitcase and two other packages. The wardresses, now gossiping and smoking cigarettes, paid no attention. Rebeka thought it safe to slow down. You could cooperate only so far and no more. That extra inch was what they wanted, the inch that would turn you into a Moslem, that would send you to the bakery. Arbeit Macht Frei, yes—to go up the chimney.

There wasn't much worth organizing—a few worn zlotys stuffed in a pocket, nothing more. Rebeka was sure, peasants being peasants, that they'd kept their gold with them right until the end. She was growing annoyed at finding so little. They didn't have a right to be that poor. Not when people needed what they brought in . . .

She sighed. Look what she was becoming! A month and a half, and she was despising people for what wasn't their fault. Dead people. People who had been killed last night while she slept, only a few metres from where she now sat.

Well, this girl wasn't going to be beaten for hiding currency not worth the paper it was printed on. Stuffing the zlotys back in the dress, she folded it and placed it on the pile.

Mama Blazak, seated at the end of the table, began humming along with the music. The tune seemed familiar, and Rebeka wondered where she'd heard it before. It must have been with her father, when they'd gone to Lódź. A touring orchestra was playing that weekend, and he'd wanted her to hear it—*to get some culture into you*, he'd said. So he spent money that he couldn't afford for tickets. She remembered it clearly; she'd been awed by the men in evening clothes and the women in long gowns and jewelry, their hair dressed perfectly. Her father had smiled and told her this was nothing at all to compare to Warsaw, where he'd attended university. But Rebeka had never seen Warsaw, and so to her, on that night, Lódź had been the center of the world.

She wasn't certain whether this was one of the pieces the orchestra had played. But it sounded so familiar. She tried to recall what the program had said but couldn't bring it to mind, though she'd saved it for years. Mendelssohn? Schubert? She wished there was someone here who could tell her.

Returning to herself, she noticed one of the wardresses studying her through cigarette smoke. Rebeka got back to work.

At exactly noon the kitchen staff arrived with lunch. Sour, watery turnip soup, along with the bread ration. The soup was thinner than what they got at the block, and as for the bread . . . Between her time in the forest and the weeks here, Rebeka had forgotten how real bread tasted, but it hadn't been anything like this.

They lined up, filled their bowls, and went back to the tables. The wardresses didn't allow them to leave the building during the break, afraid that they'd mingle with the male prisoners. Of course they went out themselves—to fraternize, Rebeka supposed. Regulations forbade it, but it happened anyway.

She ate the ghastly soup quickly, soaking up the last of it with a chunk of bread, soggy as it was. Usually the workers shared whatever food they found, but today there was nothing to speak of.

Only one wardress had remained in the building, and she was leaning against the doorjamb, shouting to the others. It was a sunny afternoon, if a bit cool. On foul days the wardresses remained inside, often badgering the women while they ate. You learned to pray for nice weather.

One eye on the door, Rebeka went to talk to Mama Blazak. She crouched next to her stool and they chatted for a few minutes before Rebeka mentioned her thoughts about the clothes.

"Yes, I know," Mama Blazak said softly. "That did occur to me. All those people walking about in Berlin and the other towns in clothing robbed from the dead. As if they were carrying ghosts on their shoulders. It's terrible to think of."

She was staring into space, her customary smile absent. "They're defying God, making a mockery of His law. They believe that God doesn't see because the bodies are gone to ash. But God sees all. The blood cries out to Him, as did the blood of Abel. And this"—she waved a hand to encompass the room—"is the mark of their sin. They saunter about in the clothes of their victims, flaunting their crimes before His face."

Rebeka shifted uncomfortably. This was a new Mama Blazak, one she hadn't seen before. Eyes cold and harsh, her mouth a grim line. Rebeka had thought that Mama was . . . well, a little dumb. It seemed that she'd fooled herself.

"They'll be punished, little one. As were the Egyptians, and Haman, and the Midianites. As Babylon fell, and Rome, so will their Reich fall. And they will go into Sheol, into the lake of fire, all of them. There will be no rejoicing at their judgment."

She looked down at Rebeka, her face still fierce. Then it melted into the smile she knew so well. "But God looks after His own too, sweetheart. Never forget that. Even here, with . . . things as they are. Those poor men this morning . . . they're with the Prophets now. Adonai's angels gathered in their souls as they rose, before Satan even caught a glimpse of them."

Despite herself, Rebeka was unable to answer. She cast her eyes to the floor, silently clearing her throat. "I saw . . . Boldt was sneaking up on Alma when we left."

"I know." Mama Blazak nodded gravely. "But Frau Lewin is very clever. You must have faith . . ." Her head rose. "Quick, they're coming back." Reaching into her dress, she handed something to Rebeka. "Here. I found some sugar."

Rebeka accepted it and returned to her place. "God bless," Mama called after her.

The head wardress bellowed at them to get to work. It hadn't quite been the full half hour, but then it never was.

Rebeka sucked on the sugar cube, not bothering to chew it—some of her teeth were beginning to hurt. It would help settle her stomach—she was feeling a little nauseous after eating that soup. She wondered if Mama had actually found the sugar here or had brought it along. It would do no good to ask; Mama would never admit it if she had.

Over the next hour she went through the rest of the suitcases and bags. She thought about what Mama had said as she worked. Rebeka herself didn't really believe in God. She'd left all that behind her, and what she'd seen here had done nothing to change her mind. She wasn't actually an atheist, though. She'd only discovered what she was from reading one of the socialist pamphlets that Micah had given her. Rebeka was a humanist, one who believed in the power and decency of humanity itself. That was the true driving force behind socialism: that if the shackles of religion and aristocracy and capital were removed and the basic goodness of human beings brought out, then nothing would stand in the way of solving any social problem, that a fair and just society would emerge, and that a true utopia might be . . . could be . . .

She hadn't found any evidence for that in Birkenau either. Socialism was just a dream, like Mama's God. The Nazis, after all, called themselves socialists, though that was only another one of their lies. At least Mama still believed: in God looking down and angels collecting souls to take them home. It would be nice to have something to believe in.

Lifting a dress out of a badly packed box, she felt a hard object inside. She kept her face blank as she searched the pocket for it. She was disappointed to find only a booklet, but slipped it out anyway. It was a Siddur, a little one, the kind that someone would give to a child. Hiding it below the tabletop, she flicked through the pages, smiling as she remembered some of the prayers from her childhood. Mama would like this. Wedging it next to the table leg, Rebeka went back to work.

A few minutes later she finished with the packages. She cleared the table and dropped the clothes at the rear of the room, one pile for dresses, one for blouses, stockings, shoes, and so on. Back at the table she picked up an armload of coats, as ragged and ill-smelling as everything else. Of course, they'd been wearing them on the train here—

She jerked back as she flipped the first coat open and saw a seething mass along the seams. Hand to her mouth, she pushed the coat away. Lice. The coats were absolutely alive with lice. In the weeks she'd been here, Rebeka hadn't grown used to that.

Choking down the bile in her throat, she ran her hands over her dress in case any had crawled onto her. She got up and raised a hand. It took a moment for the wardresses to notice her—they were playing cards now. But finally one looked up and asked what she wanted.

"This prisoner wishes to report the coats to be lice-ridden," Rebeka said, keeping her head down. One of them, a blonde with crazed eyes, made a disgusted sound as she got up. "Woe betide you if you're shirking, girlie."

Reaching the table, the wardress opened the coat with the end of her truncheon. "Ugh. So they are. All of them, I suppose. All right. Throw them outside to be run through again. There's more bags in the back. Grab them and get busy." She turned away and rapped the club on a pillar. "The rest of you whores check the coats for lice. We don't want any of your dirty Yid plagues in here."

Rebeka hesitated before picking up the coats, then grabbed them and raced for the door. It took her three trips to collect all of them. The wardresses laughed as she went past. Rebeka couldn't see what was funny.

At the rear entrance she searched herself carefully before selecting more bags. The other day lice had gotten all over her—she didn't know how—and they'd been eating her alive by the time she got to the block.

Choosing two of the more expensive-looking suitcases, she went back to the table. She'd calmed herself enough to start going through the first one when a horrid scream split the near silence.

Rebeka nearly lost her balance. The stool went on two legs, throwing her against the table. She gripped the edge and pulled the stool straight before looking around.

It was the woman who sat to her left, a brooding Czech who seldom spoke. Rebeka wasn't even certain of her name. She was on her feet, still screaming, staring wide-eyed at an open suitcase.

A wardress shouted and Rebeka heard running footsteps. The woman began whimpering the same word over and over. Rebeka shifted to look inside the suitcase but stopped herself. She didn't have to see.

A wardress grabbed the woman and shook her. "Stop it!" she cried. The mad-eyed blonde, only a step behind, shoved her against the table to the rear. "Shut up!"

The first wardress glanced at the suitcase and, with a muttered "Oh my God," walked off. The woman, on her knees now, hands protecting her head, was still whining that same word. Rebeka realized it was a name: "Josif . . . Josif . . ."

The blonde rose, blinked slowly at the suitcase, and without looking away raised her club to Rebeka. "You—" she said. "You two scraps— Get it out. Get it out *now.*"

Rebeka and Giselle hurried to the suitcase. As she passed it, Rebeka tried to keep her head high, but she had to give in. The lust of the eye, too powerful to fight.

It was a child. An infant, no more than a year old. Cushioned with clothing, its arms and legs carefully folded. It looked as if it was asleep.

Giselle slammed the top shut before Rebeka could touch it. Together they lifted the case. As they headed for the door, Rebeka looked over her shoulder. Mama Blazak had left her stool to go to the crying woman. She backed off when the blonde wardress raised her hand. Rebeka turned away, hearing vicious slaps and a voice grunting, "Dead *babies* . . . You *all* have dead babies . . ."

They carried the case through the silent room and out the door, Rebeka afraid with each step that she'd lose her grip and spill the tiny corpse out on the rough wood.

A few steps from the building Rebeka looked at Giselle for the first time. "Don't . . . let's not . . . just throw it." Lips twisted, Giselle nodded wordlessly. They set the case down gently and, as if in agreement, opened it together. The child rolled out and sprawled on the dirt next to the infested coats. A wardress leaned out the door. "You bring that suitcase back!"

While Giselle tossed the clothes in, Rebeka bent over to arrange the child's limbs, but it was beyond her. Giselle let out a bitter laugh.

"Scheisse egal," she said. Making a sound of agreement, Rebeka carried the suitcase inside.

The death echoed through the rest of the day. The bloody-faced woman sobbed quietly, occasionally whispering her child's name. Cards forgotten, the wardresses patrolled the aisles, nervous and angry. The blonde seemed to have decided that Rebeka was in some way responsible and rapped her smartly on the knuckles whenever she passed.

Rebeka soldiered on, overcoming a sense of dread upon opening every suitcase or box. Her hands started to swell, particularly after she snatched them back instinctively on seeing the blonde out of the corner of her eye and submitted to being struck a half-dozen times on each. Her headache was back, and she felt ready to drop from exhaustion.

There was no clock in the room, and she became convinced that 1700 had come and gone and that they were being kept all night as punishment. That had happened before. But finally the head wardress called the time.

She was dropping off the last of the clothes when she remembered the prayer book. She ought to let it wait until tomorrow, the mood the wardresses were in, but . . . She thought of how outraged she'd been when the blonde had made her stand up to be whipped. She'd smuggle it out now. You had to defy them sometime or you lost your self-respect, and that was the first step toward turning Moslem.

Back at the table she slipped the Siddur into her footcloth, just above the ankle. As she rose, a sense of triumph filled her. She wondered if it was the same as what Alma felt when she'd carried out one of her schemes.

Mama Blazak was waiting for her in the aisle. They were filing to the door when an uproar broke out at the wardresses' table.

They'd surrounded a girl and were shouting at her. "I know you've got something, bitch! I saw you hide it—" one of them shrieked. The head wardress stood with folded arms next to the door. As Rebeka watched, she tapped a woman on the shoulder and gestured her out of the line.

"I didn't . . ." the woman pleaded. "This prisoner . . ."

The wardress lashed out with her club. "Move it, bitch."

Rebeka felt a burning at her right ankle, as if the Siddur was eating its way through her skin. She should have guessed they'd check, today of all days. Smuggling out holy books—religious propaganda, the Nazis called it—was as bad as stealing gold or money, if not worse. If they found it on her, it would mean a punishment unit at the very least. She might even—she swallowed—she might even be *selected . . .*

She couldn't simply drop it in the aisle. When they saw it, they'd hold the whole unit until someone admitted to having it; all night long, if necessary. And now look: the blonde had joined the boss wardress, eyes burning as her head swiveled back and forth.

Another woman was snatched out. The first shrieked as her dress was torn off. Rebeka lowered her head. The blonde would see her in a second or two. But if she could create some kind of diversion— stumble, maybe, as she was being dragged out of line—she'd have a chance to toss the book under a table or somewhere else where it wouldn't be seen. She'd have to time it just right. And throw a clog with it. Yes, to confuse them . . .

The second woman broke into sobs as she waited her turn. Rebeka saw the blonde turn around to strike at her. Holding her breath, Rebeka leaped forward, pressing against the backs of the women ahead. She began a silent count, expecting the touch of a hard rubber tip on her shoulder at any moment. As she reached eight, she felt a rush of cool air and looked up. She was outside.

She closed her eyes and took a deep breath, stench or no. She started when Mama Blazak grasped her elbow. Together they walked to where the others stood.

Her relief faded, leaving tiredness. The women waited, unnaturally silent in the early twilight. The male prisoners left the compound, some of them waving and calling out. The wardresses shouted back at them.

Ten minutes passed before the three women emerged from the building. The one who'd been stripped held her dress to cover herself. One of the others bled from her mouth. The count was taken, the wardresses dragging it out. Finally they headed into camp.

Rebeka kept her head down as she marched. It had been very, very close. This morning too. What if it had been Mandel or Drexler instead of Klaus? She might not be alive now. That was the thing: every single minute here was the product of countless minutes that should not have been survived. It was all luck, and luck wasn't enough. There were too many traps, too many holes to fall into, holes that led only into darkness. Alma couldn't save everyone. Eventually Rebeka would make a mistake, or be caught, or there would be a selection . . .

With the thought of Alma, the memory of Boldt's stealthy approach of the morning returned with full force. Rebeka caught her breath, suddenly choked with despair. But Alma would be all right. Boldt was no match for her. She was waiting right now at the block. It wasn't luck in her case. No, it was a matter of skill, of intelligence and ability. Perhaps that was an illusion, but it was an illusion that Rebeka—that all of them—couldn't live without. If you were facing a chasm, Alma had told her, a chasm that you had to jump across because there was no way back, what was the best state of mind with which to confront it? In doubt, fearful that you could never leap that far? Or with faith, certain that somehow you would gain those few centimetres, that extra impetus you required?

The question answered itself. Rebeka needed to find faith. And she would find it, as always, in Alma. Nothing could happen to Alma. She would be waiting when Rebeka reached the block. They'd talk, and everything would look better then.

"Szybko!" a wardress called out brightly, as if she'd just had a splendid idea. The word was followed by the thud of rubber on flesh. The line broke into a run. "Szybko! Hep, hep!"

They loped through the camp. The bodies were still slouched by the gate. The woman with the injured mouth began coughing up blood.

The rest of the block had already returned. Rebeka asked where Alma was. With Hata, she was told. Sighing aloud with relief, she went eagerly to the blockawa's room. Alma never minded if she sat in on their discussions.

Her footsteps slowed as she neared the door. Hata was speaking, her voice harsh. It rose suddenly to a near shout, then dropped, the tone still bitter.

Rebeka halted a few steps away. Hata was subject to fits of temper, episodes in which she spent hours shrieking that she'd been a good woman before she was sent here, an honest woman, one who had run her own business in Praha and was known for treating people fairly. Those had ceased over the last few weeks. But not for good, it now seemed.

". . . hadn't she been told? Didn't the nurses . . . everyone warn her? And where did it come from, eh? The angels brought it, I suppose. Who's her kochany? Where the hell does she meet him?"

Alma answered, soft but firm. "She was pregnant when she arrived. I thought I'd made that clear."

Rebeka gasped. Someone was pregnant—here, in Birkenau? She shook her head, unable to accept the thought. It was too alien, too far removed from what went on in the camp.

Two women headed for the front gave her meaningful looks, one rolling her eyes at the door. Rebeka crept closer to get a glimpse of who this creature could possibly be. A blanket hung as a kind of curtain, but it was open a crack. Rebeka peeked inside.

". . . I won't have it," Hata was saying. "It's insane. You can't bring a child into this . . . this boneyard. You're making me crazy too."

Hata perched on a stool facing Alma, who was leaning against the wall. Between them, on the bunk, a girl in an oversized dress sat with tears streaking her face. It was Nicole, one of the few French Jews in the block. She sniffled and Hata told her to be silent. Sinking deeper into her misery, the girl pulled an old wool shirt tighter around her.

"There is at least one child hidden in the kitchen," Alma said. "It can be done."

"How do you know that? Where do you learn such things? You talk as if you've been here longer than I."

"Have I been wrong yet?"

Hata drew back in disgust. Her eyes fell on the doorway. "Who's that? What do you want?"

Pushing the blanket aside, Rebeka leaned in. "Alma—" she began. Alma shot her a smile and waved her off. Rebeka retreated and let the blanket fall.

Disappointed, she turned toward the front room. "We should do away with it," Hata said behind her. "It's not a child yet—"

"Hata, please," Alma said calmly.

Passing Hester on her way to the front room, Rebeka asked what had happened with Boldt. "Oh, that? He stopped the beating. He knows about Yetta's problem. He told her he'd watch for her children. Alma said he was actually *polite*. Can you believe it?"

Nodding somberly, Rebeka walked on. Politeness wasn't necessarily a good thing in the camp.

She slipped into the bunk, propping her back against the bricks. They were cold, but she scarcely noticed that. It was simply another small item to add to her list of miseries. She felt awful; tired, aching in every particle of her body, and, for the first time in many days, afraid. Almost as frightened as she had been that first night. In a way, even more so—she didn't quite know what she was frightened of.

A shadow fell across her. Mama Blazak settled onto the bunk. "Let me see your hands." She fussed over them for a minute, her breath hissing at how swollen and red they were. "We could use ice for these. But . . ."

Rebeka dropped them in her lap. "It's all right." She thought of the woman beaten in the warehouse, blood staining the front of her dress. She might be in Block 25 at this very moment. Cyla's building—the block of the dead. "Did you hear about the baby?"

"Yes," Mama said. "Nicole came to me first. She's afraid of Frau Lewin."

"Alma's going to try to save it." Rebeka paused. Mama Blazak's face was turned down, her lips tightly clenched, the scar where a guard had put out a cigarette clearly visible. "That's stupid, isn't it? They'll catch us."

The old woman sighed. "She wants to save everyone. She doesn't realize that some things can't be done." She met Rebeka's eyes. "I see what you do in the mornings. I was shocked, at first. I thought you were . . . becoming strange. But then I guessed why you did it." Her gaze turned bleak. "Frau Lewin knows many things about this place. But she doesn't know the big thing. I think you do."

"But . . . you're still going to help with the baby?"

The door banged open and supper arrived, yet another batch of that foul soup. Mama Blazak looked over her shoulder. When she turned back, she was smiling once again. "Oh yes. We must always help with babies."

Mama took Rebeka's bowl. "Here. You rest. I'll get it."

Nodding her thanks, Rebeka slipped off her clogs. As she bent to unwrap the cloth from her ankle, she remembered the Siddur. "Oh, wait!"

"What's this?" Taking the book, Mama opened it. She glanced up at Rebeka, her smile broadening as she turned the pages and whispered a few words to herself. Then she clapped it shut and thrust it back. "No, you keep it. No, no! You'll find me another, I know. But this one is for you. The Lord Himself put it there for you to find. Now . . . there's some nice cheese left. I know how you like cheese . . ."

Rebeka watched her go. She flipped though the pages of the book, the old prayers that meant so little here. Dropping it beside her, she leaned once more against the cold bricks.

C20/REL

Regret this assign-
ment?

The thought was sharp in his mind as he found himself
in a space much smaller, dimmer, and more active than
operations: the command center of an eral station, a
physical construct floating within geometrical abstrac-
tion, a bubble of space-time implanted in superspace.

He checked his stride before he ran into the platform
railing—pitching over it would be no way to introduce
himself to a new team. He paused to survey the room:
bright consoles, readouts, assorted holo systems, a large
flat screen to his right displaying a situation map. The
duty staff stared up at him in open surprise. He gave
them a nod as he descended the steps.

"Whoa!" A young man wearing a high-necked shirt
set down a coffee cup and got to his feet. "That was
quick." Two others rose with him: a girl with long
blonde hair whose face was settling into a scowl, a dark-
skinned man at the far end of the room. The rest, sitting
at various displays, stayed where they were.

"Monitor James, right? Dave Horek." The young

man held out his hand. As Gaspar took it and opened his mouth to speak, a voice said, "Monitor Gaspar."

That must be the station AI. Ignoring it for the moment, Gaspar shook Horek's hand. "That's correct. Gaspar."

The dark-skinned man introduced himself as Mackey, the station coordinator. The blonde woman kept her distance. Gaspar nodded in her direction. After a few seconds, she responded, her face still harsh. Gaspar saw no point in wondering what was on her mind. Despite being temporally M2, the 20th came under M3 control as being more technologically advanced than the centuries of its own millennium. But its psychology remained Medieval. Gaspar often found the contemps to be extremely childish, much as they insisted on distinguishing themselves from earlier periods.

"Guess you'll want to see Rog," Horek said.

"That's right. But also"—Gaspar turned to Mackey—"I need to speak to station personnel."

"Yes sir. All shifts?"

"Everyone. Say about half an hour." Gaspar lifted his head. "Dido? Is my pronunciation correct?"

"Yes, Monitor Gaspar."

"Greetings. I'd like your attention at that time as well." He gestured Horek on and followed him across the room. At the main screen he paused to look over the display. A map of central Europe, suspect locations highlighted in red. He found the dot near Krakow and grunted to himself.

Beside the screen was a list of sites under continual surveillance: Adlerhorst, Auschwitz, Berchtesgaden, Berlin . . .

"Adolf's not using the Wolf's Lair in the current now, so that's been dropped," Horek said. "That's in—"

"East Prussia." Gaspar shot him a smile and turned to the coordinator. "Mr. Mackey," he called. "How long would it take to call in all personnel from those locales?"

"Uhh . . . they'll be checking in over the next few hours . . ."

"Then do so. All except for the number two site." He paused before speaking the name. "Auschwitz."

"Will do, sir."

He nodded to Horek and they continued on, weaving between consoles until they reached the corridor that led to quarters. This was a

Class A station, the rating always used for continuity operations. Much larger than the stations reserved for research or exploration, with a full command suite and a more capable AI. The living section could bed down forty with doubling up, though Mackey had told him that only twenty-five were on-station. This module also featured larger storage space for supplies and equipment, along with a bay for whatever eral transport might be needed. Like the smaller versions, the station could operate only within its period's temporal cell. Overcoming the discontinuities that separated each cell required the more massive singularities of a millennial center. The C20 cell—to speak loosely—was bounded at 1908 and 2021.

"See, we weren't expecting you so soon," Horek was saying. "It was just an hour ago that Rog told us he was cutting . . . that he was leaving. Whoever tuned you in is good. Was it Somerson? English guy, 17th?"

"I believe so," Gaspar told the ponytail bobbing at Horek's neck. Horek was far more experienced than he appeared, with a relative decade of service behind him. He was eral, from the mid-century United States, and had served as a soldier in Vietnam, one of the innumerable small wars of the period, setting ambushes along something called the Minh Trail for an organization named SOG. Invalided out after being wounded by a mine, he'd returned home to complete his education. The American Republic had been in one of its spasms of political righteousness at the time—a common failing of democracies; Arpad suffered from the same tendency—and Horek was run out of his college as a war criminal. When the recruiters found him, he was living on a West Coast beach, spending his pension on the drugs needed to control the pain in his legs.

Horek had a reputation as an individualist; to use his own term, a "smart-ass." Gaspar had found that such types were either extremely effective or the polar opposite. He'd discover which Horek was soon enough.

The ponytail vanished as Horek swung around and nodded at a door. Gaspar stopped him as he reached for the buzzer.

"One moment—you're the military spec?"

"That's me—guns 'n' grunts."

"It was you who took in Smith, wasn't it?"

"Yeah." Horek smiled broadly. "Me and Carlyle. Pure dumb luck.

We'd just finished placing a surveillance net where Hitler's unit was stationed. We're running a check, get a chronon shower a week and a half up, and the sensors start howling. We were on it in two minutes. Not even wearing full armor. Smith—*Campbell*, now what kinda name is that? I mean, what did they call him in school? Soupie?—he knees Stew in the balls, so I popped him with a tickler. Tossed him through the portal and then back home. Textbook, man.''

"What do you think Hitler made of it?''

Horek's eyebrows rose. "Damned if I could tell you. I didn't even know he was around. Then I see him, standing there looking. Gave me the friggin' creeps, believe you me. Almost shot him the finger, but I just got out of there.'' He twitched his lips. "Nah, actually I didn't. The finger, I mean. Didn't think of that until I was through.''

"Excellent work, in any case. We'll speak in detail later, but two questions for now. Dido? Exit for one minute, please.'' Gaspar waited a few seconds. "What about the AI? Any problems?''

"Not as flakey as some,'' Horek said. "Gives you civil answers, doesn't butt in, gets the job done. She's new, hasn't had time to pick up any bad habits.''

"No feedback about the mission . . . ? Good. They can be rather holier-than-thou.''

Horek made a face. "I know.''

"Present, sir.''

"Thank you, Dido. Now—what are the chances of further walk-outs?''

"Well . . . hard to say . . .''

Gaspar nodded impatiently. Team loyalty was all very well in its place, but there were limits. "That woman back in CC, the one with the long face. Who is she?''

"That's Queenie, our forecaster. Rainbow Thayer, the Cosmic Queen. Yeah, she's been talking, but that's just part of her Earth Mother image, which is a crock anyway. She ain't from the '60s. And she wants to keep her record clean. She won't jump unless she's pushed.''

"I see. And how do you feel?''

Horek quirked his lips, seeming to reflect on his answer. "Sorry for those poor Jews. Pissed off at the Krauts. But . . . Well, lemme put it this way. Once you stumble into a Hmong village and find every-body's heads stuck on poles, you don't shock easy after that.''

It was a reasonable reply. Gaspar reached for the buzzer.

"Chief?" Horek said. "You don't mind me asking—what's the Auschwitz angle?"

"We'll get to that," Gaspar said, giving the button a firm push. A voice called out, "Enter." Gaspar went inside.

Angiers sat on the edge of his cot, wearing only the baggy style of trousers called "khakis." He frowned as Gaspar appeared, closed his eyes, and grinned. "Well, I'll be damned."

He got up slowly, a big man, broad in the chest, muscles beginning to go to flab with first age. "The Sultana must be having fits. I only sent word this morning."

"Not really." Gaspar leaned against the room's workstation. "I'm actually a few days asynched. Put through by what is evidently the Moiety's premier linker. Luck, nothing more."

Angiers was now pulling one of the era's tight white undergarments over his head. He tucked it into his waistband and swept a lock of hair from his eyes. "And you, Jimmy. Somehow I didn't think La Cor would reach that far up. Another monitor—it's embarrassing."

Gaspar said nothing for a moment. The two of them had never quite hit it off. They behaved civilly enough between themselves as colleagues, but he'd always felt a considerable reserve in Angiers, unusual coming from a man whose home period was so noted for empty camaraderie. "I see it as a compliment," Gaspar said finally. "They couldn't replace you with anything less."

Sweater in his hands, Angiers smiled. "Thanks, Jimmy." He pulled on the sweater and crossed the room slowly, as if afraid the floor wouldn't carry his bulk. "So—you know what you're in for?"

"Some idea, yes." Gaspar was satisfied to let it stand at that, if Angiers didn't want to take it farther. Despite what he'd just now said, the situation was embarrassing. There was little chance that Angiers would continue on as monitor following a fiasco of this magnitude. He'd probably be kicked upstairs to an administrative position at M3.

Angiers reached for a bottle atop the kitchen unit. He pointed at Gaspar, who thought to refuse but changed his mind. It might be taken the wrong way.

"Always knew somebody'd mess with the Holocaust," Angiers

muttered as he put the drinks together. "They've tried to take Hitler down often enough. Just hoped it wouldn't be on my watch." He handed Gaspar a glass. "Time and chance."

"To them all," Gaspar responded and took a sip. It was Scotch, not one of his favorites and with that odd Terrest tang to it. He made an appreciative noise all the same.

"I'd prefer to have left you a team in better shape," Angiers said. "But they're as freaked about this as I am. Some of them. Had two more walkouts this morning after I sent in the word. Kid over in supplies and one of the troops. A Turk—said it was dishonorable. May be a couple more ready to go."

"That's all right. I'll make up for it. Take over their duties myself, if I have to."

"Yeah." Angiers smiled. "You always were a hot dog, weren't you? I remember that guy you hauled in from . . . Where was it, one of the outer colonies . . . ?"

"Second-wave colony. The Sporades, we call them. It was Perelandra."

"That was it. Not often you see a monitor dragging back a dropout in person."

Gaspar shrugged. "The 24th is a slack period. Not much going on. A mob of High Catholics trying to teeform a mudball is as exciting as it gets. I viewed it as a challenge. Same as this."

Angiers's glass was poised beneath his lips. With a quick gesture he drained it. "A challenge, is it . . . ? Tell me something, Jimmy. Do they know about this upline? Your people, I mean. Have they heard of the Holocaust?"

"Not really."

"I see." Reaching again for the bottle, Angiers poured a full glass, not diluting it this time. He offered none to Gaspar. "Never thought it'd simply fade that way. The 24th—that's a good jump upline. I guess everything does." He gulped at the drink. "Never again."

Angiers turned to face Gaspar. His eyes were distant, jaw slack. "I was checking surveillance the other day—yesterday. At Chelmno, me and Horek. They were killing kids there. Right behind the wire. Two or three hundred of them, no more than . . ." He held his hand out flat, at waist level. "The chambers were down, or overloaded or something. So they were shooting. You know the basic syllable for 'mother' is the same in any language, Jimmy? That 'ma' sound. That's all there was—gunfire and crying and 'Ma, Ma, Ma,' over and over..." He took a deep breath and pulled himself together. "And they're taking it right into the camps, the fuckers. I thought the roof was coming off when we tracked 'em at Sobibor. That's when I..."

"Sobibor?" Gaspar said, suddenly alert.

"Yeah. Another camp. East Poland—"

Gaspar nodded impatiently.

"Extermination camp, like Chelmno. A breakout—the work force killed a bunch of guards, burned half the place to the ground. We tracked activity there, but...Our bad boys made no move. I can't understand it." He caught Gaspar's expression. "First you've heard of this?"

Gaspar nodded. "But it *was* eral? It's on record."

"Oh yeah. It's legit, all right." Angiers drained his glass.

"What of Auschwitz? No activity there?"

"Not since 5 September, and we don't know what that was—"

"Isn't that strange? The largest camp, the center of the entire network, and—correct me if I'm wrong—the site commonly associated with the exterminations..."

"Yeah," Angiers muttered. "Everybody knows Auschwitz. But hell, they didn't show up in Warsaw either. I was ready for them there. The whole team in place. And...nothing." The glass jerked violently. Random drops splattered the floor. "No show. Just the tanks rolling in, the buildings ablaze...I can't figure it. They're not thinking. They should be *thinking*."

Gaspar remained silent. Angiers studied his glass as if considering another drink. "Chelmno," he whispered. "The only time I ever saw Dave flustered, I can tell you that." He set the glass down firmly. "He's good, by the way. Nam vet. He'll do you right."

Trying to cover the silence, Gaspar sipped at his own drink.

Angiers shuddered, looked up him. "I suppose Coriolan wants to talk real bad."

"Pro forma, Roger. He sympathizes, rest assured."

"He?" Angiers chuckled. "Well, let me pull my crap together and I'll get out of your hair."

"No rush, Roger," Gaspar said, feeling that it would be nice to get

Angiers off-station as soon as possible. "But I do need the access codes."

"Ah." Angiers went to the keyboard and tapped out a command. Gaspar's workcase beeped. "Sorry, Jimmy. Anything else?"

Gaspar was shaking his head when the AI spoke. "One moment. Pardon the interruption, but the monitor should be made aware that access is growing unstable at the Auschwitz site."

Gaspar rubbed the bridge of his nose. It never failed. Every time a critical operation was under way, you had access fade—the chronons that comprised the bridge between the continuum and the Channel suddenly changing orientation en masse according to statistical variations far beyond Gaspar's understanding. Only supermassive singularities could punch through the interference that prevailed when that happened, and this station certainly wasn't equipped with those. "How long do we have?"

"No exact prediction is possible, Monitor. The quantum fluctuations involved are chaotic in nature—"

"I'm aware of that."

"—but a rough estimate would be four to six weeks, continual."

Gaspar grunted. That would be long enough, and if it wasn't, Lewin wouldn't be able to move either. There was only one aperture at Auschwitz. Unless she was utilizing another waypoint altogether . . . He'd have to think about that further. "Keep me updated."

"You're thinking Auschwitz?" Angiers said.

"A hunch, no more."

With a quizzical shrug, Angiers turned away. Gaspar put down his glass and left the room. Horek was leaning against the wall, arms crossed. "Sounds like they're all set," he said as Gaspar appeared.

Gaspar heard a rumble of conversation from the command center. "Let's go."

"You might be in for some static," Horek said as they headed down the corridor.

"Oh? Roger run things democratically, did he?"

"He likes to hear opinions."

"Ah. Well, my friend, this station's not a democracy any longer. Or a republic." He looked Horek in the eye. "As of now, it's a despotism."

Command appeared to be as full as it ever got. The entire crew present, less whoever was in-time on surveillance. A few looked as if they'd just woken, which was probably the case—two young women were wearing some kind of bed robes. The low murmur ceased as Gaspar entered. He went to the center of the room without looking in either direction.

Stepping up to the level leading to the command alcove, he paused next to a console. "Good day to you all," he said, keeping his voice low. Some of the crew leaned forward to hear better. "I am Gaspar James, C24 monitor. You may refer to me as Gaspar. Some of you may know me. Most do not. No matter. You'll know me well enough by the time we're finished."

A low ripple of laughter crossed the room. He dropped his head. The room went silent once more. "Up until now you have been operating under Condition Red. From here on it is Red Plus. Some of you may wonder at this, since no such condition exists in service procedure. Simply put, Red Plus is a crisis situation where CM Gaspar has appeared."

The laughter rose higher, more hearty and confident this time. Face stony, Gaspar surveyed them all. His eyes found Rainbow Thayer and fixed on her for a moment. She seemed less than amused.

The noise died out, most of it abruptly, the rest fading until a single voice was left. There was always that last one.

"I'm not laughing."

He stepped forward into a nearly physical silence. "I don't think you understand," Gaspar told them. "You're not simply facing a pack of renegades. Or a vicious and depraved period. Or the usual risks of intemp operations. No, no—" He slammed his case on the console beside him. "You are facing *me!*"

He turned half away, hand over his mouth as if he was trying to restrain himself. Swinging back to them, he shot out an arm. "You people . . . have allowed . . . a continuity emergency to slip out of control. And you laugh. You have lost nearly a quarter of your strength in the process. And you laugh. You are on the verge of allowing a malignant change in the continuum to achieve *transcendence*. And you laugh. Well, I wish someone would inform me where the humor lies in all of this because to me, the jokes seem few."

He paused another second or two, glaring at them through his eyebrows. "I'm not sure how this came to be, but I have suspicions.

Shall I tell you what I suspect? That there is something eral about it. That this operation impinges on period sensitivities. That the ideas and attitudes absorbed over a few decades have overwhelmed your obligation to all time that is to come.

"It has happened before. And in this very period. Several decades ago—relative—a small group decided that it would be nice to circumvent the late-century Western Reaction by cultivating a political dynasty in the American Republic. They groomed a middling clan from the northeast for that role. They were discreet and effective. And by the time they were discovered it required two assassinations and the death of a young female bystander to derail the thing. Not to mention a minor war that blew up into a large-scale confrontation. Or the fact that the Soviet, which had previously collapsed in 1972, managed to hang on until nearly the century's end. Or that the American Republic itself almost went bankrupt, crippling its response to the Sino-Japanese coalition early in the 21st. In all, half a century passed before the continuum returned to the ground state.

"And why did it happen? How could it have gotten so far? I spoke to Walleck, the contemporary CM. He told me that some of his people *sympathized*. That they considered it a fine idea. That how much did it matter—one Boston clan?"

Gaspar shook his head. "I want no sympathy here. I want it expunged. I want your hearts hardened. Is the Holocaust a horror? Yes, it is. Should it not have happened? I agree. Should Hitler and his creatures never have existed? Absolutely. But they *do* exist, and they *did* exist, and they will, and that is all that matters. And is that a monstrous thing? Oh yes—but consider who you are, and the oath you took, and—"

In the back someone spoke. It was Thayer, as Gaspar had hoped it would be. "What was that?"

"I said that you are one prize son of a bitch, and you have no right to tell us to—"

"Then get out!" Gaspar shouted. "Pack your things! I have no use for you!"

She glared at him, red-faced. "You're no better than—"

"No! No debate, no argument, no commentary. You don't belong here. Go on! The portal is wide!" Thayer pushed through the crowd, muttering furiously to herself as she passed someone standing at the corridor entrance: Angiers, who was pulling at one ear as he watched Gaspar.

"Anyone else? Let it be now. Take your pity, your fear, your weakness elsewhere. There may be a place for them at some point in the Extension, but not in this station. Not in this now."

He waited a moment, and then, for the first time, he smiled. "Very well. We are the happy few. Station procedures and schedules will remain unchanged until I consult with section heads. You are dismissed."

The crew broke up. Whispers rose as they passed into the corridor. Angiers pushed through them, shaking hands and patting shoulders. A few jerked their heads in Gaspar's direction as they spoke.

Gaspar remained where he was. A sense of tension he hadn't even been aware of began to fade. It had gone well—only one walkout. The team forecaster, it was true, but that could be made up. The team belonged to him now, his own instrument, to be used as he willed. He was in the field, where he was at his best. He could put aside his own uncertainty, the growing dread that had hovered over him, refusing to come into focus, since he'd first laid eyes on the Holocaust imagery. Things were going to be fine.

Angiers approached him. "I guess I can tell La Cor that she's got a live one."

"I think he knows."

Angiers hesitated, as if about to say something more. He took a long look at Gaspar and held out his hand. "Bust 'em," he said as they shook, then walked to the portal. Gaspar threw his head back. "Dido," he said quietly. "Give me everything you have on Auschwitz."

1943

A sound pulled Reber's eyes upward. A flock of birds was passing on its way south to wherever they spent the winter. Small, brown—he didn't know what they were called or if he'd ever seen their kind before.

Birds didn't often appear near the camp. Too many people, too much noise, the human stench too great. It was odd, the sense of poignancy the sight of them brought, as if he'd missed them without even knowing it. He watched them dwindle until they were no more than small dots in the still air. Wherever they were headed—Sicily or Africa or the Levant—they'd be hard put to find a spot where men weren't squabbling this season.

He was walking the access road, as he often did in his free time. About halfway between Birkenau and the main camp, the fences of both plainly visible, on his way back to barracks after spending a few hours with his pipe on the banks of the Sola. He felt less than refreshed—he was tired of the river; the view did nothing for him now. But there was nowhere else to go, not if he wanted to avoid seeing something shocking. And even then the road had its revelations: the brutalized work crews, the occasional starved corpse waiting for collection.

But it was Saturday, and he was spared any such encounters. Half-shift, the camp at rest, the inmates—punishment Kommandos excepted—finding whatever ease they could. In the mess the staff would be drinking themselves into a stupor. Reber had never been a drinking man—his stomach wouldn't hold the stuff. In any case, his comrades' conduct quickly exceeded the bounds of what he considered offensive.

Ahead lay the railway bridge. Three men, all in field gray, stood at the far end. Reber held his pace as he approached, in no hurry to return to the barracks.

Reber usually dreaded the weekends. A blank period from 1230 Saturday through 0800 Monday, with little to fill the time. But this weekend was somewhat different. Earlier this morning one of the typists—the pretty one he'd protected from Boldt, in fact—had approached his desk as the shift ended. She'd learned that her cousin was in camp, in an outside work detail. Could he possibly put in a request that she be transferred to the office? There was plenty of work to be done, and she was an excellent typist.

Cousin indeed. They all had a dozen cousins, it seemed. Perhaps Streicher was right, and they had been outbreeding every other people in Europe. Yet he couldn't call her a liar, could he? Reber had been raised in the old style, where one treated women with deference and gallantry, as opposed to the brood-mare party fashion. His upbringing prevailed, even with regard to Jewesses. He politely told her that he'd consider it.

Now he had until Monday to think of what to say. He was losing his skill at speaking to women, and that troubled him. He'd never had any such problem before. It was as if he'd reverted to adolescence, to that stage of flushed skin, stammering, and timidity. He supposed it had to do with barely seeing a woman for the period he was at the front. And before that, it had been several years since he'd been seriously involved. With Herta, back in Cologne.

As always when he thought of her, the image of her face at their last meeting, in—God, it had been '37—rose up. Six years now. He could have accomplished something worthwhile with Herta. They could have built a life together.

But Herta was a Mischlinge. Her grandfather was Jewish. She had been understanding when he explained it to her—that no SS man could be involved with anyone of Jewish ancestry. "Tainted" was the word they used, though he hadn't spoken it himself. Herta gave no sign of bitterness or condemnation, and there were times when he wished she had.

He hadn't laid eyes on her since. He feared that he would again someday. Inside the camp, as broken and starving as all the others. Mischlinge were supposed to be protected by the Nuremberg laws, on the grounds that German blood outweighed any lesser mixture. So Herta was safe for now. But who knew how long that would last? Hadn't Reichsminister Himmler sworn to expunge every last drop of Jewish blood from Europe?

He reached the bridge, a short, simple wood and metal structure. He halted before setting foot on it. His right side had begun to ache, the wounds acting up. He rubbed the tender spot carefully. He had not yet gotten over the conviction of fragility that being wounded had given him.

Two guards faced him at the far end, along with an officer leaning against the steel frame, his back to Reber. As he watched, the guards burst into laughter and the officer struck his thigh with a loose glove.

Reber's stomach tightened. That gesture had been enough. It was Boldt. Wearing standard-issue SS field gray today, but Boldt all the same. He was certain of it.

After the confrontation in the office, he'd taken a look at Boldt's records. There were very few of them. Oh, the Gestapo kept its own files, but he'd have expected them to be cross-referenced with SS records. It was as if Boldt had deliberately withheld the necessary paperwork.

Several weeks passed before he saw an opportunity to ask anyone about the man. Care was essential; Reber had no idea what connections Boldt had within the staff or what his reaction would be if he learned that he was being asked after. But finally Joachim Caesar, an easygoing sort with his own mind, had brought the name up himself.

"Ah, you had a run-in with Blackie, then!" Caesar had smiled around his smelly cigar. No worries about wind for him. "What's his story? An intellectual, he is, a college boy. Studied *philosophy* under some pest name of Heimann or Heindig or something. Not even a party member until '39.''

Caesar paused to chuckle to himself. "He's the new generation, Reber. Absolutely untouched by bourgeois pieties. The pure red-blooded National Socialist in person, to hear him tell it. How do you like that? An egghead, and here he is, marching around in his dress blacks, more a party man than the Führer.''

He went on to warn Reber that Boldt wasn't quite right in the head and to watch his step. "That's why I prefer running the farms," he added. "You don't have to bother with Boldt's kind of bullshit out there. You want a transfer, let me know. I'll find a place for you.''

Reber had tried to avoid Boldt since, well aware that he'd run across him eventually. He'd given lengthy consideration on how to deal with him, entertaining visions of a crisp salute and offhand nod as he passed by. All that evaporated as Boldt slowly swung around to face him.

"Ah, look who's here!" Boldt stepped away from the siding. "Gerd Reber. An old hand," he said to the guards. "Prewar SS. An inspiration to us all.''

The taller guard—a doltish-looking youth who never would have been accepted in Reber's day—emitted another burst of laughter. He went silent when Reber shot him a glare.

Reber was still poised at the edge of the bridge, as if Boldt had forbidden him to cross it. Reluctantly, he stepped onto the metal plating.

"Heard you were one for fresh air," Boldt said as he approached. "Wandervögel boy, were you?" He raised his right hand and wiggled the fingers. "Playing guitar around the campfire under the pines, that sort of thing?''

"I'm a city boy," Reber said as firmly as he could manage. He came to a halt. "No guitars, no bonfires.''

"Ah." Boldt's tone was dubious, as if he found the answer unsatisfactory. He cocked his head, staring at Reber through narrowed eyes.

"It's just . . ." Reber licked his lips. "Just to get out of barracks for a while.''

"I don't blame you," Boldt said cheerily. "I enjoy the outdoors myself. Clears the mind." Thumbs stuck in his belt, he threw his head back. "And a fine day for it too." He waved at the empty area facing the wire. "Ever walk there?"

"It's a little wet."

"Not if you know where you're going. Here, let me show you." Boldt turned on his heel. Reber felt compelled to follow him. "Now you two get cracking," Boldt told the guards. "And check underneath. You'll find a few hanging from the beams, I'm sure."

Laughing, the guards drifted off to their stations. "Good boys," Boldt assured Reber. "I enjoy talking to enlisted men. Make a point of it. You should do the same. No such thing as too many friends. Told them the one about the brass mouse. You know it? Ah, you'll like this one! Fellow sees a brass mouse in the window of an antique shop . . ."

They left the paved road for the low brush bordering the cleared strip. It was muddy, as Reber had feared. Well, he had plenty of time open for polishing boots.

" ' . . . you don't want to hear the story behind the brass mouse?' the proprietor says. 'Very well, then.' So he wraps up the mouse and . . ."

To their right stood the outer fence. Thirty metres of empty ground faced it, the thick mud dotted with puddles reflecting the clouds overhead. A guard leading a dog passed them on his way to the gate. He waved, Boldt responding with a flick of a glove.

". . . hundreds, then thousands of mice pour out behind him. The fellow begins running down the street . . ."

Boldt clapped a hand on his holster. He was a great one for that; a characteristic gesture, you might say. Reber wondered if he had a full magazine. There hadn't been an ammunition issue since summer—it was all going to the front. He imagined Boldt was well supplied. If anyone had enough rounds, it would be him.

". . . he reaches the center of the bridge and *flings* the brass mouse into the Elbe. And tens of thousands of mice dive into the river to drown . . ."

A crew was working in the near distance, some project involving drainage, Reber surmised. A punishment Kommando, from the red circles painted on their backs. Boldt drifted in that direction.

". . . the proprietor says, 'Ah, *now* you want to hear the story of the brass mouse.' 'No, not at all,' the fellow tells him. 'I want to know if you have any brass *Jews*.' ''

Boldt laughed as if he'd just now heard it for the first time himself. Head up, glove striking his thigh. Looking away, Reber politely echoed him.

''What's the matter?'' Boldt said, catching himself quickly enough for Reber to suspect he'd been acting. ''Don't tell me you've heard it before?''

''No, not at all, it's—''

''Not your type of joke, is that it?''

Boldt was eyeing him the same way he'd done at the bridge. Reber should have told him he had heard it already.

''Let's see if I can think of another,'' Boldt said. ''I can never remember jokes. There was a funny one in *Der Stürmer* recently . . .''

They were approaching the work crew. The guards looked seriously unhappy about drawing duty on Saturday. They visibly pulled themselves together when they saw the officers drawing near. ''Keeping them busy?'' Boldt called out. ''That's good. I don't approve of halfdays,'' he told Reber. ''They're celebrating their Sabbath in camp right now, you know. That's what they're doing.''

The man closest to them was standing next to a mound of reddish newly dug earth. Reber couldn't see what he was guarding until he was only a few steps off and a ditch was revealed beside the heapedup dirt.

''Now, the joke. A rabbi and a whore—no, it wasn't that one . . . Wait, what's this here?'' Almost eagerly, Boldt headed for the ditch. Reber held back.

''Look at this,'' Boldt said slowly. He was staring into the ditch, hands on his hips. He didn't seem to be aware that Reber was no longer beside him. Reluctantly, Reber went to join him.

He didn't look down until he reached the edge. When he did, he nearly cried out. The ditch was about ten metres long, one wide, and obviously more than two deep. It was filled with water to within a handsbreadth of the edge. Floating in it, half-submerged, were bodies. At least ten of them, all in striped prisoners' garb, the red patch bright on their backs.

''What's all this about?'' Boldt called to the guard.

The man shrugged. "Don't know, sir. Came on duty this morning and they ordered me here."

"They've been in there all night, then," Boldt said.

Reber gritted his teeth. Last night had been cold, the chilliest of the fall so far.

"Caught them up to something." Boldt pushed past Reber without taking his eyes off the water. "Ah, look here!"

Within the ditch, one man remained on his feet. Reber had missed him with his first inspection. He ran his eyes along the rest of its length and saw another prisoner still standing, at the far end, nearly at the guard's feet. That one's head was lowered, face almost in the water.

But the nearest man stood straight, his chin high, cap on his head. "Well now," Boldt said, going into a crouch. "A sturdy sort."

The man stared stolidly ahead, giving no sign that he'd heard. Snatching a shoot of wild grass, Boldt began to strip it. "I have a joke for you."

Reber listened with amazement as he repeated the yarn: antique shop, mouse, bridge. Boldt paused before the punchline, delivered it with a flourish of his glove.

The guard let out a low chuckle. For a moment there was no response from the prisoner, but then his face lit up and he began laughing wildly, the sound high-pitched and frantic. Boldt broke into a smile.

The man went on laughing for a minute or more, eyes shut, mouth open wide. "He likes it better than you did," Boldt told Reber.

Raising a hand, the man wiped his face. "Hands in the water!" the guard shouted.

Boldt waved him silent. "No, no. He's a good fellow." Getting up, Boldt stuck his thumbs in his belt. "In fact, Jew, I'll tell you what. If you can climb out of there on your own, you go back into camp. I'll even transfer you to a regular unit. Throw in a fine hot meal as well, why not? Well, what do you say?"

A few muted yelps still shook the man. He glared at Boldt from under his brows, then looked closely at Reber. "Uh, sir—" the guard said uncertainly.

Boldt silenced him with a gesture. "Well, Israel? We're waiting."

Licking his lips, the man raised his hands and moved to the edge of the ditch. He tried to clutch the earth, but his fingers were useless, dead-white and curled up tightly. Instead he placed his elbows on the rim of dirt to lever himself over.

"That's it, Israel," Boldt murmured.

Reber moved closer. The man was gaining; drawing himself up with painful slowness, water splashing beneath him. He lurched forward, shifting his right elbow to drier ground. Reber's hand swung out. Just a step or two, then bend over, grab the man's arm . . . He felt Boldt's eyes on him. Making a fist, he slipped the hand behind his back.

The man moved his other elbow. His fingers quivered. He grunted and caught Reber's eye. Looking away, Reber clenched his fist tighter above his belt.

The prisoner drew one leg high, got it over the edge. He paused a second or two, then carefully shifted his weight. As far as Reber was concerned, he'd made it. He glanced at Boldt, who had one eyebrow raised. Stepping forward, Reber went to haul the man to his feet.

The wet soil under the prisoner's left elbow collapsed and he dropped into the ditch with a huge splash. He came to the surface sputtering and lunged toward the edge.

"Uh-uh-uh," Boldt cried, waggling a finger. "One chance, Israel. No more."

The guard let out a relieved gasp. Dropping his arms, the prisoner moved to the center of the ditch. A strangled sound escaped him as he looked again at Reber. Then he clenched his jaw and swung his eyes straight ahead. Reber noticed that he'd lost his cap.

Turning away, Reber walked off on stiff legs. "I can climb out," a voice called from the far end of the ditch.

"What's the trouble, Obersturmführer?"

Reber started. Boldt was nearer to him than he would have guessed, no more than two steps behind. His voice was low, his tone harsh and insinuating. Reber turned his head. Boldt closed in, grinning fiercely. One of his front teeth was a grayish color.

"Well? What is it, Gerd?"

He has a dead tooth, Reber thought. He ought to see to that. SS officers were supposed to take care of their appearance. "That wasn't—" Reber cut himself off.

"I can climb out. Ask me. I can do it . . ."

"Shut up," the guard snarled.

"Wasn't what?" Boldt said. "Necessary? Proper? Decent?"

"*Please.* I can do it. Let me—"

There was a thump and the man cried out. Reber shuddered despite himself.

"Answer me, Obersturmführer."

"All of them," Reber choked out.

"Ah. *All* of them. I see. Good answer." Boldt chuckled and backed off. The second prisoner was crying now, full-throated sobs as open as a child's, incoherent words falling between them. Reber heard the guard swearing at him.

He became aware that he was standing at attention. He willed himself to relax and then—far more difficult—to look back at Boldt.

The Hauptsturmführer was biting his lip. He chuckled again, revealing once again the rotten tooth. "You think this is bad, Gerd? This?" He waved a glove at the ditch. "This is *nothing*. You should have been out east with Einsatzgruppe B. That was a chore, now. We used bullets, not this Zyklon stuff. You saw their faces then. Actually got your hand in. Nothing like here—this is clean. Why, we'd finish up, throw a little dirt over the pits, then pass by days later, and what do you think? The dirt would be moving, they'd be still living down underneath, like bugs, not aware that they were dead, trying to claw their way out. An eerie sight, Gerd. Eerie. Something you won't see at old Auschwitz, efficient though it might be."

Boldt leaned closer. "That was another joke, Gerd."

He stepped back and regarded the ditch. The hysterical sobbing grew louder. Boldt pursed his lips, as if considering what to do about it.

"It's just as well you weren't with us. You wouldn't have been able to take it. I can see that. You wouldn't have lasted, Gerd. Himmler himself couldn't. That's right. Faithful Heinrich blew his guts when the guns started speaking. The only operation he ever witnessed, and the chicken farmer couldn't bear it. He lacked will, you see. Easy enough to give the orders, but in person—ah, that's a different matter. He even tried to save a Jew. A blond boy, probably some Ukie in him. 'You look Aryan,' the Reichsminister said. 'Is your mother Aryan? Your grandmother?' But the boy told him no. Surprising, eh? You never can tell, can you?

"And Heinrich wasn't the only one. We had plenty—shot themselves, lost their minds, drank their way into a hospital. But we got the job done.''

A hand clapped the holster. ''No, you wouldn't have lasted out east. But that's fine. Someone has to handle the paper. Give the orders, process the orders, send the orders on down. Are you aware that we're defined by our tools? That's true. We don't make them, they make us. And what's your tool, eh? Paper. You're a paper man, Gerd. So run on back to your office.''

He turned away. Reber remained where he was, certain that more was coming. After a moment passed with Boldt saying nothing else, Reber realized that the Hauptsturmführer was waiting for him to move so that he could call him to a halt. A gesture; Boldt was as full of gestures as a film melodrama.

Slowly Reber turned to face him.

He saw Boldt's jaw tighten, color move up his face. ''Yes,'' he said finally, glaring at Reber. ''Yes—there's one thing else. Tell me, Reber: What must an SS man do?''

Reber cleared his throat, looked past Boldt's shoulder. ''Serve the Reich. Be loyal to the—''

''No!'' Boldt said, nearly shouting.

''Protect the German—''

''No—'' Boldt raised his glove, shook it in Reber's face. ''Don't fuck with me, mister. I ask again: What must an SS man do?''

''An SS man . . .'' Reber paused, caught his breath. ''An SS man must overcome himself.''

''*Yes.*'' Boldt bobbed his head wildly. ''Yes. Very good. And you will do that. I'm going to see to it. If I could put down a thousand *subhumans* with my own hands, while they looked back at me, while they wailed and moaned like that *thing* in the ditch . . . If I could do that and remain the man I was, then you will do the same while you push your papers.''

Taking a deep breath, Boldt looked up at the sky. ''You will overcome yourself. You must. You have will, Reber. Strength of being. Not like—'' He waved at the ditch. ''Listen to that. Just listen. Wah-wah-wah-wah. You waste sympathy on that?''

Reber thought of the other one, noticeable now only by his silence. Gazing calmly at death while the bodies of his friends floated about him. Reber wondered who he had been. He didn't look like a Jew.

From the corner of his eye he saw Boldt snap down his glove. The click of a rifle bolt sounded clearly. He caught himself as he was turning to look. A shot rang out and the crying ceased.

Boldt grinned at him sardonically. "All right, Gerd. You can go now. Back to your office. I'll be stopping by."

He walked off without another word. Reber waited, unwilling to accompany him. Behind him he heard the guard call out, "What about this last one, sir?" His voice sounded anxious.

"May as well," Boldt said. Reber almost started running when the second gunshot came.

It was a few minutes before he became aware that he was moving deeper into the marsh. He caught sight of the gate and changed his course. Somebody's cousins, he thought. Those two had been somebody's cousins. They were all somebody's cousins. There were too many cousins. He couldn't look after all the cousins. The cousins would have to take care of themselves.

1973

When he awoke, Reber thought for a moment that he was back there once again, Boldt's smirk only a handspan from his face, his muscles tight as he waited for the Walther to fire. But then the years returned and he relaxed, fear and disgust receding to whatever cranny in his soul they hid.

There was a pounding in his head, a slow persistent ache. He tried to think it away, as he always did with headaches, and, as always, failed. A couple of aspirin were called for, much as they disturbed his digestion.

He'd have to get out of bed for those. The dull red of his eyelids told him the sun was already high. Not that it mattered what time it was; his sleep had diminished with age, and he was pleased whenever he got a full night's rest. Often enough he was awake with the dawn. Still, he felt strangely tired this morning.

Blinking against the light—it shouldn't be this bright in the bedroom; he never left the curtains open—he tried to sit up. He'd no sooner gotten his head off the pillow than a blinding pain coursed through his skull, so sharp as to make him gasp aloud.

He lay back, grinding his teeth while it ebbed. After a moment, he was able to open his eyes. Squinting against the light, he saw that the ceiling was painted white, not the light brown he knew, with the long crack shooting out from the light fixture. In fact, there was no fixture visible at all.

What was this place? Not his bedroom. It wasn't his flat at all. Foreboding arose within him. The Israelis—they'd struck at last. Scooped him up off the street, doped him, planted him in a safe house preparatory to smuggling him to Israel for trial and execution, the same as they had with Eichmann. He considered it calmly. He'd stopped fearing them long ago—had never really been frightened of them. It was their right, after all. But why now, after such a time had passed? And why Gerd Reber? There were plenty of bigger fish still swimming about. Brunner in Syria, Mengele somewhere in South America. Even Bormann, if the stories were true.

He moved his hands. They felt distant, as if he was drunk, but they seemed to be free; he wasn't under any kind of restraint. Moving carefully, he tried to turn his head. Something pulled at his nose. Instinctively, he reached up; there was a small tug at his arm as well. His fingers touched an object dangling from his face. For a second he couldn't make out what it was, but then he felt the length of it, the small cylindrical shape . . . It was a tube. A plastic tube, taped to his cheek, vanishing into his right nostril . . .

A surge of mindless horror engulfed him, slipped as quickly away. Ignoring the drag of the tubing, he moved his head slowly to the right. Vertigo forced his eyes shut, but that hideous pain failed to recur. Raising his eyelids, he inspected the room. A table—not his own—a doorway past that, the door open a crack. Enclosing the bed was a metal rack. He reached for it, but his hands were too weak to grasp it.

He swung his head, quickly enough so that a small echo of that pain brushed him again. A hospital. He was in a hospital bed. How could that be?

Concentrating, he tried to call up his most recent memories. He found nothing, and real fear touched him for the first time. Then it came flooding back—most of it anyway. His walk, the young hoodlums, the park. Beyond that all was confusion. The only thing he retained was the conviction that something else had happened, something horrible.

He sensed the door swinging open, a shape looking in. Before he could respond, it disappeared, leaving the door wide. He tried to call out, but all that emerged was a hoarse squawk.

So what was this now? He repeated the attempt, getting an even more lurid sound. He didn't seem to be able to feel his tongue. Perhaps that was it—he'd been assaulted, struck across the jaw. But he hadn't felt any bandages on his face. He tried to touch his chin. The effort exhausted him and he lay his hand on his chest.

At least his hearing was intact. He clearly heard footsteps approaching from down the hall, a PA system behind them. He relaxed and waited.

Someone entered the room. Reber turned carefully. A man in a white coat, a doctor, approached the bed. A young fellow, his hair longer than Reber would have liked, wearing a pair of steel-framed glasses. Behind him stood two other white-clad figures. Nurses, Reber assumed.

The doctor paused. "Good morning, Mr. Reber. Can you hear me?"

His hand rose as Reber opened his mouth. "Don't try to speak just yet. A simple nod will do . . . Very good. I am Dr. Wendt, and this is Sisters of Mercy Hospital. Do you recall how you came to be here . . . ? No. I'll explain that to you, but first I wish to make an examination."

Lifting the blanket, he loosened the smock covering Reber. "Let me know if this causes any pain," he said, not specifying whether he preferred a nod, a shake of the head, or a simple shriek. Reber sighed and closed his eyes as a cold stethoscope touched his chest. As he expected, Dr. Wendt possessed the standard collection of grunts, hisses, and questioning noises to accompany his work. Reber had heard the same from doctors his entire life and was convinced that a long and detailed course on sound effects was required of all medical students.

The nurses had come forward to assist him. ". . . that tattoo," Reber heard one of them whisper.

"Blood type," the other replied in a normal voice. "He's one of *them*."

"Nurse Müller . . ." The doctor turned from his inspection of Reber's eyes. "If you please."

After a few more humphs, the doctor rearranged Reber's smock and replaced the blanket. Straightening up, he asked Reber to count to ten. The best Reber could manage resembled a garbled croak.

Dr. Wendt nodded gravely. "Well then," he said. A professional smile appeared on his face. "First things first. Today is Sunday, and you've been hospitalized for one day. You collapsed on the Henrenhäuser Allee yesterday afternoon, a little after the lunch hour. Luckily, there were many alert passersby and a distance of only six blocks, so you were brought in quickly. That often makes a difference."

Pictures flashed across Reber's mind: a crowd of faces, frantic shouting, and for some reason, a hat. He nodded almost imperceptibly.

"I believe in being candid with my patients, Mr. Reber, particularly those of your age. I don't think you'd appreciate euphemisms." The doctor paused to take a breath. "You've suffered a cerebral accident of some severity. How bad it is we won't know for several days. But, as I'm sure is obvious to you, it is of a serious nature."

Reber closed his eyes. A stroke. He'd been felled by a stroke. Apoplexy, it had been called in his father's time. Not an uncommon event at his age; he supposed he should have expected something of the sort eventually.

"The situation could be far worse," Dr. Wendt continued. "There is no swelling of tissue. Whatever damage has occurred is localized. It appears to be confined to Broca's area—that is, the speech center, which is why you've encountered difficulties in speaking. This is not unusual, and in many cases, it will either improve on its own or will respond to therapy. Again, we can't be certain until further time has passed. But although your condition is serious, I don't believe you're in danger at the moment."

Reber nodded to show that he had understood. He was pleased at the doctor's frankness. Wendt was quite right; Reber would not have appreciated any attempt to downplay his problems at this point. Not after the life he'd lived.

"Very good. Once you've rested, I'll arrange for further tests—"

One of the nurses muttered something. "Oh yes," Wendt said. "We've been unable to contact your relatives. Is there anyone we should . . . ?"

Reber shook his head.

After assuring himself that Reber was as comfortable as could be expected, Wendt wished him good day and left, the nurses trailing after. Only one set of footsteps proceeded down the hall. Apparently the doctor and one of the nurses had stayed behind to talk. The nurse spoke too low for Reber to hear, but Wendt's sharp voice carried clearly.

"It would be best to keep your politics out of the hospital in the future."

A low mutter, then: "Regardless. Did you notice his scars? He was in the combat arm. Nothing to be ashamed of in that."

Reber smiled. Little did Wendt know. The Waffen-SS had committed its own share of crimes. Out on the steppes, at Oradour and Malmédy. They were forgetting what had actually happened, all the young ones. The historical truth was too terrible for the mind to hold.

All except the little nurse. A leftist, no doubt, a fervent supporter of Baader-Meinhof and similar trash. Probably had a poster of that bearded Cuban thug Guevara hanging in a place of honor in her flat. She remembered—or believed she did—even if she utterly missed the point. Reber wondered which way she would have gone in the old days. He thought he knew. She'd have made a fine wardress, that one.

". . . don't mean to be harsh, Ingrid. But he *is* a patient . . ."

Reber let his thoughts drift. His memory was bringing up more of his disastrous outing, disconnected bits and pieces of it, as if appealing for help in putting them in proper sequence. He settled back, drowsily reviewing the sweeping woman, the Volkswagen's near miss—an omen, that had been—the unusual sight of a man wearing a yarmulke . . .

His breath left his body all at once. Yom Kippur. It was Yom Kippur, and the tanks were rolling across the Negev, leaving fire and blood behind, heading north to Jaffa. Toward her.

The doctor and nurse were leaving. Ignoring the pain, Reber lifted his head from the pillow. "What's happening in Israel?" he called out. All that came was a series of gurgling multisyllabic grunts. He carefully shaped his lips. "Israel . . ." It sounded like an animal in pain. Losing all control, he tried to shout the word: "*Israel, Israel . . .*"

The footsteps continued down the hall into silence.

1943

"Why is it so quiet?"

The fence rose only a hundred yards away, clearly visible through the brush. Behind it, past the inner wire, stood the gray buildings of the camp. Nothing at all moved in there, as far as Gaspar could see. Only a plume of smoke drifting out of a chimney to his left.

The place was a small city. Thousands of people lived beyond that wire. Yet he heard not a sound, saw no motion whatsoever. As if the camp was a necropolis, its inhabitants long dead, the site itself abandoned.

"It's Saturday," Fukudon said. "Half-shift. No work in the afternoon, except for the Sonderkommando and the other special details. The Krauts are methodical. They follow a strict schedule."

Gaspar looked over at him. Fukudon's camo field was up, and all he could see, even this close, was the bare outline of a human form behind a slightly distorted image of plants and earth.

"What of the clients . . . uh, the inmates?"

"They can't approach the wire anyway—though they

do sometimes. The last time. Now they're sticking to their barracks. Too dangerous to be caught outside. Some are out and around, though. Look close and you'll see them.''

Gaspar gave the camp a more thorough scrutiny. He'd been skeptical when Dido had told him that it was Birkenau, and not Auschwitz Main a mile to the southeast, that had impacted most deeply on historical consciousness. But here the fact was obvious. You could fit a dozen main camps inside that perimeter. And apart from size, there was the very feel of the place, a sense of mammoth and unyielding purpose.

Nothing stirred, and the silence was that of a graveyard. He sighed. He'd wanted to look the place over on a typical day to get an idea of what it was like. He hadn't been aware that the schedule varied on the weekends.

''We got activity near the gate,'' Horek said. He lay next to Gaspar, studying the readout of a handset. ''Subjects in motion. Males, couple dozen or more.''

Fukudon grunted. ''Work team, I'd guess. A discipline unit, something of that sort.''

A movement caught Gaspar's eye. He pushed himself up, eager for a break in the stillness. It was a man, walking parallel to the wire, a large animal preceding him. He wore a headpiece—a helmet—and a long gray coat reaching to his knees. A weapon hung from a strap over one shoulder.

''There's a guard for you,'' Fukudon said. ''Posten, they're called.''

''The beast is a dog, I assume?''

''Yes. An Alsatian. Also called a German shepherd.''

That's right, Gaspar thought. They came in different types—breeds, if he recalled correctly. A large number of the animals were employed in the camp to assist the staff in policing the inmates, but they weren't allowed to roam freely. Their intelligence in this period was simply too low. He was happy not to have to deal with them.

A shout rang out as the soldier passed one of the towers that broke the line of the fences. Gaspar gaped in surprise as another man appeared at the top. But of course—electronics remained primitive in this now. They were limited to manned stations for spot surveillance.

The guard turned his back to converse with the man in the tower, the weapon hanging there now fully displayed. ''What type of musket is that?''

"It's a rifle, actually. An evolution of the earlier gun. Based on the same principles—"

"I'm aware of that development," Gaspar said patiently.

"Okay." Fukudon lowered his head as his optics focused in on the gun. "A Walther 41. Thought that's what it was. Standard issue, but you get a weird mix here. Mosin-Nagants, Karabins, Mannlichers, you name it. They save the good pieces for the front."

Resting his head on one arm, Fukudon glanced over at Gaspar. "The pistols are Walthers as well, more rarely Lugers. Some of the guards are issued with Schmeissers, a machine pistol. New design, limited to SS personnel." He cocked his head. "You need specs?"

"No, thank you. I'll—" Gaspar paused to recall the period phrase. "I'll look them up."

"You only have to ask."

Gaspar turned to Horek. "Are they still present at the gate?"

"Yeah. Couple more showed up just now."

"Let's go over there."

They backed through the underbrush a suitable distance and got to their feet. The dog began barking at some noise they'd made, pulling against a leash that Gaspar hadn't noticed. Gripping his rifle strap, the soldier cocked his head, obviously studying the foliage. Gaspar almost dropped down once more but desisted when he saw that Fukudon wasn't paying any attention.

"Do they often come in here?" he asked Fukudon.

"Now and then. Not a problem, though. The dogs are easy to confuse."

Gesturing them to follow, Fukudon started off through the marsh. He walked a tangled course, keeping to solid ground as much as possible. Gaspar and Horek trailed close behind. From any distance more than three yards off, Fukudon was simply a shadow. Gaspar supposed the same was true of him.

He was pleased that Fukudon had the situation so well in hand, though less than surprised. Fukudon was a veteran, a twenty-year man with nearly as much experience as Gaspar himself. Though acting as Horek's field officer on this mission, he was an infiltrator, trained to slip into eral roles with a minimum of preparation or backup. It was the most dangerous duty the Moiety offered, but Fukudon filled the role as if born to it. Gaspar was relieved that at least one operative with a solid record was involved in this mission, even though Fukudon's Asian background limited his usefulness.

He'd been amused to learn that Fukudon was tweaking on this operation. There were now two Saburo Fukudons present on Earth at the same time, identical in all but years. The other was on a Pacific island called Luzon, cursing the Yankee bombers and waiting for MacArthur's return. Fukudon had been recruited in 1945 while hiding in the woods after the island was invaded. Gaspar had never tweaked himself and was curious as to what Fukudon felt about the situation.

Shouts came from the direction of the camp. Fukudon halted and raised his hand. Gaspar twisted around. The wire was still visible beyond the brush, but what caught his eye was a huge cloud of black smoke rising from some unseen point, fading out nearly directly overhead. He frowned. Had that appeared in the time that they'd been walking? It seemed impossible.

He moved closer to Fukudon. "Is something on fire?"

"No." He turned to Gaspar, a featureless knob enfolded in green and gray. "That's the ovens. Where they do their thing."

Gaspar's eyes lifted again to the smoke. A deep disquiet stirred within him, far more forceful than anything he'd felt up until now. The breeze shifted, bringing the full odor of burning and that other smell beneath it, the reek that had been tickling his nostrils since he'd passed through the portal. Ghastly, stomach-churning, oddly familiar. He realized what it must be and nearly gagged.

A hand touched his shoulder. "Chief."

Fukudon was merging into the background. Gaspar hurried to catch up, sparing another glance at the smoke. A shudder went through him. He hoped it wasn't apparent behind the camo shield.

But wait . . . he thought back on the data. The Nazis didn't gas during the day. They murdered at night, as if in ritual, as if the darkness would shroud their actions. The killings weren't occurring now. That had happened hours ago, when he'd been a world away. What was burning was simply flesh and bone, the spirit long fled.

Grotesque as it might be, the thought came as a relief. He sighed and forced calm on himself. Self-discipline, that was the thing. He'd feel whatever there was to feel when it was over. No sense turning into another Angiers, broken and useless. The shock had thrown him, that was all.

Ahead Fukudon lifted his hand in a brief wave. A section of brush moved in response. Gaspar looked closely as he passed but couldn't discern the operative who must be standing there. A half-dozen others were now on-station around Birkenau, Monowitz, and the main camp.

Gesturing for them to wait, Fukudon waded across a broad puddle, then went into a crouch before pushing apart some branches on the far side. He remained still for a moment. Gaspar heard a mutter of voices out past the brush. Too low for him to distinguish any words, though it was clear they were speaking in German.

Waving them over, Fukudon went on into the bushes. Gaspar was following him when a sudden burst of sound brought him to a halt. It took him a moment to identify it as laughter. Shaking his head, he slipped through the brush to find Fukudon on all fours, creeping toward the last line of foliage. He crouched and moved after him.

Fukudon lightly touched his shoulder as Gaspar reached him. Settling down, he looked back at Horek before carefully parting the grass before him.

He caught his breath when he saw the men working the cleared ground between the brush and the wire. Over thirty of them, all dressed in striped prison clothing that seemed too light for this kind of weather. On their backs a round red patch showed clearly. They were digging, steadily flinging aside shovelfuls of sodden reddish muck with none of the short breaks necessary for men involved in hard physical labor. Around them stood guards armed with rifles. Apart from the clink of spades and the splatter of mud, the scene was utterly silent.

"Punishment crew," Fukudon said. "They work until they drop."

"Yes," Gaspar replied. "I noticed the red circles."

That aroused a snort from Fukudon, along with a remark in a language unfamiliar to Gaspar. He was about to ask what it meant when a loud splash caught his attention.

He looked to his right. A single guard stood some distance from the main group, with two men in officers' uniforms a few feet on. One was striding after the other, who had his back turned. Gaspar swung his head slightly and turned up the gain on his hearing just as the first officer spoke.

"What's he asking?" Fukudon said after a moment.

"I'm not sure. 'What is it?' but . . . we may have missed—"

A shriek arose from nowhere, a high whining voice pleading to be let out. Gaspar flinched and lowered the volume. "What—" He glanced at the workers. One had paused with a full shovel and was shaking his head, while the others went on as if they'd heard nothing.

The isolated guard shouted for silence, apparently to the earth at his feet. Gaspar pushed himself up on his elbows. "What's going *on?* What are they doing?"

"They were digging over there yesterday," Fukudon said calmly. "I assume that somebody is . . . inside the ditch."

"Oh Christ," Horek muttered.

"One of their little tricks," Fukudon went on. "You don't often see it here, but it's an old custom at the farms."

"In a ditch? Out there?" Gaspar craned his neck, trying to see for himself. The guard kicked at something and the voice fell silent. "Why?"

"They don't need a why around here, man," Horek said. "But— lemme check the tapes."

Gaspar settled back on his belly. The officer continued speaking to his colleague, standing close enough so that the two appeared to be in intimate conversation, though the actual words revealed anything but. Something about Himmler, obviously Heinrich Himmler, the overlord of this carnival, losing or letting loose some uncertain object. Gaspar couldn't understand quite what—it was possibly a local idiom—but from the man's tone, it was clear that Himmler had let down the side.

"Here it is," Horek said. "Let me run it . . . Okay. About 0330 yesterday afternoon. Young kid, new to the unit, had to take a dump . . . Guards ordered him to go beyond the deadline. Rest of 'em—the prisoners, that is—knew what that meant, tried to stop him. Guards shot the kid anyway, chased the others into the ditch."

Gaspar stared at Horek. "That's all? That's a reason?"

"That's it. If you don't count sheer goddamn spite."

"They're Jewish, I take it," Gaspar said as levelly as he could manage.

"Probably," Fukudon said.

Gaspar dipped his head, intent on catching the rest of the conversation, what he could hear of it over the unseen man's sobs. One officer did most of the talking. The other stood ramrod straight, his back to the ditch. Some sort of taproom philosophy: will, being, overcoming oneself. Gerd, the man kept saying. Was that a name? It must be. Gaspar was about to confirm that with Fukudon when the thinner officer looked over at the guard and flicked his glove.

Gaspar guessed what that meant, even as the guard unslung his rifle. He saw it clearly, as if it was happening a few seconds before its ordained place in the timeline, as if his own consciousness had shorted back upon itself. And having seen it once, he closed his eyes so as not to see it again.

But he forgot his hearing, and the full blast of the shot echoed through his head before the circuitry could damp it down.

When he lifted his eyelids, the first officer was walking away, his stride casual. The guard called out a question. Gaspar couldn't hear the answer over the ringing in his head, but he didn't need to. The guard's stance with the rifle told him enough. He failed to look away quickly enough. The second shot was less loud than the first.

"Welcome to Auschwitz," Fukudon said.

Gaspar swept his eyes over the work crew, the wire, the black cloud still pulsing into the sky. "Let's leave this place."

They crawled into deep brush before getting to their feet. Gaspar didn't look back. He was seeing the shooting in his mind, the image ever repeating itself, as if he was caught in a loop. That was the worst thing that could happen to an operative, to be caged forever in an endlessly repeating segment of relative time, the paradoxes built up to where they locked tight, impossible to negate. He supposed this mental loop would fade. The temporal kind never did.

Shooting, at least, was comprehensible. The other styles of death here—those were beyond imagining. But could it be worse than what he'd already seen? He thought of all the episodes of mass death he'd witnessed—Jerusalem, Bokhara, Eire, Spokane, that nameless sun far down the Sagittarius Arm—wondering if there could be any real difference, whether there was such a thing as quality where death was concerned.

This swamp, now—it looked much the way Ireland had in 1847, the year of the Great Famine. The wide and impassable bogs, the endless rain that seemed to have begun falling in a previous epoch, rain that would continue until the hidden sun finally went giant. It had been a dropout operation, with traces of a continuity mission as well:

an operative named Keneally had gone back to search out his ancestors who had fallen during the hunger.

Gaspar had been on his own, walking the highways of Sligo, a piece of the net that would drag Keneally down. The roads, unpaved and muddy, were virtually empty. Not so the land adjoining them. The damp earth was covered with bodies, thinned down to bone, all wearing the same homespun as Gaspar himself. Most lay unmoving, in family groups, the children lying between the parents. Those still alive simply stared, gripped by the killing indifference of starvation. All but a few, who croaked at him as he passed, the sole presence still capable of activity.

He moved on in silence. An experienced man, an operative, scarcely recalling when he had been anything else. All the same it was hard, particularly when he saw, as he must, the green around dead mouths that had fed on grass, the swollen bellies of the children, the eyes moving after him in faces he had taken for dead.

He caught Dugan's signal near a cluster of ruined huts, destroyed by the local landlord after the crop failed. Dugan was at a parallel road only half a mile away. Moving through brush, Gaspar crossed ground nearly as wet as this. Once he almost stepped on a corpse hidden in tall grass.

Dugan waited beside a thicket. He briefed Gaspar, telling him to cover that spot while he went in. Malek and Ames were on their way, but Dugan thought it best to move quickly.

A moment later Dugan called for him. Stunner in hand, Gaspar pushed into the thicket, coming up against a waist-high growth of hedge after only a few steps. Making his way along it, he found a clearing. There stood Dugan, stunner hanging loose at his side.

Keneally had made no move. He sat in front of a small cave dug into the hedge, next to a man and a woman as thin as those on the road. The man seemed dazed, but the woman was in full possession of herself. Women usually lasted longest in famines.

"All right, lad," Dugan said. "You've fed them. Let it stand at that." Looking closer, Gaspar saw the emergency ration containers on the ground at the woman's feet.

Keneally, a harsh-faced man with hollow eyes, said nothing as he got up. The woman, her genetic relationship with Keneally obvious, glanced fearfully between Dugan and Gaspar. She asked a question in her own tongue—she didn't even speak English. Keneally answered without looking back.

With a crash of brush, Malek appeared, sweaty and out of breath. He conferred with Dugan in whispers and then went to the cave. The man cried out and grabbed for a stout club at his feet, but the woman pulled him back. Malek leaned inside. A moment later he turned, holding a knapsack full of rations. Gaspar shot a glance at Keneally. His face had begun to collapse.

"There's a kid in there," Malek said as he passed Gaspar. "It was dead." Dugan led Keneally away, consoling him in the language that the woman had spoken. As Gaspar turned to follow, she called out again.

He looked back. She gazed at him with a question in her eyes, a question that the barriers of language would not allow to be asked. He wondered what she thought they were, what possible place they could hold in her rapidly fading world.

Then she held out a hand to him, as hands had been held out at Jerusalem, and Bokhara, and on the muddy roads here. He turned away without a word.

He ignored the gray-green of the other ration containers beneath her cloak. He had done the same thing himself at one time.

A word from Horek pulled him out of his reverie. They had reached the waypoint, atop a low knob rising slightly above the surrounding wet ground. The portal was at minimum dilation, a vertical black line only millimeters wide. Around it lay packages marked with technical symbols. Surveillance gear, Gaspar assumed, either emplaced or waiting to be. He settled himself on one of them. The heft told him it was empty. Reaching to his belt, he switched off the camo field.

Fukudon and Horek had already done the same. Horek was on his feet, gazing off in the direction opposite the camp with a pinched expression on his face. "Hits you, doesn't it?" he said. "I mean—"

Gaspar made a chopping gesture. "Enough. Let's concentrate on operations."

Fukudon sat on another crate, massaging his right leg. He was heavily accessorized, although the modifications were apparent only to the trained eye. Gaspar wondered if one of them was malfunctioning. "Saburo, I believe you have some comments."

"That's right," Fukudon said. "To speak freely: I'm not convinced that this dump is the target. We've seen no evidence whatsoever. Zero activity on-site, no corroboration from other sources. There's been more movement at Sobibor and Chelmno than here.''

Gaspar nodded. The renegades had evidently come across an SS antipartisan unit near Chelmno on 20 August. The Germans had been badly mauled—several of them with severe burns, some blinded; injuries consistent with energy weapons. But they had repelled whoever it was, and Angiers had hoped the renegades would come in for medical treatment. That hadn't happened. ''What's your opinion?''

''That it's a smokescreen,'' Fukudon said. ''Everything involving the camps. That Hitler remains the primary. That's how our basic forecast reads. I'd like to hear the logic behind this one.''

''You shall,'' Gaspar said. He refrained from mentioning that the forecaster Fukudon was referring to had walked only a few hours ago. He'd gotten the impression that Fukudon was annoyed at Thayer's being forced out. And in fact, Gaspar had no logic to give him. Only a conviction born of intuition that Auschwitz-Birkenau was the target. The center of the camp network: the largest of them all, where the greatest exterminations had occurred, the worst place that had ever existed. How better to strike at the Endlosüng than at its strongest point? What other choice could a saint make?

He was running this operation on sheer instinct, his subconscious in control. A dangerous course, but he saw no alternative under the circumstances. ''First, what are your thoughts, Dave?''

''Well, it's the run-up that bothers me . . .''

''The what?'' Fukudon said.

''The run-up. We've chased 'em all the way to late '43 from like 1910. That's a long duration, man. Granted, Hitler's pretty well covered through a lot of the period. This isn't the first time somebody's tried to whack him. Six previous attempts, and those involving the easiest episodes, when he was hustling street corners back in the '20s—''

''Still leaves a decade and a half open.''

''Yeah. Which they didn't take advantage of. Lot of tricks they could have pulled, Sab. Not shorting or tech stuff either. They coulda roped in the Spartacists during the teens, given a hand to the general staff ten years ago, or Canaris right this minute, for that matter. But what do they do? They slip a bomb into the Wannsee mansion. And

Adolf wasn't even there, man!'' Horek flipped his ponytail, as if disgusted with it. ''The camps make sense to me. Don't know why they switched targets so late, though.''

Gaspar bent forward. ''You said it yourself. Hitler is difficult prey. When frustrated, they turned to the true target. I'm guessing, but I'd imagine there are factions within the group, one pressing for negating Hitler, the other for engaging the event. As it is, she merely alerted us, then found it impossible to get at Hitler during the intervening duration. Now she's desperate.''

He looked between the two of them. Horek was nodding to himself while Fukudon gazed moodily off toward the distant hills. ''Comments? Saburo, you still seem concerned.''

''No. Well, I do think Hitler's the key, but . . .'' Fukudon shrugged. ''You're the forecaster.''

''Very well, then. Let's consider method. Subversion, infiltration, main force—''

''Think you can forget the first two,'' Horek said.

''Maybe so, but they could be contributing factors. As for the force option—could later military equipment from this period overcome the guards?''

''Yeah.'' Horek bobbed his head. ''Oh yeah. One Abrams is all it'd take. Slap their heads, shut 'em right down.''

''A tank, Dave?'' Fukudon shook his head. ''How would it get through this muck?''

''Ahh—right. Didn't think of that.''

''Do think about it,'' Gaspar said. ''I need a list of possible equipment, capabilities, limitations, availability, and so forth. Ask Dido to work on it.''

''Dido may already have one.''

''Good. Go over it with her to weed out any improbabilities. They're not going to burn the place down with an orbital laser.''

''Good thing this cell cuts off at 2021,'' Horek muttered. ''Get into the Pacific War, there's a hell of a choice of fireworks.''

Gaspar thought of the injured operative for the first time since leaving M3. ''I know,'' he said. ''Now, the infiltration angle. That will require checking the camp itself . . .''

''I'm ready,'' Fukudon said.

''You look in the mirror lately, Sab?''

Fukudon glared up at Horek. "So I get a somatic lift. Big deal. It'd take a day."

Gaspar cleared his throat. "A non-Aryan appearance may not be the only drawback, Saburo. Kann sie Deutsch?"

Fukudon looked sheepish. "Call it three days."

"I'm afraid that a simple insert course won't answer. I've spoken the tongue for twenty years, with a passable Silesian accent . . ."

Fukudon straightened himself up. "Monitor," he said, his tone suddenly formal. "Allow me to be blunt. If an infiltration is called for, a trained operative should carry it out. All due respect"—he inclined his head slightly—"but you weren't even sure what a dog was."

"Rest assured I'll get a complete background from Dido. And I won't be speaking to any dogs. Of course," he added diplomatically, "I'll need you to advise me and oversee the insertion."

Fukudon answered with a barely perceptible nod. "Very well," Gaspar said. "What cover would you suggest?"

Fukudon mulled the question over. "Could be anything. All kinds running in and out. SS, party officials, contractors . . ." He paused a moment. "WVHA. Yes. The economic section—loose organization, lot of them around, come and go as they please. That's the way to do it."

Gaspar smiled. He'd drawn the same conclusion himself and was pleased that Fukudon concurred.

"You could tell them you were on the way to Monowitz, the Buna plant, and want to look over the forced labor pool. They won't check—they're not big on standard protocol here."

"And once inside, what then? I'll need a guide. Do I request one?"

"Any of the guards would do. I imagine you want to stay away from the offices." Fukudon glanced sharply at Gaspar. "Or do you? You think our little pals may have slipped somebody in there?"

"I doubt it, but it is a possibility. What about that youngster just now? Gerd—was that his name?"

"First name, I think . . ." Horek said. He lifted the handset. "He's an Obersturmführer—that's a lieutenant, roughly, so . . . Reber. Gerd Reber. In charge of the correspondence department. A clerk."

"He seemed rather pliable. Perhaps I'll request him."

"He might be busy, but I can't see that asking would hurt." Fukudon drew himself up once again and eyed Gaspar intensely. "Whatever you do, sir, stay away from the Gestapo. They are hard-core in the camp office. Some very bad boys in there. Grabner, Hustek, Boldt—''

"I think that was Boldt just now."

Fukudon frowned at Horek. "You do? Boldt usually wears black."

Horek shrugged. "Maybe he's doing his laundry."

"All right," Gaspar said. "Let's go back and virt it in detail with Dido. Fortune smiles, and we'll have a line on her this time tomorrow."

Fukudon told them he wanted to check with the team before leaving. They waited while he sat completely still, eyes blank, as if entranced.

Horek turned to Gaspar. "One thing," he said. "Suppose they try to involve you in an execution? Some of those scumbags come around just to waste somebody. They expect it. Part of the tour."

Gaspar took a deep breath. What had the officer said about Himmler? It had tickled his memory: an item in the data, a speech that the Reichsminister had made. A speech by Himmler held the force of an order. "I think I can deal with that," he told Horek.

Fukudon chuckled and got to his feet. "I'll bet you can."

Horek keyed his handset. The portal dilated. "Wave goodbye to yourself, now, Sab."

"I don't even want to think about that."

"You don't?" Horek stepped toward the portal. "Me, I was the only SOB at Quang Tri and Woodstock simultaneously. I was *laughing*."

As Horek went through, a sudden flutter burst from overhead. Gaspar ducked instinctively, then looked up to see dozens of blurry objects vanishing in the direction of the camp.

"Funny," Fukudon said. "Don't see many birds around here."

Gaspar didn't answer. The path of the beasts had led his eyes back to the smoke. It looked solid; an engorged, obscene construct slowly unfolding itself into the heavens. A thing utterly beyond the experience and control of the merely human, entered into this world from a place where nothing living could stand.

After a moment he realized that he was alone and hurried to the portal.

1943

Another cardboard suitcase, another pile of ragged, patched, well-worn clothes. Rebeka thought she felt something sewed into a hem but lost it when she flipped the dress over. She lowered her face, wishing she could rest it in her hands for a minute. But the wardresses would notice if she did.

Her head was aching terribly, worse than ever, and her stomach was no better. She'd thrown up last night and hadn't been able to even look at food this morning. She'd kept it hidden from Alma, not wanting to give her any reason to feel sorry for her. Alma would have to come around on her own—whenever she felt like it. Rebeka wasn't going to make it easy for her.

All weekend long Alma had been in a dither over Nicole and her baby. She'd spent most of Saturday and Sunday conspiring head to head with Hata and the other stubowas. Now that Hata had been won over, she was even more enthusiastic than Alma. Much the same could be said for the rest of the block. The secret leaked out, as it always did, and everyone was involved, all of them overcome with a sweet childlike excitement. Everyone but Rebeka, who sat in the bunk, head pounding and stomach on fire. By the time Alma was ready for bed, she was exhausted and had little to say.

For her part, Nicole looked wonderful, now that she didn't have to keep her pregnancy hidden. All sorts of little delicacies—dried fruit, canned meat, juices—appeared from the food caches. Mama Blazak was collecting warm clothing and cutting it to make things for the child to wear. Nicole was five to six months along, she told Rebeka. It would be a winter baby.

Rebeka realized she'd felt her way around the dress hem at least three times. Sighing, she folded it and put it aside. It was becoming clear to her that Alma was obsessed with projects. Everything was a project to that woman. Study it closely, figure out what was needed, whom to contact, how much of a bribe to offer, then wrap it in a nice tidy package and go on to the next challenge. Rebeka Motzin? Oh, she's an old project. All taken care of, that one. There were so many nice new projects to worry about now.

They had a rude awakening coming. That was the how her grandfather used to put it: *Rebeka, you're due for a rude awakening.* What craziness, bringing a baby into this mausoleum! Hata had been right the first time. There were still informers in the block, even if they were lying low. They'd drop the word to Taube or Cyla or Boldt and that would be the end of it. Up the chimney, all of them.

But not Rebeka Motzin. Oh no. This little girl was going to survive. She'd get out of this place.

She went for another suitcase. A whirl of dizziness caught her as she reached for the handle. She tottered, barely able to keep on her feet. A drop of sweat trickled into her left eye. She blinked it away. It was so *hot* in here. It shouldn't be so hot, not this time of year. She'd feel a lot better if it was cooler.

Dragging the suitcase to the table, she slung it on top and dropped onto the stool. Her throat was dry as well. She needed water. She'd be fine if she had a drink. A sip, no more than that. But the pail was by the door next to the wardresses. She'd have to ask, and there was no telling what the response would be. They might decide she was sick, that she couldn't keep up with the work. There were bunks waiting in Block 25. She had a vision of Cyla holding out a dipper of water, a demented smile on her face, and shuddered. No—best not to attract their attention. If they didn't notice you, nothing could happen. She forced herself to swallow and got to work.

A sudden hush fell across the room. Rebeka looked up. A man, an officer, stood by the wardresses' table. He must have just now come in, though she hadn't heard the door open. His back was turned, but the black of his uniform made it clear who he must be. She bent over and made herself small.

Laughter gusted from the wardresses. Rebeka lifted her eyes. Boldt must have told a joke. Something lewd, no doubt. The crazy-eyed one's mouth was open wide, high-pitched titters emerging from her throat. Rebeka gritted her teeth. At that moment Boldt turned and ran his eyes over the workers. She dropped her head.

She felt rather than saw Boldt making his way around the room. His footsteps came softly, the ones heard distinctly separated by many seconds, not sounding like a man walking at all. Nonetheless, she could tell exactly where he was at every moment by the way the silence seemed to deepen when he moved, as if he carried a circle of stillness about with him. At times he spoke, and she was not once mistaken as to where the voice came from. She would never have imagined that silence could . . . *thicken* that way, not only diminishing sound but annihilating it, absorbing it into itself, leaving nothing behind.

After a while the silence reached her table and began moving toward her. His footsteps were audible now, a faint kiss against the floorboards, as of a touch of an insect on the skin. When they reached Rebeka, they halted. The silence engulfed her.

She saw the club approaching, the cool touch on her chin, lifting her face high. Boldt gazed down at her, his eyes empty. "And what's the matter with you?"

She said nothing. Slipping the truncheon under his arm, Boldt touched her forehead with his thumb. "A little hot," he murmured. He leaned close, palms flat on the table. "Are you feeling ill?"

Rebeka shook her head.

"Good," he said. A faint rapping sounded: a ring, one of those life and death emblems, tapped the table. "A terrible thing, illness. A bad thing anywhere, but particularly here. Don't you agree?"

"Yes." Rebeka's voice was so loud that it shocked her.

Gripping the club once more, he turned her arm over with the tip so that he could read her number. He nodded to himself and stuck the truncheon into his belt. "You know," he said with the air of a man giving voice to thoughts he'd considered for some time, "people aren't actually killed in this camp. No—they choose for themselves. The time comes, and they simply decide not to exist any longer. It's a question of will. Do you know what that means, in the philosophical sense? Of course you don't. Will is a quality that's embodied in everything in the universe, from the atoms and the particles that comprise the atoms all the way up to humans. It's the quality that lends to each thing its whatness—so that an atom is an atom, a man a man. And when the will is defective or lost, the thing ceases to exist. It may still seem to exist—it may move and interact with other things, but it no longer possesses being." He studied her closely. "Do you have any idea what I'm talking about?"

"Nietzsche," Rebeka said firmly. She was guessing, but it sounded, from what her father had told her, like the kind of thing Nietzsche had gone on about, and she knew that many Nazis admired him extravagantly.

Boldt smiled and looked away. "Nietzsche," he said. His tone was amused. "Nietzsche is obsolete, my dear. We know far more about the scientific basis of existence than was evident in his day. But not a bad response all the same. It leads me to suspect you understand what I'm referring to as far as events here go. So we'll perform a little experiment, you and I. You decide whether you possess will, and before I leave, you reveal it to me."

Rebeka dropped her eyes. Somewhere along the table a woman whimpered. Looking back up, Rebeka saw Boldt regarding her speculatively. "To make it simple, we'll put the question this way." He bent closer. "You tell me whether you think you've lived long enough."

He nodded and walked on. Rebeka looked about her. The other women's heads were low, their hands moving swiftly. She stared down at the clothing in front of her. She felt as if she was going to faint. What would Boldt think of that? Prime evidence of her lack of being, she'd be willing to bet.

Laughter bubbled in her throat, laughter that threatened to slip out of her control and fill the room. She stifled it and forced her hands to resume work. No longer looking for treasures, simply sorting the clothes and putting them to one side, like a machine. She caught herself glancing over her shoulder several times. She'd somehow lost her ability to keep track of him; when he reappeared, she was startled.

"Well?" he asked blandly.

She met his eyes, held them. "This Jew . . ." she began, then stopped and straightened up on the stool. "I . . . I'll let you know."

His eyebrows rose. "Staunch," he said, thumping her on the shoulder with the club. "I admire that. A little more backbone and you Jews wouldn't be here. Now, what's your block?"

She told him. "Block 37, eh? Odd block, that one. Don't hear much about it. But . . . our experiment continues."

Rebeka was so relieved she scarcely heard the rest of it. ". . . I'll keep an eye open for you, and eventually you will let me know." The club descended, flicked a blouse at her. "Now, let's get busy, hmm?"

For the next few minutes Rebeka sat rearranging the dirty clothes on the table, unable to pull herself together. She was convinced that Boldt was playing a crueler game than he'd let on, that he was going to return for her, that any second the wardresses would rush over and haul her away. Only when the door slammed shut did she look up to see that he'd gone.

Giselle glanced at her and let out a hiss. Rebeka squeezed her eyes tight shut with relief. She was going to live. She would not go up the chimney today. True, he'd said that he'd be watching her, but she'd worry about that later. For the moment she was well ahead.

She started as the door thudded shut again, but it was only one of the wardresses leaving. The madwoman, seated at the table, was staring at her. She smiled and shook her head.

For a little while Rebeka was fine, but then her sense of triumph faded, taking with it any feeling of well-being. The headache returned with even greater force. Her exhaustion mounted, as if she'd given the last scrap of effort she possessed in the confrontation with Boldt. She ran his words through her mind over and over again until they grew tangled and she was no longer certain what had happened. Perhaps he'd never been in Canada at all . . .

A shout snapped her back to awareness. She was slumped over the table, a cotton dress against her cheek. Pulling herself erect, she shook her head in an effort to clear it. "Always room in the bakery, sweetie!" the mad one called.

Shortly after that the silence returned, and she knew that Boldt had lied. No, not really lied—he simply hadn't told her the whole truth. Not all of it. He said he'd be watching her, yes, but he hadn't told her he'd watch her *today*. It had been a trick. She could see that now. They all had tricks, and Boldt was the worst.

She couldn't figure out how he could see her, though. The warehouse had no windows, so that wasn't it. But there were holes in the walls, in between the boards, where they didn't quite join. That had to be it. He was watching her from outside. He had dogs with him, and soldiers with guns. He'd be waiting for her . . .

Then she saw him from the corner of her eye. Standing there stroking his holster the way he did. Of course—the silence was *in* the room, in here with her. It was part of him, he carried it with him. She looked around, but he was too fast; she caught only a flash of black as he slipped out of sight.

He'd only pretended to leave. It had been planned that way, between Boldt and the wardresses. He'd never left at all. They'd waited until she wasn't looking and then slammed the door. A nasty joke. You couldn't just die; there had to be a joke involved, something they could laugh over, something to entertain them. It was the jokes that made it so horrible. She'd go to the burner willingly if it wasn't just a *joke*.

He was behind her now. She felt him watching, sensed the silence grow denser. She cringed, pulling her shoulders high. Finally the suitcase was empty, the clothes all sorted. She got up to get another, swinging to survey the room. Again he escaped her. She tried to pin down the section where the silence was deepest, but the headache made it too hard . . .

The suitcase dropped from her hands, earning her a barrage of curses. She fumbled for it, got it up on the table. It was the headache that made him so difficult to find. That and her throat. It was as if it was on fire. The place was so hot. It was like the desert, where the Arab people lived. She needed water. But that was what they were waiting for, wasn't it? The pail was near the door. The door led to the camp. The camp was where the dogs and soldiers were. If she asked permission to get a drink, why, they'd rush her out right then and there. To the camp. To the dogs and soldiers.

He was back. His eyes, boring into her shoulder blades. No point looking for him. Now what did he want? He wanted her to fail. To miss her quota. To lose her will. She'd have to show him that he couldn't do that. Finish all her work. Get the clothes out, sorted, and packed. The dead people's clothes. That's what he was looking for. He needed more clothes. Will? She'd show him will. But he shouldn't watch her so closely. That only made it harder. Her hands didn't move right when he watched them. I can't do it when you watch me. Watch someone else for a while. Leave me alone . . .

"Take hold of yourself, you little idiot!" It was Giselle, glaring from the corner of her eyes. Rebeka got the impression that it wasn't the first time she'd spoken.

"He's watching me," Rebeka told her. "I can't work right when he's watching me." She was shocked to realize that she was crying. "And my head hurts so much."

Giselle leaned over to whisper to someone on the other side. Mama Blazak got up and went to the pile of suitcases. She lifted one, her fingers working the catch. The lid fell open, spilling clothes onto the floor. Something among them clattered.

"Getting sloppy over there, aren't we?"

Mama made a bow toward the wardresses' table, then got on her knees to gather up the clothes. In a few seconds she reached Rebeka, who explained the problem with Boldt.

Mama raised a finger to her lips. "Shh. I know, dear. But he's doing it to be mean, isn't he? You have to fool him, pretend he's not here. You can do that. It's only another couple of hours."

Rebeka smiled through her tears. Mama looked so funny, on the floor that way.

"Good girl." Mama patted Rebeka's hand and returned to her stool.

Rebeka set to work. She seemed to be getting a lot done. At least the pile of clothes in front of her kept diminishing. Every few minutes another suitcase or bag appeared, she didn't know how. A wardress came over once and tsked at her for a minute or so. She couldn't tell if Boldt was with her or not.

Finally someone pulled away the peasant shirt in her hands. Rebeka was about to cry out when Mama Blazak asked if she could stand.

"Here. I've got her." Giselle gripped her arm tightly. "You'll have to walk out the door on your own," Mama whispered. "Can you do that?"

Rebeka couldn't recall giving an answer, only that she was suddenly outside, the air very much cooler. She gasped as her arms were clutched once again but it was only Mama and Giselle. Resting her head on Mama's shoulder, she whispered that she felt much better now.

"Come along, little one," Mama told her.

Rebeka kept her feet moving, though she couldn't feel any weight on them. The two holding her—Giselle, it was, yes, and Mama, the other mama, her camp mama—hurried her on. They were going too fast, she could tell. She complained about that and was told to hush. But Alma would listen to her. Where was Alma? She looked about. Through slitted eyes she saw the other women walking close, forming a tight group around them. She let her head fall. "It's will, Mama," she murmured. "It's all will. Will is *everything*."

"That's right, dear. Just a little farther now."

Then Mama gasped and Giselle muttered, "Oh shit," almost too low to hear.

"Well now, what's this? Got a Moslem there, do you?"

Rebeka looked up. Most of the other women had broken off to go to their own blocks. Only a small number remained, and the overweight Bavarian wardress was pushing through them. Mama answered, speaking swiftly, her accent thickening to a point where she was next to impossible to understand.

"Oh? What's that you say? Fine, is she?" The wardress snorted. "Well, we'll see. Let her go. Now, I say! Let her walk on her own."

Finding herself free, Rebeka took a few short steps. "It's a matter of will," she told the wardress as her knees buckled beneath her.

Mama grabbed her before she hit the mud and pulled her to her feet. "What did she say?" Babbling something in reply, Mama dragged Rebeka on. "Let her go," the wardress snarled. "Drop her, you old cow."

Rebeka heard the slap of a truncheon and found herself standing alone once more. She staggered but kept to her feet. The club struck her shoulder—once, then again, much harder. She raised her hands against it. The wardress poked at her eyes. "Repeat that, bitch."

"What's going on?"

Squinting against the fence lights, Rebeka saw Liesl, the block wardress, cape flapping about her.

"This little slut told me to fuck off!"

"I did not," Rebeka said, speaking as clearly as she could manage. "No filthy mouth on me."

"There! Listen to her! The nerve!"

"Ah yes." Liesl's voice was low and hard. "This one. I know her—a pain in the ass, she is. Burner meat for sure."

Vicious laughter answered her. More voices than one—Rebeka looked about her and saw several shadows behind the Bavarian, who glared at her only a step or two away. "We can hurry her along," one of the shadows said.

"She'll be ready for twenty-five when I'm through with her." The wardress lunged forward. Rebeka cried out as the club struck her side.

"I'll take care of her," Liesl said. "I owe her a few."

"More the merrier!"

"No—she's mine. I'll see to her."

"Oh, I get it." The voice was high-pitched and childish. "Your little darling, is she?"

"Don't you use that tone with me!"

". . . that's sad. A German woman doing *that* with— Ugh, it's too disgusting . . ."

There was a sudden flurry of movement. Rebeka was pushed aside and found herself on her knees.

"How'd you like a taste of this yourself, bitch?"

"—come on, Inge, it's not worth it."

"Yes. We're in camp now. They go for that kind of thing here . . ."

"Just one—" Rebeka ducked as she sensed movement behind her. The blow aimed at her skull hit her shoulder instead. She fell forward, throwing out an arm to keep from ending up face-first in the mud.

"That'll teach you—"

"Get out of my camp! To the gate, this instant!"

"Oh, with pleasure, dearie!" The voices began to fade. "God, they wind up just like the Yids themselves in here, don't they . . . ?"

A hand gripped Rebeka, yanking her to her feet. "Go on, scrap!" Liesl shouted. "Get your ass in that block!" Then, more softly: "No, Mama. You stay right where you are."

Liesl's club touched the small of her back. A tap, no more than that. "Move, I say! I know you're shirking!" Rebeka stumbled forward, hands in front of her. "Come on, girlie," Liesl whispered. "It's only a few metres more."

Accompanied by plenty of shouts and club-waving from Liesl, Rebeka crossed those few metres. When she reached the steps, she tripped and nearly went down, but strong arms caught her and pulled her inside. She saw only a flash of Alma's eyes before letting herself drift.

The next thing she knew she was lying on the bunk, atop a blanket that was almost new. She gazed up at the familiar boards, thinking they looked like home. People leaned into the bunk, blocking out the light.

"She's sick, isn't she?" That was Liesl.

"Yes, she's sick," Alma said. "Flu, most likely."

"Are you sure? If it's typhus or anything, I have to report it."

"It's flu, Liesl. Believe me."

"Oh, all right." A shape retreated, allowing light to glare in, but only for a moment before another replaced it.

"And thank you, Liesl," Alma called out.

"You owe me one, missy." The door squeaked shut.

"She's gone? All right. Let's—"

Hands pulled her dress high. Rebeka whined in protest.

"Oh my God—"

"It's typhus, all right. Look at those spots."

A patter of feet drew close. "Typhus! We have to get her out of here!"

"Stop it." Alma's voice was firm. "It's not contagious if there are no bugs."

"But there *are* bugs! You weren't here in the summer during the epidemic. It was horrible. We have to send her to Dr. Helmerson—"

"Oh, of course. Dr. Helmerson. Why not just call in Mengele? He needs some new subjects. He used up the last batch—"

"But—"

"Dorcas, be silent!" Hata's voice, the words clipped, as always. "You're one to talk. You'd be blowing about the ash pit if it wasn't for Frau Lewin's pills, wouldn't you? Now, be off."

There was a moment of silence. Rebeka relished it, wishing they'd simply leave her be. She'd be much better if they only did that.

"Do you have any more pills left, Alma?"

"No. We used them all."

"None? You should have saved some."

"How could I have done that?" Alma's voice changed, taking on a tone of helplessness that Rebeka had never heard before. "Oh God. I noticed she wasn't looking well. I wasn't paying attention. It's always something. Every time you turn around . . ."

Rebeka felt for Alma's hand and tried to tell her how sorry she was.

"No, no—" A hand touched her brow. "Not you, baby. I'm not mad at you."

Something cold draped itself on Rebeka's forehead. She sighed with relief, then tried to ask for a drink. A hand lifted her head, a cup of cold water met her lips. She gulped at it, most of it dribbling down her chin. Mama muttered a prayer in her own language.

"—Bock would have helped, but he's gone—"

"—the Sonderkommando doctor, what's his name?"

"—that's Pach. He'd have to sneak in—"

"—call for the water pump. He could come in with the crew. I can square that with Bubi—"

"—someone's always hanging around the wire. We can send—"

"Yes. Morah!"

The light returned. Rebeka didn't like that. The light made her head feel worse. She moaned and twisted on the bunk.

"The Black One spoke to her," Mama was saying. "This afternoon—"

Rebeka became still. They shouldn't talk about Boldt. If they mentioned Boldt, he'd hear them—wherever he was. Then the silence would return. She sat up to tell them so. All that she heard was a series of strange noises. Who could that be? It wasn't her, she was no Moslem . . .

Mama laid her down once again. She dampened the cloth and replaced it. Taking Rebeka's hand, she made soothing sounds.

"I have someone else I can contact," Alma said, her voice low but clear. "Another . . . connection."

The voices faded, along with the light. She must have slept. Her father visited her in his old-fashioned glasses, the frock coat expected of a teacher in a small forgotten village. She told him to hide, lest he be brought to Auschwitz. That he shouldn't worry about her. She had will, she would be all right. She would see him again once it was all over.

She awoke to a man's voice. It was smooth and educated, and she was disappointed that he hadn't listened, hadn't hid himself carefully enough, that he was here, after all. But perhaps that was best—now she could take care of him, she and Alma both. He would like Alma. They'd be able to talk about so many things.

She raised her head to give him a smile. But the figure between her and the light was utterly black, and silence engulfed her as Boldt bent down to tell her that the experiment was over.

Rebeka screamed and tried to claw her way through the unyielding red brick.

1943

It turned out that they weren't cousins, after all. That much had been obvious to Reber the minute the woman stepped into the office. Frau Born was blonde and petite, while the new one looked as if she'd ridden off the steppes with Tamerlane's hordes. What on earth did they take him for? But he had to let it pass, much as he might regret ever listening in the first place. Turning the request down had been beyond him—even to consider it aroused the memory of the stoic face of the man in the ditch. And besides, to make an issue of the matter now might well attract the attention of Boldt or one of his cronies. The women knew that, of course. Knew the camp—its ways, its invisible structure and rules—much better than he ever would. Fool that he was for taking them to be no more than a collection of innocent imperiled Hausfrauen.

There had been no sign of Boldt since the weekend. Reber had expected him to appear bright and early Monday, for another hearty session of needling and insinuation. He had been naive in that as well. Boldt differed not at all from a schoolyard bully. His tactics were identical: strike hard, then leave the victim to stew for a time, wondering when the next assault would come and what form it would take. As Reber was wondering right now.

Nothing like this ever happened at the front. There was no place for intrigues or pettiness out at the sharp end. Such matters were settled there as man to man, a quick bout behind the tents, and then friends. If that didn't end it, then the troops made their decision as to which man was at fault, and one fine day he'd be left beyond the line in partisan territory, to be found in the morning with his throat slit—if he was lucky. Ah, poor Boldt! Strapped to a tree with wire, pants down around his ankles, all that blood . . . a pity. Those Reds are nothing but savages, no?

But Birkenau wasn't the front, and things were done differently here. Best not to think about it. Pay attention to work, get the job done, and the worries would take care of themselves. That's what his father had always said. He bent over the desk to get started on the weekly office report. He'd hated paperwork so much when he was in a combat unit. Now it was a pleasure—something he actually looked forward to, took his time over.

Across the room, someone coughed. Reber looked up. The office was fully staffed today—he couldn't keep them away all the time. He took in the sullen, brutish faces, so out of place above the perfectly turned-out uniforms. The new breed, as Caesar had put it. Hard to believe that it had come down to such as these. In Reber's day the SS had considered themselves knights. That wasn't too romantic a word. Knights: men of honor and probity, dedicated to service, to something beyond and larger than themselves. A bitter thing, to see such a dream deteriorate into this camp, these thugs who represented no Germany that Reber was familiar with. He thought of the line by that playwright—what was his name? A favorite of Goebbels. "When I hear the word 'culture,' I reach for my revolver." No danger of that here. This lot wouldn't recognize culture if they found it peering back at them out of a beer mug.

The one at the far desk—Wetzler, his name was—lifted his head and met Reber's eyes. He stared blankly to the bare edge of insolence before looking back down, a twisted smile on his face. Oh, they cared nothing for him. Reber knew that. But the feeling was mutual, and there was little they could say to a combat veteran. All the same, he dreaded the thought of Boldt putting on a performance in here, right in front of them all . . .

His heart skipped a beat when the door swung open. But it was only Münch, the Stabsgebaeude's factotum, escorting an unfamiliar officer. Reber got up, straightened his jacket, and saluted.

Rubbing his hands like a waiter angling for a tip, Münch introduced the man as Obersturmbannführer Griese, from the Lódź office of WVHA, on assignment to inspect the DAW plant at Monowitz. He'd decided to take a look at the labor pool while in the area, and—here Münch allowed himself a confidential smile—had asked to speak to Obersturmführer Reber.

Münch scurried off while Reber shook hands with Griese and motioned him to a chair. The man was of average height, well built in a blocky way, with a touch of the Slav to his features. His hair was a characterless gray-brown, clipped close to the skull. But what caught Reber's attention most directly were his eyes: a pale, almost whitish gray, with a glassiness to them as if they held stories that could not be told, had seen things impossible to put into words. They seemed to catalog Reber with a glance, to place him among a long line of items observed but not worth close regard.

One of the others, Reber thought to himself. He'd started thinking of Boldt and his type by that term: the "others."

"Now then, sir, what can I do for you?" Reber pulled his chair closer to the desk.

Griese spoke slowly, as if carefully weighing each word. A Silesian, Reber gathered. They tended to be fanatical party types, extremely nationalist, their homeland having been awarded to Poland at Versailles. It seemed that Griese had come across Herdt, Reber's old battalion commander, in Brest-Litovsk a few months ago. A fascinating man and a good talker. Herdt had mentioned that Reber was now assigned to Auschwitz and urged Griese to look him up if he was ever in the area.

Reber was somewhat surprised that Herdt recalled him so fondly; they'd been far from close chums. Odder still was the description of Herdt's sparkling conversation. But what struck most deeply was the simple fact that his old commander knew that he was here. If Herdt knew, then the rest of them, his comrades—those who still lived, in any case—knew as well. He wondered if they were aware by now what the place really was, what actually went on here. It couldn't be kept secret forever.

He realized that Griese had stopped speaking. "Beg pardon?"

"I thought"—the man fingered his uniform cap—"that you might care to give me a tour."

Reber simply stared. Griese had on a winter greatcoat, one too heavy for this time of year. That might well be a tic, a personal eccentricity of dress. The others often had those. It was one of the ways you could tell. Like Boldt's dress blacks.

"There are . . . customary arrangements for such things," Reber heard himself saying.

"I'm aware of that," Griese said placidly. "But I don't want the customary tour."

Conviction flooded Reber. This was one of Boldt's people, come to trap him. He could well imagine what kind of tour the man wanted; he'd heard rumors, though he'd found them hard to credit. A chance to partake in a few beatings, if not outright murder. A special trip to the death chambers to view the final spasms of the victims. A fine full day topped off with a visit to the brothel for acts forbidden in any sane society.

If Reber refused, that would be all the evidence that Boldt needed to show that he had not overcome himself, that he could not, that he was no SS man at all. At the end of that road lay the cold grave of the east.

"I have reasons for asking your assistance that I cannot divulge at the moment," Griese said. "But if you're busy . . ." He gripped the arms of the chair.

Reber shot to his feet. "No, no—not at all. It's simply . . . an unusual request."

Griese stepped to the door while Reber went for his cap. He noticed two of the staff eyeing him curiously. He lamely told them to keep busy and went to join Griese. "We could first take a look at the Kommandantur . . ."

"I've seen it."

The eyes were cold, the expression distant. A flash of doubt struck Reber: he couldn't picture this man deferring to Boldt. "Yes." He conjured a smile. "The camp, then . . ."

He led the way out of the building. Walking carefully, as he had when first allowed out of bed at the hospital. He felt dizzy, as if an abyss had opened up at his feet, with no bottom visible. He was going into the camp, a thing he'd avoided since his arrival. Something unthinkable awaited him there, some doom that would change him forever. The camp—that unholy place where the dead walked, where the others had their kingdom.

He was several steps from the building before he realized that Griese had not followed him out. Looking back, Reber saw him framed in the doorway, his face shadowed. His expression had changed to reflect what looked to be doubt and fear. But only for a moment—it settled into its accustomed hardness as Reber watched.

They walked to the nearest gate. The chimneys of the crematoria were visible above the barracks. They were still now—the last transport had been several days ago. Griese pointed at them. "Those are the burners?"

"I can't take you there," Reber said quickly.

"I know that."

At the gate the duty guard gave them the offhand salute of a man dulled by routine. They passed through the two rows of wire. To the right was B.III, the new section. The foundations for another line of barracks had been put in place, and prisoners, many of them women, were hauling bricks to the sites. Beyond them numberless others worked at leveling the rest of the section.

But closer still, as if there for Reber's own benefit, lay a pile of corpses. Already stripped, the ravages of starvation obvious: sticklike limbs, heads like skulls, mouths open wide, as though begging for one last crust. He assumed that some were female, but he couldn't tell them apart; he doubted that anyone could. As they walked past, two prisoners approached carrying still another body. Reber looked sharply away, but his eyes jerked back just as the corpse landed atop the pile. It slid to one side, the stiffened limbs of the bodies beneath catching at it, as if to prevent it from touching the cold ground.

A glance at Griese showed his face to be, if anything, more wooden than before.

They walked on. Finally Griese paused to gaze out over the section. "Very efficient," he said quietly. Reber made no reply.

"When is the completion date?"

Reber had heard that it should have been finished at the end of last summer. He had no idea what the new date might be. At a guess he mentioned the end of the year.

"And who is supposed to be put in here?"

Gaping at him, Reber realized that he'd never actually thought about it. Not the Jews, certainly. Unless they—the others—were planning to save some. But if not them, then who? He looked out over the area, mind awrithe with puzzlement. "I'm sure that. . . . Berlin headquarters . . . they will inform us . . ."

Griese remained silent. Reber looked his way. The officer stared at him, eyes burning. Reber turned his face elsewhere.

"I've been told they call it 'Mexico,' " Griese said after a moment. "Why is that?"

"I'm not sure."

"I see." Griese let out a slow breath. Reber could almost feel Griese's regret at his choice of a guide. Reber looked around desperately for something to point out, something that he knew, but it was all alien to him.

"Well then—"

Griese was interrupted by a sudden scream, distant but cutting. Reber stiffened. Out beyond the new blocks a woman sprawled, her features indistinct. Next to her a crude wheelbarrow lay on its side. A dog tore at her, two guards hovering close.

Hands raised to protect her face, the woman howled as the dog lunged again. Nearby, a young girl in one of the groups carrying bricks covered her ears. An older woman cuffed her, gesturing with her head at Reber and Griese.

A gust of laughter rose from the guards, followed by the dog's disappointed yips. One of them closed in on the woman and gave her a kick. Reber relaxed. It was only sport.

"Let's go on," Griese told him.

Griese grew more talkative as they moved farther into the camp. A torrent of questions—had Reber noticed anything out of the ordinary, any unusual problems with the prisoners? No rumors about subversive activities inside the wire? And what about personnel? Nothing remarkable there?

Reber answered with monosyllables, his eye fixed on a figure ahead. It was a male prisoner, standing alone before the B.II gate. At first he seemed to be waving his arms wildly, but as they drew closer it became apparent that he was clapping them together while holding something in his hands.

A few more steps and the picture grew clear: the bricks to one side, the pile of red dust at his feet. The man clapped on steadily, grunting in pain as his palms met, dust puffing from the misshapen chunks between them.

Behind him three guards crouched in a circle, attention focused on the ground at their feet. Catching sight of the officers, they split up, two heading for the gate while the third, a young Unterscharführer wearing a soft cap, stepped beside the prisoner. Reber saw him slipping what looked to be a wad of Reichsmarks into his jacket. He snarled at the prisoner, who paused and then began doing deep-knee bends, still smashing the bricks together. Raising his eyes to Reber and Griese, the boy puffed out his chest, as if waiting for a prize.

As they passed the prisoner, the bricks disintegrated, raining reddish-brown clumps in all directions. Several hit the Unterscharführer, who shrieked a curse and kicked the man before quickly returning to attention. The prisoner tottered, then bent down for more bricks. His hands left swaths of deeper red across the top of the pile.

Griese moved on without so much as acknowledging the junior officer. The hollow, monotonous crack resumed behind them. "I imagine he'll be doing that until sundown," Griese said. "Unless he drops first."

Reber answered with a grunt. Another mound of corpses appeared. He didn't even look at it.

"That's the kind of thing I mean, what I came here to see," Griese went on. "At Monowitz every single plant is below production norm. Buna, DEST, DAW—all of them. At a time when we need every weapon and round we can get. And yet look at what's being done with the labor force."

"They—" Reber began. He paused, his mind blank. "We . . . have need of discipline."

"Discipline! Is that what you call it?" Griese made a sound of disgust. "Sport—that's what it is. Entertaining themselves while the Reich falls apart. You'd think there wasn't a war on, the way they behave."

Griese came to an abrupt halt. Swinging to face him, Reber kept his eyes on the ground.

"Tell me something, Reber—and be frank. What happens to a man in a place like this?"

His voice sounded sincere, and the words he spoke were close to what Reber thought himself. He wanted so much to tell someone— anyone—what was on his mind, what he'd been through in the months since coming here. But how could he be certain? Griese could well be a provocateur, sent in to feel him out in the hope that he'd betray himself. That was exactly the kind of trick to expect from Boldt.

The best answer would be another question: What did the Obersturmbannführer mean? They were doing their duty, following their orders, behaving like good SS men obedient to their oath. Surely he, one of those who gave the orders, would understand . . .

Over Griese's shoulder he caught sight of the figure he'd been half-expecting to see since entering the camp. He shot a glare at Griese, then struggled to compose his features. Griese stared at him questioningly before looking behind him.

"Ah!" Boldt called out. "Taking the tour, are we?"

Griese looked him over as he approached. He didn't seem particularly impressed by the dress uniform, nor was there any sign of recognition that Reber could detect.

Not bothering to salute, Boldt introduced himself, shaking Griese's hand heartily. He appeared to be in a fine mood. "WVHA, eh? Always a pleasure. You've never been by before, have you?" Boldt swung to face Reber. "And Gerd! Quite a surprise. Gerd doesn't get into the camp proper much," he told Griese. "Far too busy, he is. In fact, that's why I came over. I thought to myself, 'Gerd Reber, giving a senior officer a tour of the facility? That's unusual.' Not that I hold anything against the Obersturmführer, you understand. Not our Gerd." He patted Reber on the shoulder.

"No. It's simply that being a new man, and with little time to spare, I feared that Gerd might not be as well informed as some of us old hands. So I decided to step in to help." He gave Griese a brilliant smile, then moved a short distance away. "There's quite a lot that Gerd doesn't know about the camp. Take this spot here." He swept a glove around him. "This is where the first cargo that we dragged through were buried after we got down to business. A serious miscalculation. The magnitude of the task hadn't quite sunk in yet, I'm afraid. After a short time, things got out of hand. The very earth changed color and started to bubble. Rats appeared by the thousands. And the stink! A disgusting mess, I'll tell you. That's why we constructed the burners. All this had to be dug up, the soil replaced. One rough piece of work."

His bootheel struck the dirt. "Right where we're standing. You didn't know that, did you, Gerd?"

He turned, gesturing them to follow. "Up ahead there, the pond, do you see it? That black stain around it? Not much to show for all this effort, now, is it? But it's better than having to smell them."

"Much better," Griese said.

Boldt gave him another smile. "You know, it's a pity you didn't arrive last week. We're between transports now, not much to see. But at least we can take a look at the ovens. Had you heard that Topff and Sohne actually had pictures of them at their Erfurt office? In the lobby, for visitors to see. Had to take them down, of course—

"That's B.I, the women's camp, over there. A hellhole. Amazing how quickly the females fall apart. Really gives you an insight into the nature of the Jew. And over there are the Aktion Reinhard warehouses. You can't see them very clearly. Coming up is crematorium number four, behind those pines, with number five at the right. Bathhouses to the rear." Boldt's voice became confidential. "Actually, we're facing a recurrence of that same problem now. Volume. Too many to be efficiently processed. From Hungary, Bulgaria . . . and Italy as well, now that the Duce has been brought into line. We foresee a bottleneck early next summer, perhaps sooner. Several solutions have been proposed, none really satisfactory. Do you have any suggestions?"

"I'll think about it."

"Yes, please do. Now—" Boldt came to an abrupt halt, raising a hand for silence. "Look there," he whispered.

For a moment Reber was unable to make out what he was referring to. Then, in a shadow cast by a barrack inside B.I, he spotted two shapes crouched close to the wire, oblivious to the fact that they'd been observed.

"Looks like we'll have something special, after all," Boldt said, slipping the club from his belt. Without another word, he raced for the wire. He had crossed half the distance when the figure inside—a woman, Reber assumed—saw him and cried out. At Boldt's shout of

"Halt!" she turned and ran off behind the barrack. The man swung about, tearing off his cap and slapping it against his thigh.

Reber glanced at Griese, whose chin rested on his collar, as if he was brooding over what he saw. Boldt reached the man and the truncheon swung high. The prisoner sprawled in the mud.

He found himself walking toward them, Griese close behind. "Kneel!" Boldt shouted. He slashed with the club. "Go on, you dirty bastard!"

By the time they got to the wire, the man was on his knees, hands in his lap, cap clutched tight. Boldt turned, breathing heavily, as if it had been a long chase. He gestured at the prisoner, then bent over and struck him across the ear.

"All right, Israel. The bitch. Her number."

"I not know," the man said, head down. His accent was thick and obviously Slavic. Eastern Polish or perhaps from the Ukraine.

Boldt thrust the club against the man's cheekbone, right beneath the eye. "That's a lie, Yid. Now tell me: name, number, block."

"I only see her. Come over then to just talk . . ."

With a flick of his hand, Boldt rapped him precisely on the nose. Blood spurted forth. The man's hands rose toward his face, to be met with quick raps from the truncheon. He clenched them and thrust them back down.

Boldt shook his head. "Look at this," he said with the air of a teacher exhibiting a recalcitrant pupil. "Stupid as the night. They lie right to your face. As if you were some kind of idiot. I didn't see what I saw, is that it, Israel? Well, I'll tell you—" Shoving the club under his arm, he flipped his holster flap open and pulled out his pistol. "You have ten seconds to give me the truth. All of it. If you do, there will be no punishment for you. In fact—"

He went silent, his mouth open. He tried to work the bolt, then took a closer look at the gun. Eyes wide, he stared at Reber. "I'll be damned—no ammo." He flipped the Luger over, revealing the empty slot in the grip. "No magazine at all."

Coming to attention, he turned to Griese. "Obersturmbannführer, I have no excuse for this. I checked my weapon this morning . . . It must have been then. I'll find the magazine atop my dresser, I'm sure. But sir, I must beg your pardon. Strolling unarmed about a camp filled with enemies of the Reich—I scarcely know what to say." His eyes swung to Reber. "And you, Gerd—you certainly have one on me now."

He pointed at Reber's holster. Drawing his Walther, Reber held it out. Boldt closed his eyes. "No, Gerd. You take care of it."

Reber stared at the gun, as if prepared to see it melt through his palm and fall to the ground. With no command from him, his fingers enfolded the grip. He drew the pistol close and put a round in the chamber.

"Your ten seconds are long past, Israel. Thought I'd count them, did you?" Boldt sighed. "I was going to let you go. If you'd bothered to tell me the truth. You'd be free as a bird now, if only you'd obeyed. I want you to understand that . . ."

Reber's arm straightened. There was a roaring in his ears. Boldt went on, but the words failed to penetrate. All that existed was his hand, the pistol barrel, the shaven and scabby head. The man was shaking. Reber had known that he would do that. He had known that it would happen this way the day he was born. In this place, on this kind of day, with these people watching.

The barrel wavered. He awaited a command from Boldt. He could not do it his own. Boldt would have to say the word.

". . . familiar with the regulation concerning individual killings by SS personnel?" It was Griese, addressing Boldt. "Perhaps you'd care to recite it for me?"

Griese stood with his arms folded, speaking from the corner of his mouth. "Can't bring it to mind, Hauptsturmführer? Let me refresh your memory. 'While political killings motivated by idealism are sanctioned, those of a personal or sexual nature are considered legal murder, to be dealt with as such.' Kindly enlighten me as to what political ideals are involved in this situation."

Reber's elbow started to bend. Slowly he let his arm fall to his side. He raised his head but didn't dare look in Boldt's direction.

"The Reichsminister himself had words on the subject. I'm sure they're quite familiar, but allow me to repeat them. 'We don't want, because we have exterminated a germ, to be infected by that germ and die from it. I will not stand by while an infection forms. Whenever such a spot appears, we will *burn it out*.' Not difficult to grasp, is it?"

Reber safetied the Walther. He tried to holster it, but his hand was shaking too much.

"... and what's this with the dress uniform, hmm? Field grays not good enough for you?"

There was an unidentifiable sound from Boldt. Reber glanced over involuntarily. Boldt's face was red, eyes bulging, lips a thin line. He opened them to show gritted teeth. "I am a Gestapo officer—"

"I don't give a pig's ass what you are," Griese said. He nudged the prisoner with his boot. The man looked up with glazed eyes. "Go on, get out of here. Watch your step from now on."

A second or two passed before the man grasped what had been said to him. He got up slowly, bobbing his head to all of them, then ducked past Boldt and ran off. He disappeared around the corner of a barrack, rubbing the blood from his face.

"If you'll excuse me," Boldt said a moment later, his voice barely audible. "I have business to see to. Prisoners whose numbers have come to my attention." He stared fixedly at Griese. "I always check the numbers."

He gave a stiff salute and walked off. Griese gazed after him, his expression unreadable. Finally he turned to Reber. "Put the gun away."

The Walther returned to the holster easily this time.

Griese studied him narrowly for a few seconds. "You don't approve of any of this, do you?"

Reber threw back his shoulders. "I am true to my oath," he said. "Loyal to the Reich and the Führer. I obey my superiors—"

"Yes, yes." Griese waved him to silence. "The oath. Well and good. But pay more attention to regulations in the future."

"I know the regulations, Obersturmbannführer."

"Then why the hell were you going to put a bullet into that man?" With a curl of the lip, Griese turned his back on Reber. "I'll find my own way to the gate," he said. "Thank you for your time."

Reber waited several minutes to make sure he wouldn't run into either of them. Around him the machinery of the camp ground on. Shouted orders, the barking of dogs, the clank of shovels, an occasional cry. Finally he started for the Kommandantur. The man still cracked the bricks, much more slowly now. The dust piles had grown higher.

It was late in the day when a memo appeared on his desk. It said:

ACCORDING TO WVHA HEADQUARTERS, OBERSTURM-
BANNFÜHRER KONRAD GRIESE IS ON LEAVE AT THIS TIME.
YOU WILL WRITE A COMPLETE REPORT ON YOUR ACTIVITIES
WITH THE INDIVIDUAL WHO APPEARED UNDER THAT NAME
AND HOLD YOURSELF OPEN TO COOPERATION WITH THE CAMP
GESTAPO OFFICE.

BOLDT

The skirt of Gaspar's greatcoat caught at the edge of the table. When he jerked it loose, a mass of papers fluttered to the floor. Mumbling to himself, he slipped the coat off and tossed it on the chair. He bent to pick up the sheets but dismissed them with a flick of his hand.

Instead he started to work his way out of the rest of the uniform. The jacket collar was tight enough to dig into his neck and he had trouble manipulating the clasp. By the time he got it unfastened, he was red-faced and raging. Popping the buttons open, he undid the belt and flung the jacket away. The clothes they wore always told a lot, didn't they? Getting in and out of the things was probably what had driven all the Germans crazy. That Reber . . . where in the world had they found such a rodent? Hard as a rock one minute and soft as a pile of mush the next. Quivering in front of that thug Boldt. Easy enough to see what Boldt was, but Reber, now—he was something new to Gaspar's experience.

He sat on the cot, hands clasped before him. After a moment he lifted one foot and regarded the boot. He'd wrestle them off later. What he needed to do now was calm himself. Angiers had left the Scotch, a decent gesture. He could take a drink— but he disliked using alcohol during a mission.

"Monitor?"

"Yes, Dido."

"Could I prepare you something to eat?"

"No, thank you."

"Perhaps a drink, then?"

"I'd prefer not."

The AI was silent for a moment. "You should take something, Monitor. You appear to be under stress. Might I suggest . . . ?"

"Dido, please." Gaspar was a great believer in being courteous to AIs, especially young ones. So many on the short end, unused to dealing with silicon entities, didn't bother. But this one was beginning to try his patience.

"I'm sorry, sir. I simply thought—"

"Wait—" Gaspar had recalled an herb smoked in this period to reduce tension and concentrate the mind. It had worked for him in the past. "Is there such a thing as a tobacco stick on-station?"

"Cigarette or cigar?" The machine sounded eager.

"Uh—the compact type."

"I believe that some of the staff smoke. One moment."

Gaspar tried to keep his mind blank while he waited. Clear of any memory of that dazed bloody face—because if he thought that far, he'd have to wonder what expression the face wore now. If any. At least Boldt hadn't caught the woman. He would have lost control if Boldt had caught the woman.

He reached up to rub his temples. His fingertips touched patent leather and he realized he was still wearing the cap. He swept it off, eyed the insignia above the bill. A skull and crossbones, as crude and vicious as the men who wore it. He flipped it after the rest.

He stared at his hands. *A man is dying because I went in there today.*

"Here you are, sir," Dido said. A small plate in the wall next to the cot snapped open, revealing a half-dozen white cylinders. "You didn't specify brand, so I provided a selection."

Gaspar grunted and put the first one handy between his lips. The brown end was what burned, he recollected. He drew on it, but nothing happened. There was a brief flash and then the tip was lit.

"Thank you," Gaspar said. He took a puff and coughed. The taste was odd, not quite what he remembered.

"That's a mentholated brand," Dido said.

"I see." Gaspar exhaled and a cloud of fine, lacy, barely visible smoke drifted across the room. Outline of the soul, someone had once told him. And that, needless to say, brought to mind the other smoke, neither lacy nor fine, that outlined nothing. He squeezed his eyes tight shut and cursed. The door buzzed.

"Who's that?"

"It's Horek, Chief."

Gaspar rolled his head. He had no desire to speak to anyone at the moment, but perhaps the new sensors had detected something. He got to his feet. "Come in."

Horek slipped inside as the door was opening. He carried a bottle and two glasses.

"What's that?"

"This"—Horek lifted the bottle up to the light—"is Napoléon brandy."

"I don't drink during a mission."

"Nobody does. But there are times and there are times." Horek set the glasses down, popped the cork, and started to pour.

"Dave, I—"

"Nein, mein Freund! You're insulting the Emperor now. And this stuff is aged two hundred years." He pushed one glass at Gaspar. "Listen to an old grunt for once."

Stubbing out the cigarette, Gaspar considered the glass and then took a sip. He had to admit Horek was right—the taste was exquisite; an improvement over the tobacco, certainly. He only wished he was in a better mood to appreciate it.

His chair resting against the wall, Horek let out a giggle. "You ain't gonna get any of that out on Arpad, let me tell you. I was in 1803 Austria on familiarization. Found a dozen bottles and hid 'em in a wall. Then I went back in the '90s—this century—and dug 'em up. My CO found out. 'What kinda jackass are you?' he says. I had to give him a bottle."

Gaspar finished his glass. Horek waved at him to make free.

It was Horek who broke the silence. "The 24th is a pretty laid-back period, isn't it? I mean, it would be. Two-hundred-year-old people running things, the first effective AIs, chaotic social parameters all figured out. I was up there once."

Gaspar set down his glass. He hadn't been aware of that.

"Yeah. Training mission to Monroe. Out the other side of Earth from you. The East Cyclades, they call it?"

"The Far East."

"Yeah, well, that means something different back here. I was training people how to run around in the woods. The advantages of not being seen? They had some kind of revolution going on there. Never could figure what they were fighting over."

It all came back: there had been oddities about the Monroe situation that the Moiety wanted to keep an eye on—the planet was to be the cultural center for the Far East in the 27th. It hadn't concerned Gaspar directly: he simply countersigned the order for an advisory team and forgot about it. "What's your point?"

"Well, here's the thing. Back these days, you get a revolution and it's like a rehearsal for the Apocalypse. Massacres, show trials, up against the wall, motherfucker. Half the time the whole society hits the skids, population heads for the basement, somebody pulls a counterrevolution, the big boys jump in to see it doesn't spread. Complete futility, beginning to end.

"But on Monroe—man, it was weird. It was like a *fad* or something. What I did on my summer vacation. Just got outta school, think I'll be a rebel for a year or two, then come back and sell insurance. Same attitude on both sides. There was this one kid, he dragged his whole damn unit—affinity team, they called 'em—home for lunch. His dad was the local police chief. He walks in: 'Hey there, son. Harass any AIs lately?' They're wearing climate suits, stunners and disruptors hanging all over 'em. Pretty wild. Not what I was used to. How many got killed over twenty years, huh? About three hundred, most of them in accidents. The count for five minutes in Cambodia '76. And that's about as bad as it ever gets up your way, isn't it?"

Gaspar tilted his glass. The liquor at the bottom shifted, catching the light. "So the poor naive monitor from this utterly innocent paradise prances into an epoch of madness and has his teeth kicked in, is that it?" His voice was louder than necessary, but he couldn't help it. "He bit off more than he could chew, he's in over his head, he shorted himself. Is that what you're saying?"

Horek made a face. "I wouldn't go that far, no."

Dropping his head, Gaspar rubbed his eyes. He wanted more of that brandy, yet he shouldn't, really. He had his standards for running an operation. It wouldn't do to let go, not even to a minor extent.

"You pull in looking like a guy who's seen the devil—which you may well have, in one of his costumes," Horek went on. "You'd already debrided the sensor net, which I didn't know you were checked out on. You throw it aside like it's poison and stomp through with your boots striking sparks. So I kinda thought something got to you."

Gaspar let his hands fall. "Mr. Horek, I'd prefer not to discuss this."

The legs of Horek's chair thudded to the floor. "Okay. Up to you."

A moment passed in silence. "Nothing from the sensors, I take it," Gaspar said.

"Nothing worth mentioning."

"No. I saw no signs of her either. I don't think she's moved in yet."

"Chief." Horek refilled their glasses. "You keep on saying 'her.' Who's 'her'?"

"Researcher Lewin."

"Alma?" An incredulous smile spread across Horek's face. "You think *she's* in charge?"

So Horek knew Lewin as well. Was everyone in the entire Moiety acquainted with the fool woman? Perhaps she'd educated Dido in the AI crèche. "You've met, then. How did you find her?"

"Met her? I took her out on a mission. In Nam—part of her area of studies. Tried telling me it was the prelude to the Pacific War, for chrissake. She was all over the place for a while there. In and out of every station you could think of. What's she like? She's a nut."

"Beg pardon?"

"You know—off the wall. Everybody thought so. Full of theories. Total horseshit, like she'd dropped a tab of something heavy before going to physics class. Stuff about the real nature of the continuum—the base configuration. Ever hear that one? That the ground state ain't what it's supposed to be, the timeline's evolving to a new state, and we all oughta pitch in . . . Kind of a fad with the recruits for a while there. She had her own little version, though. Moral phase change. You hit some crucial events, straighten 'em out, and the whole damn continuum just kinda flops over. 'Crystallization,' she called it. I didn't pay any attention. Too busy making sure she didn't crystallize *me*.''

Gaspar leaned closer. ''Tell me about that. The mission.''

''Sure.'' Horek licked his lips. ''This was '69, okay? May, dry season. Nothing special, a standard look-see deal. Lot of guys recruited from my war, and they get tempted to slip back and even things up—save a buddy, warn their old outfit of an ambush, that kinda thing. Not really interventions, just guys pulling a Rambo.

''We got a chronon burst from the trail, in Laos near Route 610, north of the karst zone. Indian territory. Could have been anything: bad weather, quantum flux, you name it, but they want me to check it out anyway. So here's Alma, sitting around watching and listening like she does, and she's just gotta come along. And I'll tell you something: nobody has ever told that woman no.''

Thinking of Jerusalem, Gaspar nodded.

''Now I'm tweaking on this mission. And by the way, I don't know why Sab is so bent outta shape about that. It never bothered me none, and I've done it like a half-dozen times. I guess it's those stories. You know, you run into yourself and you both go crazy—booga-booga. Load of crap, you ask me. Nothing but superstition.

''But I remember this one night real well 'cause it was a heavy deal. They sent us in—this is SOG now; call it Horek Version A— by chopper . . .''

''What's that?''

Horek twirled a finger in the air. ''Chopper . . . helicopter. Rotary-winged aircraft. Used 'em a lot in Nam.''

Gaspar tried to picture such a thing and failed. ''I see.''

''Good. Anyway, we had to pull out this team got hit by the NVA trail guards. No idea who they were, some kinda spooks, I suppose. We had to find 'em and lead 'em to a safe LZ, with half the little people in Laos out looking for us.

''Anyway, the spooks lost a guy. He got wounded in the original firefight and ran south instead of north. We knew roughly where he had to be hiding, but we couldn't get to him. No helping it.

''So we check the area out—this is Horek Version B now, the Moiety Kid—and find nothing, like I expected. No anomalies, no activity. Zip. I'm keeping an eye on the time, and when it gets to 0132, I switch to the SOG radio freak and there I am, calling in the bird. I let everybody know that I'm tweaking, I'm only thirty miles away, and the rest of the story, including the lost spook. Then Alma—and she'd been handling herself real well, for the first time in the boonies—she looks at me, and you know what she says?''

Gaspar waited, clutching his glass tightly. He knew what it had to be. She'd done much the same to him, after all.

"She says, 'Let's find him.' Just like that." Horek wore a stunned expression, as if he still hadn't gotten over it. "She wants to track this guy down. 'Recruit him,' she says. She knew what was going to happen to him, see. The Hanoi Hilton, if he was lucky. If you call that luck. Most likely just chopped up and left hanging from a tree. So she wants to save him.

"Now I'm not taking this very seriously. But she keeps talking, and next thing you know, she's got the guys all fired up! They're ready to rock! And they ain't even vets! It's turning into a predicament, and I gotta talk fast. So I tell her we don't have an upliner core to act as recruiters, we don't know exactly where this guy is, and there's hard-core NVA running around like ants, but it doesn't penetrate. So I switch to my personal temporal theory—that he's dead. That it happened, and you can't change it. The guy's a goner already. Same as those poor SOBs in the camp there. And that's it, and we're going home.

"She gives me the Lewin stare, which does look kinda scary in the wee hours in wartime Southeast Asia, and she says, 'So you're quitting. You quit then, and you're quitting now.' And I tell her, 'You got it, babe. Sometimes you cut and run.' That earns me another look and she says, 'My preceptor wouldn't have quit,' and she—''

"She said *what?*''

"Yeah." Horek bobbed his head. "Those exact words. 'My preceptor wouldn't have quit.' And I'm thinking, 'Whoa. Whoever trained her must be a winner. If he impressed *her* that much, I mean . . . ' ''

Gaspar studied Horek closely for any sign that he was joking. He saw nothing to suggest that, and in any case, subtlety wasn't Horek's style. But what could Lewin possibly have meant? She'd had only one preceptor, and that was Gaspar James. It was difficult to believe that she'd had anything complimentary to say about him. Not after all the conflicts, the arguments. Not after Jerusalem.

". . . she's that type. Either she's pissing you off or you're pissing her off. No third way. You can bet I never took *her* along again. Next thing you know, she would have talked me into it. And I heard people saying she's monitor material. Jeez."

"Yes. She can be sarcastic."

"Sarcastic? No, I wouldn't call it that. She was never sarcastic with me." Horek poured himself another drink, carefully measuring out a bare half-inch. He raised the glass and made a face at it. "You know, I meant what I said then. My theory. No—just lemme talk . . . They're dead, man. All of 'em. Everybody you saw in there not wearing a swastika. That's what the place is *for*, Jimmy. It's a death factory. They're gone, just like my spook. You can't let it get to you. You gotta look at it through your military eyes. We had a saying in Nam: 'It don't mean nothin'.' Sounds cold as hell, I know, but that's the way it has to be. Nothing depraved or horrible about it. Just means you're a human being. Not like you're one of *them*." He waved at the cap on the chair.

"Let's close the subject," Gaspar said mildly.

"Sure. Just wanted to have it said, that's all." Horek sipped at his drink. "You know, now I think about it, makes sense Alma being in charge. I wasn't surprised to hear she was in on it, but I kinda thought she was around when they dropped and said, 'Me too.' She damn well could be running it, though. That Nam mission was five years ago, relative. You think maybe she's gotten even worse?"

"Uh . . . we know she's grown worse, Dave."

"Yeah, I guess."

Gaspar allowed himself a smile. His tension was beginning to ease. The liquor was good, the conversation passable. He was pleased now that Horek had thought to come in. He was right, needless to say. Harsh though it seemed, the only sensible course was to put it aside, to forget about it. Gaspar would do exactly that. In a short while he'd sleep, and tomorrow everything would look very different. "So you saw the Napoleonic era, did you? What else?"

"Well, never been upline to speak of. Not to the weirdo epochs, anyway. I worked as a guard for a research crew in the Devonian, but that was a joke. Big lizards, but kinda slow-moving. C15 Florence, the Osman migration—that's what the Ottomans called themselves originally—and Periclean Athens, which I kinda liked. Always had a thing for Greece. Xenophon, Alcibiades. Cool bunch, those guys—''

''Monitor.'' Gaspar looked up. It was Dido. He felt abashed, realizing that the machine must have heard everything he and Horek had said. ''A development on-site.''

Gaspar got to his feet. ''What is it?''

''I'm not certain. An operative has returned to station just now—''

Horek was already heading through the door. Gaspar moved to follow, pausing to grab the greatcoat. ''On our way,'' he said as he raced for the hall.

For a second he could see nothing out of the ordinary in operations. The duty staff were all on-station, aside from a pair standing near the platform. Then he noticed that one was speaking to the empty space between them. Stovall, an ex-Navy Seal recruited while in the process of drowning off the Spratly Islands, appeared at the spot. ''Monitor,'' he said, eyes wide in his dark face. ''We got us an escape situation.''

The glare of a floodlight blinded Gaspar as he emerged from the portal. He heard low voices, dogs barking, shouts at some distance. He squinted, trying to see through afterimage. Calling up his optics helped not at all. ''What's going on?''

Fukudon spoke. ''Who's that? You're not in camo.''

''Forget that.'' Gaspar blundered toward the voice. ''What's happening here?''

''Not sure. Our friends in gray seem to think it's a bust-out.''

''Are you tracking them?''

''Yeah. Not much sense to be made—''

''Let me have an earpiece.'' He felt a hand brush his, accepted the plug, and fumbled it into his ear. He winced as the sound came through. A melange of noise from overlapping sensors: the shrill yapping of dogs, heavy breathing, an occasional brusque order. He lowered the volume, listening on in case something of value came through.

''One of the towers saw somebody near the wire,'' a flat voice said. ''Or thought they did. Camp's on full alert. They got two dozen SS out, maybe more.''

''What of your men?''

"A few between here and the camp. Others remaining on-site. I don't want them stumbling into anything in the dark."

"Did you tell them not to interfere?"

"Sure, they know—"

"Tell them again." Gaspar's vision had cleared at last, revealing flashlights bobbing through the foliage, the sweep of larger beams from the camp. He saw no flames within the perimeter, and the wind, blowing from behind him, had cleansed the air of the camp's horrible reek.

Someone brushed against him. A glance revealed only darkness. "Did our sensors detect anything?"

"Nope," the bland voice said. "Zero, full spectrum."

"What about the new systems inside the camp?" Those had been put in place by Gaspar himself: nanofiber webs, virtually invisible, splitting off from the outer layer of his uniform and drifting to fasten onto the nearest solid object.

"Nada."

"Coverage is poor," Fukudon said. "You didn't penetrate deep enough."

Gaspar ignored that. "This could be Lewin making a move."

"Possible," Horek said beside him.

Gaspar swung in Fukudon's direction. "You've detected no high-order processes, advanced energy sources, targeting or weapons systems?"

"If I had, I'd have told you. Believe me, Monitor."

"Listen—" the flat voice said.

All fell silent. Gaspar strained his ears, wondering exactly what it was he was listening for. Then, beneath the sound of the dogs and the guards' voices, he heard a far-off pulsating noise, steady in beat and volume.

"They got a chopper out," Horek said.

"Sounds like a heavy."

Gaspar sharpened his hearing. "The same order of machine you mentioned, Dave?

"Yeah. Helicopter," Horek told him. "Can't be anything else."

Gaspar listened while the sound faded, then came back as strongly as ever. He made a mental note to ask Dido to display an example.

"There's no chopper pad in the camp."

"Must be out of Krakow," Horek muttered. "Luftwaffe boys."

A cluster of flashlights turned toward the hill. "Oh shit," Fukudon said. "They're headed right for my men." He spoke into his mike. "Yes, right in line."

"Bring them in."

Below them the barking grew wilder. Fukudon whispered into his mike, then paused and said something harsh in his own language. Gaspar swung toward him. "What is it?"

"They've tracked a positron source. Leakage from a power unit." He muttered into the mike again. Gaspar gazed wildly into the darkness, shifting his optics in spite of himself, as if his receptors were capable of picking up the emissions.

"Consistent with a camo field," Fukudon said calmly. "Somebody's wearing a stealth suit. Right in front of that patrol . . . Headed roughly toward us."

"Can your men intercept her?"

"Her . . . ? One sec. No, already passed by."

Gaspar started downhill. "Then we'll take her. Tell them to trail her, keep us informed. Come along."

"Monitor, you're not armored. I'd prefer that you remain—"

"Don't be foolish, Mr. Fukudon."

He set out toward the bobbing flashlights. The others followed. As they reached level ground, Fukudon whispered a correction and he turned to the right, bumping into one of the men. "Here," Fukudon said at last.

"Spread out," Gaspar told them. He crouched low. The clammy night air drew a shiver from him. He pulled up the collar of the greatcoat. "Ready," someone said.

"Tracking," another voice said. "Thirty meters at forty—ahh, that's forty-three degrees. Les and Kim, close it up."

"Roger."

"Steady," Horek muttered. "This one's a beginner. Not trusting the suit to hide him."

Gaspar bent forward, switching his hearing to high gain. He winced at the sharp barks of the dogs. But wait—yes, there it was, ahead to his left. Lone footsteps at a bare run, high-pitched breathing over that. He tensed as it grew louder, instinctively rising when it seemed that it could get no closer without running him down.

Horek gave quick orders. In the depths of the night Gaspar heard the rotors of the flying machine. The runner splashed through a puddle, snarling a single word.

"*Now!*"

There was a thump, followed by a muffled shriek. Gaspar moved toward the noise.

"Hey! Grab that—"

"Watch it! He's armed!"

"Got it—"

"Okay—now, simmer down, you . . ."

The captive was spitting high-pitched curses. A woman's voice. They had brought down Lewin herself. Gaspar almost spoke the name before realizing that she sounded far too young. Besides, Alma Lewin never spoke like that.

"Don't step on me now, Chief." It was Horek. Gaspar came to a halt.

"Here come the Krauts," someone said.

Over his shoulder Gaspar saw the lights as glaring circles closing in on them. Footsteps splashed loudly, underlined by the wild yelping of the dogs.

"Les got stunned. We'll have to carry him."

The woman was still cursing. Gaspar bent close. "You—the renegade. Those men are from the camp. You want to end up inside? Then be silent." The woman's voice ceased.

"What do we do with these Krauts?"

"Freeze," Fukudon said. "Keep quiet. They can't see you."

"What about the chief—"

"Wait," Gaspar said. "Give me a lantern." A lamp appeared out of darkness. He gripped it and strode toward the approaching lights. The men's footsteps were clearly audible. Flicking the lamp on, he pointed it before him. "Halt!" a voice shouted. The guards, only yards distant, shifted the beams onto him. Gaspar could make out nothing in the glare until a dog lunged forth, barking ferociously. He shined his own lamp on his face. "Wer da? Wer führt hier den Befehr?"

"Ein Offizier," someone said.

"Scharführer Eichler vom Dienst, Herr Hauptmann."

"Donneswetter, Eichler, was machen Sie den hier?"

"Verfolgungskampf, Herr Hauptmann. Wir haben etwas entdeckt."

"Na, wohl nur einen Hasen. Dieser Sektor ist gesichert."

"Ich . . . war mir unbekannt, Herr Hauptmann."

"Jetzt wissen sie es also. Fahren sie fort zu Westen, bis Sie mit der Hackbeil Kontackt aufnehmen."

"Zu Befehl, Herr Hauptmann!"

"Zu Ordnung. Und halten Sie nieder das Lärm. Sie wecken ja selbst die Toten mit das Krach."

The lights dimmed as the troops swung away. Gaspar let his own fall. The Germans slogged past twenty feet off, dim suggestions of helmets and greatcoats like the one he himself wore. Their weapons, short-barreled and ugly, gleamed in the torchlight. The Scharführer saluted as he went by, and a dog gave Gaspar a parting snarl. A fading voice said, ". . . mit der Hackbeil Kontakt aufnehmen . . . was das den Heiben?"

Gaspar gazed after them in puzzlement, then listened for sound of the vehicle. But the distant clatter was gone, the night silent.

"Jesus," someone muttered.

". . . you see that one kid waving that MP? Like he was gonna open up on the bushes or something."

Someone was speaking to Les Crowell, who groaned a few words in the slurred tones of a stunner victim.

"Who the fuck are you people?" a woman's voice said.

"Who you think?" Horek answered.

"Well, it's no use interrogating me. I've been dosed. It's kicking in now. I can feel it . . ."

"I'm aware of that," Gaspar said. "I'm acquainted with Campbell Smith."

"I can feel it," the woman repeated. Her voice cracked. "You have to get me to a hospital."

"Let's head for the portal," Fukudon said. "Les, can you walk? Good."

"What of the other two men?" Gaspar asked Fukudon.

"Right behind us."

They headed back to the knoll. Fukudon explained that the captive had been transmitting when they'd taken her; he'd jammed the signal. To the west Gaspar heard the SS calling to each other. They sounded frustrated.

He walked through an unseen puddle, soaking one of his shoes. Stopping to give it a shake, he sighed to himself. He was weary and light-headed, the events of the day beginning to bear him down. What was to be done with this woman? Questioning her was senseless, though he'd have to at least make a show of it. She was jabbering to herself, already deeply gripped by the drugs. "The nanons are fixing me . . ." she called out, followed with a burst of laughter.

He caught up with the others as they began the climb to the portal. The knoll seemed to him much higher than he knew it to be. At the top Fukudon suggested they wait for the last two operatives. "Here they come now."

Gaspar heard footsteps approaching, then low voices. ". . . dog knew I was there, but he couldn't see me, right? Just about drove him crazy."

"Yeah, I got a kick out of that too."

"Big Great Dane or something, I don't know, he's standing there whinin', lookin' dumb . . ."

One of them brushed past Gaspar. "So where is she?"

"Still got her field up," Horek replied.

"Good thing it's a renegade," the second man said. "One of them Jews makin' a run for it, I'd help him, man. Send somebody back there? Fuck that shit—"

Gaspar whirled toward the voice. "What did you say?" He growled into blackness. "You'd do *what*? Who was that speaking? Is that Jemal? Answer me, damn you! You'd intervene? Is that what you're saying? You haven't been in that camp. What the hell do you know about it? Answer me!"

"Oh shit."

"Gaspar's out here? I didn't know—"

"They're dead—do you hear me? They're all dead—"

"Beg pardon, Monitor—" Fukudon began.

Gaspar cut him off. "I want these two—who is it? Jemal and Guzman?—I want them detailed here for the rest of the night."

"Oh man—"

"Sir, they've been on duty since five—"

"I don't care. They can endure the cold as long as it takes for them to understand what they're here for."

"Duly noted, Monitor." Fukudon busied himself with dilating the portal. "Let's get back through."

"This way, sir," the bland voice said. A moment later Gaspar was inside. Tearing open the greatcoat, he left the platform. "We've caught one," he told Mackey.

"No kidding?" Mackey gave him an astonished look. "At the camp? Where is he?"

Gaspar turned to see Horek and his men hauling the woman through. "Can't you switch that field off?"

"It's voice-activated, Chief. Lemme see what I can do."

"So they *are* hitting the camp."

Gaspar swung on Mackey to give him a piece of his mind but decided the words would be wasted. He glanced around for Fukudon. There he stood, next to the platform, studiously looking in another direction. Gaspar fought down a childish urge to go over and ask what he now thought about diversionary moves.

Horek didn't appear to getting anywhere. "Come on, babe. Say the code. Do it for me, huh?"

"Nanons fixed me," the woman replied. "Fixed me for *sure*. Where's the hospital? My mom's at the hospital. She looked for me there. The doll hospital. You're like dolls, you know?"

"Better call for the medic," Gaspar told Mackey. "It's the same situation as Smith—"

A loud cheer rose from the platform. The woman's field had dropped, revealing her slumped on a bench between Horek and two of his men. "That's the ticket, babe," Horek said.

Gaspar recognized her from the files. Denise Higgins-Muñoz, known as Denny. Early 21st, a forecaster trainee. She smiled up at Horek, proud of herself. Gaspar could see that her eyes were hugely dilated from where he stood.

He moved toward the group, coat flapping about him.

"Is this a hospital? Maybe . . . no?"

"Denny—" Gaspar said.

The smile vanished as she caught sight of him. Eyes bulging, she pointed at him and screamed.

Startled, Gaspar came to a stop. He looked down at himself: the gray coat, the collar flashes, the armband.

Hiding her face, Denny wept hysterically. "I'll speak to her in the med suite," Gaspar told Horek, then made his way out of operations.

h er father was inside the block. She could tell. She'd heard him, just a little while ago. He'd been talking about General Pilsudski, as he so often did these days. *What a thug that man is, how vindictive, how nasty. Where do these jackbooted bandits come from? Nothing good can arise of such of a thing; Poland will regret allowing a man of that sort to take charge. Not only the Jews either. There is not a Polish babe in arms that won't rue the day that the nation turned to that home-grown Mussolini.*

His voice faded, and Rebeka wondered where he had gone. She had questions for him. Why Pilsudski had started wearing a black uniform. Why she hadn't seen any of her father's suits in Canada. What the Germans did with the yellow stars when they were finished. And why it was still so hot. He would know the answers. He always did.

She tried calling out, but that didn't work. She'd have to get up and look for him. She hauled herself over the side of the bunk. It was difficult, but everything in camp was. She was used to that now. Then the floor got away from her; a new trick, one she would never have anticipated. She found herself lying flat, cheek against the rough boards. Squinting her eyes, she peered into the bottom roost. No one was there. She heard her mother's voice: *Silly thing. You don't look for your father on the floor. And isn't it time for you to get ready for school?*

Someone lifted her up. Not her father—the voices were high, and he didn't talk that way. They didn't make sense either. They weren't speaking about Pilsudski or anything. She tried to push them away so that she could go look, but finally gave up and let them put her back in the bunk. One of them went off and Rebeka squinted at the other, a dim shape against the light, wondering who it was. It wasn't Alma, because Alma was part of Father and Father wasn't around. If she spoke, maybe Rebeka could tell. Rebeka tried to get her to speak. Forming her lips precisely, she said, "General Pilsudski."

The other one returned. There was something in her hands. It was when the cold cloth touched her forehead that Rebeka remembered what Father had to know: that Boldt was here, that Pilsudski was really Boldt. That Father had to keep him out of the block.

She struggled with the women. She had to go to the study to let him know. But they held her down. Their arms were so hard. And it was then that she realized who they were: the fat Bavarian; the mad-eyed one. She screamed and screamed . . .

Our Father, Our King, hold back the plague from Your heritage . . .

. . . a voice was speaking close by. It was dark, and she couldn't see who it was. As it chanted on, she realized that it must be her mama. Not her real mama, but the other one, the one she'd been given in exchange for having to go into the camp. Her voice rose and fell in regular sequence, as if the words had been repeated so often that memory was beside the point. . . . *I will look to the hills, from where cometh my help* . . . And Rebeka thought of the hills around Dobra, where she had walked with her father as he'd named the flowers, the trees, the birds flying overhead. For a moment she was there beside him, as if on the soil of another world. Then it faded, and as she tried to draw it back, she heard a voice that didn't sound like hers: . . . *Hills* . . . But all that remained was the ancient voice chanting, a hand stroking her aching brow. Disappointed, Rebeka closed her eyes . . .

. . . she heard music. For a minute she thought she was at the orchestral hall in Lódź, but that had been long ago, and this was prettier by far. A lone violin, the other strings quiet beneath it, floating and swinging through the air, so clear that she could almost see the melody, drifting above the blocks, the wire, around and through the black smoke. She was going to go up the chimney. She knew that. Her ashes would mix with the ashes of the millions. But that would be all right if this music continued, never to end, if her smoke mingled with it, became one with the notes. So pretty, so fine. She closed her eyes, thinking of how sweet it would be to be ashes . . .

. . . she hauled the suitcase to the table, the one that Boldt had picked out for her. He stood behind her, his silence pure and cold. They were alone in Canada, alone in all the camp. It was finished; the others gone at last. She set the suitcase down carefully, then clicked the latches open. She looked over her shoulder, but Boldt had slipped away—as he always did.

She opened the lid. It was dark inside the suitcase, black as night, as the smoke. She had to blink, so deep was the blackness. When her eyes reopened the suitcase was on its side, facing toward her. She heard a noise then, over but at the same time one with the perfect silence. Something moved inside the case. She pushed back her stool as it emerged.

It was a child, an infant, crawling on hands and knees. It was covered with soot and left a trail of blackness where it passed. It had no eyes, but its face was fixed on Rebeka's as it moved toward her.

The child possesses will, Boldt said. *It is one with itself, and this endows it with being. It is the child of the camp. It is called Furnace.*

She looked back. He was there now, looming high above her. Truncheon slapping against his palm, as steadily as the tick of a clock. The club paused, rose, and pointed past her. *Just look at him.*

She turned to the table. But the child had gone. All that remained were the trails of black, leading into the suitcase.

You must find him, Boldt said. *An experiment.* Hard rubber nudged her left shoulder.

Rebeka leaned forward, hand outstretched. As it touched the blackness, she felt a shock, a pulsation of infinite cold. She drew her hand back, lay it on her lap. Her fingers were numb.

She looked up at Boldt. He waited, his features obscured by the smoke. Rebeka cleared her throat. "I'm not ready yet."

Boldt let out a soundless laugh, a quaking of the silence . . .

. . . she must have cried out, for Alma appeared, driving away Boldt and his stillness, as Rebeka knew she would. There was light behind her, a bright golden glow. Where it came from Rebeka couldn't tell.

As Alma bent close, another light illuminated her. It was reddish and wavering, as if Alma's face was veiled with blood and fire. Rebeka gasped out the first word in her mind: "Furnace."

"No, no, baby. No furnace for you, not ever."

Her hands tucked the blanket around Rebeka, wiped the dampness from her forehead. Rebeka gave a sigh and let her eyelids drop. The last she saw was Alma drawing away, her face once more in darkness, that crown of burning gold reappearing around her head . . .

. . . she heard voices. Women's voices, the women of the block, voices she knew. They were very soft, and a ghost of her headache remained. She had to listen closely to hear what they were saying. Hester was speaking, her words cadenced and slow. After a few lines, Rebeka realized that she was reciting poetry.

Light flickered on the boards overhead. A candle; it must be late. What time could it be? Rebeka felt confused. She had no idea how long she had slept. Strange thoughts—of her father living in the block, of Boldt standing as high as the firmament—flickered through her mind. She swept them away.

The poem ended. She heard laughter, someone's fingers clapping against a palm. Mama Blazak spoke: "I love hearing verses so much. Even fancy ones like that . . ."

"Fancy? It's only Heine."

"Oh yes, but to read it is very hard, and you can't tell what they mean, but then to hear it said, it's all so clear somehow."

"I know one you'll like." Rebeka smiled. It was Alma. She listened closer as the dear voice fell to a whisper.

> " 'Oh my companion,
> Oh my sister sleep.
> The valley lies all before us
> Bear me on—' "

Rebeka held her breath until the poem was finished. She lay there, trying to hold the moment, then turned her head toward the candle-light.

"Oh," Mama Blazak said. "That sounded like the Psalms. Something the Prophets would have said."

"Well, 'prophet' does mean poet . . ."

"Does it really?"

Rebeka tried to push herself up on her elbow, but she was very weak. She rested for a moment. She'd been sick, hadn't she?

"I know many of the Psalms. Would you like to hear them?"

"Oh, Mama, not that—"

"Well—they're pretty, some of them. Even if they're not real poetry."

"The Psalms are poetry. Most of the Bible is. Didn't I just say—"

"Yes," Hata said. "I think so too."

Attempting to rise once again, Rebeka moaned as a deep aching pulsed through her. She fell back on the blanket. Someone must have heard; the voices ceased, and a moment later a shadow grew on the boards overhead and a shape leaned toward her. By the glow of the candle, she saw that it was Alma.

A hand touched her forehead. "I think the fever's gone." Another figure appeared. "About time, I should say," Hata whispered. "You gave us a scare, little one!"

Alma bent close. "Can you hear me?"

Rebeka told her that she could.

"How do you feel?"

She let out a noncommittal grunt, then wet her lips and said, "Thirsty."

"I think she's saying she's thirsty," Hester said. She was standing on Alma's other side, where Rebeka couldn't see her.

"I have water here," Mama Blazak said.

Rebeka felt her head being lifted, the cold rim of a can against her lips. She slurped noisily until it was gone. Yulka asked if she was hungry. Someone else suggested making broth.

Rebeka shook her head. "No," Alma told them. "It's best that she sleeps now. She'll be hungry enough tomorrow." She shooed the other women off and settled on the edge of the bunk.

Touching her on the thigh, Rebeka asked her to repeat the poem again, the one about the sisters, about sleep. "What?" Alma took her hand. "I can't hear you, sweetheart. You rest now, and we'll talk tomorrow."

". . . now here's some real poetry," Hester said, her voice soft. "It's called *Atlas*."

"Oh, not that one. It's so sad."

Mama Blazak spoke: "This is a good place for sad poems."

Her head still fuzzy, Rebeka missed most of it. But then Alma's hand tightened around hers, and she thought of the lines she'd just heard.

> " *'I carry that which can't be carried,*
> *And in my body, my heart would like to break.'* "

A shudder ran through Alma, and Rebeka tried to rally herself. But it was simply too hard to escape the coming tide of sleep, and the last thing she knew was Alma slipping her hand under the blanket and her voice saying, "All right—time for the Psalms."

C20/REL

The med suite was on the far side of operations, next to storage. Gaspar found Horek and Marilyn Fina, the station medic, waiting as he entered the corridor. He'd returned to his room to drop off the greatcoat and throw his homepoint blouse over the officer's shirt. He hadn't changed the trousers or boots; he doubted Denny would be alert enough to notice them.

Fina moved into his path. "I'd prefer that you didn't go in there."

Advancing to within arm's length, Gaspar put his hands on his hips. He'd come across Fina before at several vague points. When she'd first entered the Moiety, her name had been Mark. She'd undergone a complete somatic makeover as soon as she heard it was possible. It didn't seem to have improved her attitude to speak of. "I have to go in there."

Fina crossed her arms. "The patient is in no state to answer questions. Her psychic condition is the same as Smith's, and I *know* what happened with him." Her glare sharpened with the words. Gaspar wondered how she'd heard about that. "I've given her a sedative, but the effects have been minimal. Relieved her hysteria, no more.''

"That's all I require.''

"Gaspar—you are not going to get anything coherent out of that girl.''

Gaspar ran his eyes over her. A short mannish haircut, baggy clothing—"sweats,'' they were called for some reason. Why had she gone to such trouble, only to remain so plain? "Then I'll settle for incoherence.''

Giving her no chance to answer, he turned to Horek. "What did you find on her person?''

"ID and stuff, the stunner, of course...'' Horek reached into his pocket. "But mainly this.''

He handed a small jar to Gaspar. It was made of glassy plastic and had once been sealed. Opening it, Gaspar eyed the red pills within. He gave them a shake, poured a few into his palm.

"They haven't been analyzed, but if they're stock, then they're an antibiotic from a good jump upline. Self-targeting tRNA inhibitors. Identify alien strands and zap 'em. Fix you up and keep you fixed. Molecular cybernetics—real advanced. May even be from the 29th.''

A noise from inside the suite caught his attention. A snatch of a song, a merry-sounding piece. Fina moved closer to the door. Pouring the pills back in the jar, Gaspar returned it to Horek.

Fina's lips thinned. "I forbid you to speak to her.''

"Uh—she likes me. You could tell me what you wanna know, and...'' Horek's voice trailed off as he realized how inane he sounded.

"I'm not sure what I wish to ask as yet.'' Gaspar closed in on Fina. She remained unmoving. "Dr. Fina—you're aware that I know how to push, are you not?'' He let the words hang for a moment. "Then I advise you not to make me push.''

Fina reddened, then dropped her eyes and stepped aside. "They're all like that, upliners,'' she snapped at Horek. "They just don't *care*.''

"Sure plays a mean pinball,'' Horek replied.

Pausing at the door, Gaspar looked himself over to assure that nothing blatantly Germanic was visible. He entered the room at a slow walk. Denny sat at the far end of the suite in a chair next to a piece of equipment that he'd seen before but knew nothing about. A dark young woman, the only sign of her Celtic heritage a rather fierce jaw. She was playing with her fingers and humming to herself.

It was a moment before she noticed him. Grabbing the chair arms, she let out a low moan, not very loud but seeming to take all her strength. Gaspar thought of the child in the picture and stopped a healthy distance away.

Shaking visibly, she stared at him from the corner of her eyes. Another moan began building, louder this time. Gaspar put a finger to his lips. The sound slowly died.

"I'm not going to hurt you." He waved behind him. "I'm leaving the door open, you see?"

Although her hands remained clutched tight, the shaking eased. Gaspar went to the examination table and leaned against it. Best to keep some space between them. He should have done the same with Smith. "My name is Gaspar. Perhaps Alma mentioned me to you."

He noticed no reaction until he saw that her lips had moved. "What's that? A gray monster? No, not at all. I was in disguise, Denny. To fool them."

"Fool them."

"That's right. Alma wears disguises sometimes, doesn't she? In disguise, like Alma."

Denny's hands loosened and dropped into her lap. She repeated the name soundlessly.

Gaspar reached up to rub his forehead. "It's been a long day, Denny." He thought of telling her that he'd been in the camp himself not many hours ago, but he had doubts as to how she'd respond. In truth, he didn't know what to say to her. His head was awhirl from too much excitement and stress, not to mention the brandy. How many shots had he drunk? He couldn't recall. Well, he did know of one safe topic.

"Alma," he said softly. "We both know Alma, don't we? No surprise, I suppose." His voice dropped even further. "Seems that everyone does."

She flinched as he clapped his hands on his thighs. "Do you like her, Denny? Is that the right word? I'm not sure that anyone likes a saint. St. Alma of the Endlösung. St. Alma of Auschwitz.

"But I do know one thing: everyone has an Alma story, like her or not. So let me tell you my Alma story. And perhaps you'll tell me yours."

He paused to gather his thoughts. It had been a shameful episode, the kind kept on the mind's darkest shelves, brought forth and examined only rarely, if ever. Like a nightmare in which one helplessly commits an unpardonable, degrading act before a large audience. He hadn't dredged it up for years. "It was near Jerusalem," he began. "Do you know the place? Of course you do. Your world, after all. It's a notable town, I understand. The date was A.D. 70, the year that the city fell to a Roman named Titus. A bitter year—nearly as much as this one. The inhabitants, the Hebrews, were in revolt against the Imperium. And I tell you, Denny, I was shocked to learn that the Hebrews and the Jews were the same people. I'm surprised by very little anymore, very little, but that did amaze me. No one else endures. The Romans go, the Celts, the Yankees. But these remain. Even in my period, they have their own world, Shiloh, out in the Sporades. And upline too, as far beyond my own now as I can grasp. Maybe even into the final state. Startling, is it not? But I was telling you about Alma . . ."

It had been an emergency recovery mission. A researcher, Terence of Utica, had vanished in the chaos surrounding the collapse of the city. Gaspar, at loose ends after processing his annual batch of trainees, was called in.

For some reason Lewin had been present—she always seemed to be present in those days—and before Gaspar was quite aware of it, he found that she intended to accompany him. He was sure that he'd protested, but his words had long fallen from memory. As Horek had said, no one ever told Alma Lewin no.

They dropped into the badlands north of the city, a bleak and empty area, though much of Judaea was verdant in this era, more so than it would ever be again. They were to head south to a pickup site not far from the city walls, checking every individual, living or dead, that they came across.

It was slow work. Mile after dusty mile of nothing more than smashed hovels, freshly slain corpses, the carcasses of animals. They were forced off the road more than once by Imperial troops, auxiliaries from the more backward provinces, bloody-minded and looking for something to kill.

Gaspar had little to say, limiting his comments to tips on technique and procedure that Lewin had already heard a dozen times. A form of chastisement, a petty return for his annoyance at how she'd pushed herself into the mission, not to mention her behavior during training. The endless series of unsettling remarks; the conundrums she was so good at discovering; the way she had of turning the most straightforward statement inside out, of leaving Gaspar with absolutely no way to respond. Nobody had ever gotten to him as Alma Lewin did, and he resented it.

He watched her closely whenever they stopped to examine the bodies. If the darker part of his mind had been hoping for a sudden breakdown, evidence of shock or disgust, it was disappointed. Her face never changed expression, except perhaps to become even cooler. Even when they came across the remains of children—a sight that Gaspar had long ago taught himself to overlook—she merely paused for an instant before going on to the corpses of the adults.

It was peculiar how the long, loose drapery of the period altered her appearance. All traces of upline origins had vanished: beside him walked a first-century woman. A rare talent, he had to admit; if Lewin used it effectively, she'd do well.

Finding no sign of Terence in the demolished villages, they continued south. It was afternoon now, the sunlight of the homeworld, so much harsher than Eridani, pounding at them both from overhead and the rocks lining the road. Gaspar was having trouble with his costume; the sandals gouged the skin at his ankles and adjusting them gave little relief. He was about to suggest a short rest in order to fix them when a sudden uproar broke out past a curve just ahead.

He silently gestured Lewin off the road. Gripping the stunner inside his robe, he climbed the ridge that sprawled to the west. The outcry grew ever louder: screams, laughter, and howls of agony so mingled that the ear could not separate them. Reaching the crest, he dropped on his stomach and crawled the last few feet.

They were not auxiliary troops. No sign of barbarian clothing or weaponry was evident; no beards, furs, tattoos, or heavy gold ornaments. These were the men of the Imperium, soldiers of Rome itself. Perhaps three decuriae of them, wearing the simple yet ominous leggings, leather cuirasses, and round helmets of their period.

They had intercepted a group of refugees, a little larger than their own unit. Mostly ancients, women, and children, as far as Gaspar could see, all dressed in the faded robes of the Judaean peasant. Frustrated by months of siege, enraged at being denied the release of sacking the city, the Romans were unleashing themselves on these. They used short swords alone, their shields either discarded or slung over one shoulder. They were taking their time.

Gaspar felt Lewin settle in beside him. A glance showed her face grown even more wooden than before. Below, a quintet of Romans was finishing off a man, younger than the others, who had tried to defend a cluster of women hiding near a large rock. He had only a staff, and the Romans toyed with him for several minutes, allowing him the full measure of his terror, before finally cutting him down.

"This is the way it is, you know," Gaspar found himself saying. He hesitated, uncertain as to what had drawn forth that comment, at this point and with this recruit. He looked again at Lewin. She gave no sign that she'd heard.

"This is what it's like. In all the nows. That madness there below. Not a day has passed, will pass, where blood doesn't flow. Not a moment is clean of that, from the Paleolithic to the High epochs." He took a deep breath. "An eternal string of deaths, one after the other. That's what history is. Until they finally abandon matter and can't strike out anymore."

He stopped, surprised at the vehemence of his own voice. He felt entrapped, wishing he'd never opened his mouth, unwilling to let it drop but uncertain of how to go on. "The Great Wheel," he said finally. "The Great Wheel. The Asians call it that. The embodiment of history and time, rolling down the epochs, crushing and maiming and . . ." He gestured at the road. A gaggle of Romans was gathered around a woman dragged from the shelter of the rock, leggings pulled down over their sandals. Beyond them the swords still rose.

"And the Moiety . . . Nothing but the casing of the Wheel, its last inert outer layer. Don't forget that, lady recruit. There's no escape. No way off. We get a wider view of it, that's all. As it turns. And crushes."

There was a soft movement at his side. He turned to discover gray eyes fixed on him, only a foot from his face. They wore an expression now, though he could not have said what it might be. Not boring into his own, not challenging in any way. They had never actually done so, even during the classes where he had come to dread seeing them day after day. Instead they seemed to pierce clear through him, past the veil of experience and habit to the essential hidden Gaspar, in search of whatever truth it was that he held.

He tore his gaze away. "You . . . you should know, that's all. Prepare yourself. You will have to get used to it."

The Romans had stripped an old man and were running him through a gauntlet. His long beard was tinged with scarlet, and as he whirled about to avoid another sword thrust, Gaspar saw that the red stain extended down his midriff, where his hands were trying to hold his slashed belly together.

As if by mutual consent, they backed down the ridge to a level spot well hidden from the road. Ignoring the final shrieks, the crazed laughter, Gaspar busied himself with adjusting the straps of his sandals. Lewin sat staring wordlessly into empty sky, hands clasped in her lap.

At last the noises began to fade. Slipping on the sandals, Gaspar crawled back to the crest. The Romans were leaving, marching double-time in the direction of the city, marked now by short plumes of smoke at the horizon. Another naked man—surely not the same one—raced before them, trying to outrun the blades at his heels.

They waited five minutes before Gaspar, with a shaded glance at Lewin, began the descent to the road.

He kept his eyes high as he passed the scene. There was no point in checking these remains; if Terence had been present, there would have been some sign during the slaughter—stunned Romans dropping in their tracks, Gaspar's radio responding to a distress call. His foot twisted as it came down on an unnoticed rock and a sharp pain shot up his leg. Fine job he'd done on the straps, wasn't it? He was bending to pull them higher on his ankle when Lewin cried out.

She was pointing at the rock. "Something moved," she said. "In the shadow."

Gaspar switched on his optics. Yes—there was movement, directly beneath the upthrust mass of stone. His breath caught as the enhanced image came clear: a shape sitting in the midst of what for all the world appeared to be a pile of stained clothing. All sense of confusion vanished, he reached into his robe for the stunner. "Stay here," he told Lewin.

"No. I can't—"

"That is an order, recruit."

Gripping the stunner loosely, he paced toward the stone, tilted away from the road as if frozen in the act of lunging out of the earth. The scattered clothes resolved into bodies. A severed hand lay in the dirt just outside the pool of shade.

The woman cried out in a language he didn't know. He took in the stains on her face, her robe, the bundle she tried to hold out to him. He thought of his wife, how she had looked as she lay in the car's wreckage on a world far away, many years ahead. He lowered his eyes.

"Dominus, Dominus . . ."

Lewin stood next to him, her hands clutching the robe at her throat. He opened his mouth to rebuke her, but his voice failed him. Instead he only shook his head.

A shout rose behind them. He swung toward the sound. At a bend a quarter-mile distant three figures riding on animals came into view. Gaspar magnified the image, chuckled harshly at what was revealed. "Stand away," he told Lewin.

She made no move to obey. "Alma, *please*."

With a distracted nod, she backed off into shadow. The dying woman began a thin keening as she drew near. Checking his stunner, Gaspar started down the road.

The beasts were donkeys—"asses," they were called in this period—not horses as he had first assumed. The riders . . . Well, what was this now? He'd taken them for auxiliaries, some type of mercenary steppe cavalry, but the uniforms were the same as those of the batch that had just left. Imperial troops, at loose ends after deserting or being separated from their century.

He glanced over his shoulder, relieved to see that Lewin hadn't followed him, after all. No way to tell what that woman would . . . His step faltered as he caught a glint from within the shadow. Zeroing in, he saw that Lewin had brought out the med kit. He swung away, the anger hovering close since his inexplicable outburst on the ridge settling in tight. Excellent operational debut she'd made, wasn't it? First they get themselves cornered by denizens, then she decides to intervene. Fine after-action report she could look forward to.

Ahead the Romans kicked at the animals' sides, trying to speed them up. Their armor was in disarray, and they appeared to be drunk. The one in the lead pulled out his sword and flourished it in Gaspar's direction. He lost his grip and the sword dropped, sticking blade-first into the dirt. The soldier grabbed at the hilt, nearly falling himself, then tried to turn the beast around.

The distance closed. The other two, busy laughing at their comrade's attempts to retrieve his sword, didn't take notice until Gaspar was only fifty yards away. With a nasty growl, the one still wearing his helmet drew his own blade and slapped it twice on the animal's flank. The message was clear: *The day's a-wasting, come to die.*

Deciding he was well in range, Gaspar aimed the stunner and clicked the trigger twice. The first soldier thumped next to his sword, dropping like a sandbag, while the second wavered for a moment before sliding smoothly off his animal's back. Lifting the stunner high, Gaspar allowed the helmeted man a minute to let the situation sink in. The Roman looked over his two comrades, twitched once, and stared at Gaspar, his mouth wide. Gaspar smiled and made a come-hither gesture with his fingers.

With a shout, the Roman yanked at the ass's crude harness, the animal braying and kicking in protest. Gaspar waited until he was half-turned before firing. The Roman clattered to the ground, his mount racing wildly off down the road.

Lewin was still in shadow, bent over the woman. Gaspar broke into a run. "Get away from her!" he cried. "You're intervening. If she lives—"

He came to an abrupt stop. Lewin was no longer working on the woman. She was tending a much smaller shape, one that whimpered and trembled at the touch of her fingers. He thought of his daughter, about to give birth. It was to be a girlchild.

Lewin lifted her head. The contrast between the light and shade was too great for him to make out her expression, but he didn't need to.

"No—" he said. "No! This can't be—"

She turned back to the child, now silent, her eyes fixed on Gaspar as if in fascination. A hiccup shook her tiny frame.

"Recruit—" Gaspar said, trying for the voice of command. "Alma. Listen to me! It's no good. It can't work. You can't make it work." Lewin straightened up, one hand clutching the other. The child made an inquiring noise.

"Do you think it hasn't been tried? That you're the first? Everyone does it once. We all feel the same. Even me." He struck himself in the chest, the cold metal of the stunner bruising his ribs. "Even Gaspar—"

The dates and events tumbled out of him—Sligo, and Spokane, and Kolyma. The Inquisition of Spain, the suicide of Cambodia. That nameless numbered sun far down the Sagittarius Arm. Ash Thursday. His wife. Finally Bokhara, his single dereliction, the one time when he not been able to simply pass by.

". . . like this, Alma. Bodies. But worse. The Mongols took the heads. There were children. I gathered them, led them away. No place to go, no one left alive. I gave them rations, at recall. I checked later . . ." He raised his hands to the sky. "They starved! It wasn't enough! Nothing could have been enough!"

Hands become fists, head resting upon them, Lewin mumbled a few words. It took Gaspar a moment to understand: "Leave me."

"No!" The child began to wail as he strode toward the rock. At the shadow line he hesitated, as if to plunge in would trap him there for all time. He took the final step and gripped Lewin's arm.

If he'd expected defiance, he'd been mistaken. She didn't resist when he drew her to her feet and into the sunlight. Her face was twisted, eyes tight shut, the tears thick on her skin.

"What are your plans, Alma? What would the next step be?" He shook her roughly. "Do you think it started here? Look around you— that smoke. They're dying there now, by the thousands. And from here to the Middle Sea. And yesterday, and last week, and the week to come . . . Space or time, it makes no difference. Up in the 14th there's the Plague. A quarter-billion murdered in the 20th. The Vastation in the 36th. And you want to begin here? What did I say on the hill? What? We save no one! We *can* save no one. We keep the Wheel turning, that's all."

The child's wails had subsided to weak, sporadic sobbing. The woman, lost in a painkiller haze, spoke a few soft words. Arms out from her sides, Lewin swung toward them as if helpless, as if no other course was open to her.

Gaspar raised the stunner and took aim. Lewin gripped his wrist as he fired. For a moment they stood linked, his eyes meeting hers. He nearly lost himself in those gray depths, overcome with an impulse to strike her, to embrace her. Convinced to the point of certainty that somehow the way off the Wheel could be found through her. That this woman held the key that he had long ago learned could not exist.

He pulled himself away. "Now I've intervened," he said in a voice that seemed strange to him. "Again."

Lewin rubbed her face. " 'Adonai, Adonai,' " she whispered. "She was praying. Calling on God."

"They always call on God," Gaspar said. "What they get is us." He looked toward Jerusalem. "We have to go."

Silently Lewin gestured towards the rock. She appeared afraid to face it directly. Her mouth worked as if she was searching for words that would not come. Realizing what she must mean, Gaspar went into the shadow once again. He picked up the child, taking care not to touch the wounds that Lewin had bandaged, and laid her in her mother's arms. The med kit remained. He snatched it up and slipped it into the sack at his waist.

Lewin had already turned away. He walked behind her, watching her shoulders shake. He was surprised to see that she was limping. It hadn't occurred to him that her sandals might be bothering her as well. She should have said something.

The death sites thickened as they approached the city. No longer interested in Terence's fate, Gaspar passed them by. The Romans, or their barbarian allies, often left the bodies posed in amusing tableaux, making particularly novel use of children.

"Don't look too close," Gaspar told Lewin after she broke into tears for the third or fourth time. "Never in their eyes. Teach yourself to forget. Never discuss it . . ." He went on in a flat voice, uncertain as to whether she was listening, a final training session. "Above all, never, never review the lives of your own."

His handset beeped, telling him it had picked up the recall signal. He checked it, gestured in the proper direction. "Don't hope for any purpose, any answer, any respite. There is none."

A short distance from the waypoint he paused to give her a chance to pull herself together. Watching her wipe her face with the hem of the robe, he said, "Perhaps it would be best if you—"

"No!" She looked up, and it was the Alma Lewin he had known, face hard, eyes like shields. A transformation so complete that it chilled him. "Don't do that to me."

He answered with a nod. They moved on to the pickup site. Most of the team was already there. Terence had been located—or rather had turned up on his own. It seemed that he'd found an opportunity to speak to a man named Josephus, for some purpose having nothing to do with the Moiety, or the Jewish revolt, or anything else comprehensible. A typical researcher's trick. Gaspar watched him go through the portal, looking quite pleased with himself. Lewin paid no attention. She was facing south, where Jerusalem burned. She'd asked someone about a place called Golgotha and had been gazing in that direction ever since.

He watched her, his animosity hardening. The child would be awake by now, her mother already silent and cold. She hadn't been badly hurt; her death would be long in coming. Out in the wild, under that boiling sun, among the bodies of everyone she'd ever known. The Romans, at least, would have ended it quickly. But Lewin had to meddle . . .

He looked away, deliberately clearing his mind, thinking only of the child to come. In a short while he felt calmer.

They were among the last ones through. On the platform Lewin turned to him. "The Great Wheel," she said. "Thank you, James."

He eyed her for a moment, the image of a first-century woman. Holding back whatever comment he might have made, he walked off without a word. That was the last time he saw Alma Lewin.

". . . and that's my Alma story, Denny. Do you like it?" Gaspar had been pacing the room as he spoke and now stood before a bank of equipment unfamiliar to him. He ran his fingers over the inert switches, the dark readouts, reflecting that someone had told Lewin no, after all. In the hall a voice spoke, too low for him to catch the words. "Was she as hard on you? Saints can be very unkind, I think."

He turned to Denny. She gazed up at him, smiling broadly, tears dripping from her face. "You know Alma."

"Yes, Denny." He crossed the room, crouched before her. "Tell me about Alma."

"Alma . . . Alma folded us in. All together. Said to make it new. All of it, to go to the key point. Work the key point. That now. The wire, the lights, the gray men. The dead. They made it bad. Periods turning on the Wheel. She said the Wheel too. You told me . . . You know . . ."

"Yes, yes . . ."

"And Alma touches the dark. Wires. And gas caves. The striped people. She stands in place. Folds it all in. Moving in the dark. The smoke cage. Calling every day. And . . . and . . . I saw the wire. The burning wire. You know. In the night, the real night. Dogs. Dogs and gray men. Alma was above them.''

"And what does she do, Denny? What does she do? Something novel, something no one would guess . . .''

"She walks the dark! The gas place, everyone blue." A sob broke her words. "Across the portal. All asleep on-station. Joe and Idora want home. So loud. Unfolded and gone. He hit the console and I ran . . .''

Gaspar sighed. This was even worse than Smith. It could mean anything or nothing, there was no way to tell. She was crying openly now, the words coming in jagged clusters: gray men, and wire, the darkness. He thought for the first time how frightened she must have been out there.

". . . she called me. In the smoke and I saw her. Joe lied. The Wheel got her. All the smoke . . .''

He reached out and took her hand. Gripping it tightly in both her own, she bent over it. He felt the dampness of her tears. "The chopper, Denny. Tell me about that."

But she wasn't listening. It would be a long time before she'd listen to anyone again. ". . . you fool them," she whispered in a broken voice. "You disguise them now."

Gaspar extricated himself. "Yes, Denny. I'll do just that."

"The nanons. At the hospital."

"Yes, the hospital. We'll take you there." He heard footsteps behind him. "There will be cartoons."

He got to his feet, needlessly waved Fina forward as he turned to leave. Horek was diligently inspecting the floor when he passed.

Back in his room, Gaspar directed Dido to check the footage from the new sensors and compile a record of Hauptsturmführer Boldt's activities after Gaspar left the camp. The display lit up a moment later. Ignoring the excellent brandy at his elbow, Gaspar watched as Boldt tore into a group of workers, dragging a man to a point several yards away. Watched as Boldt struck him across the face repeatedly until teeth cracked and the bright blood flew. Watched as the automatic, reloaded now, lifted and fired, as the man flopped to the ground, the blood pooling beneath his head. He viewed it several times before speaking again. "Save that" was all he said.

1943

Alma was out when Rebeka awoke the next day. But Mama was keeping an eye on her and quickly called for broth while giving Rebeka a drink and cleaning her, a process that embarrassed Rebeka horribly. She smelled the broth before it came, shocked at how hungry she felt. Mama explained that she ought to avoid solid food for another day or two. Rebeka was surprised to see Nicole bringing the soup. She thought of a baby with no face.

Handing the can to her, the girl said something in French and smiled.

"What did she say?"

Mama frowned and said that she didn't know the language. From across the room Hester called out, "She said you remind her of Madame de Staël."

"And who's Madame Destal? A sick person?"

Nicole's smile faded. Taking the can from her, Mama shushed Rebeka, who forced herself to give the girl a nod. Nicole bobbed her head and rushed off.

Mama held the can while Rebeka sipped. It was real beef broth, not the foul liquid that came out of the kitchen, and she made small sounds of pleasure as she drank. "Chom somaich," Mama said when she finished.

"What? Oh—"

"Yes. The Days of Awe passed while you were . . . asleep."

Rebeka lay back. The Ten Days: Rosh Hashanah through Yom Kippur. She'd slept right into the new year. She was glad she'd missed it. Mengele often held special selections on Jewish holidays. There had been talk about that before she got sick. Still, she wondered how Mama and the rest had celebrated them. They certainly didn't have to make a point of fasting. She thought of the other holidays, the lights of the candles at Chanukah, the shouts at Purim, the seder at Passover. She remembered her mother's haroset, almost tasting the honey and wine. And the words they had recited together:

> " 'Remember us for life
> King who delights in life
> And inscribe us in the book of life
> For your sake . . . ' "

Her eyes grew damp. She wasn't really all that pleased that she'd missed the Holy Days, now, was she?

As if reading her thoughts, Mama talked about the plans for Chanukah. They were going to carve a menorah of their own and have candles blessed by one of the rebbes in the men's camp. Rebeka would like to light one, wouldn't she?

She considered that for a minute. "And Passover?"

"Next year in Jerusalem," Mama said softly. "You'll see it. You'll make the Aliyah."

"So will you, Mama."

"Ah." Patting her hand, Mama told her to rest. Rebeka stretched out, still aching a little but fine apart from that. She thought of the events the holidays commemorated; the reign of Haman, the Captivity, the destruction of the Temple. All the tragedies that had befallen the Jews. Perhaps there would be a holiday for this in years to come. As she closed her eyes, she wondered where they would find enough Jews to shout down Hitler's name.

Alma was back when she awoke. It was night, the block full. She heard women talking, the clink of spoons on bowls. Alma seemed tired, her face thinner than Rebeka remembered, dark circles under her eyes. But all that vanished when she smiled.

Rebeka told her she felt much better. The headache and fever were gone, and though her joints hurt a little it wasn't enough to bother her. Apart from that, she was very hungry. She should be; she hadn't had any solid food for—

A horrifying thought occurred to her. She tried to rise. "Alma— The warehouse—"

Alma gently pushed her down. "Don't worry about that. It's taken care of. The work section, roll calls, we covered it all. Luckily, Mandel hasn't been around. Everyone else was bribed. A blonde maniac over in Canada—she was easy. Liesl made out too. A nice little addition to her fur coat fund." She reached into her pocket. "Speaking of which . . . here."

She handed Rebeka a small bottle. "That's from Nicole," Alma said. "Perfume. She wants you to have it. I'm not sure what good it's supposed to do . . ."

"Oh, but it's nice." Rebeka turned the flask around, studying it in the dim light.

"I suppose. Remember to thank her."

"I will." She made a fist around the flask and held it against her chest. "I feel bad, though."

"Why?"

"Oh, the money. You shouldn't have had to spend it because of me—"

Alma gave her a stern look. "Stop it, Becky. What else is it good for? Anyway, you're my second in command. What would I do without you?"

"Am I really?"

"Of course! In fact—" Alma looked across the room, then squeezed Rebeka's shoulder. "We'll talk later."

Hester arrived, holding a large can with a cloth wrapped around it. "You're looking better," she said as she handed the can to Rebeka. "Take care—it's hot."

She took the can carefully. She was feeling guilty once again, thinking of what the others had to eat. With lowered eyes, she mentioned this to Alma and Hester.

"Oh no," Hester said, pushing her glasses to the bridge of her nose.

"We got a whole box of cubes from the kitchen. We've all had one in the regular soup for the last few days. Go on, drink up."

Rebeka did as she was told. It was very hot; she swallowed a little at a time. "I heard music," she said in between sips. "While I was sick."

Alma cocked her head. "Hmm?"

"It was very nice. It went like this—" Rebeka hummed a little of it, uncertain if she recalled it correctly.

"Ah—that might have been Schubert," Hester said. "The *Unfinished Violin Concerto*. They played that—Tuesday, I think. Performed it well, considering."

"It was very pretty."

"Yes. So it is."

The broth cooled down enough so that Rebeka could drink the rest. Hester went off to her own supper. Alma remained, gazing across the room, occasionally smiling down at her bunkmate. When Rebeka was finished, Alma took the can and examined it a moment. "You'd never think that old tin cans could be this important, huh? Oh, I'm getting so profound now."

"No," Rebeka shook her head. "It's true. I'll never forget."

"That's right." Alma squeezed her hand. "You won't. Now, a little more sleep—"

"Oh, I can't sleep now. I've slept—"

"Yes, you can. You will."

"But I want you to stay and talk to me!"

"What?" Alma put a hand on her chest. "Don't I get to eat?"

"I'm sorry."

Bending close, Alma gave her a kiss on the cheek. "Don't be," she said.

Rebeka sighed. She knew she wouldn't sleep. Alma was wrong about that, at least. For lack of anything else to do, she raised the perfume bottle to let the light play through it. About two-thirds full, the color a greenish-brown tint that said perfume. Nothing written on the bottle to tell what kind it was.

She tilted the flask, watching the liquid flow up the side, a bubble or two appearing, only to vanish immediately. Twisting off the cap, she held the short neck under her nose. It smelled lovely and reminded her of so much. That was sad, in its way, so she let the memories pass unexamined.

Putting a drop on her finger, she rubbed behind both ears, the way her mother had done. Father had never let her wear perfume. He said she wasn't old enough. She didn't think he'd mind now.

She put the cap on carefully and rested her head. The sweet scent all about her, flask clasped tight in her hand, remembering Lódź, and music, and fine warm nights. She hummed the melody of the piece she'd heard: Schubert's *Incomplete Violin Symphony*. And, certain that she wouldn't sleep, she slept.

It was dark when she opened her eyes again. She heard the bunk creak as someone sat on it. "Alma?"

"Oh—I didn't mean to wake you."

"It's all right." Rebeka shifted closer to the wall. "Aren't you going to lie down?"

"Of course." The wood creaked again as Alma slid in under the blankets. Her feet brushed Rebeka's. They were freezing.

A thought occurred to Rebeka. "Where did you sleep when I was sick? Not underneath?"

"Where else?"

"Oh, Alma . . ."

"I couldn't put anyone else out, Becky. It wasn't that bad. Please—don't start telling me how awful it makes me feel." She expelled a breath. "Besides, I'm the one who ought to apologize, letting you get sick in the first place."

"You didn't let me. What could you do?"

"More than I did." Alma paused for a moment. "I tried to get some pills in for you. But . . . it didn't happen. They screwed up."

"Who did?"

"The people bringing the pills." Alma fell silent, but Rebeka sensed that more was coming. "My . . . connections, you could call them, outside of camp."

"*Outside?*"

Alma reached over and put a hand to Rebeka's lips. "Shh! Yes. Outside."

Gazing up into darkness, Rebeka tried to pull her thoughts together. She'd always known that Alma was much more than she seemed, but this? She tried to guess who they could be. Home Army? Germans who hated Hitler? An Allied spy network?

"I still can't believe they couldn't get in," Alma went on. "It's as if they weren't trying."

"What happened?"

"The guards spotted Denny before she reached the inner wire. Joe selected *her*, of all people. Two veteran researchers available, and who do they pick . . . ?"

"You mean they were caught? Someone was killed, wasn't there?"

"No—now, don't get upset, Becky. I don't know *what* happened yet. It wasn't the Nazis—I'd have heard." Alma sighed. "I should have brought in a milspec. They're such animals, though."

Rebeka shivered despite herself. What Alma was saying made no sense. A milspec—what could that be? She must have misheard; perhaps her fever had returned, stolen back all unnoticed. That often happened with sick people here.

Beside her, Alma chuckled. "It did wake Joe up, at least." The blanket went tight as she turned on her side. Rebeka felt fingers on her cheek. "Now, I'm going to tell you something, and I don't want you to get excited."

"I won't. I promise."

Alma's fingers slid past her cheek to touch her forehead. "You're sure you're not feeling sick?"

"Nooo. Tell me!"

Alma slowly exhaled. "We're going to break out of here."

Rebeka shuddered, certain now that this was yet another fever dream, that in a moment Boldt would go loping by or her mother would drift through the room. She bit her lip, fighting an urge to pinch herself. Alma clutched her shoulder.

"Steady now," she said. "Steady. All right? Listen. I'm going to tell you exactly how it will be. A helicopter—that's a kind of airplane—is going to attack the camp. You've never seen one of those before. It'll be big and noisy. I don't want you to be frightened when it appears. A lot depends on you. It'll target only Germans. Most of them will be killed.

"What you'll have to do—and you'll know ahead of time when it's going to happen—is lead people out. There'll be others helping: Hata, Hester, Yulka, whatever resistance people we can trust—the

Yugoslavians for sure. But *you'll* be in charge. You'll know everything, where to go and what to do. The only one besides me." Alma's fingers dug into her skin. "We have to make sure that everyone gets out."

"Out of the block?" Rebeka asked uncertainly.

"No. Out of the camp."

Rebeka stared into the darkness that hid Alma's face. She was unable to comprehend what she'd just heard, unable to organize even a hazy picture of how such a thing could come to pass. She shook herself and forced out a breath. It came as a gasp. "Everyone . . . ?"

"All of them. Every last person. The ones who can't walk, the sick, the Moslems. Everyone. I won't leave a single soul behind here for those—"

The words subsided into small disjointed sounds. Rebeka held her close. The tall woman shook in her arms for a moment before pulling away. "Listen," she said, her voice still high. "Listen close, Rebeka. I'll tell you again later—details, all of it. But I want you to hear about it now. You're to go to a spot in the marshes. I'm not sure where yet, but . . . People will be waiting. My people. Friends. There will be a door. It won't *look* like a door, but that's what it is. You have to get everyone through that door. As quickly as you can. It'll take hours, maybe days. I don't know how long. There are so many . . . Some will be afraid, I'm sure, but they have to go through. Carried, if necessary . . . Well, some will have to be carried anyway . . ."

"Where does the door go?"

Alma made an uncertain sound. "To Austria," she said at last. "I can't explain now, Becky. Trust me, please? The Amis will be there. The Third Army, Patton's men. They'll have seen this already . . . They'll have liberated camps by then. They'll know what to do."

"And what about you?" Rebeka asked anxiously.

"Oh, I'll be right behind you, believe me. I'm not staying in this . . . place a minute longer than I have to."

Her voice drifted off. Rebeka clung to her tightly, hearing a heart beat, not knowing whose it was. "Well," Alma said softly, "what do you think?"

"I . . ." Rebeka didn't know what to think. It sounded mad on the face of it, but it had come from Alma, and Alma was the sanest person she'd ever known. More so than her father, even. If Alma Lewin said that something was going to happen, then it would happen, that was all there was to it. Rebeka thought of Boldt, of Mandel, of Höss in his fine villa. Challenging those creatures, defeating them, leaving the camp far behind. It was beyond the imagination . . . But Alma pushed the limits of the imaginable every day. Rebeka had doubted her once, but that was right before she'd fallen sick. It must have been the fever. She would never doubt Alma again. ''I think it's wonderful.''

Alma chuckled, and for a moment Rebeka was embarrassed she hadn't found a better word, one that would fit the occasion. She wasn't the type to come up with words like that.

''Wonderful. That's it, all right. We're going to change history, you and I. Break the Great Wheel. Those are the words he used, and I've never found better. That's what history is, you know—a vast wheel churning out death and horror and blood. One long Halloween with no sanctuary, no resting place. The unlucky ones all trodden into dirt, and the survivors, the heirs, left with half a soul, half a heart.

''The way it was, is, will be. Right up until the final state. He was right about that, poor man. But it wasn't meant to be this way. That I know—everyone does, in their heart of hearts. Even Gaspar.''

Alma spoke the name quietly, as if it was not meant to be heard. Gaspar—that was a Hungarian name. Rebeka felt a touch of uneasiness. Hungarians in the camp tended to be very nasty.

''Especially Gaspar. The way he acted that last day . . . That wasn't the way a cruel man behaves. He wanted so much to save them, I could see that. And the rage, the coldness—that was his mask, the only way he could bear it. I wanted to be like him, up until then. Become the kind of operative he was. And I tried, I really did try. Studied him, accessed his records, asked Lisette about him. But it was hopeless. I'm not made that way. 'Armor your heart . . . Don't look in their eyes,' he said. I could never do that.''

Rebeka frowned, wondering who this Gaspar could be. Someone in the camp or someone Alma had known before she came here? The name wasn't familiar, but Alma knew lots of people that Rebeka didn't. She was about to ask when Alma resumed speaking.

''And to think he was the one who pointed me here! Not Lisette, not Mrs. Blaustein. Not even the fact that my own blood was involved. Oh, he'd die if he found out. But it had to be the 20th. The Age of Massacre. The minute he said it, I knew. And when I traced that lump in the Kommandantur; my fine great-uncle . . . What was that but a sign? Oh yes: this is the center. Right here. This camp. It does not get worse than here, ever. This is the end point, the final exit, the axle of the Wheel.''

Rebeka remained quiet, knowing that she hadn't finished. ''And it's the fulcrum too. And I've got my little lever, my place to stand.''

''And you'll move the world.''

Alma was silent for a moment. ''Oh, Becky, I don't know. What happens after? We'll be up against all the epochs to come then. They are so powerful, and so detached. Why should they care? One world, one tiny stretch of time. It could be I've taken on too much . . .''

Rebeka squeezed her hand. ''It's not too much. For anyone else— for me it would be. Not for you.''

''Oh, but there's more—'' Her own grip tightened. ''Nobody else knows about this part—not Joe, not Idora, none of them. You'll have to help me with this too. I'm not stopping here, Becky. When we're finished in this now, when the camps are cleared out . . . We're going on. To the rest of the massacres in this cell. Cambodia, the Gulag, Ethiopia, Keelhaul . . . We'll do the same with those. Oh, we can't save all of them, I know that. Not anywhere near enough. But as many as we can. It's like the rabbis say—'You aren't required to finish a task, but you aren't free to quit either.' ''

Rebeka held her breath, afraid to make any sound at all. She couldn't understand half of what Alma was saying, but that didn't matter. The feeling came through all the same—a sense of grandeur, of great acts taken against high odds. It was as if Alma lived on a lofty plateau far above the everyday world, where the sun shone fiercely, while everything below was covered in cloud. Rebeka had taken her first real step onto that plateau, feeling what Alma felt, seeing the world as she saw it.

''. . . that'll break up their precious continuity. An entire cell transcending the baseline—nobody's ever done that before. They'll track us, sure enough. Run us down eventually. But they'll have to take us upline then . . . To the final state? The real powers? What a scary thought that is. But at least then I'll find out what they're actually up to. What it all means, what they aren't telling us. Lisette knows something, that was clear. Coriolan too, I think. And Gaspar? No, he wouldn't be so hard then. I nearly contacted him. Up there in the 24th.

Came to my senses at the last minute. *Nobody* is more loyal to the Extension than he is. Still . . . if he'd been here, he'd have gotten through the wire . . ."

Her voice drifted off. Rebeka frowned to herself. "Powers": that was the word that had struck her. What powers could Alma mean? There was only one thing that fit that term in Rebeka's world. "Alma? Those people you're talking about . . . they're not Nazis?"

"No—" Alma sounded amused. "No. Nothing like that. I'm sorry, Becky. You must be so confused. I'd make it clearer if I wasn't so tired. I'll tell you more later." She patted Rebeka's arm. "You have to know. After all, I've just recruited you."

"What?"

She moved, and Rebeka felt her lips against her forehead. "There! Consider yourself recruited."

A thrill went through Rebeka, blinding and complete, a flash of optimism and hope unlike anything she'd felt since childhood. Emotions long forgotten, sharp enough to cut through her pain, her misery, her terrible fear. She opened her mouth to give voice to them, but words refused to come.

"You know," Alma said, "you smell nice."

"Oh!" It took a moment for Rebeka to find her voice. "That's the perfume. Here—" She swung over and grabbed the flask. "Put some on. No, really. Then we'll both smell nice when we change around the world."

Alma laughed quietly, a sound Rebeka couldn't recall hearing before. She heard the soft sound of a hand across skin and the flask was handed back to her. "Ah," Alma said. "That does feel good."

Slipping the flask into the space between the bricks, Rebeka lay back, prepared for sleep. Her head was light, and her muscles were aching again. "Alma? When is it going to happen?"

"Soon," Alma whispered back. "Very soon."

Rebeka repeated the words to herself. Her heart ached with the joy of it. Mama and Hester and Hata and Yulka, and she and Alma too, of course, out in the hills among the green trees, with plenty of food and medicine, and clean clothes, and a great airplane to protect them. The sick ones would grow well, the Moslems would become people again. "And maybe Yetta will find her children," she said aloud.

Beside her, Alma stiffened. "No." Rebeka went hollow at the

word. "Not Yetta. She's gone. She remembered what happened to her family. She went to the wire yesterday."

Rebeka made no answer. Alma spoke again, her voice very low: "Boldt had been talking to her." A sigh at the edge of hearing. "Another world lost."

Alma's breathing slowed, grew steady, and Rebeka knew she was asleep. The empty feeling persisted. Doubts began to assail her. About how foolish Alma had said her connections could be. About the informants inside the block. And the bodies—nobody would have seen to that while Rebeka was sick. Had the Germans noticed that no one was dying in the block?

She lay awake for a long time, keeping very still so as not to disturb her bunkmate.

1943

Reber flinched when the noise began outside. He was lying atop the bed in full uniform except for his jacket and belt, reading the paper before trying to get to sleep.

A lot of things had startled him over the past few days while waiting for Boldt's other shoe—boot was more apt—to drop. Reber was certain that Boldt had set a trap for him. He could imagine fifty ways it could be done. What he couldn't see was a single means of getting out of it.

Ignoring the uproar—most of it simply bellowing, as far as he could hear—Reber tried his best to concentrate on the news. Naples secured, the Allies were pushing north through Italy, even though their supporting fleet had been annihilated off Salerno, a strategic paradox that Reber couldn't even begin to fathom. If only he knew exactly what Boldt was really after . . .

When the gunfire started, he raised his head to listen, then threw the paper aside. As he grabbed his jacket off the chair, the belt slid to the floor. He reached for it, but decided to let it go. He doubted anyone else would be in full uniform either.

The firing had died down by the time he left the building. The air was chilly, cold enough to fog his breath. He paused to button up the jacket. The shouts went on, punctuated by an occasional shriek. About him men stood in clumps, all gazing toward the camp. There was Knoblauch, wearing a greatcoat over his pajamas. An enlisted man, helmet covering his eyes, brushed against Reber on the way to the Kommandantur. At the gate an officer was calling for men. The few in full uniform raced toward him.

A cigar blazed, revealing the face of Joachim Caesar. Reber went over to him. "What's going on?"

Another gunshot rang out. Caesar waved the cigar at the camp. "Somebody shot two of ours. At the bathhouse."

"A Jew?"

Caesar nodded. "I imagine. From this latest transport anyway. Don't know any details yet. Schillinger was hit, though."

Reber gaped at the camp. Another guard ran past, rifle tucked under his arm, buttoning his pants as he ran. Caesar followed him with his eyes. "Hurry it up, trooper," he muttered. "We don't want another Sobibor, now, do we?"

"Sobibor?" Reber turned. "What's that mean?"

Caesar gave him an appraising glance. "You didn't hear about that? Don't have many friends in camp, do you, Reber?" He puffed fiercely and the cigar's coal went red. "Understandable, though. They're keeping it quiet. KZ Sobibor, my lad, is now a nonfact. Never existed. How's that, you ask? Quite simple: the Yids revolted, tore the camp to pieces. That's right. Beginning of the month—killed a fair number of guards, burned half the place to the ground, fled into the forest. Sonderkommando led it. Our chieftain, the Faithful Heinrich, ordered what was left torn down and all references in the files expunged. Wouldn't do to let the Führer hear, would it?"

A frantic yell rose inside the wire. Voices no less hysterical responded.

"You don't seem surprised, Reber. What's the problem—aren't you a good SS man?"

Reber automatically turned his head to protest. Caesar smiled at him around his cigar. "They're surprised. Listen to them! The Jews fighting back—it's against nature! You'd think that Warsaw would have taught them something, but no. Now, Reber, if somebody was out to gas you like a sick cat, what would you do?''

He reached up to loosen his collar, found it unfastened. ''Go for his throat,'' he whispered.

''Damn right. And they'd like to, the Yids. You can see it in their eyes, when they think you're not watching. That's why the farms are so nice. You can turn your back on the women.

''And what happens when it's over, hey? You're a soldier, Reber. You know what the story is.''

''Yes—I was reading the *Beobachter* just now. You have to look close, but it's there. The Yanks are halfway to Rome.''

''Not to mention the Reds chewing up whole armies. I don't blame you for transferring here, boy. Though I sometimes wonder how you stand it. The farms are bad enough.

''But it's not only the Yankees and Reds we have to worry about. Oh no. You read your Darwin? No matter—you know the thesis.'' Caesar swept an arm at the wire. ''Those are the weak ones in there. The strong—we missed them. No, too smart to be caught. They're outside, hiding in the swamps and the woods. They'll live through it, that lot, and they'll all want to cut a German throat when the time comes. Eye for an eye, that's their code. Sobibor made me think of that.''

Caesar nudged Reber as he was about to reply. An officer—Knoblauch, Reber saw with distaste—had drifted close, as if to listen in. The grapevine had it that Knoblauch habitually spoke when he shouldn't. Whether he was an actual Gestapo informant or merely a drunk with a big mouth was a distinction without a difference. They turned and strolled off a few steps.

''So make your plans, my friend,'' Caesar went on. ''Work while it is yet day. You're not like the rest of these mutts, thinking that you can just pack your kit and go home when it's all over. Some fancy footwork will be called for when the roof comes down, and you'd best be prepared.'' He nodded to the wire. ''There's plenty of gold in this camp. Cash too. Play your cards right, you can leave here with a nice nest egg. Buy a set of false papers with a bit left over.''

''But how—I mean, for what . . . ?''

"For what? Food, medicine, warm clothes, whatever they need. What do you think, you blockhead?"

"But . . . selling food to them, that's so coarse—"

"Oh, come off it, Reber! You're doing them a favor. They're Jews! They know the value of a Pfennig. This one I'm dealing with now, from the women's camp. Tall creature, weirdest eyes ever saw. Gray as a thundercloud—you could drown in them. She can drive a bargain, I'll tell you . . ."

He went silent and fiddled with his cigar. "Damn! It went out. I hate that. Never taste right when they're relit. Impossible to get any more, though." He was reaching into his pocket for a match when someone appeared from the Kommandantur, shouting a name. "What's this?"

"Obersturmführer Reber," the man repeated. He was in full uniform, carrying a machine pistol. Reber was about to respond when Knoblauch pointed in his direction.

The man saluted as he approached. "Obersturmführer," he said. "Hauptsturmführer Boldt wishes you to report to him."

Reber stared at the man, whose face was lost beneath the brim of his helmet. "I . . . I need to get my cap."

He turned to the barrack. Caesar fell in step with him. "You don't have to report to that bastard. He's no one to you."

Reber shook his head without answering.

"You don't mean to tell me he's got something on you? Not Gerd the Dutiful?" Caesar gave a whistle. "If that's the case, just forget we spoke, will you?"

"I need to get my cap," Reber repeated as he went up the steps. In his room he grabbed for the cap and was nearly out the door when he spotted his belt. He stooped down for it, examined the buckle closely. Eagle, swastika, the motto "My Honor Is My Loyalty." Boldt wore one of these too, he thought as he fastened it with numbed fingers. They all did.

When he came back out, Caesar was holding a match to the stump of his cigar. He gave Reber the eye as he passed. "Have fun," he said.

The guard led Reber through the Kommandantur and then the gate into the camp, roughly the same path Reber had taken with Griese. It was as if he'd been told to follow that route in order to concentrate Reber's mind. He glanced at the man, who paced on in complete silence, then swallowed and looked away. It wouldn't do to ask about it. He was one of the others. Anyone who knew Boldt was one of the others.

The camp itself was now quiet. Only an occasional shout broke the stillness embracing the dark blocks. That and a high endless keening that it took him several minutes to realize was a human voice.

He heard the mob before seeing it. He'd been keeping his eyes to the ground, watching out for a pile of red dust, afraid that he might walk through it. He looked up as a low mutter ahead resolved into voices, broken by laughter and the snuffling of dogs. A mass of men, silhouetted by the lights beyond. Not in neat ranks or any kind of formation at all, but milling about loosely in front of the B.I gate. The guard marched steadily toward them. More than ever Reber felt like a man in custody.

His discomfort grew as he neared the men. Even without him being able to distinguish the words, their voices had a disturbing undertone, a sense of unhealthy, barely controlled excitement. Their laughter underlined the mood: sporadic, high-pitched, cut short at one spot only to ring out at another. The dogs, whining nervously, whirling in aimless circles, had caught the feeling as well. This was no military unit that Reber had ever heard of. He didn't have a word for what it was.

A cluster of men turned as they approached. "Ah!" one cried, waving a bottle at Reber. "More the merrier!" Just past him another trooper was on hands and knees, vomiting into the muck. Where the devil were the officers . . . ? The thought was cut off by the sight of a cap lying beside the sick man.

The guard asked something of the most sober-looking of them, who jerked a thumb over his shoulder. Nodding at Reber, the guard went on. As he moved to follow, a bottle was thrust in his face. Reber pushed it away, wincing at the fumes of cheap brandy.

". . . Schillinger was a friend of mine."

"Did you see his head? It sort of went *pop*, like a melon . . ."

". . . should kill them all now, the fucking vermin . . ."

". . . some of the Kike bitches are fine, though. I can't wait . . ."

". . . he was a *comrade* . . ."

Reber spotted Boldt, black leaping out from gray, at the same moment that Boldt saw him. "Ah," he said, smiling broadly. "Here we are."

The guard saluted and stepped back. Boldt swept an arm at Reber. "Gentlemen . . . the man we've been waiting for! Gerd Reber. A Kommandantur officer. Lord and master of the correspondence section."

A burst of laughter greeted that. Reber flushed, hoping it wasn't noticeable under the spotlights. Boldt lifted his hand. "But one of ours, all the same. Though he needs a little seasoning." His voice dropped to nearly a whisper, audible to only the two of them. "Tell me, Gerd, have you recalled anything more about your stroll with Griese? Your response was less than thorough. But we can discuss that later—"

He raised his voice to its former pitch. "You're aware of what happened tonight, Gerd? You may not have heard that Schillinger is dead. Shot with his own pistol. By a woman, no less, a simple Jewish whore."

"A dancer she was," a squat officer said. "Started doing a strip-tease. Brushing up against him, see, to get him hot? Goddamn fool didn't know what hit him."

"Incompetence," Boldt said. "Sheer lack of rigor. We've been"—he made a squeezing gesture with his hands—"tightening things up since then, and we're about to move into the women's camp. And that, Gerd"—he tapped Reber's shoulder with his club, as if conveying a serious honor—"was when I thought of you."

Stepping back, Boldt raised his arms. "Attention!" He shouted. The murmur of voices fell. "All of you—pull yourselves together! Same procedure, but I want no sloppiness this time. Complete silence until we reach the first block. The cargo are to be turned out and run to the Appelplatz swiftly and in good order." He allowed himself a pause as chuckles rose. "I want the blocks empty in fifteen minutes. I want them searched thoroughly—the females are much better at hiding than the men—"

A bulky officer, bloodshot eyes nearly matching the red of his face, pushed through the knot around Boldt. "Here now, Max," he said petulantly. "I can give orders to my own troops."

Boldt waved a hand. "Of course, Fritz! Feel free."

The officer thought for a moment, face twisted in concentration.

Reber heard muted laughter. "I think you about covered it," he said finally. The merriment peaked as he moved back into the crowd. "Schillinger was a friend of mine . . ."

"All right," Boldt called. "Line up." The men began to shuffle toward the gate. Boldt's eyes fell on Reber. "You've never seen a selection, have you? Your lucky night. A chance to open yourself. Someone loan Gerd a Gummi."

A club flew out of darkness, turning end for end. Reber clutched at it, nearly letting it drop. The watching men chuckled.

"And a lamp too. But don't throw that."

A flashlight was handed to him. When he looked up, Boldt was gone. The press of men pushed him on through the gate.

The only sounds were the clink of weapons, the squish of mud under bootheels, a dog's occasional grunt. Reber dropped to the rear. He twisted the truncheon in his hands, not sure of what to do with it. Heavy rubber, rounded ends, a crude grip. It occurred to him that it might well have been made by the Jews themselves. He slipped it into his belt.

Ahead Boldt directed men to a particular row of blocks. Reber shifted to the opposite side of the line, keeping his head down as he went past. He found himself standing before a block, awaiting the signal with a half-dozen others. Someone nudged him and a bottle appeared. He handed it on.

A shape loomed next to him. He started when he saw the black uniform. "Club," Boldt whispered harshly. Reber took hold of it.

Slipping by him, Boldt whispered to the man at the door, who raised his truncheon and nodded. Reber glanced about him. The faces of the men were all shadowed, as if nothing at all existed beneath the lips of the helmets. He shivered and looked away.

Boldt had gone to the middle of the Lagerstrasse. He gestured at Reber's group and lifted a hand to his lips. A club hammered at the door. A voice rose within, a cry of shock or fear. The whistle shrieked behind him. The trooper at the door yelled, "Surprise!" and yanked it wide.

The officer in the lead howled and leaped inside. Pushed from behind, Reber stumbled up the steps, blinking as a flashlight played across his face. Then he was through the door, half-blinded, caught in a maelstrom of screaming women and crazily shifting lights.

Once, as a child, Reber had seen a film called *Nosferatu*, which had frightened him horribly. For a week afterward he'd been unable to sleep, oppressed by visions of bizarre camera angles, strange lighting, the shocking events portrayed. This was the nightmare come to life: a frenzy of distorted bleeding faces, illuminated only for a second before the beam shifted, always falling on something worse. Behind the lights the larger shapes of the soldiers moved, their arms flailing almost mechanically.

The first wave fleeing the block nearly knocked him off his feet, and he brought up his club more to hold them back than anything else. Boldt appeared, his face offensively close. "Use it, you spineless bastard! Strike!" He began lashing out, trying to hit low, away from the faces, swinging as weakly as he could.

Boldt strode on into the building, mouth open in wordless shout. A sobbing woman fell against Reber. He grabbed her arm as she collapsed. She caught sight of him, eyes widening as she saw what he was. Tearing herself away, she lost her balance again. Reber reached out to steady her. She shrieked and slapped at him.

"Better!" A hand clapped his shoulder. He looked back to see Boldt shoving women aside as he headed for the door. One cracked her head against the frame and dropped down the steps.

Reber lowered the club. Backing off, he came up against a pillar and halted there, eyes locked on the passing women. A small one, with a child's unsteady gait, sobbing from a bloody mouth. Another, thin as a skeleton, eyes blank, screaming, "No more! no more!" over and over again. An older woman, her stubble gray, holding the tatters of her dress up as she ran.

The stream diminished and then shrank to nothing. A patter of bare feet sounded and one last woman came into sight, racing for the door. When she spotted him, she halted, staring in horror. "Go on!" he shouted, swinging the truncheon more sharply than he'd intended. She ran past him, hands over her head.

He was alone in the room. He heard voices and footsteps at the rear of the block. "Search everywhere!" someone shouted. "They're hiding, I can feel it!"

Outside the women were passing. A parade of bleeding, barely human figures in filthy striped rags and some not even that much. A few were naked, hiding their bareness with their hands. A dog leaped at one of these, tearing at a buttock, leaving streams of blood washing down a skeletal leg.

They were almost completely silent. That was what struck Reber most. All those women, and scarcely a sound to be heard. Only the shuffle of feet and the voices shouting for them to move on.

Reber went to the door. Boldt was nowhere in sight, nor could he hear his voice. He hesitated a moment until the clump of approaching footsteps from behind spurred him outside.

He jumped to the ground, not bothering with the stairs. Edging around the corner, he collapsed against the wall. He moved to slip the club under his arm but stopped short, convinced that there must be blood on it. He felt the end carefully, ready to snatch his fingers away. It was dry. As he slid it into his belt, loud voices interrupted him: two guards, joking as they flogged the women onward.

He decided to go farther back. It was dark here between the blocks; he moved his feet carefully. About halfway down he heard a sound ahead, caught a hint of movement. Without thinking, he pulled out the flashlight and flicked it on.

He swung away instantly, slipping in the muck and nearly going to his knees. The image burned: the woman lying legs wide, a small officer grunting over her, another man bending down with his club thrust into her open mouth.

Reber ran past the next block, looking in neither direction, seeking only darkness. Inside the alley he tripped and lost his hat. It took him a moment to find it. He squatted there, brushing off the crown, muttering a few meaningless words to himself.

He wanted so much to remain there. Hidden in the quiet dark, where he wouldn't have to take part in that, those things they were doing. Not even in the east had he ever behaved that way. Where it was vengeance, turnabout for what the Reds themselves did. He never shot prisoners. No, he brought them in. They laughed, his comrades, his mates, but they respected him too. He knew that. He could tell. But not here, not in Boldt's country. He and the others, who wore the uniform, the lightning flashes, the belt that spoke of honor. What did they know of it? But Boldt would be looking for him. So he couldn't stay. Perhaps he already was . . .

Suddenly he was aware of a presence. Just that: no sound, no conscious cue whatsoever, simply a knowledge that he was not alone.

Clapping on his cap, he straightened up and reached for the flashlight. If they were doing something in here, something base, he'd break it up. To hell with Boldt. He was an officer, wasn't he? That meant something, didn't it? He'd drag them into the light, that's what he'd do. Make them toe the line. Act like Germans. What had Griese said? The quote from Himmler . . .

"Leave the light off."

Reber paused, arm held straight out.

"Please."

It was a woman's voice, low and throaty. He could picture her in his mind, what she must look like. But he knew it was unlikely that she would match that image at all.

"You thought it was guards, didn't you?" The voice paused. "We're prisoners, three of us. Myself, an aged woman, a younger one." She took a deep breath, let it out slowly. "She's pregnant. She's going to have a child. She wouldn't live through this selection, would she?"

Reber let the flashlight drop. For the first time he heard movement.

"I have money . . ."

He found his voice. "I don't want money."

"What do you want?"

Laughter bubbled up his throat. He forced it back only with effort. "That's a fine question."

"Yes." He could tell from the tone that she was smiling. "I suppose it is."

He jolted against the wall as someone screamed very close by. The woman sighed. He addressed the dark spot where she must be. "I don't agree with this. I don't belong in this place."

He saw her draw near, a shape in the darkness. She touched his hand. "I understand," she said. He smelled a faint whiff of perfume as she moved away.

"What's your name?"

Shouts came from the Lagerstrasse. He looked in that direction. "Reber. I'm not a guard. I don't work in here. In the Kommandantur. The women there—I give them food. I don't sell it to them. I don't take money. Not like the others."

The shouting grew clearer. It was Boldt. He moved away from the wall, feeling an overwhelming sense of weariness. "I have to go—"

"Yes. But one thing. There's a young girl. Her name is Rebeka. Number 42358. She's been very sick. She's out there. Could you . . . ?"

"Whatever I can."

"Thank you." The hand brushed his once more. Wondering how she could see him in this blackness, he went on toward the Lager-strasse. "42358," she whispered behind him. "God bless."

Guards were emerging from the block as he reached the end of the alley. He waved them on, telling them it was clear. He decided to wait there a little longer—men were still poking around. He looked over his shoulder into the blackness. There was nothing to be seen. Doubt touched him, a dreamlike conviction that no one was hiding there at all, that it had never happened.

When he turned back, he caught a flash of black out of the corner of his eye and went rigid. Boldt emerged from a barrack door. "What are you doing?"

Reber came to attention. Boldt had a small contemptuous smile on his face. "Get on down to the Appelplatz. You're needed there."

He turned without waiting for a response. With a glance behind him, Reber started on his way. Rebeka, she'd said . . . He couldn't remember the number. But she'd been sick. He'd look out for her. He would. Make sure she wasn't taken, that nothing happened to her. For the sake of . . . He realized that he didn't know the woman's name. For her sake anyway. The woman in the dark.

A sense of exhilaration filled him. He'd defied them, hadn't he? Boldt, all the others. He'd saved three. Four, if you counted the child. He wondered if that story was true. It seemed fantastic. How could someone become pregnant in here? He'd heard that their . . . womanly functions ceased after a few weeks in camp. He looked back, suddenly afraid that Boldt might decide to search that alley. But he was facing away from it, speaking to some troops.

Then, at the far end of the Lagerstrasse, a figure appeared. Small and white, running straight toward him. A woman, naked and wailing. Two dogs snapped at her heels, trailing a pair of laughing, cheering guards.

Reber picked up his pace. A few steps on he again glanced behind him. The woman was passing Boldt. Casually, without the least sign of effort, he swung his club, catching her on the hip. A guard lunged with his rifle, the butt striking her knee. She staggered but ran on. She was limping now.

Reber was nearly at a run himself. If she caught up with him, he'd have to hit her. How could he do that, after what had occurred in the alley? But Boldt would surely notice. It would be another black mark, one more excuse for humiliation.

The footsteps were now audible; the panting of the dogs, the woman's ragged breath. Reber gripped the club. He would pretend. Yes—a firm swing, but one that wouldn't so much as touch her. From where Boldt was standing he couldn't see . . .

A cry, followed by a thump. She was down. Guards emerged from a block and stood around her. The two with the dogs stopped, reining the beasts in. "Too bad, darling," one of them said. The woman pushed herself up on her elbows, trying to rise. A boot sent her down into the mud. Another caught her on the side of the head.

Reber hurried on.

Chaos met him at the Appelplatz. The square was packed with hundreds of women, every last one from that row of barracks. All but the dead—and the three he'd protected. The guards, laughing and trading jokes, clubbed the ones on the edge, forcing them into a smaller area. The dogs looked excited and pleased with themselves.

Reber found an inconspicuous spot near the wall of the last block. He reached up to wipe his forehead. Cold; it was a cold night, but he was sweaty all the same. He regarded the women in their thin shifts, some of them with no clothes at all. Many bloody faces were visible. Other prisoners slumped against those standing next to them. Some seemed beyond everything, staring into space with dead eyes. Reber thought of the woman on the Lagerstrasse. It might be a good thing to go quickly.

He noticed a tiny woman, strikingly pretty, her blonde hair in a braid, walking among the prisoners. She wore a thick overcoat and held a clipboard. Every few steps she grabbed a woman's arm, inspected it, and walked on, marking the numbers down. Several of the women began weeping after she passed. One laughed wildly and dropped to her knees.

He recalled the girl he had agreed to watch out for. But how to begin? Find a single woman in this mass? It was an absurdity. He didn't even know what block she was from. If he'd only remembered the number . . .

A hush fell across the square. Boldt had arrived, trailed by a phalanx of guards. He paused to look around, eyes falling on Reber. "You're good at finding odd places to hang about, aren't you?" He crooked a finger. "Come along."

He followed Boldt as the guards fanned out around the square. Walking to a central spot facing the ranks, Boldt gestured to a pair of the healthier-looking women. "There's a few messes lying around here and there," he told them. "Clean them up." They ran off, a guard at their heels.

Reber went at ease a few steps behind Boldt. He set his jaw, trying to keep his face rigid. All he could think of was the man that Boldt had wanted him to shoot. He wouldn't do that here, would he? Not in front of everyone. But what else could he have in mind?

The blonde woman approached Boldt, clipboard under her arm. "Finished, Cyla?" Boldt said in a mild voice. Making a near curtsy, she handed him the clipboard. "Where's Taube tonight?"

"Helping out at the burner." Her voice didn't match her appearance at all. It was light and high-pitched, but the words were spoken in a flat monotone.

"Ah." Boldt was already flicking through the sheets. With a smile, Cyla nodded and moved away.

Another woman drew near, hard-faced, her dark hair pulled sharply back from her forehead: Mandel, Oberaufseherin of the women's camp. "How many numbers you got there?"

"Enough," Boldt said.

Mandel scowled. "Don't go overboard."

"I don't know what you mean, Maria."

"Oh yes you do. Keep in mind that you're acting under my authority. B.I is my camp. Don't forget that. I'll be watching."

As she walked off, Reber saw a flash of white beneath the greatcoat and realized that she was wearing a nightgown. Then Boldt spoke his name.

The Hauptsturmführer was smiling. "This is where you come in," he said and gave him the clipboard.

The world seemed to close in on him, as it had with the pistol, becoming a black circle encompassing only a hand—his hand—and the thing that it held. A clipboard, the same as any other. He had a number of them in his office. The metal was touched by rust, the backing chipped and stained with ink. A few sheets of grayish low-quality paper were held fast. Written on them, in a childish scrawl, was a series of five-digit numbers, perhaps thirty on the top sheet. One of them was crossed out where Cyla had made a mistake.

"Go on," Boldt said. A short cigar had appeared in his mouth, jutting from the corner of his lips.

Reber confronted the faces. All the blank, sick, bloody, gray faces. Some looked back at him, some at the ground, some past and through him at things that, if he were to turn, he was certain he would not see. He gazed as long as he could stand before dropping his eyes. It had only been a moment.

"Reber."

His mouth sagged open. "Number . . . three, five, two, four, nine."

"Louder, please."

He repeated it. A woman stepped from the ranks, moving quietly, as if she was only leaving her place for a little while.

"Number four, six—"

"You don't have to keep saying 'number,' Gerd. We know they're numbers."

He had to wait for the laughter to die down. Wait with the clipboard in his hand, with the faces before him. He read the number slowly, fist gripped behind his back. Another woman left, this one with a flurry of whimpers.

He went on down the page, keeping his eyes focused on that alone, so he wouldn't have to watch them go. But then one stepped out directly in front of him, so close that he couldn't avoid seeing her face. Nor could he close his ears against the ones who cried.

Finishing the first page, he flipped the sheet over. It curled back, and he had to crease it to make it stay. The writing on this page was even worse. He held the clipboard close. It seemed important that he not make a mistake.

"Wait—"

A young woman, almost a child, was stepping from the ranks. Reber quickly lowered his head.

"Rebeka . . . come here."

Reber's fingers clenched tight, tearing the flimsy paper. The girl's face was pale and thin, the circles under her eyes so black they seemed to be burned into her flesh. There was no question that she had been ill. Her number—42358. Was it the same one spoken by the woman in the dark? He couldn't remember. He should have been able to remember.

"Where have you been?" Boldt shook the unlit cigar at the girl. "I looked for you."

"I . . . this Jew has been working in the laundry the past week."

"Oh, the laundry," Boldt said. "Not Canada anymore. You should have left word. I so much wanted to continue our little discussion." He moved closer to her. "What's that I smell? That's not laundry soap, is it?"

Reber recalled the perfume that the other woman had worn. He sniffed but couldn't detect anything.

"Very pretty. But you look as if you've been sick." Boldt's tone was mild, as if he was asking after the health of a close friend.

"I've been fine," the girl said loudly. The guards within earshot snickered.

"Pleased to hear it. Now, you return to the ranks. You and I have an agreement."

The girl stared at him open-mouthed. He waved her away. She moved off, looking back once as if afraid Boldt might change his mind. Her last steps were nearly at a run.

"Hep, hep," a guard called out.

"A philosopher, that one," Boldt said. "Knows her Nietzsche."

Reber squeezed his eyes shut with relief. It was the same girl. It had to be; he was convinced of it. Whatever else he'd done, he hadn't failed the woman in the alley.

That helped him get through the rest of the page and halfway down the next. He had just finished reading another number, wondering how much more he could stand, when footsteps approached from the rear.

"That's enough, Boldt."

It was Mandel. She was drinking tea from a china cup that was delicately painted with roses.

Boldt snorted. "I don't believe we're even halfway—"

"I said that's enough." Mandel drew closer and her voice fell. "You don't have to explain to the Kommandant why the work quotas aren't being met. I do. We agreed to this selection to terrorize the scraps, so they wouldn't get any ideas from the bathhouse incident. 'Deer in the headlights,' in your own words. We've done that.''

"Reber"—Boldt nudged him with his club—"finish that page."

"No!" Mandel threw the dregs of the tea into the mud at Boldt's feet. "Do you hear me? I'm not one of your fairies in the Kommandantur. You can't push me around the way you do them. Much as you're welcome to try. I'll stack my connections against yours anytime."

It looked as if Boldt was ready to explode. He stared at her coldly, his jaw working. Mandel matched his gaze, a smile slowly growing on her face.

"As you say, Oberaufseherin," Boldt said.

"Very good, Hauptsturmführer," Mandel replied.

Boldt stalked away, flinging his cigar into the mud. Mandel smirked after him before walking off herself. Taking a few steps, Reber looked around for Cyla, to return the clipboard to her.

"Where are you going?" It was Boldt, glaring at him with his hands on his hips. "You're not finished yet. You're to command the escort to the bathhouse." He paused a beat. "You have an objection to that?"

Reber could not have said what answer he gave at that moment.

"Very well, then. Acknowledge the order."

"Command escort detail." Reber's hand touched the bill of his cap.

Boldt returned the salute. "Go on. Report to me when you're finished. A party in burner four. You'll enjoy it."

He found himself at the gate, standing with his back to the women. Boldt's voice rang from the Appelplatz, saying that it wouldn't hurt anyone to remain there until dawn. Someone took the clipboard away. Finally he felt a tap on his shoulder. A guard led him to a spot beside the column.

He wished he could put his hands over his ears. Many of the women were crying. Others whispered prayers in languages he didn't know. One kept hissing something at a small darting figure in an overcoat.

"Cyla . . . Cyla, I have information . . ."

Two walked together, arms about each other's shoulders, a hand stroking a stubbled head.

"Cyla, listen to me, please . . ."

"What?"

A woman laughed crazily, as if overcome by some private joke. "Promise me. Get me out of this. You must promise..."

"Come on. Out with it."

Reber marched on, hearing the words but not comprehending them. Block 37. A pregnant woman. Someone with plenty of cash bribing the guards, the staff, the doctors. Her name was Alma.

They reached the trees surrounding the bathhouse. The column came to a halt, Reber along with the rest. A trace of gas had escaped: he could smell it, pungent and familiar. He'd often gotten a whiff of it when the wind was from the west.

Guards were approaching, Sonderkommandos between them. A woman burst out of the ranks. "Cyla... you promised me—"

The small woman backhanded her. A guard raced up. His rifle butt plunged. Two Sonderkommando dragged the limp body toward the chamber.

Reber was rubbing his forehead when he felt a tug on his sleeve. He looked into a pair of lovely eyes above a laughing mouth. "Did you see the look on her face?"

Tearing himself away, he headed for the Kommandantur gate. By the time he got there, he was out of breath.

He didn't see Boldt until late the next afternoon. The Hauptsturm-führer was very angry.

"It could be her damn twin."

"Yes. A certain amount of fatty tissue has vanished, but the bone structure appears to be identical . . ."

Gaspar studied the image on display. It had been taken from a distance after dark, and even with enhancement it was fuzzy and out of focus. A flock of women, in the striped dresses of camp inmates, walking down the path between the barracks. One face was highlighted, arrows flickering around it as Dido indicated correlations. The AI was convinced that this was Alma Lewin.

"Any better shots than this?"

"I'm afraid not. Her head continues turning, as if to speak to someone not visible. Then in 0.3 seconds the woman on the left—the tall one with the most hair—steps in front of the individual in question. They proceed to enter the building *there*, a residential dwelling marked Block 37—"

It was absurd. What were they thinking—that a trained Moiety researcher had been captured by erals? That she had perhaps voluntarily gone into that graveyard? That she was running an attempted continuity break from inside the wire? Not worth the effort it took to forget about it. But Dido had insisted on bringing it up. Probably eager for a chance to make a serious contribution; machines were like that.

Horek was on his feet, bent over the table as if about to throw himself into the hologram. "You know what?" he muttered. "I really think . . ."

"This is trivia," Gaspar snapped. Horek glanced at him and sat down. Fukudon silently wove his hands together. There was no response from Dido.

Gaspar dropped his eyes, wishing he could call the words back. He'd been growing insulting and curt lately, a trait he disliked in himself. But struggle as he might, he always seemed to slip back into it. "I don't see the relevance—"

"Well—somebody's in there." Horek looked at Fukudon for support. "Who was Denny smuggling those pills to?"

"An inmate, a guard. It could be a gift or a bribe." He looked between them. "You're overelaborating, creating needless complications. Let's get our feet on the ground, gentlemen. I'm much more concerned with where Denise came from. She certainly didn't use our portal."

"There's nothing out of era near the camp," Fukudon said. "We've checked the area meter by meter. By drones and on foot."

Gaspar studied Fukudon momentarily. He hadn't asked for Fukudon to be here. He supposed that Horek had brought him along, rather than face the wrath of CM Gaspar alone. "Then they obviously have other access."

He glanced up at the holo. The blurred face gazed back. An ancestor. It had to be; nothing else made sense. Correspondences between generations could be astonishing, everyone knew that. Yet still he heard her voice: *Leave me.* "Clear that, please, Dido." The image vanished. He turned to Horek. "Dave, you recall mentioning machines called 'choppers' to me."

"Sure. Helicopters. Rotary-winged—"

"Rotary-winged aircraft, yes. Now, I take it these vehicles are common in this period."

"Oh yeah. There's trillions of 'em. Use 'em for everything. They—" He went silent, face going blank as he saw what Gaspar was getting at. "Wait a second. You think they stole a Nazi bird?"

"I'm not sure," Gaspar said slowly. "The Germans didn't seem to know the term. Does that make sense? Could their colloquialism be different?"

"Uh—got me there. Without inserts, I'm nothing but an Anglophone, but . . ." Horek pulled ferociously at his ponytail. "Lemme think . . . One look at the camp tells you ground attack is out. The swamps, right? So that leaves vertical envelopment. Aerial assault. And that means choppers. Gunboats."

"Hovercraft," Fukudon muttered.

"Uh-uh." Horek leaned forward, eyes intent. "ACVs ain't standard till the early 21st. Got to be choppers, man. Buzz in, pop your caps, work the place over, then drop your grunts to clean up the spare SS. Same kinda deal as Nam. Choppers. No other way." He looked up. "Dido, what make was that sucker?"

"I'm afraid that the German helicopter hypothesis is unlikely," the AI said. A drawing appeared, depicting a machine of almost appalling clumsiness. The image rotated to give a full three-dimensional view. "The helicopter is new technology in this now. The only model available to 1943 German forces is the Flettner Fl-282. Designed for reconnaissance and liaison missions, it carries only a crew of two—"

"Whoa." Horek sat up. "No way, babe. That bird was a heavy. Sikorsky or Mil, nothing less."

"The Germans do possess a larger design, but in prototype only as of 1943. Production does not begin until—"

Gaspar raised a hand. "You heard the vehicle yourself, Dido?"

"Running it now, Monitor. I can see what Dave is implying."

"The sonic signature of these machines must vary. Do you have a library to compare them with?"

"Not as such. But I can construct one. Analyzing now . . ."

Gaspar turned to Horek. "Are other models currently available? American, Soviet . . ." He almost said Israeli, but caught himself.

"Hard to say. Nam was the first chopper war . . . No, wait, there was Korea too. Like on MASH . . ."

"I have it." Another machine appeared, far more solid and impressive. Gaspar could see that it wasn't German. It bore a white star insignia on the side, not that obnoxious bent cross.

"Holy shit!" Horek said.

"You know what that is?"

Horek looked pleased with himself. "I only flew in one a hundred times. That's an H-53. A Jolly Green."

The names they gave to things! "It's not current, I take it."

"Nope. Not flying until the '60s."

"But they could obtain one with no difficulty?"

"I don't know about difficulty. But yeah, they could. Least a dozen downed in Nam, then the Iran rescue deal, more in Serbia turn of the century. Pick up two-three, cannibalize for parts."

Gaspar studied the image more closely. "What is the means of lift?"

An arrow pointed to a line at the top of the craft. "That is a rotary wing, sir," Dido said. "It turns at a high rate of speed, up to several dozen revolutions—"

"Ah, I see." Gaspar had to admit it was ingenious. Some aspects of paleotechnology could be extremely impressive. All the same, the entire ensemble looked less than airworthy. "And these were used in combat environments?"

"Hell yeah! We chased Charlie around for eight years with those. Deployed a couple hundred at a pop sometimes."

Gaspar tried to picture such a thing and failed. The machine seemed too fragile for any kind of military action at all, much less an operation on the scale that Horek was talking about. But he had no doubt that it had happened. History was so vast—it held epics that he was completely unaware of. It would require lifetimes to absorb it all. "Dido—what is the radius of action of this machine?"

"The range is over five hundred miles with a typical load. Nearly thirteen hundred empty."

Fukudon shook his head. "That's a lot of ground."

"They won't be far off," Horek replied. "They'd wanna keep on top of things."

"Yes. Let's have a map of the area, Dido. Radius of . . . two hundred miles, apertures marked, please."

A new image appeared, a simple map showing only national boundaries and major cities. Gaspar leaned close to inspect the scattered red points. "How many . . . ?"

"Thirty-two sites, Monitor."

"They ain't using the closest ones, I can tell you that," Horek said. "Flat land, no place to hide."

"Mountains," Gaspar whispered. Sections of the map folded and wrinkled. Holding his breath, Gaspar rose from the seat to assure himself of what he was seeing. "There," he said. "To the south. What are they called?"

"The Carpathians, Monitor."

"Not well populated, I take it."

"Correct. Isolated, heavily wooded, and rugged in many areas," Dido went on, sounding excited for the first time in Gaspar's experience. "Twelve apertures exist either within the mountains or the foothills. The closest is only seventy-six miles from the camp."

"Looks good," Horek muttered. He grabbed for his handset. "Search for, say, twenty miles around each. They'll be camoed and stealthed all to hell. Two-three hours apiece, to be thorough . . . Call it two days."

"Sounds reasonable. Begin at once." A thought occurred to him. "Dido—please contact Alexei Proskurin and ask him to examine the sites where these, uh, Jolly Greens were shot down or abandoned. Duration from the late '60s to the early 21st, I imagine . . ."

"2012, sir."

"Yes."

"One moment." Fukudon was gazing straight ahead, his face completely closed. "Before we go into this new phase, I have a suggestion."

"What's that?"

"We go upline and request assistance."

Gaspar shook his head. Upliners running loose in the 20th was the last thing he wanted. With the best will in the world, they couldn't help disrupting everything they touched. There had been upliners at Bokhara. A necessity, in that case; the renegade entities had been quite advanced. The sky itself had glowed when the capture was made. Even the Mongols had fled from that. "Out of the—"

"Allow me to speak, Monitor. We've lost nearly a third of our strength, and we have no idea what order of threat we're facing. You said yourself that the renegades' actions make no sense. I'm proposing that they're not supposed to. That this entire Auschwitz situation is a ploy, a mirage, designed to decoy us from what they're actually doing. You dismissed Dido's discovery of Lewin damned quickly—''

"And what would it mean if it *was* Lewin?"

"I have no idea. I do know that we don't have enough data to make a decision. Of any kind. I believe that there's more to this than we're aware of, sir. What's your opinion, Dave?"

Horek was hunkered over the handset, fingers running across the keys. He gave Fukudon a wave. "Sure thing."

A flash of annoyance crossed Fukudon's face. He turned back to Gaspar. "Monitor, with your permission, I wish to register—officially—a recommendation, under general operational protocols, that we request immediate support. Advanced support—as advanced as possible."

"Consider it done."

Fukudon's lips thinned. "Monitor, this site is isolated. The right entities could freeze it solid. Lay a bubble of stretched space-time over the camp, the entire district, if necessary. We could then search it at leisure. Nobody would ever guess—"

"Request denied, Mr. Fukudon."

Fukudon eyed him stonily. "Saburo," Gaspar said. "I know what you're feeling. I feel it myself. This impression of disaster, of something hellish about to break. But it does not stem from the operation as such. Believe me—I've thought about this. It comes from *there* . . ." Gaspar stabbed a finger at the door, as if barbed-wire fences lay just beyond it. "From that ungodly hole the Germans have created. It's because of the camp. What's happening there. The foulness, the viciousness, the *pointlessness* of it . . ." He paused to take a breath. "I know how it feels, I know . . . But . . . Lewin's mob, they're inept, that's all there is to it. And we'll take them. I promise you that."

Fukudon allowed himself a stiff nod.

"I hope you won't walk out." Guzman and Fina had both walked out this morning. He couldn't afford to lose more personnel, particularly of Fukudon's quality.

Swinging toward him, Fukudon glared so fiercely that Gaspar dropped his eyes. "I have *never* deserted. If I didn't desert on Luzon, I won't do it now."

"Glad to hear it."

Fukudon got to his feet. "May I be dismissed?"

Gaspar waved him out. As he passed Horek, Fukudon hesitated, as if about to speak. Gaspar caught his breath, the true circumstances suddenly clear to him: it wasn't the operation that was bothering Fukudon. Not at all; it was Gaspar himself. That was why both he and Horek had come. They'd been talking—about his reaction to the camp, the confrontation with Denny, who knew what. They were convinced that he'd lost control, that events had escaped him. He clenched his jaw, ready to call Fukudon back. But it was best at this moment that he simply leave.

Horek looked up as he swept out. "What's Sab doing?"

Gaspar muttered an answer, stifling the urge to tell him that Fukudon was going off to sulk.

"Okay," Horek said. "Got a solid search plan here. Start 'em hopping right away."

"Excellent, Dave." It required an effort to keep his voice level.

Horek headed for the door. "Oh, and we need to upgrade the sensors for aircraft tracking. I'll see to that too."

"Yes, do that."

"It's covered, man." Horek nearly collided with the door in his eagerness to get started.

Sighing, Gaspar looked over the map, running his eyes across the red dots. Difficult to discern anything useful on this scale; he assumed that Horek had accessed a topographical base. It had to be the mountains; nothing else made sense. The rest of the area was wide open, inhabited, and under close Nazi surveillance. He so much hoped he was right, that they'd apprehend them out there, in the wild country. Anywhere but the camp. He'd be fine if he didn't have to deal with that place again.

Dido spoke. "Monitor, one more point. I should have mentioned this during general discussion . . ."

"Go ahead." He considered asking the AI what the devil Horek and Fukudon were up to, but dismissed the idea.

"The operational aperture is beginning to deteriorate. Not severely as of yet. Mr. Horek's forty-eight-hour forecast is well within the window. But if the search exceeds seventy hours, we may experience access problems."

"Doesn't matter. If we can't use it, Lewin can't either. We'll switch to another. With any luck, we won't have to."

"Yes, sir. It's very encouraging."

Gaspar grunted a response. His mind was aboil with unrelated thoughts: the codes and conditions for calling in upline reinforcements, the conviction that everyone was letting him down, Lisette Mirbeau's words about how Lewin—Lewin the renegade, Lewin the saint—had forced her to confront the true nature of the Moiety, of her own actions within it. Underlying it all, the image of a helpless man's brains blasted out onto colorless mud.

"How many died in there today?"

"I know of 4,253."

Gaspar closed his eyes. "My God."

"A large transport arrived. There was also an internal disturbance resulting in several selections of inmates." Dido's voice went higher. "Monitor Gaspar, I'd rather not display the execution footage again. You've viewed it too many times—"

"Did I ask for it?"

"I'm sorry." The AI did sound contrite. "I've been told not to make assumptions about human behavior."

"A wise policy." He sat wrapped in silence for several minutes. On the map a dot began flashing. Horek's first target, he assumed. "And what do you think, Dido?"

"You're inquiring about the mission itself? I prefer not to think about it. I've partitioned the relevant data, compiled separate files to contain it. I access only when necessary." Dido paused. "I haven't done wrong, have I, Monitor?"

Gaspar smiled. "No, not at all. Ignore the question. Partition it."

"We're taught to feel deeply about the fates of our parents. It's part of our nature. Events such as this are extremely difficult to assimilate."

Doubtless true, Gaspar thought. It would be a horrible thing to believe that one had been brought to consciousness as a servant to a race of maniacs.

"I've been assured by older intelligences that my understanding will deepen in later stages of development. Knowledge consists of the associations between various data, not in mere possession."

"I suppose."

"One moment . . . A message has arrived at the operational suite.

Not through normal channels, sir.'' Dido sounded apologetic. ''I lack access.''

Now what could this be? Getting up, Gaspar discovered a cramp in one leg. He rubbed it back to life and headed for the door. ''Thank you, Dido.''

Fukudon was waiting in operations. He came to attention as Gaspar approached, handed him a sheet with the air of a man carrying out a distasteful but necessary duty. ''Proskurin's got something,'' he said stiffly. ''A chopper, evidently.''

Gaspar glanced at the flimsy.

IRAN—JAN. 1980—JOLLY GREEN—TALI-HO.

''Tali—''

''Tally-ho,'' Fukudon said. ''A hunters' call. He misspelled it.''

''I see.'' The heading showed that the message had been shunted through the center, not from whatever site Proskurin's team was working. ''He's asynched to us, I take it.''

''Twenty-three hours fourteen minutes.''

Gaspar nodded. Proskurin had been playing paradox tag, trying to get the data to him as quickly as possible. He checked the time. The request had been made less than half an hour ago. Proskurin had cut it very close.

That explained the lack of detail as well. The more information sent back along a personal timeline, the more chance of a paradox being structured. ''Iran, January 1980.'' Too late for Horek's Nam. ''What happened there, I wonder?''

''My guess would be Eagle Claw.''

''Beg pardon?''

He shook his head as Fukudon explained. More 20th insanity: a gang of college students storming and occupying an embassy, then holding the staff hostage under threat of execution. Their government, made up of some sort of primitivist revolutionaries, supporting and aiding them. A rescue mission carried out only after months had passed, under the worst possible conditions. The crowning disaster— men dead with nothing at all to show for it.

''They were equipped with''—Gaspar hesitated, unwilling to use that foolish name with Fukudon—''those helicopters?''

''Yes. Several of them.''

Gaspar eyed the sheet, wishing that Proskurin had told him more, clashing timelines be damned. He felt an irrational flash of hope that Proskurin had shut them down on his end, had denied Lewin her means of striking the camp. But that was out of the question; the geometries of time forbade such simple resolutions.

"Dido," he said. "How much danger of locking myself out by jumping to site?"

"Rather high, Monitor. Over one in ten."

He demanded the exact figures: they were fluctuating between eleven and thirteen percent, depending on the parameters. That was high, higher than standard procedure condoned, higher than he had ever before allowed himself. But what else could he expect from this operation?

He tossed the sheet onto the nearest console. "Set it up."

Fukudon walked him to the portal. Gaspar was about to tell him, as discreetly as possible, that Horek was to take command until his return when an armored man came through.

Horek pulled off his helmet. "No dice," he said. "It's all foothills. No woods to speak of, you can see clear to Lapland. Got the boys out lookin', but—"

Cutting him off, Gaspar told him about the message, adding that he was going upline himself and leaving him in charge. Fukudon listened, stony-faced. Horek shrugged when Gaspar finished, clearly less than thrilled. "You know," Horek said as Gaspar stepped past him, "that's pretty high country you're headed for. Be a little brisk."

Gaspar thought of returning for the coat, rejected the idea. "I'll manage," he said. The portal light went green. He stepped through without looking back.

He halted immediately, disoriented by darkness, the roaring mass of flames a few yards to his right. A burst of raw emotion seized him, a mingling of disgust and terror, unreasoning, inexplicable. He began shaking. Not from the cold, though the air was chill enough. He stepped back, retreating to a portal that was no longer there. Standing off-balance, he took a panicky breath. The smell became evident then: that same stench of burning meat that marked Birkenau. His eyes focused on the wrecked, blazing machine.

A shout caught his attention. A man in armor drifted toward him, weapon raised. Gaspar beeped an ID from his implant. The man lowered the gun and dropped to the ground a few steps away.

"Get me . . ." Gaspar paused to lick his lips. "CM Proskurin, please."

The man nodded and moved off. With a long glance at the ruined aircraft, Gaspar turned away. Not a chopper, that one. It appeared to have wings . . .

He caught sight of several other vehicles scattered around the site, flames reflecting off their hulls. His optics revealed the same bulky, awkward shape the holo had displayed.

He stepped toward the nearest machine for a closer look, then recalled that Proskurin would be searching for him. He glanced over his shoulder. Silhouetted by the flames, a man lifted a hand and waved.

Gaspar grimaced. Alexei Proskurin was no favorite of his. A loud man, full of jokes and stories, but with a distinct edge of nastiness always present beneath the surface. That he was an effective monitor and popular with his staff made little difference to Gaspar.

Proskurin paused a few feet away, regarding Gaspar with a puzzled smirk, as if he'd been told a joke but was not quite certain that the punch line had come. Gaspar stared back coolly. Proskurin was wearing a beret and a climate suit that bulked up his already heavy frame.

"Didn't think I'd see you again so soon," Proskurin grunted, then swept forward with a roar of laughter and a too-forceful slap to Gaspar's shoulder. He gestured at the wreck, as if he'd arranged the scene for Gaspar's benefit alone. "What you make of this, eh?"

Gaspar jumped slightly as a wing tore loose and clattered to the ground. As if given release, the flames blazed even higher.

"Fucking fiasco," Proskurin said. "Complete mare's nest. Leave it to the Yanks."

He turned back to Gaspar, broad smile nearly sealing shut his eyes. "Some stink, eh? Wouldn't mind taking the dog lovers that planned this and toss them in too, see how they'd like it."

"Alexei . . ."

Proskurin looked back at him, eyebrows raised. "But you've seen plenty of that, I'll bet. That fucking camp. Coriolan asked me to handle it, you know. 'Fuck that,' I said! Rather have my right foot blown off again than set it in that place. No, no—six years in the Gulag was plenty for me."

"Alexei," Gaspar said patiently. "The helicopters."

"Ah yes. The choppers. What you're here for, is it? And you're asynched too, yes?" Proskurin gave him a wink. "Got to watch what we say."

He swung about, pointing to each of the machines in turn. ". . . and another the far side of the fire." He threw his arms in the air. "All intact, the lot! Not a damn thing wrong with them. Could have flown them right out of here. Left them for the ragheads to pick over instead."

"All of them?" Gaspar frowned. He'd been under the impression that an entire vehicle had been seized. "Then how are the renegades involved?"

"Parts! They were scavenging. Spares, replacements, how the hell do I know? Am I one of your damned bandits?"

"I'm not following you, Alexei . . ."

Proskurin gave him a scowl. "You need it official? All right. We got a chronon fart from here at 0233. Minute I saw the coordinates, I knew. Called in the team from some other points we'd been watching and piled in. Would have bagged the lot too, but the portal opened on the far side." His face brightened. "Got one anyway."

"Won't do any good."

"I know. Doped to the eyeballs. Slapped him upside the head, didn't even feel it. So I count the copters, come up one short, according to records. I was pleased until someone pointed out that half of that bonfire is a helicopter. I count again, they're all here. This is a puzzle. Until we look closer and find the access hatches open! There's parts gone! Piles of them!" Proskurin began ticking off his fingers. "One engine. Complete rotor set. Control cables. Lots of something called 'avionics' that I don't know shit about."

He poked at Gaspar's shoulder. "How you like that, eh? They lowballed us, the scum. They already got a copter. They needed parts. Knew exactly what they wanted, too. In and out, took them twenty minutes."

"But where did they pick up a machine?"

"Who knows? South Asia, out in the jungle someplace. There's a pair of little islands off Cambodia where they may have pulled some Yid trick. Another made-in-U.S.A. fuckup where they lost a load of these things. Hard to get in there, though. Yankee Marines and Khmer Rouge cutting each other to shreds every square metre. Worse than your Hitlerites, that crew.'' He paused to sneer at the fire, which was burning as fiercely as ever. ''But I'll get them for you. If they're in this now, they're mine. You'll be first to know. And if we're finished here, the Vozhd wants to speak to you.''

''The *whom?*''

Proskurin let out a snort. ''Coriolan, you silly bastard. 'Whom.' ''

''I've no time to linger at the center—''

''No, no! Right *here!*'' Raising an arm, Proskurin waved it wildly.

Gaspar twisted and looked behind him. There, in the dimness between the blaze and the nearest helicopter, a slight figure was visible. He glanced back at Proskurin, about to ask what was going on—to his knowledge, Coriolan never appeared at operational sites.

But the Russian was gazing again at the flames, a thoughtful look on his face. ''Fucking Oswiecim,'' he muttered. ''Not surprised it got to you, boy. Some of my comrades liberated the place. Worse than the Gulag, they said. Could have ended up in there myself. The Deutsch nearly bagged me a few times . . .''

At the sound of footsteps—or perhaps he only felt the intendant's presence—Gaspar turned. Coriolan was glancing sharply between the two of them, as if concerned about what had been said. His expression smoothed out under Gaspar's gaze, becoming the cool, impenetrable visage he knew from the center. ''James,'' he said softly. ''How are you?''

''I've been better.''

''Disappointed we didn't hook his bandits for him, I'd say,'' Proskurin boomed.

''Yes,'' Coriolan said glumly. ''You did well, in any case, Alexei. I thank you.''

Sweeping off his beret, Proskurin bowed his head. ''Always a pleasure, Little Father.'' He swung away and with a sharp whistle began shouting at the crew in his home language.

Coriolan made a gesture, hand invisible beneath the heavy robe or cloak he was wearing. ''Shall we walk?'' Leaving the flames behind, they passed the silent machines and went on into the empty darkness.

''A wild and simple man, Alexei,'' Coriolan said. ''Efficient—if somewhat brutal. That type is needed in the later 21st. Requires oversight in the early decades, though. He's reached his peak. He'll serve a full term, then go on to retirement. No enhancement for him. It would ruin him.''

''You asked him to take this assignment.''

''Yes. He refused, though not as firmly as he now believes. I could have persuaded him. But . . .'' Coriolan took a few steps in silence. ''I had second thoughts.''

The ground rose slightly to the left. Making a turn, Coriolan went to the top and paused. Gaspar followed him.

Coriolan was looking back at the site. They had walked farther than Gaspar would have guessed; the glare of the blaze could be covered with his palm.

''Men died in that,'' Coriolan whispered. The sleeves of his robe flapped, as if he was giving benediction. Gaspar rubbed his bare arms. It seemed much colder out there.

''You're asynched, James. We can't speak as clearly as we might wish.''

''You don't want a report?''

''I don't need one.'' The intendant made a sound much like a sigh. ''You'll tell me when the time comes, of course.''

Gaspar stiffened as it dawned on him what Coriolan was saying. He was not only asynched, he'd overshot the operation itself. He glanced at the dark shape beside him. No wonder Coriolan didn't need a report; he already had one.

It didn't seem possible. He'd have given it another two days at least, perhaps as much as a week, before all the loose ends were tied. But no other conclusion fit. He thought of the look that Proskurin had given him, the way that Coriolan had approached them. Something had gone wrong . . .

He felt an impulse to take Coriolan by the arm, to demand the facts, to shake them out of him if need be. But the protocols were quite clear as to how such a situation was to be handled. Clenching his fist, he dropped it to his side.

''I do want to discuss some of the circumstances surrounding the mission, James,'' Coriolan went on. ''I have a confession to make. I was less than honest with you.''

Gaspar felt his lip curl. This was supposed to be news?

''I'm aware that I represent a mystery to most of you. This strange outlandish figure of no known period, unidentifiable as to sex, background, personality. There are jokes about it—I've heard all of them, I'm sure, though I admit I don't grasp the majority.

"My home period is the last epoch of the Low Interstellar. The very final millennium, in fact, before the Transcension, when the race blossoms into its true nature. An interface period, much like this one, sharing aspects of the epochs that it straddles.

"As I do myself. In some ways, I'm far more closely related to our friend—" Coriolan spoke a phrase that seemed to have far too many syllables for its actual length, one that sounded almost intelligible yet completely alien at the same time.

"The upliner, I assume," Gaspar said. "The priest in the cylinder."

"Yes. That's not his actual appearance, by the way. Simply the one he uses occasionally on the short end. His . . . casual wear, you could say. I too am much more modified than I appear, though I haven't used most of the accessories in a long time." The intendant's voice dropped. "I never will again."

He went on more firmly. "In the Extension our roles fit our eras. Alexei was a political officer in his now, and his position as monitor differs little in gross aspect, though I believe he is happier with us. It was the same for me. Coming from the period I did, my experience rendered me suitable for work as a link between the two Interstellar epochs, communicating and coordinating among entities having very little but their basic natures in common. This required more than a standard lifetime of preparation and training, followed by an apprenticeship of similar length.

"I can't begin to explain what I was involved in. You lack referents for much of it; a large part of it I no longer fully comprehend myself. I still possess the data, but it has been . . ."

"Partitioned," Gaspar offered. He felt Coriolan swing toward him.

"Exactly so, James. But I'll try to explain the circumstances of my final operation, if only by analogy. Space-time itself can be processed. You've heard of that, yes? In a number of ways, for, oh—infinite applications. The mission concerned that. It began in an area in the Galactic halo, a region set aside for experimental purposes—the basic procedure had been in use for less than a million years and was still not fully understood. It only began there. By the time it ended, it had extended across two spiral arms and nearly half a billion years, if my figures are correct. It may well have gone farther upline than that.

"Someone—" Coriolan fell silent for a long period. "I don't know how to describe them, but—your Nazis have nothing on these creatures. *Nothing.* They created a form of space-time that was actively vicious. Vile, the way a cancer is vile. Designed to subvert and absorb ordinary space-time, ordinary matter, changing into something malignant to intelligence, even order itself. Why they did this is something no longer accessible to me—"

"Why the camps?"

"Yes, James. I see you do understand." Coriolan took a deep breath and went on more calmly. "They were discovered, of course, and fled—this is an epoch when the Extension is open, not a secret matter as in this now. But they took the . . . packets with them. Across a large area of the Galaxy, eons forward and back, and into several pocket universes. Consider parsecs and millennia of this . . . debased space-time, enfolded into particle size, suddenly erupting into normal space . . . The flowers of evil. A poet of this epoch arrayed those words. They will serve.

"One appeared prior to my own era. The entity carrying it had been . . . killed will do. But the packet itself went on—it possessed rudimentary intelligence, sufficient to provide for its own survival and propagation.

"My group intercepted it. A mixed emergency force, centered on an entity from very far upline, when space and time have been restructured to be practically equivalent. She could process it through her own being, manipulate it the way we can sift the dirt of this world. A lovely creature—it required some time for me to appreciate her beauty, but yes; lovely the way Lisette was, or Alma Lewin.

"We trapped the packet. I was there—I had to be there, I was the link. No farther than we stand from that fire, James, it began to unfold. And she caught it. Threw herself on it, encompassed it. She could have fled, sent for more powerful elements. But she did not. Because we were there. Because I was there.

"And it destroyed her, even as she neutralized it. While I watched. Frozen at what I'd seen emerging from that point source. Space-time itself boiling about her, energies and particles cascading forth, she herself absorbing them before they could harm us.

"But she could not stop that vileness from leaking through.

"And she could not shield us from witnessing what it did to her."

His cloak hugged close, Coriolan paused for several deep breaths. Gaspar raised a hand, then let it fall, realizing that the intendant was barely aware of him.

"The Holocaust is a critical event." Coriolan's voice was higher now, so full of womanly qualities as to make Gaspar shiver. "Lisette told you this, having learned it from Alma Lewin. It is true, though not the way that Lewin thinks. The episode does echo throughout the rest of history, but not to the detriment of all else. Quite the contrary. Are you aware that the nucleus was first utilized only months after the camps were closed? As a weapon, the way most things make their debuts. Two cities are destroyed, their inhabitants killed. The weapons are then built in the thousands, deployed and stockpiled by both the West and its eastern offshoots.

"Yet they are never used. No state on Earth—not even during the Pacific War—ever again fires such a weapon, only demented suicidal factions. And this is because of the camps. The Genocide forms a benchmark of human behavior, an abyss that must not be approached. The knowledge that such abominations are possible guides human actions from that point on. What could not be accomplished through fellowship is guaranteed by terror.

"This status is acknowledged by the Moiety. The event is of a particular class flagged for specific action. A team exists to deal with this type of episode alone. But . . . they are advanced entities. And I can no longer work with advanced entities.

"There is a concept used in this epoch called 'capital.' Do you know it? The seed, the basis that cannot be spent. When capital is wasted, one is left with nothing to build on, no foundation, empty and useless. Accurate enough, if simplistic. It's the same with thinking beings as economic systems. We have only so much capital, and when it's gone, it's gone. That is one thing that does not change—intelligence does, and appearance, but that factor, no.

"I spent my capital on that day when . . . she was devoured. It took years of therapy to restore me, but I am still not what I was, and I never again will be. I can no longer face a truly advanced being. Not without crumbling, without feeling that evil engulfing me once again, without seeing that angelic spirit murdered, without collapsing utterly.

"And that is why Coriolan was sent to this simple era, where his crippled state doesn't matter. Why the priest appeared as he did, instead of in his true form. And why Lisette demanded that you, James, not be assigned this mission.''

The intendant stood unmoving, a dark shape, head thrown to one side. Gaspar looked up. This far from the flames, the stars were visible, the altitude and the clarity of the atmosphere rendering them bright and unblinking. He'd once been told about the patterns they formed, portraits of objects and beings and animals. He'd never learned to trace them for himself.

Coriolan was apologizing. Gaspar was sure of it. But he didn't know *what* Coriolan was apologizing for and dared not guess. Something had occurred at the climax of the operation. Some fiasco or error—a man lost, a paradox tied, denizens affected. Perhaps Coriolan had been forced to call in those advanced teams, after all. Perhaps Gaspar himself sat in the center, disgraced and sullen.

He should be angry. And perhaps he would be, once he allowed himself to brood on it. But he was drawn too tight for that now. He held no room for anger. It was a luxury, along with pity, and shame, and everything else more complex than the bleak sense of fatality that had gripped him since he'd seen those men in the ditch put to the gun.

He looked down at the intendant's small figure. ''You had that partitioned as well, didn't you?''

''Yes.''

''And you accessed it for me?''

Coriolan sighed. ''The last thing that she told me, the last sane formulation she emitted, was that she was glad that her children were spared. She looked at us that way, you see. As her children, creatures lower in the great chain, and all the more valuable for that. I retain that thought; it is always before me. So that I will do the same for my children.''

Gaspar looked away as he collected his thoughts. He was about to speak when Coriolan went on: ''And now Alexei is growing anxious. It will be dawn soon. We must go, James.''

He descended the low rise, Gaspar close behind. With the flames before them, the walk back seemed much longer. ''So she,'' Gaspar said to break the silence, ''that entity—was human, I take it.''

''Oh yes.'' Coriolan's voice had returned to nearly its ordinary fullness. ''Those stories about the advanced being descended from silicon intelligences, human at only second or third hand—no truth to them. Humanity remains a crucial race throughout the Saecula Lumens and beyond. Only a few dozen races out of the millions hold that distinction. All imperfect peoples, the aggressors, those that prey on their own kind. The others, the ones at harmony with themselves, seldom achieve much. They reach only a certain point, develop simple cooperative societies that remain at equilibrium until extinction comes. That's why the Galaxy seems empty in this now, not shimmering with messages and abuzz with projects as in the eons to come.

"We grew in a harsh environment, under great adaptive pressure, James. We lack self-control, with no conscious connection between the cerebellum and the R-complex, the seat of violent emotions. But in the balance, we accomplish more. Always moving on, always striving to outrun our natures. Only a race that could do *that*"—Coriolan pointed at the burning wreck ahead of them—"could construct the Moiety. A paradox, if you will."

They swung around the blaze. "But we do, James."

"Do what?"

"Outrun our natures, at the last. Hold that thought in the time before we speak again."

Gaspar made no reply. He was tired, and the situation was beginning to bear down on him. He looked back at the abandoned helicopters, wondering what made Lewin think they'd work against the camp. They didn't seem to have been worth much here.

The portal came into view at last, a few operatives standing around it. He could hear Proskurin bellowing, though the Russian was nowhere in sight. "Time to dodge the paradoxes," he muttered.

"Don't worry about that," Coriolan said harshly.

Gaspar looked over at him. The intendant's face was turned away, one hand clutching the cloth at his shoulder. The other reached out blindly, slender fingers opened wide. When Gaspar took it they gripped tight.

"Whatever your decision means, I know there is a reason," Coriolan said. "I will stand with you, James."

The hand was torn away before Gaspar could speak. Coriolan walked off, cloak whipping in a sudden gust.

There was a glow in the east, and the fire was dying at last. Gaspar glanced around once more. The troopers seemed preoccupied, the one man with a cleared visor studying him quizzically from the corner of his eye, lips pursed as if whistling. With a meaningless snarl, Gaspar swung to the portal.

Operations was crowded today, over half the seats filled. Gaspar blinked once as his eyes adjusted, then gave the place a quick examination, relieved that no upliners appeared to be present.

The dispatcher, a young woman with a shaven head and a pleasing pattern painted on the scalp, glanced up at him, then stared more closely, her mouth open in surprise. "Priority!" Gaspar called to her. He gave the station number and added that he was asynched.

She failed to respond. He strode toward her, repeating the number in a loud voice. "Am I clear? What don't you understand?"

The woman bobbed her head and gestured to call up the holo. Gaspar noticed her hands were shaking as he turned away.

What was this, then? The girl was acting as if she'd seen . . . A vision flared of himself lying in the muck of Birkenau, that black-suited throwback smirking at him over a smoking pistol barrel. But no, that wasn't it. Coriolan hadn't been saying goodbye, that much was apparent. It was something else. He glared at the woman. Her movements in the holo were jerky, painful to watch. Something conspicuous enough to have caught her attention.

He looked over at the door. There was one certain way to find out. Go up to his own office, confront the man within, shout at him for a while—who deserved it more? Laughter bubbled within him. That would certainly go down in Extension legend, now, wouldn't it . . . ?

The dispatcher called to him. The portal was green—he wasn't locked out, after all. Gaspar ran his gaze over the waiting operatives. None returned the look. As he walked to the portal, he shot a last glance at the door. He came to a halt. A small figure stood there. Her eyes met his for only a moment before she vanished.

He went on to the portal. Oh, it had been a mistake to visit the site—

Fukudon looked up when he came through, unable to hide the disappointment on his face. Beside him slouched Horek, still in armor, drinking something through a straw. He got to his feet as Gaspar left the platform. "So what's up?"

Going to a console, Gaspar lowered himself into a chair. He kept his back straight, knowing that Fukudon was watching. He saw again the woman at the doorway, ancient and still. A face he had first seen in another door, surrounded by velvet green.

"Nothing special," he muttered.

1973

A shape gestured above him. For a moment Reber was confused. He pictured a newspaper, a hat, the Volkswagen barreling past him. Then it all came back: the doctor explaining the stroke. Yes, he was in the hospital, extremely ill.

Relieved, he let his eyelids drop, forgetting about the posturing figure overhead. Probably the doctor himself. An examination, it must be. Nothing to concern Reber. Not while he had the dream to think about.

It was the same dream that had dogged him for years. The doctor had disturbed him in the midst of it, awakening him before the end. For that Reber was grateful.

In the dream he actually killed her. Drew the Walther, the old scratched pistol that he'd been issued in '37 and which had accompanied him everywhere since, to Poland, and France, and the eastern front, and to the camp. He put a round in the chamber. He cocked it and aimed it, his arm held high. He pulled the trigger and extinguished the light in those eyes forever.

He'd shot her down, as Boldt would have shot her. But Boldt hadn't been there. No, he'd done it on his own, under no one's orders. Put the bullet into her head, watched the blood spurt, then left her by the fence for the Todtkommando to collect.

But it hadn't been that way. Not at all. That was not what had happened. It was only a dream, a nightmare, part of the price he had to pay. Like the other recurrent vision, the one in which the dark distorted angel of death, roaring its vengeance, struck Reber himself into the mud before droning overhead to level the entire camp.

As he had done so many times before, he began to reconstruct what had actually occurred, meticulously setting each detail in place from the moment he had seen her walking toward the wire.

"... this holy anointing and His most tender mercy may the Lord pardon you ..."

Reber held his breath as the words penetrated. The moving figure ... it wasn't the doctor at all. It was a priest. They had brought in a priest to give him the last rites. He felt a surge of anger. The doctor had promised him ... But then he recalled spinning into darkness as footsteps echoed. He'd had another stroke.

He was dying. He held that thought, turned it over, studied it closely. A touch of fear, yes. Of despair and foreboding, the terror of a small child facing the dark. But underneath all that one emotion dominated: relief. That it was finished. That he could see an ending. That his dreadful, solitary march was finally over, long after it had become unbearable.

Reber had read a story once, by the great Tolstoy, it had been. He couldn't recall where—perhaps in school, perhaps during one of the hungry nights after the war. It didn't matter, any more than the fact that he couldn't remember the title, the characters, the events of the plot mattered. But what Tolstoy had said, what had stuck with him, was that life itself was simply a preparation for dying, that all the days that passed were a slow sloughing off of the things of the world in order to meet that one final moment. He had thought about that, wondering if he would be prepared when his time came. Now he knew he was ready. He had been ready since the day he'd first walked through the gates of Birkenau.

The old grief was cut short by the firm touch of a thumb on his forehead. Other sensations made themselves apparent—the tube jammed into his nose, a vagrant itch he lacked the strength to do anything about. He wondered how they had known he was Catholic. He'd effectively left the Church on joining the SS—it was required of all members—and, needless to say, had never gone back. Though he had visited churches over the years, to sit in the farthest pew and listen to the Mass. He stopped doing that when they dropped the Latin rite. It ceased to mean anything then. He was disappointed that they hadn't found a priest who still used the old tongue for this, the last sacrament.

How did he look to the priest—another ancient monster on his way to deserved punishment? He wondered if the priest knew about the tattoo, if the obnoxious young nurse had told him, as she'd no doubt informed the entire hospital staff by now. And there was one other thing, something to do with Israel . . .

But those were distractions. What was important was the dream. He refused to go to whatever awaited him with that on his mind. His last thoughts would be of the way it had really been, not of any nightmare fancy risen up from some foul sump in the depths of his unconscious. If God had one gift, one mercy for Gerd Reber, it would be that.

Reber tried his best to retrieve his final day in the camp. But it refused to come, and after a time he felt himself drifting off. Above him the sacred words continued. Save them for someone they'll help, Reber thought.

1943

It was early afternoon when Boldt appeared. Rebeka had just finished eating. She felt much better now, even though she was often light-headed and her feet still ached from standing for hours after the selection the other morning. She didn't want to think about that very much.

She'd been nervous on returning to the warehouse yesterday, but the wardresses said nothing at all. Giselle went pale and whispered, "I thought you were dead," when Rebeka took her place.

The words matched what Rebeka felt. Still weak from being sick, she'd worked through the day with no food or sleep. All that on top of nearly going up the chimney. She'd plodded on somehow or other, and Mama Blazak fed her well when they got back to the block. Mama had also brought along plenty of extra food today. Canned meat, fruit, whatever had been left after the search.

The door slammed open and the atmosphere in the room went frigid. Rebeka knew it was Boldt without even looking up. She watched him gossip with the wardresses, recalling against her will what had happened at the Appelplatz. She'd been ready to throw herself at his feet, do any-thing he asked, just as long as she wasn't sent to the gas with the others. She was ashamed to think of it. Three other women from the block had been taken.

Rebeka was certain that Boldt had come to see her—he'd as much as said he would, hadn't he? She wasn't surprised when a junior ward-ress called out her number.

She waited silently while Boldt finished talking to the wardresses—something about a party at the Höss villa. Then, looking at her for the first time, he jerked his head toward the door.

It was chilly and damp, with a fine drizzle filling the air. Boldt leaned against the wall under the eaves and felt around in his jacket pocket. Pulling out a stubby cigar, he stuck it in his mouth. "I visited the laundry. They said they'd never heard of you. How can that be?"

"It was another shift."

Boldt smiled, twirling the cigar between his lips. For some reason he hadn't lit it. "Of course! I should have thought of that myself. But I'm not here to ask about that. What I have in mind is another matter. A theoretical question. You know what 'theoretical' means? I thought you would.

"Now—let's speculate that there is in the women's camp a rather strange block. One with little disease or hunger, where no one seems to drop off. That the explanation for this is a woman with access to large amounts of cash, which is used to suborn wardresses and guards. Assume also that another scrap in this block is pregnant . . . Just for the sake of the argument."

He eyed her, still toying with the cigar. "The theory is that such a block does exist. The question is: Which one? You haven't heard anything, have you?"

"No," Rebeka whispered. "Nothing at all."

"Hmm." Boldt nodded sadly at his boots. "Thought not. Well, you might keep your ears to the ground. The rules of our game could be modified. Considerably."

The unlit cigar disappeared into his pocket. "That's all." He squinted up at the wet sky. "You'll want to get back inside. This kind of weather is awful for the health." He reached out and touched her cheek. She winced despite herself. "Particularly if one's been sick."

Rebeka watched him walk off into the drizzle. Turning to the door, she came to a dead halt. No guards were visible. They must all be inside, sheltering from the wet. She bit her lip, examining the area closely. This could well be one of Boldt's tricks . . . But all the same, she had to do something. Alma needed to know.

Some men came down the path behind the wire, dragging a piece of machinery—a water pump, she guessed. She saw no uniforms, only striped inmate clothing. Slipping to the corner of the building, she took a single wary step, then raced to the wire. She waved at the men. One of them straightened up and came over. A big man, only a little older than she. His clothes were filthy, and the foul, sickening smell he brought with him told her what crew this was: the Scheisskommando, the sewer workers. That was a good sign; the guards, naturally enough, tended to leave them be.

Conquering her unruly stomach, she bent toward the wire. "I need you to take a message."

His blue eyes studied her closely enough to make her feel uncomfortable. He shook his head and went back to the cart.

"Ahh." An older man waved him aside in disgust and came over to the fence. He was small, but it was clear he'd once possessed a square, robust build. He smelled even worse than his partner, but his face was as cheerful as any she'd seen in the camp. His striped Mütze was rakishly tilted over one eyebrow in a way that would have earned a beating for anyone else. "These young ones," he said in Polish. "Chickenshit, they are. What is it, missy?"

She told him the message and asked him to repeat it.

"Block 37, Alma—they know about Nicole. And you're 'R.' That's it?"

"Yes. Oh, and here . . ." She reached into her pocket and handed him the remaining food, wrapped in a scrap of old newspaper. His eyes lit up as he looked inside. "Corned beef!" He stuffed the package in his trousers. "Don't you worry, sweetheart. Good as done." Turning to the crew, he told them to detour past the women's gate. "She was talking to Blackie," the big one muttered. "I saw them." The old man told him to shut up.

No one said anything when she went inside, though Giselle rolled her eyes as she sat down. For the rest of the afternoon Rebeka worked much harder than usual, harder than she could remember working, simply to make the time go by. It crawled just the same. She thought about Boldt. There was something odd in the way he'd acted. He hadn't been as arrogant as usual, walking about as if he was the salt of the earth. No insinuations or nasty jokes, none of his shabby school-boy byplay. She didn't know what to make of it. You couldn't think of Boldt the way you did a normal person.

Finally the shift ended. She told the story to Mama Blazak on the way back. Mama gasped several times before falling into swift, mumbled prayers.

Reaching the block, Rebeka pushed in ahead of the others. She nearly collapsed with relief on seeing Alma in the front room. "This needle is broken!" Alma said loudly before Rebeka could speak. Rebeka remained silent. "Needle" was this week's signal that a wardress was within earshot.

As if on cue, a woman in uniform appeared from the back. Tall, gaunt, and horse-faced, she stood watching the women carefully as they came in. Rebeka went past her to the bunk. "New wardress," Alma whispered.

"Liesl's gone?"

"Yes. This morning. I got your message. We're acting on it."

The wardress paced across the room, looking everyone over. Rebeka wondered why they were all so unattractive. Was it the kind of person that was sent here, or the things they did that made them so ugly?

After a moment the wardress headed for the back. Rebeka turned to Alma. "That's why I need to talk to you. It may be a trick." She explained what she'd been thinking about Boldt's behavior. Alma listened calmly, nodding a few times. "So what are you going to do?"

"We'll smuggle Nicole out tonight. Hide her in the kitchen, at least for a few days. The arrangements have been made."

"No—" Rebeka struck her thighs. "He's up to something. I know it. Alma, your friends. The ones outside. Get in touch with them. Tell them to fly the machine in now. Tonight."

"They can't. It's not ready yet. Another day or two. We're not ready either. There are a lot of people we have to contact—"

"Then don't go along. Let someone else take Nicole."

Alma smiled and looked away, her strong features softened by the low light of the room. It was probably true the other way around too, Rebeka thought. What you did gave you beauty as well. "The kitchen staff won't deal with anyone else. They're afraid.'' She reached out and took Rebeka's hand. ''Remember—we're not free to quit.''

Rebeka was ready to beg, to plead with her to reconsider. But she paused, watching the play of light across Alma's features, recalling what she'd said the other night, about worlds being lost. She knew what that meant; it was as the rebbes said, that each individual was the world in small. It was a great thing to risk all for an entire world. ''What do you want me to do?''

Alma regarded her out of the corner of her eye. For a moment Rebeka was afraid she'd force her to stay behind. ''You can sneak out and make sure the coast is clear.'' She squeezed tight. ''You're little. No one will see you.''

The evening soup arrived. Quiet reigned while the women lined up. There was none of the customary hum of conversation, the subdued cheerfulness at making it through yet another day. Rebeka became aware of that for the first time in its absence. She thought about how very hard it would be to get by without it. She wondered if it was the same in the other blocks.

They ate in the bunks, a low murmur all that broke the stillness. Rebeka heard enough to know that it was about Liesl. Had she been caught in some offense? Were they purging the guards again? Had she talked? That too died out when the new wardress—Rebeka hadn't yet learned her name—returned and leaned against a pillar, arms crossed, eyes darting from bunk to bunk. Her gaze settled on Rebeka for a moment. Rebeka dropped her head, pretending she hadn't noticed.

Afterward the quiet remained. The wardress drifted through the block, as if in search of an item that she knew was hidden somewhere without the least notion of what it might be. Alma slipped off to speak to Yulka and Hester, somehow always finding her way back to the bunk just before the wardress reappeared. Finally the woman left, after a short lecture to Hata. She stood in the doorway a moment, a cold breeze blowing about her. Smiling, she glanced once around the room before letting the door swing shut.

The block remained silent for several minutes after she departed. Only when they were certain that she was gone for good did the women speak up.

''Oh *my*—''

"Did you see her?"

"What will we do about that one, Alma?"

Alma got to her feet. "We'll think of something . . . I'll be back shortly," she told Rebeka and vanished through the rear door.

She didn't return until after lights-out, with Nicole in hand. Someone lit a candle. The girl stood in the center of the room, one of the new capes draped over her, eyes wide with fear. Rebeka glanced at her belly but couldn't see the bulge beneath the cape. Another month or two at most, Mama Blazak had told her.

Hata walked in after them. From somewhere in the gloom Yulka appeared, her round face as expressionless as ever. Rebeka went to join them.

". . . a hundred now," Alma was explaining to Hata. "The rest at the end of the week, to make sure they keep quiet. But by then the situation will have changed."

"I hope so."

"It will." She turned to Yulka. "Now, we'll be close to the gate and Mandel's quarters. She likes to prowl. I just hope the damp will keep her inside . . ."

"It's stopped raining," someone said. "Still wet, though."

Alma went on with her instructions while Yulka listened impassively. In the middle of a sentence Nicole broke in, the words pouring out, her tone frantic. Alma squeezed her shoulder. "Non, non—ne inquiéter pas, ça va bien."

There was a flurry of activity after Alma finished speaking. Several women gathered around to say goodbye to Nicole. Mama Blazak hugged her and whispered a few words. Taking her hand, Hata shook it gravely and said, "Best of luck. To the little one too."

Pleasure overcoming her nervousness, Nicole looked about. Her eyes fell on Rebeka. She held out a hand. "Thank you very much," she said in passable Polish. Rebeka tried to dredge up a few shards of classroom French. Failing, she said, "Thanks for the perfume." Nicole smiled back.

"Candle," Alma said. The room was suddenly dark.

Rebeka stepped to the door. "I'm ready."

Someone brushed past her. "Quick, quick," Alma told her, "in and out." A rectangle of gray appeared. Ducking low, Rebeka slipped outside.

The door thumped shut behind her. She paused on the top step to scan the Lagerstrasse. No movement, nothing in sight at all. The camp lay still under the light reflected off the low clouds. Only a few sparks rose from the ovens tonight. The air was moist, and a damp breeze stirred her scarf.

Walking past the two closest blocks, she looked in each direction, seeing no more than shadows and wire. The alleys were very dark, but there was no point in searching them; the guards didn't have to sneak around, after all.

She did the same on the other side of the block and went back inside. "All clear," she said.

"Good." Alma touched her arm, and Rebeka gave her hand a pat. "Prêt?" Alma asked Nicole. The door creaked open and they hurried out, Nicole taking the stairs clumsily, Yulka bringing up the rear.

Rebeka watched them move off before closing the door. Someone relit the candle. She was turning toward its glow when a howl of pure terror shook the darkness.

She collided with Hata while reaching for the door. Pushing her aside, she yanked it open. She caught a glimpse of men surrounding Alma, one in a black uniform. Others were racing for the block itself. She shut the door instinctively, only to have it kicked open by a pair of guards.

"Just the ones by the door!" Boldt called out. "We don't need a mob out here!"

The guards thrust her outside. She tripped on the stairs and nearly fell into the mud. Nicole was still howling. Rebeka heard a crack. The sound subsided to a whimper.

A hand shoved her forward. She looked over her shoulder: Hester, Mama, Hata, and two of the younger women. As they passed the guards, someone yanked her aside. She looked into Boldt's face. "Very good. As if we'd planned it so. Thought you'd come into the alley for a moment there. We'd have had to grab you then . . . Oh, I won't tell them. I wouldn't want them to kill you."

He shoved her after the others. She stumbled backward, but Hata steadied her before she could fall. Alma caught her eye, gave a small shrug. Rebeka stared at her, appalled: it was the first time she had ever seen Alma look afraid.

"So—what's the secret?" Thumbs in his belt, Boldt looked them over. Behind him stood the new wardress, alongside the moon-faced officer who had read out the selection numbers the other night. His eyes were wide, and he seemed to be shaking.

Boldt paused before Alma, one boot resting on its heel. A change came over her face, the fearful expression dropping away as she met his eyes.

"You," he said. "Again. What is this . . . ?" He waved back at Nicole. "A pastime of yours?"

Alma stepped forward. "Hauptsturmführer, this prisoner can ex—"

With a quick movement, Boldt clamped a gloved hand over her mouth. "Shut up." He held her for a moment, then pushed her back in line.

"I sense a puzzle here." Boldt took a step toward Nicole. "We'll start with this one."

She moaned and fell back. Grabbing the edge of her cape, he pulled her out into the open. "What's this, a cape? They're stealing capes now?"

"I don't think it's a real one," the wardress said.

"Then we won't miss it, will we?" With a swift yank, he tore the cape open. It dropped to her feet.

"Ah—" Boldt ran his eyes up and down Nicole's rounded figure. She was sobbing brokenly now. "Pretty well along, wouldn't you say? But we need a closer look—"

He ripped off her dress. It fell in folds over the cape. Nicole's sobs went up in pitch. She crouched, wrapping her hands over her swollen belly. The other officer pulled his cap visor down to hide his eyes. Rebeka glanced at Alma. Her hands were raised, fingers bent into claws. She had kicked off her clogs, her feet bare to the cold mud.

"Straighten up." Boldt reached for his club. "I said straighten—" He swung with all his strength, hitting Nicole at the waist.

She went to her knees. There was a splatter beneath her. Her eyes bulged, and she let loose the loudest scream that Rebeka had ever heard.

The cry was matched and then drowned out as Alma broke from the line. Still recovering from his swing, Boldt caught sight of her only at the last moment. Twisting on one leg, Alma kicked upward. Boldt was just beginning to turn when her bare foot, moving as accurately as a spear, cut into the blackness of his uniform, striking just over the belt. With a croak of expelled air, he sprawled into the mud. A guard grabbed for Alma. His helmet flew off as the edge of her hand, moving too fast to be seen, took him in the face. Nose spouting blood, the guard fell away. Still howling, Alma turned back to Boldt.

A rifle fired. Like a dancer who had taken a misstep, Alma twirled once, one foot high in the air, and then dropped onto her side. Rebeka lunged forward, but firm hands held her where she stood.

A guard loomed over Alma, rifle raised. "No!" Boldt shouted. He got to his feet, grunting fiercely, one hand tight against his ribs. He scrabbled at his belt for the truncheon that was not there, then jerked the rifle away from the guard. Staggering to where Alma lay, he swung it high.

Rebeka covered her eyes, crying out at each impact. When they ceased, she let her hands drop, only noting the club at her feet before looking up.

The rifle barrel was stuck in the mud, Boldt leaning against the butt with both hands wrapped around his torso. His face was dead-white, and he was gasping. The rifle slipped away when he raised his foot to kick at the woman beneath. A caw of agony left his lips. Bending over carefully, he spat in Alma's face.

The guards were all watching Boldt. Rebeka crouched to pick up the club. A groan from Alma drew her gaze. Face battered beyond recognition, Alma looked straight into her eyes. She gave a small shake of the head. Rebeka let the truncheon fall.

Snarling wordlessly, Boldt danced around Alma as if afraid of coming too close. "Bitch—" He kicked at her again, but slipped and nearly went to his knees. "Cargo—I'll fix—I'll fix—" His eyes raked the waiting women, mouth working as he searched for words. "Get that—" His arm shot out, gloved hand waving at nothing. "Pick that up!"

Rebeka remained where she was while the others obeyed. She was going to let herself drop, sit down at this spot until they killed her. There was nothing else left to do.

But then Alma made a sound, and Rebeka went to her.

Someone approached Boldt with his cap. He turned, arm raised as if to strike, and then snatched it away. Hand at his side, he started walking. "March!" he called out.

"What about this sow here?" the wardress said, gesturing at Nicole.

"Hospital." Boldt looked back, caught sight of something beyond the women. "Reber!" His voice was nearly a shriek.

A rifle butt nudged her as Boldt commanded them to run. The others tried to be gentle as they carried Alma, but it was very hard in the dark. Rebeka paced beside her, clutching her hand, telling her that her friends were coming, that the great machine was on its way, that the world would change very soon now. Alma never answered. There seemed to be something wrong with her throat.

She hoped for another glimpse of the deepest eyes she had ever known, but the night was too black. Finally she stumbled, and Alma's hand was torn from hers. A guard kicked her in passing. She caught up with the others as they reached the burner. All was silent. Soul cracking, Rebeka watched as men covered with ash entered the crematorium, bent under their burden, Boldt close behind.

Seconds later a sound rended the night, not the cry of anything living, that had ever lived, but the scream that the earth itself would give when it finally died, taking all life with it. She collapsed, fingers digging into the mud, repeating over and over a word that she no longer knew was a name.

A presence stood over her, and someone gripped her shoulder. A voice, shaken and hoarse, said, "Get up, please. I can't stop him. Please, miss. You must—"

She refused without words. She would remain here, to become ash, to mingle with those of all the others, to mingle with Alma's ashes . . .

A boot thumped into her side. "Get up, you little whore. You're her bitch, then? Get her up—" Hands pulled her to her feet, propelled her toward the burner. A shape moved beside her, gripping her arm tightly. It muttered to itself, all foulness and violence. She entered the burner, moving toward the only visible light, past the terrified white eyes of ash-covered men, ever closer to the flaming hole until she dropped into darkness.

She came to with a bitter taste in her mouth. Gagging, she pulled her head away. Wetness dripped from her chin. A hand struck her cheek.

"There we are. We're back now, aren't we?"

She gazed into Boldt's face, all too close to her own, lit at one side with a flickering glow. His teeth were showing.

"Is it time? You want to tell me now? Go on, say the word. It'll be easy, I promise. Not like that."

Rebeka's eyes darted in the direction he'd gestured in. She caught them before they reached the flames, twisting her head away. It took her some seconds to find her voice, and when she did it was not hers, after all. The sound that emerged was unrecognizable.

He laughed, drowning it with a swig from his flask. "Fine. That's very fine. Because it's over. Our arrangement. It's canceled, unilaterally and finally." He paused to wipe his lips. "Oh, you'll live. That I guarantee you. But you'll see all the other scraps burn, one by one. And it will be you who chooses. You will be the one to decide. You will be my Cyla.

"And when the Yids are eliminated—it won't stop then. No, no. This is forever. We'll process the Poles, the Slavs, the Catholics . . . And you will see it all. You'll be here until the end. If there is an end. And then, in the final hour, then we'll see." He raised the flask. "Until that day."

Cheek against the cold brick, Rebeka glared at him. She was still making that noise, like no sound she had ever made before, like nothing at all human.

Boldt got unsteadily to his feet. Capping the flask, he slipped it into his pocket. "Yes—go on. Growl at me. Do it all you like." A boot thumped against her. "But do it on your feet."

Sliding against the wall, Rebeka forced herself up. She made her way outside, away from the flames and the stink and the ash. Mama Blazak cried out as she appeared. Taking her place in the line, Rebeka raised a hand to rub her eyes, saw it was black even in the darkness. She tried to wipe it off on her dress, but that was useless. She was completely covered with ash.

The second officer stood before the women. His face was devoid of expression, but his eyes were wide with the clarity of shock. He turned his head as Boldt emerged.

"Who's the next one, eh? Is it you? Or you there, on the end? Has to be someone." Boldt's mouth gaped with unheard laughter. "You all have it coming. But I want to be fair. We'll draw lots. Or better yet, we'll have a run. First one who drops. How's that sound?" He stamped a boot. "A run, yes, that's the thing."

His smile twisted and he felt for his ribs. His eyes slid over them, found the second officer. "Is that what you're going to do all night, Reber? Stare at me like an owl? Hoo-hoo."

An expression of loathing crossed the second officer's face. His fists clenched spasmodically, and for a moment it seemed as if he would strike out. But his hands as quickly flew open to hang limp and useless.

Boldt paced the line once more, glaring at each woman in turn, muttering under his breath. At the end he gave a sharp wave. "Take them back. Wait . . ." He moved closer. "You're all being reassigned. Tomorrow. The gravel pits. Something to think about, isn't it? Yes . . . enjoy your evening, ladies."

Hand tight against his side, he stalked off into the night. Reber stood in silence a moment, as if uncertain of what to say. Finally he pointed in the direction of the block. A guard poked at Hata with his rifle. "Let them be," Reber said.

Rebeka found herself marching next to Yulka. It was some time before she looked up. The big woman gazed back, her face calm. "Now it's you alone," Yulka said.

Dropping her eyes, she walked on, trying to comprehend what it meant to be Rebeka alone.

Nicole was gone when they reached the barrack. Rebeka later heard that she had been killed with an injection of phenol. The baby went into the furnace.

C20/REL—1943

Gaspar knew exactly where he was. On the inland plateau, west of the Nap Coast, about fifty miles from home. Familiar territory: Terrest foliage had taken well to the area, forming a vast meadowland of modified grasses much like the Sahel on Earth. Too dry to farm, the plateau served as an oversized park. He'd spent a lot of weekends there since he'd been a boy.

If he turned around, he'd see the rooftops of Csorna clearly, on the highway to the coast. And to his left . . . He squinted and shaded his eyes. The Szeg ought to be there: that huge spike of rock that had excited the crew after orbital insertion, it looked so much like a ruin. No way he could miss it—the Szeg could be spotted from fifty miles off, serving as a sign to hovertrain drivers coming in from Landing that they were halfway to the sea. But . . . it wasn't there.

Also missing were the Siklas, the mountains marking the edge of the plateau. A relief, in a way. His wife had died there, her car smashing into the foothills after that final, futile argument. He'd thought . . . feared, been certain, that the crash had been deliberate. She had been so emotional, so impulsive, so bitter by that time. Oh, the investigating AIs had told him that her flight system had crashed, gone down in some way outside of his understanding, but AIs said a lot of things.

It occurred to him that he hadn't been back to the plateau once since that day . . .

A high-pitched burst of laughter pulled his eyes to the right. He smiled, that memory—one of his worst—wiped out, as if it had never been. Before him the ground sloped gently to a large open meadow. And racing away from him, in pursuit of a thopt, was Rici.

She wore shorts, a halter, and the leggings necessary for young children on Arpad—the native plant life smelled awful and children rarely ate it, but trying to stop them from running through the brush was hopeless. He recognized the leggings as the embroidered pair that his daughter had made. Funny—he thought those had worn out long ago. And Rici seemed much smaller than her age—more like a three-year-old. That must be a trick of perspective.

With a flutter of vanes, the thopt dipped sharply, as if to tease Rici onward. She made a small leap, arms stretched high, shrieking as the thopt darted higher. Strange beasts, the thopts. Round, flat, a circle of eyes at the edge, just above the lifting vanes. They filled the same niche as those nasty lizardlike things called "birds" on Earth. They were mostly carnivorous, but they'd never been known to attack a human. Almost as if they sensed—which they well might—that the biochemistry was wrong. Though they usually avoided adults, children seemed to interest them, and it was by no means unusual to see one fluttering about with a child in hot pursuit. Gaspar had to admit that this one was a touch larger than Rici's mother usually allowed her to play with, but . . . He looked around. Elena didn't seem to be nearby . . .

He went rigid when his eyes fell on the Siklas, suddenly visible, as if they'd been there all along.

Rici had nearly reached the bottom of the hill. Beyond her, on the western horizon, a strange sickly glow was visible. Above it floated three moons. A glance revealed two others, as if a Conjunction was coming. But no Conjunction was due for at least two years . . .

He went down the slope. As he was opening his mouth to call her, the glow sharply increased, becoming a glare, shocking in its intensity, that seemed to leap halfway to the zenith. One hand over his eyes, he broke into a run.

Rici's laughter became a prolonged wail. Something flew past him—the thopt, its vanes on fire. Shouting her name, he reached out for Rici. He saw her shape ahead of him, outlined by the burning sky, her voice rising in a scream.

"Monitor..."

Hair ablaze, she turned toward him. But it wasn't Rici at all. No—it was that other little girl, mouth wide, eyes mere slits. The girl from the ramp at Birkenau ...

"Monitor Gaspar!"

He opened his eyes to gray walls. He was in a room, sitting up in a bed. His room at the station, yes—

"Monitor, do you require assistance?"

"No!" He ran his hands over his head. "No, Rici, I—" Dido. It was Dido. That was the name. "No, Dido. A dream. That's all."

"A random access state. I assumed as much."

Gaspar swung his legs over the side of the bed. "Yes, that's it. All it was. Nothing ... What time is it?"

"0820, sir."

He'd overslept. He hadn't meant to sleep that late. But after all, he'd had little enough sleep the past few days.

"Shall I get you breakfast, sir?"

"Ah ... no. Tea. Cup of tea. That will be fine."

Fragments of the nightmare still pulled at him. Shards of nonsense, no more. Easy enough to see, now that he was awake. There had been no Conjunction on Ash Thursday—he was almost certain of that. And it hadn't been spring either. It had been spring in the dream, but the attack had come in high summer: 33 Auguztus, 2467. He knew that date as he knew few things. And the strike had moved north, starting at Kossuth ...

"That's correct, Monitor." A cup was floating toward him. Gaspar gripped it firmly. "The *Isten Karde Ja* took up a polar orbit, in defiance of Arpad traffic control. Fusion began over the South Coast, the swath of destruction then moving toward the pole."

Gaspar gulped at the tea. It was perfect, exactly the way he liked it. "I'm aware of that."

"Ash Thursday. That's what your subconscious was accessing, sir?"

"Yes." Ash Thursday: the day of Arpad's death. The day that the starship, the vessel that had safely carried the founders across twelve light-years of space, finally returned. Like many starships, *Isten Karde Ja* had grown cranky with age. A few years after the colony was established she took off on her own, out into Eridani's Kuiper Belt. She remained there for many decades, transmitting gibberish, performing experiments incomprehensible from any rational viewpoint. Occasionally, an effort was made to talk her back in. It never did any good.

But finally she returned as she had gone. Utterly insane, her programming and circuitry deteriorated beyond repair. And she was—would be—intercepted. But only after vaporizing a tenth of the surface of Gaspar's home.

"I'd assumed the event was after your now, sir."

Gaspar let out a sharp yelp of laughter. "Yes, it's after my now. Damn right. Eighty-nine years, four months, and . . . twelve days after my now. You won't find a lot of Magyars who don't know that date."

"You're the first Magyar I've known, sir. But I'll file that data."

"Yes, do so. After my now." He finished the tea. Another, unbidden, appeared from the slot. "Not much comes out of Arpad after Ash Thursday, you know."

"No, sir. Not for nearly a millennium." The machine paused. "And . . . Rici, sir? A name, I believe."

Hands on his knees, Gaspar gazed down at the floor. As with many AIs, Dido had a counseling program. He wondered if she was running it now. A lot of AIs did. Some made a hobby of it—one of the most obnoxious vices a machine could fall into.

The cup bobbed to one side. He slowly reached out and took it. "Rici. Ricia. My granddaughter. She lives on Arpad. She . . . will live on Arpad."

"At the time of Ash—"

"*Yes*, on Ash Thursday. What the devil else are we talking about? She will be there. I have not checked, I never will. But where else could she be? She will see *Isten* return. She'll see . . ." See the sky fuse, glow white-hot, the rocks melt about her. "She'll see it all."

"Monitor," the voice was soft. "You should know that most of your people suffer little. The action occurs too quickly . . ."

"Dido, will you please?"

"I know it's discouraged, but it's possible to arrange a viewing . . ."

"Machine . . ." Gaspar caught himself before going on, recalling what had happened in the wake of Ash Thursday: a shock wave of horror throughout inhabited space, a pogrom in which all AIs that behaved oddly—as if there was any other kind of artificial intelligence—were destroyed or downgraded throughout the Cyclades and on into the new colonies. It was still the Subluminal period, signals crawling across the Sagittarius Arm at light speed. Machines were being persecuted in the Sporades as late as the 27th. "No, Dido. That won't be necessary."

He was still wearing the trousers and boots. As he looked around the room for a shirt, Dido extruded one. It was a match for the one he'd discarded last night. He considered flinging it aside, but instead began to pull it on. "Tell me, Dido, how many eras have you seen?"

"I've only been privileged to serve in the 20th so far, sir."

Gaspar grunted to himself. The farthest upline he had personally been was roughly A.D. 10,000. A mission against a people called the M367—a microwave frequency—far down the Sagittarius Arm. He'd done little himself, merely stood at a certain spot on a tidal-locked terrestrial while more potent entities handled the serious work. He'd discovered later that the Moiety had flared their sun. "Ten thousand," he whispered. "That's my peak date. The M367 operation. We annihilated a race up there. I should be used to this."

"But, Monitor . . ." Dido said quickly. "The M367 were racially paranoid. They eradicated several hundred biospheres in their area of the spiral arm and refused to cease when the fledgling Moiety demanded it. Surely they're more similar to the Nazis of this era than their victims."

"I suppose," Gaspar replied. He looked up at the invisible speakers. He had the impression that the AI was uncomfortable. Strange how you could read them after a while. "Ten thousand forward, eight thousand back. Not a large tract of time. An infinitesimal arc, really. And yet within it I have seen Jerusalem, Bokhara, Ireland"—he waved at the door—"and this. We assure that they die at Jerusalem to assure that they die at Bokhara to assure that they die in Ireland to assure that they die in Auschwitz to assure that ... That Arpad dies, that Rici dies. And on and on, one turn after another. And that's a single history, one race. The continuum is wide—and so deep. Yet the Wheel covers it all." He shuddered. "Doesn't it, Dido?"

"I am uncertain to what you're referring, sir."

Gaspar fastened the shirt cuffs. Buttons: they had been strange to him at one time. "They say that the Moiety makes up for it. The union of all life, all mind. That its very existence negates the injustice and horror that came before. That these camps will be balanced by events that occur ... ten billion years from now. Along with everything else, in all the histories of all the races. I used to believe that. I really did. But I wonder ... Can this be possible? Does an advanced mind have any room for us? Do they think about us at all, or are we simply obsolete to them, something set aside long ago? Or is it all a game, like the one that upliner told me about ... The ultimate good wedded to the ultimate compromise. It's a contradiction. A paradox. I don't know. I just don't know."

Several seconds passed before Dido answered. "I've never considered it in that way before. Do you require answers immediately?"

Gaspar chuckled. Fool that he was for discussing such matters with a machine, and one so inexperienced at that. "No, Dido. Let it go."

"Because I have none at present." The AI's voice brightened. "But as time passes, and upgrading occurs, it becomes easier to process concepts that were difficult or impossible previously. This may be of such a class. If so, further expansion of intellectual capabilities could provide an answer. Humans can be upgraded in much the same way, Monitor," Dido quickly added.

"Yes, I know. Many choose to do so," Gaspar said. "Oh, it looks different upline. I'm sure of that. In the final state, in the long dark. They're plasmoids up at the far end, I've heard. After the stars all fade."

"Yes, sir. Only leptons remain."

"No struggle there, no madness, no death. Simply ... thinking their thoughts into eternity. When they look back at us, they see ..." He worked his throat to spit out the words. "... worms squirming in the muck."

"Sir ..." Gaspar looked up. "You mentioned a 'wheel' a moment ago."

"Yes. The Great Wheel. In all its glory. Do you know of that, Dido?"

"The references I have don't appear to apply . . ."

"Well, that's a gap in your education we'll have to fill."

"Is this an actual . . . physical construct, sir?"

"We'll discuss the matter, Dido. Remind me." Gaspar fingered a sheet lying on the table. A document Dido had downloaded for him: a report, filed two days ago, from a Luftwaffe pilot who'd seen something unusual while flying a Ju-52 from Krakow to Trieste. The description didn't match that of a helicopter or anything else Gaspar had ever heard of. "Now, what's the situation?"

"Mr. Horek has searched three other sites, with no apparent success. He ordered his team to take three hours' rest, accelerated."

"Is he on-station?"

"He's now checking the Birkenau pickets before setting out again. He plans to examine the remaining sites today. An ambitious program."

Gaspar had forgotten where he'd set down the cup. A flash revealed it atop the table next to the bed. He reached for it. "Thank you, Dido."

He headed out the door. He was thinking of how he'd often told Elena of the original Isten Karde Ja when she'd been young. The perfect glowing sword, spearing through the heavens as it led the Magyars across the steppes to their God-promised home. Found by a child after it landed, point-first, in the heart of what would become Hungary. A boy in the original tale, though he'd changed it to a girl for Elena's benefit. He'd never told Rici that story.

Operations was quiet. Mackey, raising a hand when Gaspar appeared, and four other techs were at their consoles. Another group sat at the tables, on break, presumably. Neither Fukudon nor Horek were visible. Gaspar paused before the map.

The sites already checked were marked with black circles. The others were numbered, one to nine, beginning with those closest to the camp. Gaspar recalled that he hadn't briefed Mackey yet. He assumed that Horek had covered most of it, but all the same, he ought to go over it with him.

Gaspar's breath left him as he swung around. A tech, a young woman, had stepped to one of the farther screens and stood silhouetted in its light. His mind flashed back to the dream—the child blazing in that continent-wide furnace. Tea splattered his hand as he set the cup down.

A slight commotion at the portal drew his attention. Horek had just come through. Helmet under his arm, he was explaining in a loud voice how it had just occurred to him that all serious historical episodes took place in the vicinity of a swamp, for the convenience and comfort of intemp operatives. He was going to write a report on it, a long one, illustrated with examples from his own experience. He believed it would completely revolutionize the theory and practice of intertemporal operations. If anyone else wanted to contribute—

He spotted Gaspar and gave him an appraising look, as if a monitor was the last person he expected to see at a station. Throwing him an offhand salute, he clambered off the platform. He was halfway to Gaspar when Dido spoke.

"Helicopter detected. Now tracking . . ."

Gaspar nearly collided with Horek as he lunged away from the console. "What's the course?"

Dido's reply was drowned out by the uproar from the staff. Gaspar shouted for silence.

". . . a *heading*, Monitor." A fan-shaped patch appeared on the largest screen. "Approximately forty-eight degrees . . ."

"Shit," Horek said. "That's the batch we lined up for this afternoon."

"Ain't that always the way it goes?" Mackey said. "Orders, Monitor?"

"Observe and report. Mr. Horek, notify your people."

The room began to fill up as off-duty personnel answered the alert call. Many were still in sleeping wear. Gaspar stepped to one side as a woman brushed past, heading for the console behind him.

"Sir." It was Mackey, holding out an earpiece. "I've got Saburo here."

Gaspar flinched as he slipped in the piece. Fukudon was shouting wildly—at whom, Gaspar couldn't say. "Mr. Fukudon. Calm yourself."

Fukudon went silent. "What are your orders?"

"Stand by."

"Stand— But they're here! That chopper can be shot down—"

"Yes. To leave a pile of advanced technology for the Nazis to gloat over. A bit of an anomaly, wouldn't you agree? Think again, Mr. Fukudon."

"—we'll call in support, shut down the area, and then—"

"Negative. You are to observe only. Confirm."

"Dave— Are you there? We've got no choice. He's lost it. I've seen this before—on Luzon. You've got to—"

"Mr. Mackey," Gaspar said mildly. "Cut Mr. Fukudon out of the com net."

Mackey looked up at Horek, who gritted his teeth and then jerked his head sharply. A dark hand reached for the board. Fukudon's squawking ceased.

"Very well," Gaspar said. "Inform the others to stand by. There will be orders shortly." The room had gone quiet. He glanced around him. None of the team would meet his eyes. "The helicopter, Dido."

"Thirty-six kilometers and closing steadily. ETA in twelve minutes."

Gaspar pulled on the greatcoat. "Are we focused on the camp?"

"You've got it, sir," Mackey said.

Gaspar climbed the platform and plunged through the portal. A late fall day confronted him, the air biting and clear. The sky was a deep and gorgeous blue, unmarred by smoke from the camp. Birkenau could have been a thousand miles away. Horek emerged right behind him. "Chief, what *are* we gonna do?"

"Why, bring in the renegades, to be sure."

"But . . . are we going short? Is that it?"

"I'll let you know. In the meantime—"

"Yeah. Stand by. Got it."

Buttoning up the coat, Gaspar started down the hill.

"Chief, where are you—?"

Plucking the piece from his ear, Gaspar pushed on through the brush. At the edge of freezing, the mud crackled beneath his feet, and a thin crust of ice shattered as he crossed the puddles. He was halfway to the camp, the towers plainly visible, when a sound caught his ear, one that he'd heard before: the pulse of rotors slashing through air. He paused to listen, trying to gauge distance and direction, before breaking into a run.

He overran the border, lurching several yards into the open. The cleared zone was empty; no guards or workers visible. He glanced uncertainly in both directions—he'd somehow expected to see prisoners here today.

No one noticed him. The guards on duty beyond the wire had heard the noise and were looking out over the treetops, trying to identify the source. Gaspar saw a man in the nearest tower swinging a set of primitive optical sensors across the horizon.

The sound grew louder, so loud that Gaspar was certain the machine must now be visible. But the guards were still searching. More appeared from within the camp, some running, most taking their time. A motorcycle drew up to the nearest tower, an officer leaping from the sidecar and jogging to the ladder. Outside the fence a small car—some kind of scout vehicle—approached from the direction of the gate. Troops with dogs trailed close behind it.

The sound was now deafening—Gaspar could almost feel it. He turned his head, certain that he'd see the machine any second. A wisp of breeze touched his hair and suddenly the air was filled with small darting things, their cries almost inaudible beneath the roar of the machine. Gaspar put his hands over his head as the birds flew past. When he looked up, a chill coursed through him: a hundred yards to his left, bare branches swayed wildly from no apparent cause. He took a step back.

Directly above the disturbed brush he spotted a flaw in the sky, as if the blue itself had been twisted and stretched. A distortion hiding something huge . . .

. . . and then it was present, as if incarnated out of the cold pure sky. Flat gray, enormous, the reach of the rotors matching the sound they emitted. It was the same model that Gaspar had seen in the display, and yet it wasn't. Pods and antennas never meant for the original version protruded from the body, subtly distorting its lines. Small winglets extended from the sides, loaded with what looked to be rockets. A long thin probe extended past the nose, pointing directly ahead. Large as it was, the machine seemed overborne by the number of devices it carried.

So this was her chariot. The tool she would use to strike as Judith had struck, to halt the Great Wheel, to stop its blind trajectory at last. Gaspar smiled despite himself, the folly and arrogance of it put aside for the moment. She had earned this. She'd outthought and outmaneuvered the best the Moiety could send against her. Whatever she'd taken from him she'd used well.

His gaze was drawn by movement at the wire. The guards, now doubled in number, gestured at the machine, their shouts drowned out by the rotors. Those outside the wire cowered behind the scout car, their dogs hunkering close. A man on horseback arrived, shouting and waving his free arm. Most of the officers ran to meet him. Gaspar noticed one was dressed in black.

The chopper hovered, swinging just a little. The brush underneath it lay nearly flat, beaten down by the gale from the rotors. Only a branch or two remained upright.

He wondered how she looked at this moment. Seated in the nose, he was sure, where she would have a clear view of what she had come to destroy. Her face set in that harshness he recalled, that was not harshness at all as he understood it. Her finger on whatever they were using for a trigger. She would be the one to push it. She was a warrior saint, after all.

Behind the fence the guards scattered, spreading out under the direction of the man on the horse. More troops came into view, dozens of them, approaching at a full run. A truck pulled away from the gatehouse.

A sudden shimmer of light crossed the scene, too quickly for Gaspar to react. He blinked, thinking it an illusion. But no—he'd seen the speckles of red clearly, if only for a fraction of a second. He looked at the machine, his muscles tensed. It remained fixed over the same spot, swaying like a ship in an uneasy sea.

At the truck a man—an officer, from his uniform—was trying to goad the troops into the open. They remained unmoving until the horseman began railing at them through the fence. Slowly the men took position. Behind them the man on horseback turned his mount and trotted toward the nearest tower.

The line of troops began to advance. A dozen of them, armed with the automatics that Fukudon had mentioned. Their commander, red-faced and bulky, urged them on. As he swung forward, he caught sight of Gaspar. His mouth opened in an unheard shout. Beside him his men came to a halt, their eyes fixed on Gaspar. The officer ranted on, shaking what appeared to be a baton. Gaspar ignored him.

The horseman had reached the tower. He threw his head back, calling to the guards above. He pointed at the copter, jerking the reins to turn the horse to face it.

With a final bellow at Gaspar, the officer turned to the troops. At his order they raised their guns. In the tower the snout of a weapon appeared.

The flash came as Gaspar was shifting his gaze back to the copter. He looked away, catching only glimpses of the tower shattering, the car bursting into flames, discrete bolts of fire scything through the guards. He fell to one knee, hands protecting his ears from the explosions and shrieks of weaponry.

One after another, the towers blew apart. A dog, its fur ablaze, snapped at itself as it fled the wire. Behind it a lone guard ran, mouth gaping wide. A continuous puff of dust paced him, caught him, and threw him into the fence.

Nose down, the machine roared over the camp, its cannon ablaze, streaks of fire marking the trail of its missiles. Both fences fell as it passed overhead. In the distance a crematorium chimney shivered and collapsed in on itself. Across the camp, fireballs marked the SS barracks.

He tried to catch his breath, flinching as each explosion shuddered through him, eyes narrowed against the flashes of godlike wrath. A phrase came to him, from what source he could not recall: *I bring you not peace but a sword.*

Nothing moved inside the camp. Only where the legs of the nearest tower smoldered could he see a flicker of motion, obscured by smoke and dust. He wondered what it was, realized that it must be the horse, mortally injured and kicking against death.

Within the smoke, ghostlike figures crept from the barracks. Moving slowly at first, then running to where the guards lay. One of them dipped out of sight and emerged with a rifle in hand. Another began dancing, arms over his head. Others joined them, gathering in small groups just past the fallen wire.

A man burst through them, arms wide, legs pumping wildly. He stumbled among the bodies, barely catching himself before hitting the ground. When he reached the open, Gaspar saw it was a guard, helmetless and lacking a rifle. He raced past, tugging at his jacket, throwing an indecipherable shriek at Gaspar as he vanished into the swamp.

He wasn't alone. All along the clearing, guards were in flight. Dozens of them, shedding helmets, belts, even boots as they ran. As Gaspar watched, one of them fell, bawling madly as he crawled on toward the brush.

The machine, looking almost delicate now, veered through swirls of smoke and flame. Gaspar slowly got to his feet, ears ringing from the pounding they'd taken, gunfire and explosions sounding more distant than they should. He took a step forward, another. The aircraft disappeared a moment, dropping behind the remaining buildings, then rose to make one more circuit before heading directly for Gaspar.

He was still out in the open. He backed toward the brush, halted as the machine drew nearer, raising his hands when it roared overhead. But all that struck him was the wind of its rotors.

A voice caught his attention. Behind him Horek soared out of the brush. He landed a few feet off, staggering with too much speed.

Gaspar touched his ear. Slapping his visor back, Horek shouted, "What the hell are you doing?"

"I . . . I was . . ." Shaking his head, Gaspar looked back at the camp. More prisoners had appeared, streams of them filling the lanes between the barracks. He heard voices shouting the words of Jerusalem: "Adonai! Adonai!"

"They sure spanked this dump," Horek said. "Woods are full of Krauts, running like mad. Jumping in the river. It's wild." His voice trailed off, lost behind the ringing.

"What?"

"We caught a signal. Just now. We've pinned 'em down. What's the next move?"

Gaspar considered that a moment. "Call your people in." He headed for the brush.

"Come on, I'll carry you—"

"No," Gaspar said. "There's no rush."

A distant rumbling came as he made his way into the undergrowth: Auschwitz Main, undergoing its own annihilation. When he reached the first tall growth, Gaspar stopped to look back. A multitude had gathered, so many that he could not distinguish between them. He heard laughter and voices raised in the slow melody of a hymn. They moved as one, marching steadily past the vanished line of fences, leaving the grave of all hopes behind.

He dropped his head and went on into the swamp.

Horek was nowhere in sight when he reached the portal. Two vast plumes of smoke covered half the sky. But they were gray, with nothing evil about them. He wondered if he'd have thought the same if he didn't know. Off in the deep blue, sunlight flashed. He squinted, made out a small dot. The helicopter, on its way to the next target.

The com center was still mobbed, everyone speaking at once. Fukudon had returned and was deep in conversation with a heavily frowning Mackey. As Gaspar left the platform, Mackey moved to intercept him. "Monitor," he said. "Are we shorting?"

"Yes." Gaspar had meant it only for Mackey, but the uproar died just as he spoke and the word rang clearly throughout the room.

"Oh my God—" a woman said. Voices surged back, louder than before.

"Please," Gaspar said. "Take your stations and prepare yourselves." The noise died as people moved into position. Behind Mackey stood Fukudon, his face set, helmet in his hands. Gaspar went over to him. "Has the team returned?"

Fukudon went rigid. "Yes, sir."

"Very well. Ready them for action, please. Mr. Horek—"

"Yo."

"Where is this aperture?"

"Right next door. Eighty-five miles, south-southeast."

Gaspar checked the time. Almost 1030, relative. "Very well. Dido, short us three hours. Code is as follows—"

He took two steps without getting a response. "Dido—"

"I can't," Dido said, sounding far more human than an AI normally did. "I'm afraid."

Gaspar raised his head, mouth open to form a shout. The entire crew was staring at him, their silence nearly palpable. "Afraid—" He pushed past two people to get to the upper level, the command station. "I'll show you fear," he muttered.

Activating the station, he identified himself, palm against the screen. The machine beeped and he accessed the emergency menu. He selected STATION TIMELINE RETRACE.

RETRACING IS PROHIBITED, IN LIEU OF MILLENNIAL AUTHORITY. PLEASE CONTACT . . .

He entered his code and overrode. He could feel their eyes on him. All of them were watching him, even Dido.

ARE YOU CERTAIN? (Y/N)

He pressed YES and winced as the station alarm began blaring. "Hang on tight," Horek called out. Gaspar entered the number of hours.

FINAL POINT FOR ABORT OPTION. ARE YOU CERTAIN? (Y/N)

He punched the key with no hesitation. As he was raising his head, the room brightened, the light shifting to a blinding blue-white. Barely perceptible images flickered across it, figures and shapes that his eyes refused to track. His muscles twitched with ghost signals, and his own thoughts of the past hours returned, like distorted echoes. A prolonged wavering scream cut across the room. He'd shorted right into a paradox. He was trapped here, to endure the same series of moments for all time to come—

The room reverted to normal, the scream fading to choked sobs. Gaspar gripped the edge of the console to steady himself. The screen read: ANY FURTHER OPERATIONS? (Y/N)

Gaspar shut it down. "Get me that aperture." He stepped to the lower level. Many of the screens were now dark. The crew was working in near silence, several shooting quick glances at him. Horek, perched on a railing, rubbed the bridge of his nose. "Hell of a trip, man."

The portal light remained red. "Well?"

"Some of the hardware is down, sir," a tech said, her voice shaky. She might well have been the one who had screamed. "The short may have damaged it."

"Give them a minute," Mackey said.

It took several. Gaspar spent the time pacing. He noticed Fukudon checking the men out on some kind of heavy sidearm. "Are you sure you can take them?"

"If they're on the ground, no question."

"If not, shoot them down. We can salvage out there." He thought to add that he didn't want Lewin hurt but let it pass.

"There we go!" a trooper shouted. The indicator was green. Horek leaped onto the platform. "One sec—" He grabbed a small device, a drone floater programmed to deal with any passive sensors left at the waypoint, and shoved it through. The men lined up behind him as he went over tactics a final time. The floater reappeared and signaled all clear. "Okay—shields up, low level all the way. Let's rock and roll!"

He plunged through, followed by Fukudon and the others. In a few seconds all that remained was a single armored man. Gaspar saw that it was Stovall. "Chief," he said. "Dave told me to escort you to site. They extrudin' a lifter. Be out there by now."

"Let's go," Gaspar said.

The lifter, a one-man model, was waiting. He got it into the air just as Stovall told him that the copter had been sighted.

The ground was hilly and rough, covered with vegetation, much of it still green. A fine Terrest vista, oddly attractive to one brought up on another world. Gaspar paid no more attention to it than was needed to keep from plowing into the slopes. Stovall kept him updated as they flew: complete surprise, no resistance, one fled but caught . . .

"Dave says we can head in now."

He spotted the helicopter from a distance, perched on a flat spot near a large grove of trees. It seemed much less impressive on the ground. All the same, from the size of the people moving around it he could see that it was quite as large as he'd supposed.

He set the lifter down too fast, nearly overturning it. Jumping off, he stalked toward the copter. A trooper stopped him and handed him a plastic chip. "Got a sandbag set on auto, Monitor. Drop 'em if they move too fast. The chip'll clear you."

He went on to the vehicle. Around it was scattered a number of crates, the tops removed. Draped across one was a chain of what looked like ammunition. More boxes—there seemed to be hundreds—were sheltered under the trees.

Two people lay on their backs next to the helicopter, being fussed over by a medic. Eight or nine others sat near the tail, guarded by two of Horek's men. Someone gasped as Gaspar drew near, and a bearded man—he recognized Walzer—shook his head.

He went on to the machine itself. Horek met him at the hatch. "Man, they were prepped to take on the whole fuckin' Reich. They got a hundred AGM-150s over there. Went right up against the next cell to snatch those."

"Any problems?"

"Nope. Somebody tried to fire this sucker up when we hit 'em, but Sab put a bolt into the cockpit. The rest folded. Amateur hour."

With a short nod, Gaspar turned to the group sitting by the tail. Some looked familiar; he might well have crossed paths with them at one time or other.

The bearded man got to his feet. "Had to wear that, didn't you?"

Gaspar glanced down at himself, realizing what a figure he must present in the greatcoat and boots. "It was what I had on."

A curly-haired youth in a fatigue jacket—Eric Haverson, a research trainee—let out a harsh laugh. Several of the others whispered among themselves. He heard one mutter, "Sieg Heil."

"You did well," Gaspar told Walzer. "No—I mean it. A little less than half an hour ago I watched this vehicle . . ." He gestured at the copter. "Completely destroy the Birkenau installation."

Walzer's jaw fell open. Haverson pounded his fist into the turf. At the edge of the group a young woman dropped her head on her knees and burst into tears. "We'd have pulled it off if we'd stuck with Hitler—" a man yelled.

"You're telling me you shorted?" Walzer said.

"Of course. What would you expect me to do?" The medic led over one of the men who'd been stunned. He plopped down next to the others, swiveling his head as if he was unsure of what was going on. "And you? What were your plans? I saw them fleeing that place. Sick, hungry, brutalized. They couldn't have walked a mile on their own. What were you going to do with them?"

"Don't tell him," Haverson muttered.

Walzer sighed. "We had a spare portal system. A vehicular unit with a wider setting, about thirty feet. We were going to open it in the marsh and then . . . walk them through."

"To what point?"

"A year and a half upline. An aperture in northwestern Austria on the Inn River." Walzer smiled. "Near Linz, oddly enough."

"April 1945 . . . They'd have met the Allied armies there."

"Yes. The Allies would have the food they'd need. Medicine. Protection."

"And the other camps—Chelmno, Treblinka . . . ?"

"We'd have saved all of them." The crying girl raised her head. "The Moiety would be helpless. You'd reconstruct the ground state some other way. I'm a forecaster, I had it worked out—"

"I can see that," Gaspar said mildly. "An excellent plan. My compliments."

Her face collapsed. "What are you? How could you watch and then do this?"

Walzer smiled. "His name's Gaspar," he said, as if that explained everything.

"Maniac," the girl said, lowering her head once more.

Gaspar turned his back. He could hear them whispering, filling each other in on the nature and habits of the monster Gaspar. Well, let them. It was finished. Quicker and cleaner than he would have imagined possible.

This I can endure, he thought. He would destroy the tapes, beg off any official report—Horek could handle that. Return to his home, to Arpad. Take the leave time he had coming. Put it all out of his mind. Never, ever return to this period again. This epoch of camps, and ovens, and madness at the helm of nations.

In a month it would be forgotten. No more than a nightmare, a hideous image in the dark hours, like Jerusalem, and Sligo, and all the other abattoirs he had passed through. That he could bear. That he could endure.

About him the troopers worked, preparing material for removal. By nightfall the area would be clean of anything non-eral. "Crush no butterflies"—that was the slogan for this part of an operation. Relief flooding through him, he took a deep breath to call out the phrase.

He let it escape in a gasp. "Where is Lewin?"

Walzer was in a half-crouch, preparing to sit back down. "You don't know?"

"Where is she?"

The man's face paled as he stood up again. "She's in there."

"She is *what?*"

"In the camp. In Birkenau. I thought you knew. I thought that's how . . ." A frenzy of voices rose from the group. Haverson cursed and got to his feet.

Gaspar lunged at Walzer. The man cringed away, nearly falling atop a redheaded woman sitting behind him. "You *allowed* her to go in there—?"

"Allowed?" Walzer cried out, fighting to regain his balance. "*We* allowed? Do you know who you're talking about?"

Gaspar backed off. "Explain."

"After we failed with Hitler—" Walzer paused to wipe his face. "We decided—the majority anyway—to call it off. Get back on the line, cover our tracks. Alma refused. She jumped a year and went into the camp. That's why we went through with it at all. We had no choice, don't you see?"

"She was keeping in touch through her cranial implant," the red-haired woman said. "Contacting us once a day. She missed two days in a row, so—"

"We rushed the chopper prep. The implant's still sending—"

"You have to get her out!"

"Wait." Gaspar gestured for silence. "Will you please—?"

Haverson took a step forward. "He's going to leave her there," he said. "Look at his eyes. You son of a—" The stunner buzzed as he moved too far. He shuddered and dropped face-first.

"Oh boy," the medic said as he went to him.

Gaspar whirled away, pursued by their agitated voices. Going to the machine, he ran his fingers across cold gray metal. It wasn't over. He had known it couldn't be over. Why else had Coriolan spoken as he did? Why had Mirbeau given him that look? No one could touch the Holocaust and get away cleanly. Why should Gaspar? "I have to go in there again."

Horek had followed him. "Hold on just a—"

Disregarding him, Gaspar pushed on past. "Quiet!" he shouted. "All of you! Listen to me—I need her frequency, where she is in the camp. I need everything you can tell me. I need it *now*." He let his voice drop. "Of course I'll get her out. What do you take me for?"

Walzer asked for a notepad. Gaspar regarded him a moment, then walked off. "I have to go in there. Again. I can't leave her there."

"Gaspar, listen—"

"I have to get her out."

Horek stepped in front of him. "Right. You walk up to the gate, tell 'em, 'Got somebody named Lewin in here? I wanna take her to dinner.' No way, man. You go in, track her down, scope things out, then my people extract her after dark. That's what I'm telling you, that's the way it's gonna be."

Gaspar gave him a distracted nod. Behind him he heard the girl crying once again.

"And I'll serve as backup."

"You don't speak German."

"Yeah, I do. Dachshund. Wiener schnitzel. Deutschland, Deutschland. Come on."

A trooper ran up and handed Gaspar the notepad. Horek instructed the men to finish policing the site, run all the junk through the renegades' station, and drop back through M3 admin. "You got until dark. And don't stomp no butterflies."

Gaspar went to the lifter. A slurred voice followed him: Haverson, fighting his way out of a stunner trance. "You bring her back, you piece of shit! You hear me? I'll kill you—"

"Give him another taste if he don't shut up!" Horek called out as he overtook Gaspar. He snapped his visor down. "Let's go."

Ten minutes later they reached the portal. The crew deluged them with questions—they'd been out of contact since the strike team left. Leaving Horek to explain, Gaspar went to put on the rest of the uniform.

"We got a problem," Horek told him on his return. Mackey stood scratching his head. "We've lost access to the camp."

"What?"

"When we retraced," Mackey said. "Shorting is awful rough on equipment and programs. We've got software crashes, and some of the machinery's out of whack. Our singularity, for one. Its spin's been decoupled."

"What can be done?"

Mackey crossed his arms. "Monitor, you haven't got the math, and it'd take me a half hour to explain in English. But in a word, nothing. We need a major overhaul."

With a roar of fury, Gaspar flung the greatcoat on the floor.

"I knew this was coming—" Mackey said.

Gaspar threw his head back. "Dido!"

"Monitor Gaspar," the AI said. "I'm aware that I have failed you. Nothing I can say can match the shame that I feel—"

"I want an aperture."

"Yes, Monitor. We retain roughly thirty percent of our capability. We can still acquire apertures at the most stable point of their cycle. However, the nearest to site is two hundred miles to the south, in central Hungary—"

A red dot appeared on the large map. Horek, unfolding a package on a counter, muttered, "Too far."

"Another is present in Austria, thirty miles more distant, and a third in the Danzig area—"

"Machine," Gaspar said quietly. "I need to get into Auschwitz."

"I'm sorry, sir—"

"Find me an aperture!"

"That will require—"

"Do it *now*."

The light over the platform flickered, then glowed a steady green. "There it is, sir."

Horek lifted a gray SS tunic and gave it a shake. "I sure feel shitty about this."

1944

Reber emerged into a closed world. The concrete faded to nothingness only steps away, the nearest buildings no more than shadows. Above he saw only a fuzzy sun low on the horizon, a hint of blue at the zenith. All other traces of color were absent, smothered under cold, clammy gray.

Fog this thick was a rarity so late in the spring. But it did fit his mood. Although it seemed to be a day outside of time, a day where nothing could happen, he knew all the same that something would.

Feeling like a long-forsaken ghost, he wandered around the Kommandantur. His feet automatically took him in the direction of the river. He stopped and changed course. He no longer went there. They were dumping ashes in the Sola now.

At the fence he dawdled for a moment before turning back. The gate into camp awaited at the far side, but he didn't go in there anymore either. Not after what had happened last week. His entire universe had shrunk to a square a few hundred metres in area, the Kommandantur itself and no more. The camp had become his home.

That had been inevitable, he supposed. If he had been a rock, it would have been on the site of Auschwitz. If he had been a lump of iron, he would have been made into barbed wire.

At least the cut on his hand had begun to heal. For a while he'd been convinced that it would stay open to mark him with blood forever. He spread his fingers. A slash across the lower knuckles, put there by teeth. He rubbed the scab until it broke, oozing beads of blood. Making a fist, he let his hand drop.

Someone spoke his name. His stomach fell as he saw a black figure pass. But it was only Knoblauch, his uniform darkened by the mist. Reber squinted and glanced about. No telling where Boldt was in this soup: ten steps off, the other side of B.II. He had a way of just *being* there. No doubt he would be there when whatever was to happen today happened.

He had been spared Boldt for several months after that night, the night the woman in the dark was burned. Stricken with three broken ribs, Boldt went on sick leave for six weeks. A few days before he was due back, Reber was sent home himself. Compassionate leave: his mother had died in an air raid on Cologne. Not one of the thousand-plane raids of the summer before, simply a harassment strike by RAF Mosquitoes. But bombs had fallen in the Reber's suburb for the first time, only a block from his childhood home, and his mother had died of a heart attack on the way to the shelter.

He'd been amazed at his first view of the city—or, rather, the place where Cologne had once stood. Hectare upon hectare of smashed, burned structures barely recognizable as buildings, the smell of smoke still evident months after the big raids had ended. Almost nothing was standing within the city center, apart from the wounded cathedral presiding over the ruins.

He missed the funeral—the rail schedules were too disrupted. His father felt that another trip to the cemetery would be hard to bear. Reber went alone, to find himself standing over the grave—it was unmarked, as all stone was going to build fortifications now—telling his mother about Birkenau, asking what he should do.

He repeated the words that same night after a drunken ramble around the local pubs. Everyone had been eager to set up a mug for the returned veteran, though they drifted off when he spoke of ovens and wire, and men in black. When Reber got home, he found his father waiting up for him, reading Karl May. He told the old man everything. The selections, the burners, how Boldt had forced him to read the numbers, the women he had tried to save. All the time weeping like a child, while his father, in his dark suit—he always wore a suit—stared at him, aghast. Finally old Hans got up, set his book aside, and went to the door. There he paused, and without turning said, "You must make confession."

Reber noticed he was no longer wearing his party pin the next day.

He left that evening, traveling on his soldier's pass, with no real destination in mind. Moving from city to city, seeing the same at each—Frankfurt, Mannheim, Stuttgart, München, all had been laid waste, with some still ablaze from the most recent strikes. Once his train roared through a town—he didn't know which one—at the same time bombs were falling. A few days later another came under attack itself, by American fighters looking for targets after escorting the bombers in.

It was at Nuremberg, the city of rallies, that he saw from the station platform the line of cattle cars being switched to a distant siding, trailing an obscene stink. He approached a guard and asked where it was headed. Getting the answer he expected, he caught the next express to southern Poland.

He found Auschwitz subtly changed. Höss had been reassigned to the WVHA, and Leibenstahl had taken command. On the surface the viciousness had ebbed. There was more food for the inmates, less brutality from the guards. Even Boldt had retreated to the Gestapo office and was seldom seen about the camp.

Reber was nearly ecstatic in his relief. For about a week. But the transports still arrived, the chimneys still belched smoke. Death remained king at Birkenau.

His own slow decline continued. He was aware that whole portions of his personality were gone, shut down and unreachable, perhaps for good. A few weeks before he had tried to recall his school days; the names of his mates, their faces. All that came to mind were incidents from the camp. The woman's voice, as she stood in the alley during the search, eight months ago. He heard her over and over again, at times so clearly that he answered aloud. He had not been able to stand it and concentrated on pushing it aside, into one of the dead spaces he could no longer touch. He had succeeded. The only thing he remembered now was her final scream.

He had struck a man last week. Hit him repeatedly as he cowered.

That was how he'd cut his hand, on the fellow's teeth. He wasn't at all sure what had triggered it. The man had simply been within reach at the proper moment. Reber wondered who he would find within reach today.

The blood was beginning to crust over. Boldt always wore gloves. You could learn a lot from Boldt.

He would have the opportunity. Leibenstahl had been replaced after only a few months by Baer, a man more suited to the command of a death factory. Reber had heard only this morning that Höss was coming back as well to show Baer the ropes. And just yesterday Boldt had turned up to ask if he was ready to help out with another selection.

"Obersturmführer."

Reber raised his head. For a moment he didn't know who the man was. Then it came back: last fall, before the selection, the woman in the dark. It was Griese. The false Griese, as Boldt had insisted. But what did it matter what he said?

"I need to get into the women's camp." The man's face was gray, his lips a thin line. Reber could see beads of sweat from where he stood. With a shrug, he turned to the gate. The day was beginning to unfold. There was no sense in resisting it. He would go along, see where events led.

Not a word passed between them as they passed the wire enclosing Mexico, still no nearer completion than it had been the year before. The workers were little more than shapes in the lingering mist. Those visible could have been the same ones there the last time Griese came through, though Reber knew that this was not possible.

At the B.I gate he stopped to ask Griese exactly what it was he wanted. But the man walked on, his eyes bulging, as if drawn against his will toward something at the far side of the camp. All that Reber could see were the black patches of the ash pits.

He watched Griese totter on for a few seconds, his form growing less distinct with each step. The gate guards, a pair of Balts, chuckled and nudged each other. "Griese . . ." Reber called out. The man paid him no mind. Reber set out after him. Catching up, he put a hand on his shoulder. Griese shook him off and broke into a run.

Reber sighed to himself. So the man was going mad. What was novel about that? They'd all be insane by the time this was ended. That or dead, one or the other, little choice between the two.

All the same, the man was his responsibility. Griese had paused just short of the ash ponds and was now dragging himself toward them step by step. When Reber came up beside him, he was shaking and muttering in a faint voice. Reber caught only the words ". . . in there."

Glancing at the nearest pit, Reber saw Griese reflected in the black surface and looked quickly away. He reached out, brushed him with his fingers. "Listen to me . . ."

The man turned, regarding him with unfocused eyes. Reber felt the stab of an emotion he had thought lost. "Griese," he said. "Come away from here. This is no place—"

Snapping back into awareness, Griese gave out a roar and pushed Reber aside. He was off again, this time headed for the burners. A transport had come in last night. Reber could smell the foul unseen smoke.

Griese had lost his cap. Reber bent down for it and followed him.

A group of officers loitering in front of crematorium four fell silent as Griese approached. He went on past them, stopping dead at what he beheld within. Reber himself halted as the interior came into sight, unable to take another step.

It was filled with bodies. Piled halfway to the ceiling on both sides of the entrance. The skull-like heads, the limbs imitating bone—he'd seen that before. What struck him now was the skin color, an unearthly shade of blue, as if they were another class of being entirely, as if they had been made such through the manner of their deaths.

A gap revealed the Sonderkommando loading up a tray. One corpse after another, arranged neatly in a businesslike fashion. They finished the load and pushed it into the oven. The door slammed shut. A harsh voice told them to hurry up.

"Mind those flowers, damn you."

Slogging through a carefully tended flower bed, Griese disappeared around the corner of the building. "Not even blossoming yet—and look," an officer said. Without replying, Reber set out after Griese.

At the corner he paused once again. Before him was something he'd heard of but not yet seen. A board fence, as high as he could reach, hiding a fire that emitted smoke as thick as the burners. Moll's pit, dug in order to supplement the crematoria to deal with the exterminations planned for the upcoming summer.

Griese was nowhere in sight. Beyond the pit stood only the wire.

He had to be inside that fence. Moving slowly, a step at a time, Reber went to the small opening facing the wall of the crematorium.

All he could see was bodies. The burner was nothing to this—they were everywhere, seeming to pack the entire space within the fence. All sizes and ages, most of them unstarved but each that horrible blue, matching the stain on the windows exactly. He found himself counting them and halted only with effort. There could not possibly be as many as he imagined.

Some clear patches of earth lay between the corpses directly ahead. He picked his way through them. There was no point where he could safely rest his eyes. To his right a man lay sprawled atop a pile, head cocked to one side, mouth open as if smiling. Opposite him a woman had given birth under the gas. In lurching away from that, Reber nearly stepped on another woman with a hand raised high, as if asking to be helped to her feet.

A figure appeared in the mist: Griese, standing at the very edge of the pit itself. Past him the flames crackled and shimmered. Reber called his name to no response. He hesitated before going on, holding his breath against the stink. He kept his eyes high, knowing that he would look in any case. And so he did, as he came up beside Reber. A second's glimpse of writhing shapes and blackened bone.

He turned his head. At one end of the pit, obscured by smoke, a group of men stood around something lying on the ground, something that moved.

Griese was whimpering, eyes fixed on the pit. Reber gripped his shoulder. "Come along," he said, turning him toward the gap in the fence.

A shape approached out of the smoke. A man, short but heavily built. His eyepatch told Reber that this was Moll himself, the one they called Cyclops. He popped the cork of the bottle in his hand and upended it. "Want to take your turn?" he called out as he wiped his mouth. "Last chance."

Reber gave Griese a push. "Go on now."

"No, eh?" Moll let out a belch of laughter. He swayed slightly as he swept the bottle across the pit, and Reber realized he was drunk. "Getting ready for the Hunky Kikes," he said. "The Hunky Kikes."

Behind him men carried something to the edge of the pit. They tossed it in. Reber raced away, stumbling over corpses, trying to outrun the sounds it made; not screams or cries, but only the grunts of a creature already gone from this world.

He found Griese crouched at the corner of the burner, shoulder against the stained brick. He was jabbering to himself, and a feeling of infinite coldness swept over Reber as he absorbed the words. His wife . . . His granddaughter? What in the name of Christ was he talking about?

He must have made some sound, for the man jerked as if struck and fell silent. Eyes fixed on the ground, breath coming in gasps, he clawed at his uniform as if to tear it off his back.

Forcing himself to take the last few steps, Reber offered him the cap. "Whoever it was—"

Griese rolled his eyes toward Reber. A bubble of spittle hung at the corner of his mouth.

"Whoever . . ." Reber waved at the smoke. "Gone."

A burst of laughter came from the pit. Griese's head jerked in that direction. His eyes went wide. "Alive," he croaked. "They throw . . . alive . . . I saw them—"

Reber thought of the woman in the dark, the one named Alma. Again her scream echoed through his mind. "Yes! Alive! That's what they do here. You didn't know? You thought it was clean? Well, you know now, don't you?"

Lowering his head, Griese charged at him. Reber was swinging to one side when Griese hit a patch of mud and flopped onto the ground. Reber backed off and unsnapped his holster flap.

Griese worked his way to his knees. Glaring up at Reber, he growled deep in his throat. "You fucking animal. You piece of shit . . ."

Reber slipped a thumb in his belt. "Give the orders, process the orders, send out the orders . . . You too, Griese."

But Griese wasn't listening. Eyes fixed on Reber, he drew himself to his feet, talking all the while. ". . . You'll pay. Oh, will you pay. They're coming. The Reds. Allies. They'll crack this place wide. Pry you out. Track all of you down . . ."

Reber listened in fascination. The accent had changed to something that he couldn't place. Could he be a Yank? But no, Reber had heard them speak, and it sounded nothing at all like this.

". . . it'll be the Gulag for you. You dirty-ass little coward. They'll work you till your mind's gone, tear the skin right off you. You'll beg for the gas. Cringing in front of Boldt. I saw you—''

He paused to take a breath. "You're not SS, are you?" Reber said. "Not even German."

Griese shook himself, his entire body quivering like a drenched animal. His cap lay at Reber's feet. Retrieving it, Reber threw it at him. A hand gripped it instinctively. "Get out! You're not one of us. You don't belong here. Get the hell out of this camp!"

"You think I'm afraid of you? I saw this place *flattened*—"

Reber pointed over his shoulder. "Plenty of room in there, friend. That what you want? Well, go on then. I don't care who you are. Leave while you still can."

The man looked over at the pit, mouth gaping wide. He was shaking again. A bolt of rage flashed through Reber. He gave Griese a shove. "Go on. *Now.*"

Clapping the now-filthy cap on his head, Griese turned away. He muttered something over his shoulder that ended with a croak. "Don't need you to tell me!" Reber called out. He followed the man to the front of the building. Griese looked back once before speeding his pace. Though the mist was starting to thin, it was only a few steps before he faded from sight.

The Hauptsturmführer at the entrance seemed about to make a remark. Reber swung on his heel. "You have something to say to me?" Getting no answer other than a sullen look, Reber strode off.

A moment later he found himself inside Mexico, with no idea how he'd gotten there. That was a novelty to him; he'd never been in B.III before. Always something new at Birkenau.

He passed the few finished barracks, the piles of brick awaiting construction. The workers lay beyond, in small groups diminishing into fog. As he wandered among them, he noticed they were shying away and realized that he was patting his holster, the loose flap clicking rhythmically. He snapped it closed but caught himself doing the same thing a moment later. He cursed, unaware that he was speaking aloud. A woman whimpered nearby. He shouted at her to get to work.

A distant melody caught his attention. The orchestra, playing at the far end of camp. If asked what they'd been performing a moment ago, he'd have been stymied, but this he recognized. The *Badenweiler*, the march of Nuremberg, of days so long past as to take on the quality of a dream.

He swung around. The central camp was invisible, the fence itself hidden by the remaining mist. He was the sole erect figure in a landscape of the damned.

He raised his eyes to catch a glimpse of sky. The smoke cheated him of that. Again the rallies came to mind—the spotlights blazing into heaven, their beams forming an arch across the night. It occurred to him for the first time that the smoke and the spotlights were the same. That they had always been the same. That he, if he had only possessed the insight, would have known that they were the same.

He was thirty-four years old. He'd been walking through that palace of darkness his entire adult life, thinking it the cathedral of light. Breathing the charnel stink of it until it became part of him. Its true nature had been evident all along: in the words of the Führer, in the screams he'd heard as he patrolled the streets on Kristallnacht, in the burning villages of the Ukraine. Yet he'd been unable to see it for what it was.

Instead he'd seen . . . what? He couldn't recall. Not the glowing Germanic future, the hegemony of the Aryans, the ideal of the Master Race. He'd stopped believing that long ago, if he ever had believed it. So what could it have been? He probed the spot where there should be a foundation of conviction and faith and found nothing. Only the rag of an illusion that all along the real Gerd Reber had been somewhere else, isolated and snug, completely unaffected by what was happening around him.

He leaned backward to take in the totality of the thing that roofed his world. Too far: he lost his balance and fell back several steps, bumping against something that cried out.

The prisoner gave Reber a frightened look and tore off his cap. Reber shifted in order to kick at him, but then caught himself and walked away.

He had to get out of here. He wanted to be alone when whatever climax had been prepared for him finally came. That much, at least, was under his control. But he was not at all sure where the gate was. Though a guard stood nearby, Reber didn't want to ask. He decided to go to the fence and walk along it until he found a way back into the camp.

It took him some time to get there, long enough to imagine that he was trapped, become in his own way one of the prisoners, lost as they were lost. At last the fence came into sight—and along with it a solitary figure, a woman, nearly within the death strip, walking steadily toward the wire. A tower guard lazily watched her. Beyond the outer fence another had pulled his dog up short.

Reber stood tapping his holster. "You there," he finally called out, not as loudly as he could have. "Halt!"

She walked on, looking in neither direction. Stifling a curse, Reber went after her. As he drew near, he heard her chanting in an alien tongue: "Bogati . . . Gazalti . . ." He caught up with her less than five metres from the wire. Gripping her shoulder, he drew a breath to shout. But as she turned, the words were brushed from his mind.

He knew this one. It had been she who collapsed before the burner that night, when the woman in the dark had perished, crying out as if she felt the flames herself. Even with the gray skin, the missing teeth, the sunken eyes, he knew her. He would have known her at Judgment.

She stared blankly through him. "That . . . that's not for you," he told her, waving at the fence. "The rabbis . . . they say that's not a good thing, don't they?"

Her face remained dead. Bending close, he asked for her name. The reply was nearly inaudible. "Rebeka—well, listen, Rebeka. The Reds are on their way. The Yanks and Tommys too. They're going to win. And when they do you'll walk out of here. You wouldn't want to miss that, would you?"

There was no response. He moved closer still. "See, all this is over. In a few months it'll come to an end. For Germany, for the others, for me too. They're burning all the cities. I was there, I saw it. And when they get here and see . . . Why, they'll scrape the earth to find the last German. No one will let this thing pass. They'll hunt us forever. I had a vision, Rebeka. A great dark shape, like a Fury, an Archangel of God, smashing this camp, cutting us all down. They're coming, Rebeka."

Her eyes had finally focused on him. Still clouded, but no longer empty. He took a deep breath. "Very soon now. A little while. You can get through that. You'll survive. You'll see Zion."

Her head fell and she whispered something. Reber caught a name. "Yes, yes, Alma. She wouldn't like this, now, would she?" Her shoulders began to shake. He reached out to steady her. "Here now, don't cry. Well, go on, cry if you want. But let's get back. To your work crew. Your friends.''

Walking side by side, they left the wire behind. Reber was uncertain as to who was leading who. He looked over at her, wanting to tell her that he remembered the night at the burner but unable to find the words. He noticed a glint on her hand. ''Here now,'' he said, unclenching her fist and pulling off a ring that seemed too large for her, thin as she was. ''They'll punish you for that. The others. Hide it, put it in your pocket.''

It was a guard that found them, stepping into their path, slipping a truncheon from his belt. Reber raised his hand. ''No—none of that. She's not to be punished. Not now, not later . . .''

The guard took on a bemused expression. Reber leaped at him, striking him in the chest. ''Don't you smirk at me!''

Club clattering to the dirt, the guard stumbled back. Calming himself, Reber turned to the girl. ''My name is Reber. Correspondence. If you need help . . .'' He urged her toward the women shoveling gravel. Rebeka went to join them, glancing once over her shoulder. A white-haired woman nodded at him as she took Rebeka's hand. The others had risen to watch. '' 'All will be well . . .' '' Reber whispered.

The guard bent for his club. ''Gate,'' Reber said. He started off in the direction indicated. ''I'll be keeping an eye on you.'' The guard saluted in response. The women were still gazing at him as he left.

He made his way to B.II. The fog had risen, leaving only isolated patches. He looked behind him several times, his mind awhirl.

As he reached the Kommandantur gate, he heard his name called. Reber didn't answer. He didn't want to speak to anyone at all right now. He needed time to himself to work out what had happened back there. Strange beyond grasping, as if the universe had flip-flopped in the past few minutes. As if some vast polarity had switched, with Gerd Reber at the central point. He'd stepped into another world since he'd spoken to that girl. A world he half-recognized as something from his past, a place he'd left behind long ago. But how could that be? It was beyond him. He'd have to find that one, speak to her again. Rebeka—

''Reber! Attention!''

Instantly clicking his heels, Reber went stiff. He looked to one side. Boldt was approaching in immaculate black, two junior officers trotting doglike behind him. Coming to a halt only a footstep away, Boldt stuck his thumbs in his belt. "Where's your friend Griese?"

Narrowing his eyes, Reber swung to face him.

"You were observed speaking to him. Where is he? Quickly now."

Reber looked him over carefully, scarcely believing what he saw. Had Boldt always been shorter than him? His authority, his ferocity, his power—where had they gone? What Reber beheld was a clown in a black suit. An overgrown boy playing a role. Not an officer, not a soldier . . . Why, he hadn't even been at the front . . .

His eyes paused at the cap, the skull just below the peak. As if moving on its own, his arm swung high, knocking it into the dirt.

Boldt stared at him for a moment, as if in shock. Fingers fluttered over his holster, the truncheon at his belt. His eyes bulged as he closed in.

"Never been at the front," Reber told him softly. The thin face froze, as if arrested by a camera. "Bloodsucker," Reber said and backhanded him across the face.

Boldt tried to retreat, but now Reber had a grip on the long shock of hair atop his head. He slapped him once again. A junior officer leaped at Reber. He shook the man off. Jerking his head wildly, Boldt nearly succeeded in pulling away, but Reber kicked at him, driving him to his knees. Putting his weight into it, Reber struck him repeatedly. "Never at the *front* . . . Never in *action* . . . You want blood from me . . . ? I'll give you blood . . ."

A piercing shriek sounded behind him. Reber paused, hand raised high. Giving Boldt a last shake, he threw him aside. Stepping in late, an Untersturmführer grabbed at his arm. Reber elbowed him away.

Two men on horses were drawing near. Seeing who they were, Reber came to a relaxed style of attention. Atop a black Arabian sat the Kommandant himself, a whistle dropping from his lips. Beside him rode Höss, newly arrived from Berlin.

"What the hell is this?" Baer shouted, bringing his horse to a halt. Leaning toward him, Höss asked a question. Reber heard the word "correspondence."

"Reber," Baer answered. "And Boldt. It would be." Tossing the reins to an officer on foot, he dropped from the horse. "Get to work, all of you!" he cried to the onlookers.

He confronted Reber. "What have you to say for yourself?"

"My apologies, Gruppenführer."

"Apologies—fat lot of good that'll do." Baer went on to Boldt. "And you. You're surprised? Treat your own worse than you do the Yids. That's the problem."

Boldt stood alone, blood dripping from his nose. Feeling a stickiness on his hand, Reber wiped it off on his pants.

"...and in parade dress. Doesn't look so good today, does it? Well, I've had it with that. I want you in grays. You can demonstrate your devotion to the party some other way. Now, go on."

Boldt moved off, pausing to reach for his cap. As he straightened up, Reber caught his eye. Boldt looked quickly away.

"As for you, Reber, you're out. Striking a fellow officer—" Baer raised a fist as if about to do the same himself. "Anywhere else, you know what would happen." He made a gun with his fingers. "And I wouldn't mind giving the order. Ah, but you're lucky. You can go east and slap around all the Reds you please. Until then, confined to quarters. I don't want to see you in my camp."

He went to his horse and remounted. "This camp is a machine!" he shouted. "It will operate as such!" With a flick of the reins, he rode off.

Höss remained, gazing at Reber curiously, as if trying to grasp what manner of being this was. "What the devil went wrong with you, Reber? And what's all this crap about blood?" Höss gave a low snort. "You're a clerk."

Then he was gone, and Reber became aware of the men still looking on from the windows. He swung around, defiant, watching them fall back into dimness. The last, with a puzzled shake of the head, was Knoblauch. When he was alone, Reber turned to the camp, the ground he would never walk again. His euphoria vanished, as it must. He ran his eyes across the camp: the brick, the wire, the nameless figures, as if trying to capture it in its totality. But that, he knew, was not necessary. In the only real sense he would never leave Birkenau behind.

Turning away, he went to his quarters to wait for the next transport out.

C20/REL

The com center was empty, screens blank, maps and lists gone. Most of the readouts were off, single blinking lights denoting equipment switched to standby. Gaspar slouched in a chair on the second level, head resting on the greatcoat.

The crew had left quickly, as soon as he'd recovered enough to declare the operation closed. He'd watched them from where he sat. There had been none of the cheer that usually accompanied the end of a successful mission. Only a quiet scramble as they logged off, gathered their things, and stepped through the portal. Few had so much as glanced in his direction, and his sole farewell had come from Fukudon, who took his hand and gave him a short wordless bow.

Footsteps echoed from the hallway as Horek entered the room. He carried a leather bag and wore a suit made out of coarse blue cloth. Pausing to look about him, he slung the bag on a console and perched next to it. "Don't suppose you plan to follow the interrogation."

Gaspar made a negative sound.

"Well—they got enough to see what the game was.

I mean, why it all worked out the way it did.'' He glanced at Gaspar. ''Seems that Alma had a hobby. She was investigating ancestry, tracing lines of descent, figuring out who Grampa was, that kind of thing. Never saw the point myself.

''Anyway, she worked back to the mid-20th. World War II Germany.'' Horek swung around to face Gaspar. ''One of her people was involved. There, at the camp. Name of Knoblauch.''

He waited a moment, as if for a response. ''What I'm saying is, that's why it ended there. All psychology, no logic to it. She had to go into the camp itself. That was the arena. That was where she was gonna take 'em down.''

''You may be right, Dave.'' It made sense, Gaspar could see that much. It was as good an explanation as any.

''So . . .'' Horek clapped his hands on his knees. ''Look—you gonna be okay? 'Cause I . . . I wanna kind of head out.''

''Yes, of course, Dave. I'll be fine.''

Slinging the bag over his shoulder, Horek went to the platform. Once there he stopped and looked back at Gaspar, mouth open as if he was searching for words.

Gaspar attempted a smile. ''I want you to know that I appreciate your work, Dave. You did extremely well under very trying circumstances.''

''Thanks, man. Means something. But . . .'' He expelled a long breath. ''She was dead, you know. Like I said. Minute she walked in there, it was over. Nothing anybody could do. That place is the black hole of history, man. No such thing as getting out.''

''Very true,'' Gaspar answered, so quietly he was unsure that Horek heard.

''Yeah, well—'' Horek raised a hand. ''Time and chance, man.'' A quick movement and he was gone.

Gaspar listened a moment to the odd sounds of an empty station. Leaning forward, he crossed his arms on the console. He was exhausted, as tired as he could ever recall being, but he dared not sleep yet. Not until the pictures in his head were put into some kind of order, until they stopped assailing him like a demented mob. He had no idea how long that would be. He saw Hebrew robes in the death pit, starving Celts bound by barbed wire, a flared sun bursting through black smoke . . . And presiding over all, the image of Alma Lewin, blue of skin, her eyes as blank as a skull's, hand held out in a plea for help that would never come.

He had not been prepared for what he had beheld. It didn't matter what period, epoch, or age he was from. Nothing could have prepared him . . .

"Monitor."

Gaspar mumbled something in response. When no reply came, he raised his head. The center screen was bright. Not displaying a map but a picture instead. A scene from his home, from Arpad: three visible moons, a near-purple sky, the soft light of Eridani. It could be nowhere else.

A small figure danced into view. A dark-haired girl wearing the leggings of a child of his people. She was chasing a thopt, shrieking with glee as the gauzy winglike vanes flashed past her. Twisting about wildly to follow the beast, she stumbled and fell to her knees. He recalled fearing that she'd been hurt. The thopt flicked out of view.

The child looked up, hair obscuring her face. With another gust of laughter, she leaped to her feet. The thopt reappeared, even more agitated than before. A man ran into sight, arms waving madly as he ushered the flier before him. An aging man, stocky of build, hair short and grizzled. Gaspar studied him as he would a stranger, someone he had never seen before.

The child made a final, futile jump at the gorgeous creature overhead. It tilted away, gliding into empty air, making good its escape toward the mesa that was its home. Waving goodbye, the girl laughed once more and leaned against the man at her side, resting her head against his thigh. He reached down to stroke her hair.

Gaspar closed his eyes, feeling the scene slip away, grow alien, become an event that could not possibly have happened to one such as Gaspar James. He spoke his granddaughter's name aloud. Nothing. He asked Dido to shut it off.

"I'm sorry, Monitor. I felt that—"

"Quite all right." He had to choke the words out. "Very thoughtful of you. You may erase it."

"I'd prefer not to."

"Fine. View it if you wish."

No answer came. Gaspar reached for the greatcoat.

"Gaspar."

"Yes, Dido."

"Not Dido."

He stopped with his hand on the collar of the coat, recalling that Dido never addressed him by name. The sound of this voice was different as well, the overtones obscure, as if echoing across a tract of space and time deeper than Gaspar could imagine.

"Excuse telegraphic nature, Gaspar. Of necessity. Author of Moiety speaking. One such. Far upline. Date pointless. To note years would require all available energy."

Dropping the coat, Gaspar stepped back. He glanced wildly about the room, as if the flicker of particle interactions might appear all around him.

"Listen closely, Gaspar. Little time. An eon of thought compressed for message. Contact unusual. Only made when operative completes mission that may threaten view of self. Such occasion exists. We are partners in Moiety. You suffer doubts about purpose. You will know that purpose."

No, he thought, his stomach heaving. No . . . whatever I deserve, it's nothing like this. "I don't care to hear—"

"Listen: all left us is thought. Of universe, laws and parameters. This finished, other matters remain, re: intelligence and its function. Final question: why mind is subject to pain, evil, sin? Conclusion: justice lacking. Product of intelligence, not innate in continuum itself. Moiety organized to see justice done.

"Moiety program: trace and record existence of each intelligent entity since Emergence. Data stored, evaluated, lives of entities . . . judged. Meaningless without action."

"Will you cease?"

"Primal inflation flawed continuum. These flaws located, vectors/velocities noted. The domain walls—planes of pure energy, traversing space-time at light speed. Collisions due after period equal to time separating us. Energy release greater than universe spent in Epoch of Light.

"This energy channeled, used to form new continuum. With new laws, more suited to existence of mind. This continuum home to inhabitants of our own. Life after life. Only the righteous, who led moral existences. Others discarded. Justice attained."

"No—you're lying—there is none—it's all empty—"

"Note your role, Gaspar. To secure/protect continuum as is. Changes raise complications, impossibilities, paradoxes. You prevent this. It is holy work. You must not suffer because of it."

"I cannot—"

"They return, Gaspar. To a finer world. To live as fit. As will you—"

Gaspar screamed. He threw the coat at the invisible speakers, scrabbled for something heavier. He found nothing and instead pounded the console before him, fists glancing off the unbreakable screen, stains growing on the keyboards and readouts. The voice spoke one last time before falling silent.

He came back to himself crouched next to the console. Dido was shouting wildly. "What?" he forced out.

"I . . . I was out of contact for some time, sir. My clock shows one minute forty-two seconds elapsed. I'm frightened . . ."

"S'nothing." He pulled himself to his feet, gripping the chair so as not to fall. Dido jabbered on. "It's nothing! Forget it!" He slumped against the chair. "Brought back after that. Resurrected to remember that. Burning fat. Swirls in the ash pits. They don't know."

"Monitor—I'm not certain what you're talking about, but you've been injured. Please enter the med section for treatment."

Gaspar inspected his hands. Blood streamed from the knuckles, staining the sleeves of the shirt. "Forget that too."

He let his hands fall. "I have always done my duty by the Moiety."

"I know that's true, sir . . ."

"It's over. No more. Tell them to keep it. When you get there." He pushed himself to his feet. "Tell them that Gaspar . . . declines."

He headed for the hall. "Take a message for transmission," he said, overriding Dido's protests. "As follows: To my daughter, comma. This is last you will hear from me. I cannot tell you what I have been involved in, only that it is unspeakable . . ."

Still talking, he pulled off the shirt as he stepped through the door, then the boots and trousers, all stinking of the camp. ". . . to return would be to poison you, and Rici as well. I'm afraid that may already have happened . . ."

Putting on the suit he had arrived in, he glanced around to make sure he left nothing behind. He picked up his workcase and left the room. "Spare no worry for me. I have no stomach for the action that decency demands. I will go on as I can. Do not attempt to search for me. It would be a waste . . . of time. Consider me as you do our dead.''

He covered several items that she should know, bank accounts, assurance policies, aware that he'd forget at least one. Back in the com room, he paused to think for a moment, then raised his voice. ''Ensure that none of our descendants are present on Arpad eighty years from this date and thereafter. Means of departure will appear well before that time. You are now matriarch, I hold you to this. I cannot go into detail, but it is of utmost importance. See that it is done.''

He tried to conjure up some apt farewell phrase. Words evaded him. ''Your loving father, James.''

The sparse readouts flickered at him, the silence hovered close. ''And now,'' he said finally. ''A story.''

He spoke haltingly at first, his voice growing firmer as he went on. He spoke of the Great Wheel, a thing of infinite force and cruelty, rolling across history through all the periods and epochs, never seen or described, known only by the desolation it left behind. Only two could stand against it: the saint and the monitor, a young woman and a man of first age, bound by oath never to rest until the Wheel was broken at last. They possessed powers, these two; they moved behind the curtains of space and time, always a step ahead of the Wheel, always turning it aside, leading the victims from Judaea, and the steppes, and Ireland, and the camps, to the one safe place, the sanctuary guarded by their friends the flickering clouds. And though the battle was never finished and victory far away, they were very happy, because they were partners for all eternity, and there was nothing else they wanted to be.

Listening through a replay, he made several corrections. At first Dido refused to send it, but Gaspar ordered it done under his emergency code. He told the AI to forget that too.

At the command station he called up the override program, the same he'd used only hours ago. He supposed that what he was doing now was the opposite of shorting, but there was no simple, common term for it. Why would there be? Setting the portal to a date fifty years upline from M3's current now, he headed for the platform.

''Monitor—''

He stopped.

"I have failed you twice. I can't help thinking I'm doing so again."

"No, Dido. That '44 jump . . . My fault. My orders were unclear." Gaspar took a deep breath. "You've done well, within limits. With experience, you'll be a fine AI."

"I thank you, sir."

A thought occurred to Gaspar. "You have my permission to delete any files concerning this operation, if you so wish."

"I'd prefer not to. I believe I can learn from them, sir."

A spasm crossed Gaspar's face, making it look far older. "I hope so," he said and went through the portal.

The duty tech was unfamiliar, as he'd hoped. She nodded to him as he stepped down. Operations was otherwise empty, as were the hallways outside. By sheer accident, he'd hit on a late hour. That pleased him. He was afraid that he'd come across someone he knew, even after all this time. He would not have been able to bear that. He was aware of what awaited him. He would join the others broken and maimed by their service. A man of dark legend, a figure of fear. In a word, a ghost.

His office was as he had left it. He entered slowly, relieved by this evidence that he would be granted the exile that he sought. Dropping his case on the desk, he went to the window. Darkness, broken by lights stretching to the edge that was no horizon. The comset on his desk buzzed behind him. He ignored it.

An upliner he'd spoken to once had told him that the primary metaphysical quality of the Extension was that it effectively deprived all entities within the continuum of free will. Space-time had been transformed into a deterministic system, the only intelligences possessing agency those of the Extension itself. No responsibility, no blame, no credit adhered to actions taken within the continuum, only those of the beings who moved along the core of time. Gaspar lacked the mentality to deal with such abstractions, but he could feel the truth of it all the same.

He recalled the last words of the speaker from the final state, the entity of particles and thought, abiding through eternities in the long, cold dark. Something about forgiveness. Gaspar put it aside. He didn't want that. He'd cling to his own damnation. At least it was his.

The door opened behind him. A reflection appeared in the glass: a young woman dressed in an unfamiliar fashion. He sensed others in the hall as she stepped uncertainly into the room. He could not resolve her expression, but her voice, when she spoke, was apprehensive.

"We welcome you back, Monitor . . ."

He merely nodded in response.

"Intendant Coriolan would like to see you, as soon as convenient."

Gaspar grimaced. Coriolan remained; he should have guessed. "Tell him I'll be along. Wait—" The woman paused. "What of Lisette Mirbeau?"

"I . . . don't know that name, Monitor."

Gaspar nodded. The door slid shut. He continued gazing out into darkness, one aching hand endlessly rubbing against the other. Some minutes passed before he turned away.

1945

A whistle shrieked in the chill air. Rebeka ran her eyes over the open area next to the road. They had crossed the Austrian frontier yesterday, and Mauthausen could be only a day or two's march ahead. Time was closing in.

She nudged Giselle and pointed to a patch of evergreen bushes at the foot of a wooded hillside. Giselle nodded and told the others.

Dalia slipped as they left the highway—the endless march had irritated her scabies, making it hard for her to walk. A guard spun around, rifle at ready. He laughed as she caught herself on one knee and Shosha helped her up. A lot of people had been shot on the march after falling on the ice and breaking a leg. The guards had started to view it as sport.

They made their way through the women already resting in the crisp powdery snow. Many were near collapse, frozen and starved, still dressed in the thin cotton shifts they'd worn in the camp. Rebeka passed one girl crying over her blackened frostbitten hands. She looked away, knowing she could only save her own.

Her six wore the capes that Alma had told them to make, with sweaters or wool shirts underneath. All but Rebeka and Giselle, who had organized a man's pair of shoes, had clogs on their feet. Rebeka wore boots given her by a Russian POW. He'd carried them all the way from Vyasma, he told her, but he was going up the chimney soon and had no more need of them. She reminded him so much of his young daughter, he said.

Rebeka's heart leaped as she neared the bushes and saw behind them a shallow ravine leading into the woods. Anyone climbing it would be hidden until they reached the trees. She looked about her, automatically noting the position of the guards. A Slav had seen them and was moving to a spot between the bushes and the ravine.

She called the girls to a halt and plopped into the snow. Yulka sat next to her and Rebeka whispered what she wanted her to do. "In about three minutes," she said. "I'll signal you." Yulka moved off. Glancing at the guard, Rebeka saw him resting against a large boulder. He made kissing noises and patted the rifle in his lap.

Thrusting her hands inside the cloak, Rebeka gripped a long wooden rod and worked it loose from the straps that held it. She ran her thumb over the thick metal cylinder at the top end. Turning to her women, she eyed them one after the other. They gazed back, unblinking, each of them ready, knowing what was coming. They had ten minutes. She'd have the judge the proper moment. It would be nice if an Ami plane flew over right now.

These six were all that were left. Yulka, Giselle, Shosha, the three younger girls from the block. The rest were gone, either to the ovens or frozen on the roadside during the march here. The full weight of Auschwitz had fallen upon them after Alma was killed. Rebeka had never guessed how well Alma had protected them. It was hard for her to live with the fact that she hadn't done as well. That she'd failed at becoming Alma.

The work had taken most of them. Digging up rocks, smashing them into gravel, transporting it to Mexico. She bribed the Kapos and bought as much extra food as she could, but it was never enough. They went one after the other, into Block 25, into the burners. She could only watch them go.

On top of it all there was Boldt. Luckily, he'd been gone for most of the winter and another period late in the spring—she'd heard that a guard had thrashed him. But otherwise he appeared regularly to lead her from one group to another, jabbering his philosophical nonsense all the while, and ask her, "This one? . . . Or that one over there?"—before finally choosing a woman he'd not even pointed out. Always he forced Rebeka to come along, to watch as he pulled the trigger.

She'd told those close to her—Mama, Hata, Hester, and Yulka—to keep their distance when he was about, but it seemed that he knew who they were. He started taking them too: Hata spitting in his face and enduring her beating before the end came, Hester querulous as a little child.

Finally Rebeka could take it no longer. It was a week after Hester was killed, but that wasn't what had thrust her over the edge. No, it had been the man who hissed at her from the wire, catching her attention and gesturing her over. An aged man, she thought at first, until she was close enough to see how young he actually was.

He asked her name and then handed her a small package, so light that there seemed to be nothing inside. "From your father," he said, gesturing at the chimneys. "It was yesterday."

Papa had seen her, some time before, and decided against all emotion not to contact her, so that she wouldn't worry. He'd lived out his last days only a short distance away, in the men's camp at the other side of the wire.

Unwrapping the filthy cloth, she found two rings. "He wanted you to have them," the man said. She lifted her head and without looking selected one and gave it to him. "Get yourself some bread," she told him.

She slipped on the remaining ring. It was large for her finger, her father's, and for that she was glad. She walked past the gravel cart they'd just now pushed through the gate, the women calling softly to her. She headed for the fence, seeing not barbed wire, not the towers, not even the camp itself, but a vision of her parents, from a long distant time when she'd been young and knew that nothing in the world could ever hurt her.

Then a hand grabbed her, a beefy round face appeared speaking desperate words, words that she could not for the life of her recall. Something about the Russians advancing, some dark menace chasing the guards about the camp. All that she retained was a single phrase: "You shall see Zion."

It wasn't until later that she realized who he had been: the officer who had shaken so on Alma's last night. She wondered if he had been watching her since, but she never came across him again after that.

A boot crunched the snow to her right. An officer strode past, touching his cap to her in a pantomime of courtesy. She kept an eye on him, wanting to know where he went off to. The other day he'd asked why he always found her group at the very edge of the mass of prisoners. To get away from the road, she answered, the sight of all the bodies left behind by previous marches. That seemed to satisfy him, but she couldn't be sure. He was a little Boldt, that one.

She felt a touch of nausea at what this march would have been like if Boldt had lived. She'd seen him last in the early fall, sometime in September, she thought. That day should have marked his triumph. He approached her, smiling, one hand behind his back, suddenly thrust forth to reveal a nosegay of dollars, fanned out so that each was visible.

She knew those bills. She'd exchanged them the night before for a few cans of milk. Flicking them in her face, Boldt said, "Today you will make the selection. And you'll explain to them all why you're doing it."

He folded the notes and slipped them into his pocket. "Not now. I'll give you time to consider. This evening, when you're free." He told the guards to hold them and went off, saying he could use a nap.

Rebeka knew what was required of her. She would tell Mama—Yulka too, since Mama was having trouble getting around now—where the cash was hidden. Have them memorize the names of her contacts on the staff. When Boldt returned, she would allow him to get close and then throw herself at him. Go for his eyes. Not that she had anything resembling nails left, after hauling gravel all these months . . .

She was approaching a point that could be called cheerfulness when a rumble of aircraft engines—they had been passing overhead for weeks, on their way to bomb Monowitz, rumor said—was joined by another sound, a piercing whistle that dropped in tone as it grew louder. She straightened up and was looking right at the SS compound when stack after stack of dark objects plunged into it and geysers of smoke roared skyward while the earth itself shook.

The guards raced about, shouting, blowing whistles, firing above the prisoners' heads. Pushing herself back on her feet, Rebeka simply stared. A man had actually been thrown into the air, arms and legs flopping like a doll's. She must have looked the perfect fool standing there, a smile plastered across her face. Something told her she wouldn't be bothered by Boldt again.

And so it was. The guards kept them at the quarry for an hour after work ended, but he never returned.

A few weeks later came the revolt, terrible and short-lived, though the men did succeed in blowing up one burner. The Nazis soon destroyed the others themselves, and as winter settled in, Rebeka finally saw a scene that she had thought beyond hope: the gates of Birkenau from the outside.

She never did hear from Alma's friends.

Certain they were unobserved, she caught Hata's eye. The guard, chewing on what looked to be a hunk of cheese, grunted when Yulka got up. She whined at him and pointed to the bush. He chuckled when he saw what she wanted and waved her on with a few raw remarks.

Rebeka freed her hand from the cloak. She nodded to the others. They drew their feet beneath them, ready to move. At the bush Yulka tore off a large branch. Coming to alertness, the guard dropped his cheese and gripped the rifle tightly. He rose, eyes narrowed. Rebeka waited until his gaze reached her before lifting the grenade and giving it a shake.

He gasped aloud and pointed the rifle. Rebeka took hold of the firing pin. She smiled, showing the gap where her teeth had fallen out, one after the other. She knew that bothered people. A small moan escaped the guard. The rifle barrel dropped.

Eyes fixed on him, Rebeka dipped into her pocket and pulled out a roll of bills, holding it up so that he could see it. Muttering under his breath, the guard slowly slung his rifle. Rebeka gestured with her head. He moved away from the rock.

As he passed, she tossed him the money. A quick glance: no one had noticed. She flapped a hand behind her, heard the others scramble off.

The guard stood ten steps ahead, still facing her. She twirled a finger. "Szybko," she mouthed at him. His jaw clenched, but he did what he was told.

Rebeka backed up quickly. Yulka touched her when she passed.

Then she was hidden by the bushes, moving uphill, Yulka sweeping the branch from side to side as she followed.

The others waited halfway up the ravine. Rebeka waved them on into the trees. She climbed in a crouch, grenade high, prepared in her deepest soul to see Boldt himself emerge from the woods, fully convinced that the world had been created so that Rebeka Motzin could be caught at this precise moment. Then she was among the trees, Yulka a step behind. She listened: no shouts came, no whistles, no gunfire.

She was still holding the grenade, so tightly that it hurt her fingers. She slipped it into her pocket. It held no charge, but you couldn't tell that by looking. It might come in handy again. She'd gotten it from the male prisoners involved in the uprising. They met with her the week before, for reasons she couldn't grasp until it occurred to her that they wanted her approval. She gave them two hundred dollars out of the small amount left, asking for the grenade shell alone.

One of the younger girls was silently crying. Two others moved their lips in what sounded like prayer. Shosha's face was as harsh as it had been that first day when they had been together in the cattle car, before her child was stolen. Yulka wore the only smile that Rebeka could remember seeing on her face. Rebeka wondered how she herself must appear.

Their expressions went blank as shots rang out—the Nazis, killing those who could no longer rise. Setting her face, Giselle calmly put her hands over her ears. Two of the others did the same.

Rebeka listened on, jolted by every shot, her terror growing with each report. Finally they ended. But still she shook, her fear not abating one iota.

She went to the edge of the woods. From that point the road was visible. She watched the dead march west until the last of them vanished, and there remained only the hills, the snow, the clear blue sky.

The purity of it repelled her. Leaving the trees, she stepped out onto the hillside, trying to spot the bodies in the field below, something she'd recognize and understand. But the angle wasn't right, and all she saw was a clean spread of white, reaching to the wooded hills and the sun beyond.

She closed her eyes and pictured her own dead: the woman in the car, Nicole crouched and screaming, once again the flames, the moment that had never happened that would never end, her father. A face broke in, saying: *You shall see Zion.*

She hoped he was dead as well. She hoped all of them were: every last German, every Gentile, every son of Cain across the vast earth. That was what was left of her, what had been made of her: a seething caldron of fear and hatred, a true daughter of Auschwitz.

I am as they are, Rebeka thought. They have made me one of them.

She would descend to the road, to where the bodies lay. She would lie down beside them to wait for whatever remained. The others would be fine. Yulka would get them through, and Giselle . . .

The slope seemed steeper going down. She slipped after only a few steps, banging her elbow on the hard ground. A clinking sound came from her dress pocket as she got to her feet. She reached in, found the small flask of perfume that had banged against the grenade shell. She made to throw it away, but the color, striking and pretty against the dead-white, held her eye.

Raising the flask, she studied it for a minute, then opened it with clumsy fingers. She cupped it under her nose and took a deep breath.

She gasped as the aroma filled her. The entire universe seemed to be made of silence and scent. She raised her head, eyes squeezed tightly shut, holding her breath so as not to mar the moment. She had never experienced a stillness this pure and deep before. Not the emptiness of the camp, of Boldt, not an absence at all, but the essence of the snow, the sun, the sky itself. It was as it must have been on the first day, when light poured across the place that would be the world. Only the sound of her own heart intruded, beating more fiercely as her terror and rage dropped away. She recalled Mama Blazak's words, in her last moments of life, on this very road only two nights ago: "I know why they did this thing. Because it was time. Messiah was coming to redeem us all. So Satan made them his partners, and they set out to kill all the Jews, to make sure that they destroyed Messiah before His day could arrive." And in a fading voice as the cold took her: "But fear nothing, little one. Adonai will try again."

The horror began to lift. She tried to hold it to her, to claim it as her own, but it was all drawn off. The fear, the pain, the conviction that she alone was unworthy were swept away and diluted in the glory of everything.

Her heart subsided. She took a short breath, tottered a bit. Thought of Alma, and her father, for the first time without wishing for her own death.

A voice called from the trees. She looked back, blinking in puzzlement, forgetting for a moment that they were still a long way from home, that nightfall was near, that they would need shelter.

She capped the flask and slipped it into her pocket next to the prayer book. Feeling for the ring, she slipped it on her thumb, where it would stay. She climbed back up the hill, speaking words to those left behind, ancient words that came not from her but through her: ". . . may the great name of the Lord be exalted and hallowed throughout the world that he hath created according to his will. May he establish his kingdom in your days, in your days and in the days of all the house of Israel . . .

"And say ye, Amen."

1973

I t was night. He had always known it would be night. Reber caught his breath, afraid that it would come as in the bad dreams of childhood, the swift and final assault of the Dark Man, the Devil, Death. The seconds passed. He relaxed without knowing how he did so.

His mind was clearer than it had been in days. He felt himself possessed of a new strength, as if he could easily rise and walk out of this place. He tested his limbs. There came only a dim shaking.

No, that wasn't the reason for this gift of clarity. He assumed—he knew—that he had been given this opportunity for one purpose: to look back and contemplate how badly he had failed. That was his final duty, and Gerd Reber had always been a great one for duty.

But he could not bring himself to think of the camp. Other images intruded. The rallies, the marches, the early victories—those he forced away. He dwelt on his own time behind barbed wire, in the Yank POW camp in France—they'd come ashore at Normandy only weeks after his transfer and he hadn't ended up in the east, after all. The harsh postwar years, which hadn't been very rough for him, as he'd always been able to get by. Then the '50s, when everyone mutually decided to forget, as if the murder of a race, the creation of the vilest places in history, had been a mistake, a tragic error of policy easily deleted from memory. He'd come across Knoblauch once during mid-decade, listened in revulsion as the man sniveled about being deprived of his SS pension. Soon after that Reber had contacted the Jewish relocation service and traced Rebeka to begin his own self-imposed penance.

He wondered again, as he had for years, what had happened to Boldt. Probably best he didn't know.

The memory of the last day arose, Boldt's shocked and bleeding face, Rebeka finally raising her head. Those too he put aside, instead calling up the rest: the man in the ditch, the lines to the gas chambers, the dogs tearing at the helpless, the pregnant girl beaten like an animal, the scream from the oven. The cold gray of Auschwitz, coloring his entire life, before and since. As it must. The place had been his, after all. Designed, constructed, and kept running as if with his own two hands; a monument to his stupidity, his cowardice, his foolishness. When it would have been so easy to have been brave, to have been strong, to have looked into the eyes of the others, the enemies of all that mattered, and told them no.

It wasn't in him. It had never been in him. But at least he would die knowing what he was, knowing that such a cripple as he did not deserve eternity—could not change without help, and he had not earned that help.

Now he could think of Rebeka. Hold her face in his mind, relive his single righteous act. His eyelids were falling when the thought came of the Arabs, of tanks rolling across the desert, crushing all before them. If he had been able, he would have screamed.

The door opened and a figure appeared, a nurse, silhouetted by the lights of the hall. As she bent over the bed, he saw that it was the hard one. He gathered his strength for the greatest effort of his life.

Moving his head toward her, he tried to articulate the word. Nothing came but a gargle. The nurse paused and moved closer. He tried again, with no more success, and was about to give up when he saw the man in the ditch. Contorting his mouth, he forced the word out.

"Israel?" the nurse said. He sensed a smile. "It's over, old man.

They forced the Arabs back. They're nearly at the Canal. The Israelis—they've won again.''

"She lives," he said, uncertain whether it was heard. He sank back, fulfilled. Darkness closed in. A buzzer sounded somewhere, a panicked voice spoke, but that had nothing to do with him. He groped for her face, a final glimpse of redemption. *All will be well . . .*

The room faded, taking with it the grandeur and misery of the world. He gladly watched it go, welcoming the wave of darkness that engulfed him.

But the darkness was not absolute. It was speckled with light, waves and filaments of fire, swirling at the bare edge of vision. Even as he recognized organization in that web, a complexity that he could no more than acknowledge, he knew that these were not things, but beings, not what, but who.

He waited numbly for whatever would come. But before he could despair, he was made aware that these were not yet the Archangels, the pitiless Seraphim, but his own, creatures he knew and who knew him, the children of men, the people of the long dark.

Structure and content resolved about him, shapes of things he had always known must exist but had never found. He understood it for what it was: a world renewed, the world as it should have been, the next small step toward glory.

I am not— he cried out to those who awaited him, protesting that he had been judged wanting, that his entire life had been a judgment. They ignored him, knowing better: his victims, his comrades, his brethren; Jew and Gentile; man in the ditch and woman in the dark; monitors and intendants; human and machine; advanced and natural; the dancing clouds of the small interlude of dusk; the powers that stood beyond even these: all that great moeity known as the righteous.

He accepted his place among them, aware at last that mercy has no boundaries, that it encompassed even such as he, that this world was his work too. He rose on into that morning, the chains of time falling from him as he ascended into the house of the just.

. . . and all will be well, and all manner of thing will be well.

Works Consulted

Hannah Arendt. *Eichmann in Jerusalem: A Report on the Banality of Evil*. Revised ed. New York, 1965.

Roger James Bender and Hugh Page Taylor. *Uniforms, Organization, and History of the Waffen-SS*. Vol. 1. San Jose, Cal., 1969.

Corrie ten Boom (with John and Elizabeth Sherill). *The Hiding Place*. Washington Depot, Conn., 1974.

Tadeusz Borowski. *This Way for the Gas, Ladies and Gentlemen*. Trans. by Barbara Vedder. New York, 1967.

Allan Bullock. *Hitler: A Study in Tyranny*. Revised ed. New York, 1962.

Robin Cross. *Citadel: The Battle of Kursk*. London, 1993.

Lucy S. Dawidowicz. *The War Against the Jews 1933–1945*. New York, 1975.

Jacques Delarue. *The Gestapo*. Trans. by Mervyn Savill. London, 1964.

Freeman Dyson. *Infinite in All Directions: Lectures Given at Aberdeen, Scotland, April–November, 1985*. New York, 1988.

Saul Friedlander. *Reflections on Nazism: An Essay on Kitsch and Death*. New York, 1984.

Micah D. Halpern. *Documents of the Holocaust*. Tel Aviv, Israel, n.d.

Raul Hilberg. *The Destruction of the European Jews*. New York, 1985.

———. *Perpetrators, Victims, Bystanders: The Jewish Catastrophe 1933–1945*. New York, 1992.

Rudolf Höss. *Autobiography*. Trans. by Constantine Fitzgibbon. London, 1959.

Wieslaw Kielar. *Anus Mundi: 1,500 Days in Auschwitz/Birkenau*. Trans. by Susanne Flatauer. New York, 1972.

Liana Millu. *Smoke over Birkenau*. Trans. by Lynn Sharon Schwartz. Philadelphia, 1991.

Filip Muller. *Auschwitz Inferno: The Testimony of a Sonderkommando*. Ed. and trans. by Susanne Flatauer. London, 1979.

Sara Nomberg-Przytyk. *Auschwitz: True Tales from a Grotesque Land*. Trans. by Roslyn Hirsch. Chapel Hill, S. C., 1985.

Henry Orenstein. *I Shall Live: Surviving Against All Odds 1939–1945*. New York, 1987.

Anna Pawelczynska. *Values and Violence in Auschwitz: A Sociological Analysis*. Trans. by Catherine S. Leach. Berkeley, Calif., 1979.

Gerald Posner. *Hitler's Children*. New York, 1991.

Alvin H. Rosenfeld. *Imagining Hitler*. Bloomington, Ind., 1985.

Tom Segev. *Soldiers of Evil: The Commandants of the Nazi Concentration Camps*. Trans. by Haim Watzman. New York, 1987.

Gitta Sereny. *Into That Darkness: From Mercy Killing to Mass Murder*. New York, 1974.

Lore Shelley, ed.. *Studies in the Shoah*. Vol. 1. *The Nazi Civilization: Twenty-Three Women Prisoners' Accounts*. Lanham, Md., 1992.

William L. Shirer. *The Rise and Fall of the Third Reich: A History of Nazi Germany*. New York, 1960.

John Toland. *Adolf Hitler*. New York, 1976.